call 01823
or visit www.toursite.som...

06. JUN 06	26. MAR 07	17.
28.	23. APR	
10. JUL 06.	24. MAY	29. FEB 08
22.	13. JUN 07	
11. OCT 06.	29. JU	10. MAY
	31. AUG 07	13. JUN
NOV	21. SEP	07. JUL 09.
JUL 06.	23. OCT 07	26. JUL 08
		27. AUG
	28. JAN 09	

CANCELLED

CL8C

Please return/renew this item
by the last date shown.

SOMERSET
County Council
Libraries, Arts
& Information

I SO
1 3 0015030 3

29 JAN 2010

AN OPEN DOOR

Recent Titles by Claire Lorrimer from Severn House

BENEATH THE SUN
THE RECKONING
THE REUNION
SECOND CHANCE
THE WOVEN THREAD

AN OPEN DOOR

Claire Lorrimer

SOMERSET COUNTY LIBRARIES	
1 3 0015030 3	
Morley Books	18.5.99
	£17.99

This first world edition published in Great Britain 1999 by
SEVERN HOUSE PUBLISHERS LTD of
9–15 High Street, Sutton, Surrey SM1 1DF.
This title first published in the U.S.A. 1999 by
SEVERN HOUSE PUBLISHERS INC of
595 Madison Avenue, New York, N.Y. 10022.

Copyright © 1999 by Claire Lorrimer.

All rights reserved.
The moral right of the author has been asserted.

British Library Cataloguing in Publication Data

Lorrimer, Claire, 1921-
  An open door
  1. Love stories
  I. Title
  823.9'14 [F]

  ISBN 0 7278 5426 7

All situations in this publication are fictitious and
any resemblance to living persons is purely coincidental.

Typeset by Hewer Text Ltd
Edinburgh, Scotland
Printed and bound in Great Britain by
MPG Books Ltd, Bodmin, Cornwall.

1949

One

"Have you ever thought of marrying again, Sue?"

The question ended the short silence that had until then lain like a comfortable cloak over the fire-lit room, broken only by the steady, regular clicking of the knitting needles held by Susan Parish. Watching Susan, waiting curiously for an answer to her question, Jane Everett studied her companion.

Susan was, she mused, in every way her own opposite. Perhaps that was one of the reasons that they had struck up such an easy friendship. Susan's was a quiet, somewhat reserved nature whereas her own was impulsive, carefree, perhaps even a little irresponsible. And, of course, Sue was far more intellectual . . . went in for reading a more serious type of book, loved ballet and opera and things generally on a higher plane than she, Jane, enjoyed. For her, reading was the last resort to prevent boredom and then she preferred a brightly coloured woman's magazine with a story on which one didn't need to concentrate too much.

Even in looks they were opposites. Susan was dark with large, soft brown eyes and the kind of complexion that looked tanned even in midwinter. Sue had had her hair 'short cut' and the style suited her, making her look a little older perhaps than her twenty-six years, but more sophisticated. Somehow it suited her in a way that was both feminine and yet *gamine*.

"Now I could never wear my hair short!" Jane mused. Hers was the 'little girl' type of prettiness and she always wore her fair, silky hair in a long bob that fell over her shoulders. Sometimes she tied it back in a ribbon and knew that she looked about fourteen rather than her real age, which was but a month younger than Susan's. With her tiny, slight figure she was fully aware that she attracted men as honey attracted bees. A smile from beneath her lashes, a pout of her curved lips and they were at her feet.

But Susan could attract men, too, Jane allowed her mind to run on its usual inconsequential meandering. Not any man, but certain types who liked a quiet, thoughtful manner, a rather deep, husky voice, and a tall, beautifully proportioned body. Sue would have made a good model. In really well-cut clothes she would look exotic. As it was, she could barely afford to buy a new Utility dress once a year. One way and another, life had been pretty hard for Susan Parish and Jane felt sorry for her. At twenty-six, Sue had already been a widow for five years and although this little old thatched and beamed cottage was hers, it couldn't be easy trying to clothe and feed and educate a small boy on just a widow's pension; and the little she earned doing part-time secretarial duties while young Teddy was at school could barely pay for her own personal necessities. Now if only Sue would marry again . . .

Jane's mind came round to the completion of the circle, bringing her back to her question which Sue had still not answered.

"*Have* you thought about it, Sue?" she repeated.

Susan looked up for a moment from the intricate Fair Isle pullover which she was knitting for Teddy for his birthday next week . . . a brilliant red and blue and yellow affair he himself had specially chosen . . . and her large, gently curving mouth twisted a little into a half-smile.

"Yes, I've thought about it, Jane, but quite honestly, my dear, I don't think there's much likelihood of my meeting anyone who'd fill the bill. You see, my position is a little different from yours after your Hamilton was killed. You were more or less single again, weren't you? But I have Teddy. Apart from having to choose the right kind of father for him, it isn't every man who wants to take on a wife and a ready-made family. And then, again, I think I'd find it a little difficult to give to anyone else the same kind of love that was Edward's. I could only offer second-best. And last, but not least, there aren't any eligible young bachelors around here, are there? And as I'm pretty well tied with young Ted, I don't think I should have much time or the opportunity to go husband-hunting."

She was smiling properly now and laughing at herself even while she knew that every word she had spoken was true. Often in the last year or so . . . when the first shock and grief of losing Edward had worn off and he had become rather more a treasured memory than a pain in her heart . . . she had wondered about her future . . . hers and Teddy's. At first she had been certain she would never marry again. With Teddy still a baby, she had had her time and her heart filled to capacity. But he had been growing up slowly and relentlessly and now her fat, chuckling little baby had developed into a tall, wiry boy. He had started to make friends at school, spent more and more time out of his home, growing independent of her as he was bound to do, needing her only to supply his meals, to answer his innumerable questions, mend his clothes, read to him or play with him when no one else was at hand.

It wasn't that he loved her any the less . . . merely that as he grew up, he needed her less. Only when he was ill did he become her baby again, someone for her to fuss over, to coddle and then he would nestle up against her and they would be close once more. But at present, he was a little ashamed of his 'softness' for his mother. It amused Susan even while it hurt her just a little bit. But she understood it . . . in the same way that she understood that he was beginning to need a father. At times he was quite beyond her control. She had always believed that it was wrong to chastise children, and until recently, she had controlled Ted fairly easily with small punishments, with an appeal to his honour, his age, his duty. Now, suddenly, he didn't seem to care. He would stand before her, his lips, so like her own, set in a thin, hard line, his brown eyes glowing in anger, his small square jaw set in a determined line. And no matter what she said to him, if he wanted a thing badly enough, he would go ahead and do it and accept his punishment with seeming indifference. And there was no one of a higher authority . . . a father's more frightening wrath, perhaps . . . to whom she could refer Ted in these unmanageable moods.

She turned now to look at the girl, curled up like a kitten in the deep armchair opposite her. Jane, so recently come to live down here, was the first friend she had made since Edward's death had put an end to her 'camp following', and her casual friendships with other officers' wives at the various stations where they made their homes. In a letter Edward had left for her in the event of his death, he had stressed that he hoped she would be able to make a home for herself and Teddy, in the little old-world cottage he had bought when they were first married; mainly so that they could have somewhere to spend their leaves. Neither she nor Edward had had any near relatives living. Ted had an uncle somewhere in the north of England, she, a cousin and an aunt in Australia. Edward had known that she would not want to make her home with them, and once she had adjusted herself, not without many bitter tears and much heartache, to living without Edward, she had been happy enough here in this remote Essex village. She had, of course, met one or two other neighbours, become almost friendly with these cheerful village folk. But their common interests were somewhat limited to domestic details . . . their children, their houses, their gardens. Friendship with them had never been intimate.

Then Jane and her husband, Gareth, had bought two cottages at the far end of the village, and Sue and Jane had met in the village store. That was only three months ago but in that time they were often in and out of each other's houses. Jane, with her quick laughter, her impulsive ways, was so easy to get along with. Teddy had taken to her immediately, and although Jane was not the type of girl one might expect to get on well with children, she had a way with Teddy that was almost funny, it was so elemental. She appealed to him in exactly the same way as she would appeal to a grown man. She referred to his opinion as though he were an adult, spoke to him as an equal, asked him to help her lift heavy logs and such things, so that with her, he felt the man he longed to be.

Susan had wondered at first why Jane took such trouble with Teddy. Then, as she got to know Jane better, she realized that with Jane it was simply second nature to go out of her way to make people like her. Teddy was a charming little boy when he chose to be. He had beautiful manners, when he remembered them, and he seldom forgot them with Jane; opening doors for her, handing her plates at meal times, running small errands for her that Susan often had to bribe or cajole him into doing for herself! It pleased Jane to receive such attentions. Teddy's obvious devotion flattered her insatiable vanity.

For all her vanity, however, and the more frivolous side to her character, Susan liked Jane. There was something clear cut and simple about her that made friendship with her possible. One always knew where one was with Jane . . . could understand what made her do and say things, know at first glance at her face what particular mood she was in that day; know the best way to cope with it. And Jane's moods were seldom of lasting duration. Her main problem was her boredom. Having no very deep interest in life, she found it hard to stay long in her own company without being bored. She wanted always to be 'doing' something. Hers was, consequently, a restless nature, made more so by the life she was leading.

She and Gareth had lived in London for the first two years of their married life. Gareth was managing director of a large company and could afford to take Jane about a good deal, in the evenings. They had lunched together most days, too, at one or other of the more popular restaurants. Jane used to spend what was left of the morning after she got up, dressing for her luncheon appointment. In the afternoon she would fill in the time at a cinema, and when Gareth came home at five, she would start dressing up again for wherever they were going that evening; to a dance, a cocktail party, or the theatre.

But Gareth was a good deal older than Jane . . . nearly thirty-eight, Jane had told her. And he wanted to 'settle down'.

"Jane, what made you finally decide to come down to the country?" Susan asked, following her own train of thought.

Jane tossed the fair hair away from her face and reached for a cigarette from the enamel and silver case in her handbag, both beautiful, costly presents which Gareth had bought her but which she scarcely seemed to value – she had so many beautiful things. Susan sometimes thought that on the money Gareth spent buying presents for Jane she could afford to send Teddy to the public school his father had attended!

"I don't know, Sue. I think I must have been a bit bored with life in town. After all, we'd been doing the same round of parties for two years. When Gareth said he wanted to buy a cottage in the country it sounded rather fun. I thought we'd make a lot of new friends, give weekend parties and go to point-to-points and all that sort of thing. And then Gareth said I could have a free hand with the furnishing. That was fun, I'll admit. But quite honestly, Susan, I wish we hadn't come. It's just not working out the way I thought it would. Gareth's home so much later now with the trains being what they are, and by the time he gets home, he's too tired to do much – or so he says! And now he's so garden-mad he doesn't even want to do the things I want at weekends. I'm not like you, Susan. I can't fill my life with bottling fruit and making jam and all that sort of thing. I don't know how you've stuck this way of life so long."

Susan laughed. Jane's pretty face was so screwed up with distaste.

"Well, I've got Teddy," she said. "He keeps me pretty busy. There's always a mass of washing and mending and sewing to do. *And* meals to get. And then I'm at work quite a bit during the day."

Jane sighed.

"Perhaps I'd be happier if I had a job," she said without conviction. "But it would be a bit silly, wouldn't it, Susan, when Gareth has so much money?"

"The idle rich!" Susan teased.

"Oh, but we're not *rich*!" Jane said quickly. "I mean, Gareth's often saying we can't afford to do this or that. I wanted to go abroad this winter but we couldn't afford it. And he's put so much into the house."

"You've made it beautiful!" Susan said with real admiration in her voice. The pair of tumbledown cottages had been entirely restored, rebuilt and installed with all the most modern luxuries. There was even a washing machine which Jane never used, as she still sent most of her things to a laundry! Practically every labour-saving device had been bought for the place without in any way detracting from its old-world charm. And struggling round her own home, Susan had wondered how Jane could have thought it necessary to have someone in from the village to "do" for her. That was part of Jane's trouble . . . her discontent. She hadn't enough to do to keep her busy.

"Jane, aren't you and Gareth going to start a family soon?" she asked. "A few babies would keep you busy enough."

A slight frown creased Jane's smooth, white forehead.

"Don't mention that subject," she said, and typical of Jane, promptly proceeded to elaborate on it. "Gareth's always on to me about it being time to start a family. Honestly, Susan, I don't mean to be selfish, but I really don't *like* babies. Now if they began at Teddy's age, I wouldn't mind. But *babies*!"

Susan couldn't restrain her laughter.

"Jane, you really are a ninny! Babies are wonderful, they really are. You're just judging other people's, but you'd feel quite differently if you had one of your own. I'm sure you would. They're so cuddlesome and sweet and endearing. I wish I'd had another one before . . . before it was too late."

Jane's eyebrows shot up in amazement.

"You don't really mean that, Sue. Why, whatever would you have done with two of them to bring up?"

"One wouldn't have been so much more since I had Teddy anyway," Susan said. "I might have had a little girl."

Jane shook her head.

"I don't understand you, Susan, but I certainly do admire you. I suppose we're just about as different from one another as we could be. I must be abnormal. At any rate, Gareth's beginning to think so. He says *all* women want children if they're happily married."

"Perhaps you've just not reached that stage yet," Susan said, meaning that maybe Jane hadn't really grown up sufficiently yet. "I'm sure you will want kids eventually. And you know, Jane, Gareth is bound to be a bit impatient. After all, he's a good deal older than you."

Jane's lips pouted a little, and reminded Susan of a small girl who wasn't having things her own way.

"I sometimes wonder if I ought to have married Gareth," she announced, but in such a matter-of-fact tone that Susan recovered a little from the implications of her words. "I thought I might be happy with an older man and Gareth was so persistent. I used to know him before the war, Susan, did I tell you? I was only a schoolgirl then, of course, and Gareth was a young man of twenty-eight or so. He used to tease me then and tell me he was waiting until I was old enough to be proposed to! I never took him seriously but he *was* serious, although I didn't find out till later. Then, soon after the war broke out, I met Hamilton. There was something about the Americans . . . I don't know what it was . . . that was so much more attractive than the Englishmen, don't you agree, Sue?"

Susan shook her head, smiling.

"Frankly, no! But then I married an Englishman, Jane."

Jane returned the smile.

"Well, of course. All the same, I liked them, and Ham was just everything I'd ever dreamed about. Gosh, Sue, I was so happy with him I just didn't know how to hold so much fun inside me. One glorious mad year and then he went abroad. Even then I didn't feel too miserable. I had cables and letters and gorgeous parcels and Ham was always talking about getting leave. Then quite suddenly, nothing, no letter, no cable, days and days of silence until I thought I'd go crazy. I tried to get news but all I could find out was that his regiment – he was in the Tank Corps in Italy then – had gone into action. Then suddenly I heard he was missing. I kept on hoping he'd turn up, Sue. I prayed and prayed and hoped and hoped and the months went by until finally I got notified that he was presumed killed. It was awful."

"You never heard what happened?" Susan asked gently.

"No! They never found his body. He was just one of the many who disappeared. Blown to bits. I didn't believe it even then . . . went on hoping until the war ended. I thought he might have been a prisoner, lost his memory . . . anything like that and he would turn up. He always called himself the bad penny. In the meantime, of course, I'd met Gareth again. After Ham was presumed killed, I went home on leave . . . we were living in London at the time . . . and started doing some war work. I got a job as secretary to one of the wallahs in the War Office. One day who should walk in but Gareth. He was a colonel then. He'd been fighting abroad and had got the M.C. along with a bad leg wound. That was how he got the job in the War Office.

"Of course, he started taking me out a bit and was very sympathetic and understanding about Ham. I told him I was waiting for the war to end . . . that I wouldn't believe the worst until the war in Europe was over. So he never proposed, although he's told me since he wanted to often and often. Finally, of course, the war did end and I heard nothing, and then Gareth asked me to marry him. It seemed the sensible thing to do. I told him I'd never feel the same way towards him as I had to Ham, but he seemed to understand. He said he'd help me to forget and start again. He was always very kind. I'm terribly fond of Gareth but I don't think I make him a very good wife."

Susan carefully turned a row in her knitting as she considered Jane's outburst. There was something a little pathetic in someone of Jane's inconstant nature, to have gone on hoping and believing for so long. It had been easier for herself. Edward had crashed in his plane in this country, had been killed outright and she had been forced to accept the truth from the first. Perhaps for that reason, she had found it easier to start life again.

"Gareth adores you, Jane," she said. "And he takes such care of you. He wouldn't be so devoted if you were the bad wife you're trying to tell me you are to him."

"I've never said this before to anyone, Sue," Jane said, in a low, confidential voice, "but I think that's the whole trouble. Gareth takes too much care of me. It's as if he were sorry for me and is trying to make it up to me all the time. I can be perfectly beastly sometimes, bad tempered and horrible and thoroughly nasty, but he never turns round on me. I wish he would. I wouldn't feel so guilty then. Besides, it's no fun having a bust up if it's only *you* letting off steam!"

"That's just Gareth's nature," Susan said. "He's more controlled than you are, Jane."

"I know, and more sensible. Honestly, Susan, I think you're more suited to him than I am!"

Susan laughed.

"I'm sure Gareth wouldn't like *that* idea!" she said. "I don't think he likes me very much. He hardly ever says two words to me."

"Oh, but you're quite wrong, Sue," Jane cried, uncurling her legs in their beautifully tailored slacks and stretching them out before her. "Gareth thinks you're wonderful. He's always saying he never knows how you manage the way you do. He respects you enormously."

"Gareth respects me!" Susan said. "It doesn't make sense, Jane. I honestly believe he doesn't even like me. At any rate, he always seems to avoid coming round here with you."

"That's just because he's so gardening mad," Jane said. "And he's shy, Susan. Lots of people think he's unfriendly because he's shy. Only of women, I mean. He's really much better with men. In fact he's the sort of man one expects to be a bachelor."

"But men like Gareth often make wonderful husbands," Susan argued. "I think you're very lucky, Jane."

Jane stood up, yawning and stretching her arms above her head.

"Uh-huh. I guess I am. I suppose so, anyway. I ought to be going, Sue. It's nearly teatime and young Teddy will be home from school."

"Won't you stay and have tea with us?" Susan asked, putting down her knitting and stooping to give the log fire a poke, so that the embers burst into small flames and the room became noisy with the sharp crackling of the wood.

"I'd love to, but for once we're going out tonight. Gareth's getting an early train and we're going to a dance at the Mayflower. It's a special 'do' . . . evening dress and all that. So I want to have plenty of time to get dolled up. I wish you were coming too, Susan. I feel mean leaving you behind."

Susan put her arm round Jane's shoulders.

"Don't feel any such thing. I've plenty to do tonight, believe you me . . ."

"All the same, it would be rather fun. I must see if I can find a boyfriend for you, Sue. In fact, I've just got a wonderful idea. My brother, Jim, has been promising to pay me a visit. He's great fun and a lot of girls find him very attractive, but so far he's not been trapped. I'm going to do a bit of match-making and throw you two together."

"We shall probably hate each other on sight!" Susan laughed. "Besides, who'll look after Teddy while I go gadding?"

"My Mrs Mendall will baby-watch!" Jane said airily. At the door, she turned and called back to Susan. "Jim's fair, like me," she said.

"But I like them dark!" Susan called back, laughing.

"Then you can have Gareth," Jane called back from the open door. "Jim's a better dancer. 'Bye, now. See you tomorrow."

The door closed behind her and the room suddenly became quiet again. It was a silence Susan usually did not notice . . . a gentle peace that seemed to pervade the room until Ted returned from school, filling it anew with noise and laughter and chatter. But today, for some reason, the silence grated on Susan's ears. The fire had sunk once more into a cone of red embers, and with Jane's departure, twilight had given way to dark.

Slowly Susan lit the oil lamp and placed it on the beam above the fireplace. Beside it, the mirror reflected the soft glow, and with unaccustomed impulse, Susan leaned over and stared at her reflection in the mirror.

How pale and sad her face looked, how dark the brown pools of her eyes! She traced her finger along the lines of her forehead, smoothing out the frown, considering with sudden sharp fear that she looked older . . . so much older than Jane, and yet they were of an age. Was it living alone that gave her this maturity . . . or just motherhood? Was she lonely? Had a little of Jane's restlessness transferred itself to her?

She turned away from the mirror and went slowly towards the kitchen, carrying the oil lamp. Automatically, her hands started to cut and butter bread for Teddy's tea. But her mind remained poised, aloof from her actions. It was as if there were another self watching above her, seeing for the first time the loneliness of her life. Soon Teddy would be going to boarding school, living away from her. Soon she would be quite alone here, during the evenings as well as the day. And there would be less to do, with him away, less to keep her hands busy and her mind occupied.

'I should have had other children!' she thought in sudden desperation. 'I want more children, another baby in my arms.'

The thought brought back her conversation with Jane . . . Jane's refusal to grant Gareth's wish for children. At the time it had seemed unimportant . . . a whim of Jane's, like many of her other light-hearted remarks. But now Susan felt a swift, deep compunction for Gareth . . . for the man who had so much materially but so little of the spiritual needs he craved. He must know that Jane was restless, if not actively unhappy, must wonder if he were to blame . . . he, who gave her so much.

'You don't recognize the value of what you have, Jane!' Susan thought silently. 'Gareth is a wonderful person. He'd make a wonderful father for your children.'

She had a sudden flash of memory, of Gareth on the lawn in her garden last autumn soon after they had arrived. She had been in the kitchen and looking through the low, diamond-shaped window, had seen Teddy sprawled on the grass, and a long, lithe figure standing over him, laughing down at him.

"Now who's king of this castle, my lad?" Gareth's voice, low, deep, full of quick laughter.

"Let me up. Let me up." Teddy's shrill, high tones.

"I'll have to give you some boxing lessons or you'll never be able to hold your own at school. Up you get, then. We'll have one more bout."

Teddy's small figure, arms squaring up to the man towering above him. A quick movement of those long arms and the small boy was lifted high into the air and swung head downwards in a dive-bombing movement. A screech of delight from Teddy and then his shrill voice as he came scampering into the kitchen.

"I say, Mum, that new man *is* nice. He's going to teach me to box properly and next summer he says he'll teach me cricket, too. I say, Mum, he's *ever* so strong. He lifted me right up in the air. Did you see me? I was a dive-bomber. Were you watching? Gosh, I wish that man was my daddy. Why can't he be, Mummy?"

"Well, he's married to Aunty Jane, dear."

"Then you marry him, too. I'm hungry, Mum. What's for tea?"

And later, on the lawn, when Jane and Teddy were down by the stream at the bottom of the garden, the look on Gareth's face when she said, "My son seems to think you're perfect, Mr Everett. In fact he considers you're nice enough to be his daddy. That's a high compliment from him."

"He's a nice little chap," Gareth had said, obviously pleased but embarrassed.

Since then, Teddy had been constantly in Gareth's company, helping in the garden, running errands. And Gareth had given him the promised boxing lessons.

She, herself, had seen very little of Jane's husband and yet through Teddy she felt she knew him so well. "Uncle Gareth says" was always on Ted's lips, and "Uncle Gareth thinks". She knew from Ted what a satisfying thing was gardening for Gareth, the reward of man's communion with the soil. Knew of his love for all small helpless things. His dislike of towns and society with its shallowness. His love of music, his immense repertoire of quaint, strange folk songs which he hummed aloud when working in the garden with Ted. Knew, also, through her son, that he was a man of upright character and almost fanatical honour. Ted's stricken face one afternoon, when Uncle Gareth didn't want to speak to him any more that day because he'd told him a lie. Ted's weird adult remarks, so obviously repetitions of his hero's; once even a swear word that couldn't be wrong because Uncle Gareth had said it.

Strange, to know so much of a man and yet to know him so little. Gareth was almost a stranger to the house, silent for the most part when he did come, leaving it to Susan or Jane or Ted to do the talking; once in a while smiling at her but for the most part avoiding her company, her eyes.

Now, as she heard Ted's footsteps, the banging of the front door and his voice shouting, "Mum? Is tea ready?" she wondered for the first time if perhaps Gareth's awkwardness was because he, too, knew her so well. Did Teddy say, *"Mum thinks; Mum says; Mum doesn't like"*?

Teddy burst into the room, his brown eyes shining.

"I'm early, aren't I? Uncle Gareth gave me a lift back in his car. He caught a much earlier train than usual. He had another man with him. It's Aunty Jane's brother and his name is Jim, and Mummy, Uncle Gareth says they are going dancing tonight and they've got to find someone to be a partner for Uncle Jim, and I said you danced jolly well so you're to go with them. Isn't it a spiffing surprise?"

A slow flush spread over Susan's face.

"Teddy, you shouldn't have said that. I can't possibly go. They surely don't . . . ?"

"But it's all fixed!" Teddy said indignantly. "It's my surprise for you. Listen, there's the telephone. That'll be Aunt Jane. I'll answer it. I'll say you're going, won't I? You will go, won't you? You'll have ever such a wonderful time."

Suddenly Susan laughed.

"How do you know I will?" she said above the noise of telephone ringing.

"Because you're going with Uncle Gareth," Ted shouted back. "Yes, she says she'll go, Aunty Jane. Isn't it spiffing?"

Susan stood helplessly by the plate of bread and butter, suddenly afraid. And wondering, above everything, what she could find to wear.

Two

"It's quite fantastic!" Susan thought, leaning back in her chair, surveying the room full of dancers, all so elegantly dressed, so full of self-confidence and *savoir-faire*. It was like stepping into another world . . . a world she had glimpsed once or twice during leaves with Edward, but almost completely forgotten.

All the way here in the car she had been afraid, reluctant, unwilling, regretful that she had allowed Jane and Teddy between them to talk her into stepping out of her comfortable domestic rut. She had worried stupidly about her dress . . . just a plain, full black taffeta skirt with the white embroidered Hungarian blouse which she had cleverly contrived to slip off the shoulders, in order that it should seem more suitable for dancing and more in fashion. Beside Jane, in her flowing pink net, sparkling with sequins – a creation from Paris – she had felt dowdy, insignificant. She had been self-conscious, too, about the narrow band of black velvet round her throat with the gold locket containing the picture of her mother . . . her only remaining piece of jewellery other than her engagement ring. Jane wore a beautiful triple row of tiny cultured pearls – a diamond wrist watch – exquisite ear-rings. Jane looked dazzling – glamorous!

But somehow, none of Susan's deficiencies seemed noticeable to her companions. Jane's "Why, you look wonderful, darling!" had been genuine enough by virtue of the very surprise in her tone! And Jim, Jane's brother, quite clearly found her attractive. Already he had danced five times with her, giving her no peace even through the elaborate four-course dinner Gareth had ordered for them. Only now Jane had insisted he should dance with her, and with brotherly reluctance he had allowed himself to be dragged away.

'He is a nice boy,' Susan thought. A year or two older than Jane and herself. Yet to her he was only a boy. Perhaps marriage and motherhood had added a few extra years to her twenty-six, for it seemed that for all his man-about-town manner, Jim was still too 'boyish' for her to take very seriously. Nevertheless, it was fun to feel admired, to realize that he was very definitely flirting with her; to know that she was attractive to him, who was, himself, undoubtedly attractive from a woman's point of view. With his lithe slim body, fair curly hair and laughing blue eyes, Susan could very well believe Jane's statement that girls "went silly about Jim". All the same, she could not feel any very serious leanings towards him herself and so satisfy Jane's light-hearted whim for a little match-making.

"You're very silent, Susan. A penny for them?"

Her attention was brought back quickly to her companion. Gareth was leaning a little towards her on his elbow, a cigarette held lightly between his fingers. Meeting her gaze, he stubbed out the cigarette and said, "Don't really care for the things. Wish I could smoke my pipe!"

"Can't you?" Susan asked, glancing round the room. "I suppose it's 'not done' here! Would you like to go into the lounge and smoke?"

He shook his head and gave her a quick, shy smile.

"No, let's dance instead," he said. "I'm not very good, Jane tells me, but I can keep in time if there isn't too much 'Be-Bop' or whatever they call it. I must be a bit old-fashioned, I think."

"Me, too, then!" Susan said, standing up as he moved her chair back from the table. "I haven't danced once in . . . why, six years!"

They joined the other couples on the dance floor and moved into a slow foxtrot. Without difficulty, they seemed to match steps and Susan thought how wrong Jane was about Gareth's dancing. He was far better than average and moved with a lightness and ease unusual in a man of his height and build.

They were silent as they danced, enjoying the rhythm that was quiet and yet at the same time exhilarating. The band was playing a selection of old favourites, such tunes as 'Night and Day' and 'My Blue Heaven'.

Once Gareth looked down into Susan's face and said: "Want to give it up for a bit?" But she shook her head, knowing that she could go on dancing like this for ever; that she never wanted this dance to end.

He seemed tireless and it was only when the band stopped for an interval that they were forced reluctantly back to their seats. There was no sign of Jane or Jim, and Gareth, after a quick look round the room, suggested they were probably in the bar.

"Would you like to join them or shall we have our drinks here?" he asked.

'Here!' Susan thought, but realizing he might be anxious to find Jane, she said it was up to him. Gareth elected to stay and ordered drinks for them.

While they waited, Susan studied her companion, thinking for the first time that evening that he was without doubt the most distinguished-looking man in the room. In his dinner-jacket he looked somehow taller and older than when she had seen him around the garden at home in old tweeds and flannels. His dark hair, usually a little unruly and apt to curl, was brushed smoothly off his face, making it seem longer, thinner. Only his eyes were the same, a gentle, shy blue, and his gaze never stayed long on her face.

Then he turned suddenly towards her, his face breaking into a grin.

"I'm sure you must find me a bit of a bore, Susan. I'm afraid I'm not much of a talker."

Susan felt a little of her own restraint in his company relax. "I'm not much of a talker, either. I expect we're both a bit shy!" she said.

He nodded in agreement. Then suddenly, his face turned from her, he said, "You see, it's a bit tricky, really. We've hardly said two words to each other and yet I know such a lot about you . . . far more than anyone should know. It's that young son of yours.

I can't stop him talking about you. Why, I even know you've just made yourself a pink nightdress!"

Susan laughed with quick amusement. So Teddy had been talking on both sides of the fence! Somehow that made it all so much easier. And to think he had mentioned that new 'nightie'!

"Really, I apologize for him. But he is so curious, and living alone as we do, I suppose I forget sometimes he's just a little boy. He wants to know what I'm sewing and when I tell him it's to be a new nightie, nothing else will do but that I show him. Then he criticizes it and I'll admit, I sometimes even take his advice. He's amazingly fashion-conscious, and quite devastatingly frank. 'You can't wear that old hat, Mummy. You look like old Aunt Higgins', or 'That makes you look terribly thin, Mummy'. He's mostly right!"

"He's an intelligent kid," Gareth nodded thoughtfully. "And very knowledgeable. Especially about music. He can recognize any number of pieces by various composers. The other day I played a bit of Brahms to him and out he comes with 'Oh, that's the 'Lullabye', isn't it? We heard it on the radio the other night'."

"We often listen to music on the wireless," Susan admitted. "Edward, my husband, was very musical. He played the violin. I think Teddy has inherited his gift. I'm fond of music myself but I can't play anything."

"You ought to have the boy taught," Gareth was saying, and then quickly added, ". . . if you can afford to. I think he has talent. I've heard him picking out tunes on the piano when he thinks no one is listening."

"I hope he hasn't been touching your piano without permission!" Susan cried aghast.

Gareth smiled at her reassuringly.

"No, he has permission, provided he washes his hands first. But he won't touch it if he thinks anyone is around."

"Not even you?" Susan asked surprised.

"I don't think I'm all *that* popular!" he said. "It's just that – well, I suppose a boy of that age listens more to a man than to a woman."

"I know, and I'm so grateful to you for all the time and attention you give him," Susan cried warmly. "Please don't think I haven't appreciated your kindness. It's just that there doesn't seem to have been an opportunity to say so to you before."

"There's nothing to be grateful for," Gareth said awkwardly. "I like the boy very much, and he's a lot of help to me in the garden. As a matter of fact, I had wanted to say something to you about him. I hope you won't think it very presumptuous . . . but, well, if you have any serious difficulty with him, perhaps I could help."

Susan listened with a mixture of gratitude and tenderness. Gareth was so painfully transparent at times, in this instance so clearly anxious to avoid appearing to interfere in matters that didn't concern him. And yet he had seen, as she herself had done, how much Ted needed a firmer hand than hers at times, a man's hand. But he'd been too shy, too embarrassed to say anything. Even now, she could see by the flush on his face, that he was regretting the sudden impulse.

"I should be so very happy to know you'd be somewhere in the background," she said simply and sincerely. "Teddy takes so much notice of everything you say and do. It's far more of a punishment for him that you should refuse to speak to him for an afternoon, than if I send him to bed with a favourite treat withheld into the bargain. I see immense improvement ahead if I can say 'Very well, I shall see what Uncle Gareth has to say about this!' "

They both laughed and then Gareth became serious again.

"I'd like to help in other ways, too. In fact, I've tried to do so already. Explaining to him about life and trying to find the right answers to his questions. It's not always easy to give a truthful answer and yet children ought to be told nothing but the truth, don't you agree?"

"That's what I myself believe. Does Teddy ask you a lot of difficult questions?"

Gareth smiled.

"Well, not so many. Things sort of go in circles in his mind, one thing leading to another. We started last week with Ted asking me what happened when people died. That led to God and Heaven and then graves and bodies and from there to the morbid subject of ashes to ashes and dust to dust. Back where we came from, so to speak. That, of course, led to where did we come from. At that stage I thought it best to refer him to you!"

"He asked me last night," Susan said laughing. "I told him the truth. Perhaps he's a bit young but he took it all as a matter of course and said, 'Oh, then that explains Smoky's kittens, doesn't it?' and forgot all about it!"

"It's a fascinating world, the mind of a child," Gareth said. "Seeing glimpses of it reminds one of one's own childhood. I remember all sorts of things I did as a kid from chance remarks of young Ted's. He's really a fine boy, Susan. I'm sure you're proud of him. He's quite touchingly devoted to you."

"He doesn't show it much nowadays," Susan said, feeling suddenly near to tears. "It's good to know it's there underneath. He's just at that stage where he's finding it difficult to express his feelings and is shy of emotion."

"Most boys go through that. Some of them never grow out of it," Gareth remarked. "Frankly, I'm still awaiting release from that tongue-tied state, and here I am, nearing forty!"

"Not quite, yet!" Susan reminded him. "And besides, surely you have no objection to growing older?"

There was no answering smile on his face . . . only a look of innate sadness.

"I do mind in some ways," he said shortly, thoughtfully. Then, quickly changing the subject, he said, "Shall we see if we can find the other two? Jim will never forgive me for monopolizing so much of your time."

His sudden politeness, his withdrawal into himself, jerked Susan back to her own customary reserve. She realized suddenly how frankly they had been talking, how personally; knew that it was unusual for both of them to reveal so much of their thoughts to strangers. And yet for that short space of time, they had not been strangers, but two people brought close together by their common interest in a small boy . . . in her son. Now, because of that tactless remark of hers about his age, Gareth had become a stranger again.

A little of her pleasure in the evening seemed to fade away, She rose without further speech and went with him in search of Jane.

As Gareth had supposed, his wife and her brother were in the bar, sitting on high-legged, red leather stools, holding glasses in their hands. But they were not alone. Three young men and another girl were gathered round them and there was much noise of laughter and excited talking and above the din, Jane's high giggle.

With a little shock, Susan realized that none of these people were very sober and that Gareth, beside her, was frowning in obvious annoyance. She felt a sudden irritation herself with Gareth for the scene she felt he would precipitate. There was a thin line to his mouth, a line of unmistakeable anger.

"Why, it's quite a party!" she said brightly. And before Gareth could speak, she moved over towards Jane.

Jane raised a glass to her – flushed and smiling.

"Hallo, darling? Come to join the happy family? Let me introduce . . . John, Bill, Snooker and Jean . . . don't know their other names . . . this is Susan. Great friend of mine. And Gareth, my dear old hubby. Come and have a drink, my poppets."

"I came to ask you to dance, Jane," Gareth said quietly. But Jane shook her head. "Not just now, Sweetie-pie. Jim's danced my feet off. Come and buy me a drink instead, I'll have another gin. What's yours, boys and girls?"

It was obvious even to Susan that Jane had already had enough to drink; that the three young men and the girl had also had sufficient and were drinking, so it seemed, at Jane's expense. The girl was too flashily dressed, the three young men a little too sleek and dapper. They were noisy and far too free with their 'darlings'. The man called Snooker, leant across Jane, resting his arm round her shoulders as he addressed the barman and Susan was painfully conscious of Gareth's swift intake of breath, of his hands clenched at his sides.

"I really think I ought to go home soon, Gareth," Susan said quietly. "If Mrs Mendall is waiting up, I oughtn't to keep her too long, ought I?"

Gareth jumped at this excuse to leave. He went up to Jane and tucked his arm through hers.

"Time to go home, Jane!" he said firmly. "Susan has to get back to Teddy and Mrs Mendall won't stay after midnight. Coming, Jim?"

Jim, still sober and a little anxious himself about Jane's behaviour, nodded his head and turned to Jane.

"Coming then, Sis?" he asked.

But something in the compelling force of her husband's fingers on her bare arm aroused defiance in Jane. She frowned.

"I don't want to go home yet, Ga!" she said, pouting childishly and frowning through the lock of fair hair that had fallen across her forehead. "It's early."

"It's nearly midnight," Gareth said.

"Well, that's early, except in the damned old country!" Jane said loudly. "You take Susan home and come back for Jim and me later."

"I'm not a taxi service," came Gareth's voice, cold and angry now, but still controlled.

Jane giggled.

"That's right darling, nor you are. Then tell you what, I'll get myself a taxi home later."

"Oh, come on, Jane, let's all go together now," Jim said persuasively. The three young men and the girl looked on in silence, a little awed by Gareth's manner and appearance and not wishing to cause trouble. Something in their silence seemed to challenge Jane to show her independence. It was quite clear to Susan, if not to Gareth and Jim, too, that Jane was now "showing off". She had so often seen Teddy do it.

"I shall stay!" she announced firmly. "Jim can take Susan home and then you can stay, too, Gareth!"

Gareth's lean brown face went an angry red. Susan felt his embarrassment for her and said quickly, "Please don't bother bout me, Gareth. I mean that. The porter will find me a taxi and I'll slip off. I don't want to break up the party. Please!"

Gareth bit his lip and spoke quietly to Jane, as though he had not heard Susan, "We're going now, Jane. Are you coming?"

"No, I'm not!" Jane said, raising her voice. "If you don't want to stay, then Jim can take me home later."

"Very well, my dear!" Gareth said, his voice so low now that Susan wondered if Jane heard him. Already her blonde, pretty head was turned towards the barman. "Are you ready, Susan?"

Helplessly, Susan looked from Gareth to Jim. There was something in both their faces as they looked back at her, that made her turn in silence, and go to the cloakroom to fetch her coat.

She knew that Jim had wanted to take her home. Knew, too, that although he had spent so much time with Jane at the bar he had imagined there would be more time later to dance again with her, Susan, had anticipated the drive home in the back of the car with her. But in Gareth's face, too, there had been determination to take her home. Not for the same reason, but because he wished his wife to know that he had meant what he said; wished her to know that he felt it was her duty both to him and their guest to leave now when Susan had to go. He would take her home now, only because he had said he was leaving, and he would leave this minute even if it killed him. Jim had understood how he felt, known that his brother-in-law would count on him to get Jane home as soon as he could.

Susan sat in silence beside Gareth as he drove home, his face obscured by the darkness, only the rigid line of his profile turned towards her. She sensed his anger, and something in her made her plead for Jane who was, as usual, merely following a whim, but a whim she knew Gareth neither understood nor countenanced. She had no right to interfere in their private quarrel and yet she had to say what she could for Jane.

"It really was a shame that I should break the party up so early," she said into the silence. "After all, there aren't parties every day, are there, and Jane was so looking forward to this one. She told me this afternoon how thrilled she was to be going."

"Jane is not a child!" Gareth's voice sounded cold and deliberate.

"Perhaps not, yet in some ways she is, Gareth."

"You mean, she's spoilt!" It was not a question. Just a statement.

"A little maybe. But then, you've helped to spoil her, Gareth. You do so much for her."

Suddenly it seemed wrong for them to be discussing Jane in her absence. Susan fell silent and it was Gareth who said:

"Perhaps the fault is mine. But it certainly isn't right that *your* evening should be spoilt. You go to parties less than any of us. And I'm sure young Jim wanted to take you home. So his evening is spoilt too."

A hint of laughter broke his voice and Susan felt her taut nerves relax. A faint smile glimmered in her face as he drew up outside her gate.

"Then you've done me a good turn, Gareth. I don't really feel much like flirting with Jim. I'm not one of those people who make friends very quickly."

Gareth switched off the engine and turned towards her.

"You honestly mean you wouldn't have liked to have been kissed tonight?"

"Perhaps, if the right man wanted to kiss me," Susan said lightly. "But Jim isn't the right man."

"No, I suppose not!" Gareth said. "You know, Susan, I think your Edward must have been a wonderful fellow for you to have loved him, I mean. And a lucky fellow, too. You must be lonely sometimes, without him."

"Don't be sorry for me," Susan said lightly. "You know, it can be less lonely, sometimes, to be by yourself than to be with people who . . . well, who aren't congenial . . ."

It hadn't been the way she meant to end her sentence, but at the last moment she realized that Gareth might take the words personally . . . as applicable to himself and Jane. For she knew as the words crossed her mind, that Jane didn't really love Gareth

That she didn't even respect him very deeply. She knew, too, that Gareth was aware of it, as much aware as he was of the fact that she, Susan, had been about to end her remark with "than to be with people who don't love you". It was as if some electric wire of understanding ran between them which needed no words. A great depth of pity welled up inside her with this new awareness of his unhappiness, of the loneliness in his own life.

"Perhaps we're both a little sorry for each other," Gareth said intuitively. "It's been a strange evening."

"I've had a lovely time," Susan cried impulsively. "I was a little afraid to come out of my rut but I'm glad I did. I enjoyed it all. And I want to thank you."

She held out her hand and for a moment, he held it in his own. As his hands closed round hers, Susan knew that for her this was more than just a good-night and thank you. A painful yet sweet thrill seemed to course from his fingertips along her arm, piercing her heart with trembling arrows. Swiftly, as if she had been stung, she withdrew her hand and her voice, trembling a little in spite of herself, said breathlessly, "Shall I tell Mrs Mendall you'll run her home?"

"Yes, yes. I'll do that. And . . . good night, Susan!"

"Good night!" she whispered, and before he could move to open the door, she lifted the handle and slipped quickly away into the darkness.

Mrs Mendall had heard the car and was waiting in her hat and coat.

"I'll settle up with you tomorrow, Mrs Mendall," Susan said. "Thank you very much indeed for coming."

"It's been a pleasure, dearie. And no need to settle anything. Mrs Everett fixed that before I come. Good night."

Susan sat down in the armchair as if her legs would no longer support her.

She heard Mrs Mendall's footsteps down the garden path, the gate click, Gareth's voice and then the soft purr of the engine as it drove off into the night.

Then her hands unclenched from her sides and went to her

face, cupping her burning cheeks as if their icy touch would cool the feverish heat on her face.

"Oh, Jane, Jane!" she whispered. And then, not in bewilderment but in low wonder, she cried: "*Gareth*. Even your name. Oh, Gareth! And I have no right to love you. Dear God, help me! Tell me what to do!"

Three

Unlike Jane, who, Susan realized, would probably remain in bed until midday, she was up at her usual hour of seven-thirty to give Teddy his breakfast before he went off to school. She felt hot-eyed and weary, for she had not slept well and Teddy's eager questioning as to her enjoyment of the party battered on her mind, which felt bruised and shaken.

Somehow, she managed to answer him; was glad that she could tell him truthfully how much she had enjoyed dancing, both with his new Uncle Jim and more particularly with Uncle Gareth. This seemed to content her son and the fact that she merely nodded her head in reply to his assumption that she must have been "spiffing well glad she went after all" passed almost unnoticed.

At last Ted went off in high spirits with life in general, leaving Susan alone. From habit she started her customary round of domestic duties, but for once her mind was not on her job but wandering in a queer, unhappy, undecided way around the subject of Gareth . . . and Jane. In the sharp clear-cut morning light, the violent and unexpected emotions she had experienced the night before, seemed less factual, more imagined. That unaccountable thrill that shot through her arm when Gareth's hand held her own, was somehow the least believable of all the unsettling emotions that had beset her. Logically, she told herself firmly, she could not suddenly fall in love with a man who was almost a stranger to her . . . one moment having no awareness of him at all, the next being 'in love' with him. That was not the way she had fallen in love with Edward, whom she had grown to love steadily through the years since their first meeting until, as a natural conclusion, they had become engaged for a short month and were then married. Her love for Edward had grown with her knowledge of him, her admiration of his character and her increasing awareness of her physical need for him, as their love-making made new and wonderful discoveries. In some ways, she had continued to love Edward more every day that she knew him, more with the intimacy of marriage and with the birth of their child.

Sitting down to a much-needed cup of strong coffee, Susan lit a cigarette, something which was a rarity for her, since she could ill afford to smoke and seldom felt the need, and convinced herself that she had been behaving like a stupid, romantic schoolgirl . . . that her feverishly beating heart and sleepless night had been brought about by her inexplicable restlessness of mind and not by any definite emotion.

'I've been living alone too long,' she told herself firmly, 'when I start thinking I'm in love with the first man who touches me . . . holds my hand for a few minutes. What a sure sign of repression!'

She was able to laugh at herself for a moment and then her laughter gave place to a feeling of self-disgust. Gareth Everett was a married man . . . the husband of one of her friends, and Jane, for all her faults, had been a good friend to her . . . generous, with small gifts of things "I really haven't any use for it any more, Sue; I'd like you to have it"; her thoughtfulness in paying Mrs Mendall for sitting with Ted last night, sparing her the embarrassment of offering the money to her, Susan. It seemed disloyal even to have believed for an instant that she had fallen in love with Gareth . . . disloyal and ridiculous.

"What a silly little fool I'm being," Susan told herself sharply. "It's time I pulled myself together . . . and quickly! I'll not give the matter another thought."

She took her cup through to the kitchen with a lightened heart and, humming a little beneath her breath, began to prepare the vegetables for lunch. Then the telephone rang, and all her new resolutions were wiped away before she had time to consider them. Her heart thudded wildly and the colour rushed to her cheeks in a swift burning wave, to recede as quickly leaving her white and trembling.

"Pull yourself together, Susan Parish!" she said aloud. "It couldn't be . . ."

She lifted the receiver and relief flooded through her as Jane's voice, sleepy and somewhat muffled, reached her.

"Darling, is that you? My dear, I'm desperately apologetic about last night. Frankly, I was just the weeniest bit bottled and I never realized how selfish I was being. You will forgive me, won't you, Sue?"

"Jane, for goodness, sake, there's nothing to forgive!" Susan cried quickly. "Why should you have left just because I had to? It was wonderful of you to include me in the party at all, and I'm the one who must apologize for spoiling your evening!"

"Goodness, *you* didn't spoil it, Sue. It's that old bear of a husband of mine. He's as stubborn as a mule . . . or rather as the Scot he is. He gets a bee in his bonnet about a 'principle', and that's all there is to it as far as he's concerned. He was jealous – didn't like seeing me have a good time with those people and nothing would do but that he should break the party up. Honestly, who'd be married!"

"Jane, don't talk like that!" Susan reproved her friend. "You know you don't really mean it. Besides, you'd hate it if Gareth gave in to you *all* the time; you said so yourself only yesterday."

"Oh, I know, I know!" Jane's voice came, slightly irritable. "I suppose I'm just one of those people who want their cake and eat it, or whatever the silly old saying is. Gareth gave me a good dressing down when Jim got me home and went off in a temper this morning, without even saying good-bye. That's to punish me, I suppose. Well, I don't feel sorry – as far as he is concerned. But I am sorry about you and I agree with Gareth – on that point I behaved badly."

"Jane, I won't listen to any more such nonsense," Susan broke in.

Jane laughed.

"Okay, darling! It's too damned early to be intense, anyway. I've got a frightful head and Jim's screaming at me to get him some breakfast. Heaven knows what's happened to Mrs Mendall, so I shall have to get up."

"You'd better both come round and have breakfast here," Susan suggested. "I'll be frying some eggs while you're getting up."

"Sue! You are a dear! That's a perfect idea and Jim will be tickled pink. He's really smitten with you . . . keeps waking me up to ask me when he's going to see more of you! Tell me, darling, how did you like him?"

"Get up this minute or your breakfast will spoil!" Susan parried the question neatly, and replaced the receiver on Jane's tinkling laughter.

Five minutes later there was a knock on the door and Jim arrived.

"Good morning, Sue. It wasn't any use waiting for Jane," he said as he came into the little hall, removed his Burberry and looked at Susan with blue, eager eyes. "I should think she's gone back to sleep again and I just can't go another minute without something inside me."

"It's almost ready!" Susan comforted him with a smile. "Warm up by the fire while I'm dishing up."

"Something smells good!" Jim said, pushing the wet, curly fair hair from his eyes and moving over to the blazing fire. "I say, what a dear little cottage."

"It's not quite up to Jane's standards of luxury I'm afraid," Susan called from the kitchen. "I've no electric light yet and only a miserable oil cooker."

"All the same, it's got a lot of charm which I think The Willows lacks, with its strip-lighting and so on. I like these old places like yours – untouched."

"So would I if I didn't have to clean it!" Susan said, as she carried a tray with two fried eggs and a rasher of bacon through to the sitting-room.

He took the tray from her and she sat down on the sofa, watching him tuck in. Now and again he paused to give her a satisfied grin. When at last he pushed the tray from him, holding out his cup for a third cup of coffee, the grin had spread over his whole face.

"You look like the cat after a bowl of cream!" Susan said.

"And I feel like it. You *can* cook, madam. May I ask if you're otherwise engaged or will you marry me tomorrow? Give me a breakfast like that every day and I'll willingly support you for life."

Susan joined in his laughter, thinking once more what a nice boy Jane's brother was . . . friendly, unaffected, amusing, full of charm.

She could grow to care for him very deeply, she thought . . . but as a brother. She hoped Jane was, as usual, exaggerating when she had said Jim was "smitten". It would make friendship with him so much more difficult and she had so few friends down here that it would be a shame if she were to lose one for that reason.

"Thank you for the compliment, but I regret I am already engaged to cook similar breakfasts for Master Ted Parish," she told him in the same light, bantering tone he had used. "So I must decline your offer."

"A great pity, gre . . . aat pity!" Jim said, looking at her consideringly from beneath his long, fair lashes. "Oh, well, first come first served. I'll bet poor old Gareth didn't get a dishful like that, all the same."

The smile became fixed on Susan's face but Jim didn't seem to notice.

"Frightful bust up last night," he went on with typical brotherly candour. "Jane's fault, of course, but then she can be a little . . . well, you know what, when she chooses. Can't think why Gareth married her myself. Shouldn't have thought she was his type, would you? Still, he's taken her on, poor man, for better or for worse and I guess he had some of 'the worse' last night."

"I'm afraid it was mostly my fault!" Susan said helplessly. Jim, like his sister, was so outspoken. In her own family they would never have discussed family upsets with someone who was practically a stranger. Or did Jim imagine that she knew the Everetts more intimately than she did?

"Your fault! My dear child, you're the golden-eyed girl. I'm only sorry old Gareth marched you off when he did. I'd wanted a few more dances at least. But I got roped in by Jane for a drink at the bar and frankly, I didn't care for those types she got in with and I thought it best to stay and keep an eye on her until old Ga-Ga turned up. Damn shame."

"I enjoyed myself very much," Susan said firmly, and was relieved to hear Jane's light knock on the door.

Jane's hangover had no lasting effects. By the time she, too, had had breakfast, she was in fine spirits. Before long she had it all arranged that Jim should take them both out to lunch at the local pub, Teddy, too; deliver him back to school, and then take the two girls on to the cinema in the afternoon. In spite of the fact that she had quite a few jobs to do, Susan agreed to fall in with these plans. She did not really want to stay alone all afternoon with her introspective thoughts and her oddly depressed mood. Somehow, in Jane's and Jim's company it was impossible not to catch a little of their bantering, light-heartedness – their inveterate devil-may-care good spirits.

Ted, of course, was thrilled to be lunching out. His conversation kept them in fits of laughter throughout the meal and with sudden lapse in her usually strict discipline, Susan said he could forego afternoon football at school and come to the cinema with them. It was so unlike her to act thus impulsively that even Ted found it difficult to believe his mother really meant it. When he saw by her face that she did, he flung his arms round her and, unmindful of the onlookers, gave her a resounding kiss and hug that touched her deeply.

It was, to Ted's delight, a real old-fashioned 'Cowboy' . . . something the adults would have found tedious on their own but from which they derived huge enjoyment merely through Ted's wild excitement. They had as much fun hissing, clapping and booing as he did.

When it was over, Susan wanted them to go back to tea at her cottage but Jane insisted it was "her turn".

"Besides, Gareth will be home early. He always is on Fridays," she told them. "I'd better have a decent tea ready or he'll really be cross!"

"I think perhaps we *ought* to go home," Susan murmured, but Ted, over-excited now, shouted that it was just *silly* to go home when they might see Uncle Gareth and have tea with *him*.

'That's the trouble, my boy,' Susan thought wryly. 'I'm not sure I want to face Gareth. I'm still afraid!'

But she went, not having the strength of will to find a suitable excuse, and because, she admitted as they drove up to Jane's cottage . . . she knew she would have to face Gareth sooner or later.

She was in Jane's beautifully compact little kitchen cutting sandwiches when Gareth came home. Standing, her hand poised by the loaf of bread, she heard Jane's voice saying lightly, "Hallo, darling! Tea's just ready. Susan and Ted are here, too. We've all been to the cinema and had a crazy afternoon."

But his reply was too low for her to catch the words. Then Jane reappeared in the kitchen and there was nothing for it but to follow her back into the sitting-room, carrying her loaded tray.

It was some moments before she allowed herself to look at Gareth . . . then only when she knew he was deep in conversation with Teddy and not aware of her gaze. Looking at him, seeing his tall figure in its immaculate town suit, his eyes a little strained and tired but smiling, she knew that after all, she had not been imagining. There was no shock this time, no unexpected jab at her heart, only a swift rush of certainty that she loved this man; that no matter who he was, what he was, or if he were a much-married man, she could feel no differently towards him. It was a certainty beyond doubt, beyond human control and although she would admit it to no other living soul, it could not be denied to herself.

'Gareth, Gareth!' she thought. 'What has happened to make me feel this way? To know so surely? Is it that so slight physical contact of last night? Or is it the dear way you are smiling now at my son . . . your kindness to him? Or just that you look tired and I long to go to you as I would to Teddy and smooth out those lines beneath your eyes? If only I knew where to find the root of my love for you I might be able to drag it out and destroy it.'

And yet, deep within her, she knew she did not wish to be without that knowledge of love, so sweet even while so utterly hopeless, so right in its instinctiveness, so wrong by the very commandments. Gareth belonged to Jane. But . . . Jane, dear restless, impulsive, unhappy Jane . . . did not really love *him*.

"It's amazing how well those two get on," Jim's voice said at her elbow.

With a start, Susan turned towards him, her cheeks aflame, as for a moment she imagined Jim had read her thoughts. Then she followed his gaze to Ted and Gareth and knew that he had spoken of them.

"Teddy adores his Uncle Gareth," she said more calmly.

"Ga-Ga's so confoundedly good with the kid," Jim said. "Quite honestly, I shouldn't have thought he was the type to get on with kids, but it just goes to show. Shame, really, that he hasn't any of his own. It's about time young Jane gave me a nephew or two."

The thought swam around in Susan's head . . . not a new thought, this one that Jane should have children . . . a suggestion she herself had made, and yet how new it seemed in the light of her feelings for Gareth. It was as if she could not see him as a father to Jane's children any longer . . . only . . . only . . .

'I can't go on like this!' she pulled herself up mentally. 'It's so wrong . . . so unfair. And I'm deeply fond of Jane. Nothing in the world would make me hurt her willingly and yet even these thoughts harm her in my mind. I wish I could go away . . . far away . . . get this whole stupid business out of my system. It will spoil my life. And Edward would be so ashamed of me.'

Yet she could not believe that last mental assertion. Edward, who had always understood her so well, would understand this, too. He would know that she couldn't help herself, couldn't do more than fight against it inside her and try to deny it, even to herself. Once he had said, "You either love or like or dislike. You may change your opinions but once those feelings are within you, only circumstances can change them . . . you cannot change them by just wishing them changed."

For the first time, Susan felt able to look at her new emotions, objectively. It was as if she stood apart with Edward, looking down on that other self, seeing how hopelessly she was caught in the web and yet part of it, too. It had all happened so unexpectedly, so differently from the way she would have wished it. It was not as she had imagined it, either. She had once said to Jane, "I loved Edward so much I couldn't fall in love again. If I married again I could only give second best of myself."

But even this was untrue. A different love asked different things of one; aroused quite separate emotions. It was as if loving were like dreaming . . . the dreams could be as different as were the ways of loving.

"I do wish you'd tell me what you are thinking about, Susan. You look a thousand miles away. I've never met anyone so full of day-dreams."

Susan gave her head a tiny shake as if this would bring her mind's eye back into sharper focus. She turned once more to Jim and replied, "I'm afraid I am a woolgatherer."

"Then you won't tell me what pearls of wisdom were passing through your mind?" Jim asked, half banteringly, half seriously.

A faint spot of colour touched Susan's cheeks but he only glimpsed it before it was gone.

"Really, they weren't worth knowing," she said. But he didn't believe her and longed, for a swift moment, to *make* her tell him. What an unusual, strange girl was this new friend of his sister! She was amazingly attractive . . . not just to look at . . . for in Jim's mind she was more than just pretty, she was fascinating in other more lasting and tantalizing ways. To be with Susan was like staring into a deep pool . . . perhaps an illusion from those dark eyes of hers . . . an unfathomable pool across which reflections rippled, a little sunlight when she laughed, a cloud or two when she dreamed, and all the time there was a feeling of hidden depths beneath that readable, yet obscure, mirrored surface.

Yes, there was something tantalizing about Susan that went right to the heart of a man, Jim decided, and it intrigued him. A kind of challenge which he, personally, was a little afraid of but had to accept.

'If I'm not careful, I shall find myself falling in love with her,' he told himself warily, for he had determined he wouldn't marry for some years yet. And in the past his choice of a girlfriend had been something more of the glamour-girl type. He was doing very well in his job for a man of twenty-eight, as one of the junior executives in Gareth's firm. It was a job he owed in the first instance to his brother-in-law who had taken him on at Jane's request after his release from the army. But since then, he had made his own way, and he knew that Gareth had never regretted giving him that chance.

Gareth was a decent fellow. Jim contemplated his brother-in-law. In many ways he was a lot too nice for Jane. Fond though he was of his only sister, Jim knew she was spoilt . . . that there was no depth to her character. It was not so much her fault as the way she was made. Nothing touched her very deeply . . . unless it was the one time in her life when she had been powerless to get her own way . . . when her young American husband was killed. Oddly enough, Jane had shown unexpected depths of character over Ham. She had really suffered a good deal and, in some ways, she had never recovered. It had made her restless and dissatisfied, whereas when a kid she had skimmed along the surface of life, taking things as they came and getting the best out of them.

A funny girl, Janey, reflected her brother. A generous-hearted kind of kid, but for all her generosity she was paradoxically selfish as only her type of woman could be. Not that he ever thought of Jane as a woman. She was too much of the "little" girl, and not just because of her blonde hair and childish, china-blue eyes, but in her ways and mannerisms she was immature.

Her pout now (as she looked toward Gareth) was so little changed from the five-year-old who used to pout at Jim when he'd refused to give her some toy she'd wanted! Withal, she was lovable and he was very attached to her; felt protective towards her too. He'd hate any harm or real unhappiness to come her way.

Not, thought Jim, that it was likely, with Gareth for a husband. Gareth could cope with Jane, if she needed it. He was stubborn enough at times and had all the innate Scottish characteristics . . . a fierce integrity, an almost fanatical sense of loyalty and duty. Gareth was a strong man . . . as strong in spirit as in physique, and age was on his side. He had surely enough experience of life by now to be able to deal with young Jane in her tantrums!

Jim smiled contentedly to himself, thinking how pleasant this unexpected visit was turning out to be. As a matter of fact, he had been going to stay the weekend with the parents of his latest girlfriend, Margaret, down at their country house in Suffolk. But they'd had another of their usual quarrels and this time he'd felt he'd put up with Margaret's nonsense just once too often. The quarrel had gained fervour and ended with Margaret saying she didn't want to see him any more and himself returning the compliment. So that was that. He'd expected to regret his hastiness when he cooled down a bit, but for all that he was really in a way quite fond of old Margie, this time the inclination to eat humble pie hadn't attacked him. And travelling down in the train with Gareth the evening before, he'd felt as if he'd thrown off a weight he'd not known, until then, was there! So much for Margaret. In the meantime, there was Susan Parish on whom he looked very differently. He could not imagine entertaining a light flirtation with this young widow, such as he had been having with Margaret these last few months. Somehow, Susan did not seem the type of girl one took out to the cinema or to dances several times a week, and just kissed and petted inevitably as was expected of one, on the way home. No, Susan was the kind of girl a man might consider as a real friend, or, more possibly, might wish to marry.

'I must pump old Jane to tell me what Susan thinks of me!' he thought, with an inward laugh at himself and his reflections.

Except for Gareth who was still busily talking to Teddy, or in fact more often listening to the small boy's chatter, the three adults in the room were lost in a companionable silence, each following their separate train of thought. Jane, her high spirits of the afternoon now suddenly evaporated, looked around her drawing-room and the people in it with a faint feeling of discontent to which she could give no real cause. Gareth, talking to young Ted, was as handsome and debonair as usual, she reflected dispassionately. He really was an exceptionally handsome man and yet he had never been able to give her that same thrill she had known when she looked at Ham, with his snub nose, his freckles, his mop of curls. Not that she had expected to find it with Gareth, and yet she had hoped there'd be other things. At first there were. It was fun to go into a crowded room and know that every woman's head was turned in her husband's direction, admiring him, envying *her*. Fun, too, to have almost *carte blanche* for shopping; time to go to mannequin parades at the big fashion houses and say before leaving, "I'll have the black model made up in emerald!" Spending fifty pounds as she had once spent fivers! Fun, too, to be taken around town by Gareth who knew the best places to go to; who managed waiters so perfectly and was such an effortless host. And not least, it had been strangely exciting knowing the power she had over him . . . still had at times, though not quite so often as before, she reminded herself with unusual candour.

Gareth had been so much more in love with her than she with him when they were first married. He had never really thought about any other girl that way as far as she knew, even when she had married Ham and was seemingly beyond his reach. Of course, he had been abroad during the war and not met many girls, but it was she, Jane, to whom he had written;

for whom he had longed and thought about, and when finally, she had married him, he had hardly been able to believe it true. In a way, he had never really believed she would ever belong to him.

Gareth was a deeply passionate man, Jane reflected. His intense love-making had frightened her a little, even while it had flattered her vanity to know she could have such an effect on him. From her own point of view, her relationship with Gareth was pleasantly satisfactory, but it was really the flirtation, the leading up to love-making that exhilarated her more than the act of possession itself. But Gareth, although in many ways a finer lover than Ham had ever been, was too idealistic for Jane; too poetic in his approach. His emotions, so much deeper than her own, were less controlled once they were aroused. It amused her to carry on a flirtation with Gareth, looking at him provocatively through her lashes, moving her body closer to his and then, when his arms went round her, to draw away with a little laugh, tantalizing him. At first he hadn't minded, but once or twice recently, to her annoyance, he had got up and left her bedroom . . . and not come back.

But the thought that Gareth was not now so easily attracted by her physical charms as he used to be did not deter Jane for long. She felt certain that she had only to make an effort and Gareth would once more be her slave. But for the time being, she simply couldn't be bothered. Gareth was a dear and she was still as fond of him as ever, but there was no getting away from the fact that at times he bored her, or that living here alone so much with him had taken the spice out of life.

'It's the country!' she told herself petulantly. 'And this house.' It was all perfect in a way and yet still she was bored with it. 'I must be getting flu,' she comforted herself. "Oh, I wish something really *exciting* would happen!'

As if she had but to wish, the telephone rang. Jane jumped to her feet and a smile now replacing the frown on her face, lifted the receiver.

Susan, watching her friend, saw Jane's smile broaden. Saw

that Gareth had stopped talking to Teddy and was listening to his wife's conversation.

"Of course I remember you. Fancy you turning up. . . . Why, I'd just love to. Nothing very smart round here, I'm afraid . . . well, the Mayflower isn't too bad . . . All right, Bim. One o'clock, in the bar. So long!"

The phone clicked and Jane faced the room with a bright smile.

"Just fancy that!" she announced to the room in general. "An American friend of Ham's. He's over on a 'vacation' and was so determined to look me up, he's taken all day tracing me. Of course, he didn't know I'd remarried but the War Office finally told him."

"Is it . . . someone I know, Jane?" Gareth asked, his gaze searching her face, his voice low.

"Bim! No, you never met him. His real name is Bartholomew Ignatios Merlin . . . can you believe it? No wonder everyone calls him Bim. It *did* seem strange hearing an American voice again. I suppose he's one of the dollar tourists we're trying to lure to the country."

Her voice was happy and excited, her high spirits had returned. Something in the silence of the other people in the room made her pause, look again at Gareth.

"You don't mind my going, darling, do you?" she added lightly, taking his agreement as a matter of course.

"Not in the least if you wish to go," Gareth replied.

Only Susan, over-sensitive as she was just then to every intonation of his voice, heard the defiance, felt that if it had not been for herself and Jim in the room, Gareth might have said, "Go if you wish, Jane, but I can't honestly say I like it. You can't expect me to approve of your raking up the past."

Small wonder if Gareth was jealous, Susan thought. He loved Jane so much and Jane would never be wholly his. She stared at Gareth's dark head, bent now over a pipe he was lighting, and an immense pity flowed through her, suffusing her eyes. As if there had been a moment of telepathy between them, he looked up at that instant, straight into her face and even as she dropped her own gaze quickly to her trembling hands, she knew that *he* had known what she was thinking. Knew, too, that no man of Gareth's pride could tolerate pity.

"We ought to go now, Ted. It's bed-time!" she said hurriedly. And was glad that it was Jim, not Gareth, who showed them to the door.

Four

Susan had hardly expected to see the Everetts or Jim during the following day. Jane had mentioned they might drive over to some friends for tea on the Saturday, and probably wouldn't be home until late. She was surprised, therefore, when there was a knock on the door soon after tea and Jim's voice asked if he could come in.

Teddy was busy doing an elaborate jigsaw puzzle on the floor, and when Susan went to remind him to get to his feet when someone came into the room to say 'Hallo'! Jim shook his head and prevented her by laying a light hand on her arm. He nodded his head towards the kitchen and, surprised, Susan led the way he indicated.

"Is anything wrong, Jim?" she asked, seeing the serious expression on his face.

"I don't suppose there's anything seriously wrong, but it's a bit tricky. Jane went out just before lunch and left us something cold, saying she'd be back about three-ish, or certainly in time for tea. I never thought any more about it and Gareth and I were busy doing the crossword most of the afternoon. Then I noticed the time. It had gone five. I wouldn't have said anything as Gareth hadn't seemed to notice Jane wasn't back, but he saw me looking at the clock and said he was going to phone the Mayflower. So obviously, he had been wondering what Jane was up to. They told him at the Mayflower that she'd left soon after two, but they had no idea, of course, where she and her 'escort' had gone. I wouldn't think anything of it in the normal way as I know Jane is as unpunctual as the devil, but Gareth's like a bear with a sore head, pacing up and down the house and not saying a damn word. I'd say he's just about as angry as any man could be. I suppose you've no idea where Jane and this American chap could have gone? I thought I'd pop over and ask you which were the likely places and try and tip Jane the wink."

Susan considered this for a moment then said, "I'm sure Gareth's not angry. He's probably just worried . . . in case she's had an accident or something. Did she go in Gareth's car?"

Jim nodded.

"Mind you, I don't think she's hurt herself . . ." he said. Something in the way he stressed the last word caused Susan to look at him closely. He gave a short laugh which was slightly embarrassed. "My own view is she's just forgotten about the time and is too damn thoughtless to give Gareth a ring."

"I can't think where they might have gone, unless it's to a cinema," Susan said helplessly.

"The first house would be out by now. It's nearly six. Oh, lord, what a mess! I'm getting pretty angry with Jane, myself. Personally I think Gareth's a fool to let her go lunching *à deux* with a Yank she used to know in the days of old Ham. Different if he was at work, but when Ga's home for the weekend, it's a bit too steep."

"I don't suppose that angle ever occurred to Jane," Susan said. "Besides, I'm sure Gareth knows he can trust her."

"More fool Gareth, then," said Jim shortly. "Personally I wouldn't trust young Jane a yard farther than I could see her, but then, I'm her brother and I don't wear rose-coloured spectacles!"

His voice and words were indeed so brotherly that Susan had to laugh.

"Surely she'll be home in a minute," Susan said after a moment. "She must realize you'll soon be getting hungry!"

"Soon! We're both hungry now . . . or Gareth would be if he wasn't so angry he can't feel anything else. Jane's a fool, Susan. One of these days she'll try Gareth's patience too far. The way she spoke to him last night he might have been the coal man. She thinks he doesn't mind being pushed around but Gareth isn't the henpecked husband type. He's just too darned good-mannered to say anything on the subject in front of me."

Susan listened to these confidences in perplexed silence. Her own position was so awkward . . . so much more so now that her personal feelings as well as her principles were involved. She didn't want to know about Jane's and Gareth's domestic quarrels; didn't want to be made to feel this hurt that became hers just because it was Gareth's; to be made to feel suddenly that she disliked Jane and wanted to shake her back to her senses . . . make her appreciate her wonderful good fortune in having the love of a man like Gareth.

"I . . . wish I could suggest something," she said again. "I just can't imagine where they would go. There's no other pub or hotel Jane would consider going into but the Mayflower . . . unless they decided to go up to London. But surely there wouldn't have been time to do that!"

"Seems as if Jane considers she has all the time in the world," Jim retorted. "Oh, well, I suppose I'd better go back and console the irate husband. Maybe she'll turn up soon."

"I'll listen for the car," Susan said. "If she's not back by seven, will you and Gareth come and have supper with me?"

"That would be imposing . . ." Jim began, but Susan shook her head, smiling.

"I really enjoy cooking . . . if there's an appreciative palate around," she broke in. "And I see so few people. It's always a treat for me to have company."

"I for one will accept the offer, then," Jim said firmly, "And unless Gareth is twice an idiot, he'll do the same. *Au revoir*, then, Susan. And thanks!"

Teddy heard the front door bang and as Susan joined him in the sitting-room, he asked his usual unending string of questions. She answered absent-mindedly, one ear listening the while for the sound of a car engine. Once or twice a car went by but not Gareth's smooth-running Triumph . . . only the noisy clattering of lorries and farm wagons.

By half past six, Teddy now safely tucked in bed listening to

Dick Barton before his light was turned out, Susan stood in the tiny hall by the telephone, certain now that Jane would not be home in time for supper. She asked for the Everetts' number and waited for Jim to answer. But it was Gareth's slightly deeper voice, a little sharper than usual, which answered her.

"Hallo? Who is that?"

She knew then that he had expected to hear Jane's voice and her heart ached with the idea that her own must be a bitter disappointment to him.

"It's Susan. Susan Parish," she said gently. "I just wanted to confirm you and Jim would be coming to supper."

There was a second's silence during which Susan could hear nothing but the angry beating of her heart.

"Really, we can't impose on you. We'll manage very well here. It was . . . very kind of you to suggest it . . . Susan."

Disappointment flooded through her. For a moment she, in turn, could think of nothing to say. She heard his voice again:

"Of course, if you've already prepared the food . . . ?"

"Well, not exactly," Susan said hesitantly. There was another short silence and then Gareth's voice . . . this time in a firmer, brighter tone said, "Look here, if you're sure it's all right, we'll come. We'd love to, you know. It's just that it doesn't seem right that you should be put to the trouble."

Happiness took the place of misery.

"In about half an hour," she murmured and rang off before he could change his mind again.

"I'm crazy!" she told herself as she rushed upstairs to change her dress and settle Teddy down. "I ought to know better. I've no right to care whether he comes or not."

But she couldn't help caring, couldn't refrain from giving her hair an extra brush, touching up her lips. Staring at her glowing reflection, she halted for a moment in wonder at this new bright-eyed, flushed Susan staring back at her.

"I look . . . different!" she whispered, and covering her burning cheeks with her cool hands knew that *it was love* . . . only love that could change her so.

A little ashamed, but filled with eagerness, she ran down to the kitchen and hurriedly started to prepare a meal, her mind still listening for the car, hoping and praying now that it would not come. Not just yet. She must have this one evening, just an hour; this once to cook a meal for Gareth, to see him sitting at her table; to hear a word of praise . . . and she was beyond caring that now, in spite of her resolutions, she was caught, firmly and irrevocably, in the net.

Jane did not return and soon after seven, Gareth and Jim arrived at the door. They were loaded with bottles and their faces were bright with the cold night air . . . and with laughter.

"A party!" Gareth said. "Sherry to give us an appetite, white wine for the meal and beer to follow."

"It's wonderful!" Susan murmured as she watched them take off their coats, too weak still with relief that they had come, to make any move.

"Shall I come and fetch some glasses?" Gareth asked.

She nodded her head again, acutely conscious of his tall figure behind hers, stooping as he passed beneath the big beam into the kitchen. He held the tray while she put on glasses, a bottle-opener and corkscrew. He sniffed the air.

"Nice smell!" he said, screwing up his nose appreciatively.

"It's Mousaka . . . a Czechoslavak dish," Susan said smiling. "Used by housewives nowadays to camouflage the horrible truth!"

"I don't believe it!" Gareth retorted, joining in her laughter. "Anything I can do?"

She shook her head, still shy of him, still unable to believe he was really standing here beside her.

"Then I'll take this through," he said.

She had laid the table in the sitting-room by the blazing fire. There had been no time to light the fire in the dining-room. But the two men seemed happy enough with this informal arrangement. When Susan joined them they were uncorking the sherry and talking and laughing as if they hadn't a care in the world.

Gareth handed her a glass, Jim a cigarette, and then Gareth, making room for her by the fire, raised his glass and said, "To our very charming hostess!"

"Hear, hear!" cried Jim, but she barely heard his voice, so happy was she made by the look of friendliness and admiration in Gareth's eyes. It seemed as if he had all of a sudden lost his shyness; as if he had gained self-confidence in her company, with her own loss of it! And as for Jane . . . nobody but Susan appeared to be giving her a thought. It was Gareth, moreover, who switched on the wireless and Susan could not help but wonder if he had created this noise to drown the possible arrival of the car as an act of defiance.

Throughout the evening, it seemed to Susan as if this must indeed be the case. Gareth was almost flirting with her . . . as if he were trying to show Jim that Jane's behaviour mattered not a tinker's cuss to him. A kind of 'Let her gad about as she chooses . . . I can enjoy myself too'. It was a bitter knowledge and yet to be near him, be praised by him for her cooking, have her dress, her hair admired by him . . . all were sweet enough joys, whatever his motive. And she was happy. She sat between them, hearing their spontaneous laughter, Gareth's voice, deeper and stronger than Jim's, savouring these few hours; knowing now that she had missed so very much by leading her life alone as she had done these past years; knowing, too, that tomorrow the loneliness would return; realizing now that it would be a hundred times more painful. But she could not regret it. Not yet, anyway. She thought of a little folk tune Teddy sometimes sang . . . 'Let tomorrow bring it's sorrow, For today I shall be gay'. That was so exactly as she herself felt tonight . . . reckless and improvident, but very happy.

Soon after the ten o'clock news that had ended the dance music, the telephone rang and Susan knew that it was all over. She could understand now the sinking sensation Teddy once described to her when, after a particularly lovely outing, she had said to him, 'Time to go'. She knew it would be Jane and a strange, protective numbness seemed to close down on her as she walked towards the telephone and lifted the receiver.

Jane's high bell-like voice said, "Susan? My dear, are my menfolk with you? I've just got back and the house is empty."

"They came to supper," Susan said briefly. "Would you like to speak to Gareth?"

"Yes, I should!" came Jane's angry little voice. "He might at least have had the decency to bank up the fire. I'm frozen!"

Her voice carried through the microphone across the room and Susan, turning to hand the instrument to Gareth, saw the two men look at one another like schoolboys, eye-brows raised.

"Of all the nerve!" Jim murmured. Then Gareth's lips tightened and he took the telephone from Susan's hands.

"Well, Jane?" was all he said, but his voice was ominous.

"Well, what?" came Jane's voice. "I've just got back from town, Gareth. We decided to run up and do a matinee after lunch and then I was talked into having a meal. You're not angry, are you?"

"Certainly not. Far from it! I hope you've had as pleasant a time as we have had." His tone was still too quiet, too steady.

There was silence the other end, then Jane's voice, a little higher, sharper, "Well, are you coming home now?"

"Quite soon!" Gareth said casually. "In case you're asleep when we come in, I'll say good night now, Jane."

"Oh, if that's the way you want to take it, *good night*!" Jane shouted and slammed the receiver down.

"Phew! That'll teach her a lesson!" Jim said admiringly.

Gareth was looking at Susan.

"I do hope you'll excuse these domestic upsets, Susan," he said, his voice no longer hard but gentle once more. "And I hope you don't think I've been making use of you to . . . well, to teach my wife a lesson, as Jim suggests. I'm afraid I have given that impression but I'd like you to know that that wasn't my reason for coming. And I have really and truly had a wonderful evening. It's been . . . wonderful. I wish . . . well, we'll have to do it again some time . . . soon. Won't we, Jim?"

Susan felt the tell-tale colour flame in her cheeks as she listened to Gareth's impulsive speech. She believed that he was telling the truth, for he *had* been enjoying himself. He'd seemed almost ten years younger, talking, laughing, fooling around with Jim.

"I've been very happy to have you," she said, hoping that her words did not sound too formal, too strained. If only he knew it, they were so very true!

"I suppose I really ought to push off!" Gareth said, seeming older again, shyer. "Jim?"

Susan knew that Jim was looking at her, asking her with his eyes if he might stay a little longer, but she did not feel able to give him the answer he wanted. Once Gareth was gone, the spirit would go out of the evening for her.

"I'd like to ask you both to stay, but I'm a little tired, and Ted is sure to wake me early. Sunday makes no difference to him."

Jim rose reluctantly.

"How about the two of you coming out to tea tomorrow with me?" he asked. "That is, if there is anywhere to have tea out on a Sunday?"

"Ted would be thrilled with the idea. But I'm afraid the nearest place open is at least five miles away."

"Jim can have my car . . . if there's any petrol left in it," Gareth said.

"Then it's a date?" Jim persisted.

Susan had no alternative but to accept. She could not trust herself to look at Gareth as he said good night, and was glad that he did not offer his hand. But Jim lifted her hand from her side as Gareth went through the door, and before she could stop him, dropped a kiss into her upturned palm.

"Pleasant dreams, Sue!" he whispered.

But it was of Gareth she dreamed, not Jim.

When Gareth entered his house that night, it was with the firm intention of making as little noise as possible, to avoid further discussion with his young wife, and a possible scene with her. He was so utterly tired – in mind rather than body. His feelings about Jane and her casual inconsequent behaviour, were in chaos – the more so for the contrast to Susan Parish's charm and dignity during the evening. Her utter difference from Jane; her sweet, soothing personality, her steadfast nature which had so much loyalty to her dead husband, yet was human enough to respond to the call of today. Gareth – without daring to dissect the affair – was psychologist enough to know that Susan was no longer content with widowhood and isolation with only her small son for company. He had felt her hand quiver in his . . . seen the swift, startled, starry gaze from her warm, dark eyes . . . realized that she thrilled to his touch, and in his turn been curiously enthralled. But only momentarily. The fundamental man in Gareth was far too steady, too faithful, to be easily lured either by mere vanity or curiosity from his intrinsic love for the girl whom he had desired so long and devotedly and whom he had married.

But for some time now he had been forced against his will into the bitter realization that he had hitched his wagon to no star, but to a wavering light . . . an elusive will o' the wisp, to Jane, who was half-child, half-woman and wholly egotistical. Jane, who took so much and gave only when she felt inclined. And lately he, himself, had not been so inclined towards giving all the favours. He had withdrawn from her because he was far too proud to force himself, unwanted, upon any woman. He had waited, aloof and wounded, hoping that she would return to his arms, and be yielding and tender and as seemingly responsive as she had been in the first days of their marriage. Yet, he had asked himself since, had Jane ever really loved him? Had he mistaken that fleeting pleasure she showed in being kissed and caressed, for the deep passion in his own body? Was she charming but insincere – utterly without depth? Had he been striving hopelessly for a fire to match his own but which no man could light unless, at one time, Ham, her American husband, had ignited it?

Weary and troubled, Gareth tiptoed into his dressing-room. But almost immediately the room adjoining was flooded with light and a quick, imperious voice, sharpened with irritation, said, "Gareth . . . is that you? I want to speak to you."

He raised his brows. So there must be a peroration . . . not of his making, but of hers . . . the spoiled, thwarted child, furious because he had not countenanced her escapade and immediately made her feel pleased with herself again. But he felt no particular desire to conciliate Jane tonight. He was, himself, smarting under the lash. That subtle whip of inconsideration for *his* feelings that Jane flicked whenever she chose against a heart, a consciousness, already all too aware of growing indifference to him.

He walked into her bedroom. It was warm, redolent of 'Arpège' – her favourite perfume – and gracelessly untidy; gossamer stockings on the floor; silk lingerie flung here and there; a dress in a heap where it had dropped from its hanger; Jane, too lazy or too tired to pick it up; cigarette ash on the silk eiderdown. Jane, lovely – impossibly so – with golden hair floating on ivory bare shoulders lay there eyes flashing at him from beneath frowning brows, curving lashes; lips flouting defiance, pouting.

"And may I ask why you let me come back alone here like this to a stone-cold house? You might at least have asked me to join your party at Sue's!" she flung at him.

Gareth's anger suddenly evaporated. He could even laugh. He sat down on the edge of the bed and put out a hand to take hers, which she immediately snatched away.

"Don't!" she said.

His fleeting desire to be understanding and make it up at once with a kiss, died.

He said stiffly, "Perhaps I may ask why *you* stayed out as you did and left Jim and me in mid-air wondering where you had gone and whether you intended to come home for dinner or not? I think I am the one to be angry – not you, my dear child. You succeeded in making me look a nice fool!"

"I'm not your dear child!" She was tired, sleepy, cross and wholly illogical, knowing deep inside her that she was the guilty one but furious because Gareth did not give way so easily. For a moment she convinced herself that he had dared to neglect *her*, tonight. She said, between set teeth, "And I object to being treated as though you couldn't care less whether I was home or not."

He rose and pulled a cigarette-case from his pocket.

"My dear Jane . . . I object very strenuously to being treated as you treated me. Don't try to switch the blame for this evening's affair."

She answered violently, dramatically.

"Am I in purdah . . . your Persian slave . . . forbidden to be seen or spoken to by any other man, even an old friend?"

"Don't be ridiculous, Jane. I never treat you as a slave. And I raised no objection I can recall to your going out with Bim or whatever his name is."

"You're just jealous – you hated it."

Gareth's face tautened. He did not look at her now.

"If that is what you think, then you might have had the decency to refuse his invitation. That is, if you considered my feelings in the least. Or your duties as a wife."

"So you admit you've become beastly jealous lately."

He gave a thin smile.

"No more than I've always been jealous of you. A man who loves his wife is naturally jealous."

She lowered her lashes, fuming, glowering.

"I can't stand jealousy. It's so childish!"

"Don't let's get this out of proportion, Jane. I showed no particular jealousy and I said go ahead and go out with your American friend. But you could have telephoned to say you meant to prolong the lunch."

Jane flung herself back on her pillow.

"It's all the same now whether I did or didn't phone. You're just a dull old wet blanket. You spoil all my fun!"

She had not meant to be so frank, nor so rude. But he goaded her into it. And she had just had a wonderful day with Bim . . . Bim, whose accent, whose wisecracks and jokes had reminded her so poignantly of those mad, carefree, happy days with Ham. The orchids in a cellophane box on her dinner plate . . . the flow of absurd, amusing compliments. "Gee, honey, you're as sweet as molasses sugar and as golden as a Georgia moon. I'd like to eat you right up . . ."

Then suddenly, her mind reverted from Bim to Gareth again, and with a shock she realized how much she had hurt him by her last remark as she saw the look in his eyes.

He turned on his heel and she leapt out of bed and ran after him. She could not bear to hurt anybody.

It was the old, childish, light-hearted Jane who flung herself into his arms, crying, "Darling, do forgive your Jane. I didn't mean to be beastly. You know I love you, sweetie, and you were jolly decent really to let me go at all. I've had a super day and I'm grateful. Honestly I am. I was just annoyed because my wonderful evening was spoilt by such a homecoming. Poor darling. I suppose you and Jim were a bit bored at Sue's. I ought to have stayed home to entertain you both."

Automatically his arms had gone around her. Her hair floated against his face. The old fragrance . . . the charm was there to lure his senses, but . . . tonight it was his brain and not his body which was aware of her. So typical of Jane to suppose that she had done nothing really wrong but that it could all be put right with a kiss. Typical, too, for her to suppose that his own irritation was due to the fact that he had been bored and miserable without her. Even the kiss which she asked for and received held only the vestige of a thrill for him tonight, for he could *feel* the utter shallowness of her emotions and knew that any man might drive himself mad hoping for a deeper, truer meaning behind her lightly expressed, lightly given embraces.

Almost as soon as her lips left his, she was back in bed, lighting a cigarette, chatting eagerly, laughing . . . telling him about the band, the dancing, Bim's efficiency at the Samba.

"You'll really have to learn, darling."

He did not even bother to reply to that. Despite himself, there came into his mind the memory of the perfect dance which he had had with Susan Parish. Jane had never considered him a good dancer . . . too 'staid', she had always complained. But Susan's style had been his own . . . a more dignified style which she liked and shared.

Jane did not even notice that he was silent. He wondered with a sudden unaccustomed bitterness if she ever stopped to consider his feelings . . . or if she saw only what she wanted to see.

For the first time in his life, Gareth faced the truth, and long after the lights were out and Jane was curled up in his arms asleep, he lay awake, still thinking, deeply troubled in spirit. For he knew that the very thing which had first drawn him to this young wife of his . . . her nymph-like quality of eternal youth . . . had now become the most important barrier to their happiness. For he needed something more . . . a deeper, wiser nature to match and understand his own. And that understanding Jane could never bring to their marriage . . . not necessarily through her fault, for Jane would always be the perpetual child. But he had hoped and waited so patiently for her to grow up a little and he knew now that she never would. Stripped of hope and illusion and with fear catching at his heart, he wondered what kind of a future lay ahead for them both. For the one thing which he had counted on to give Jane a full sense of responsibility was the process of motherhood, which he realized now she would always seek to avoid.

And, as was inevitable, his thoughts turned to the child . . . alas, not his own . . . who had filled the void in his heart . . . Susan Parish's son.

Five

Susan lay back against the pillows, her hot, feverish cheeks cooled by the soft smoothness of the linen case. Outside, she could see through her window the grey windswept skies filled with lowering clouds that foretold rain. Although only three in the afternoon, it was so overcast as to be nearly dark . . . turbulent, restless weather that matched her physical and mental state.

For two days now she had been feeling wretchedly low, with a heavy cold that had since developed into influenza . . . the first illness she had suffered for years. And circumstances made her a bad patient, a restless invalid. She had kept Teddy home from school on the doctor's advice, fearing that he might carry the germ to the other children and start an epidemic. With no one but herself to look after him, cook his meals and put him to bed, there had been no alternative until now but for her to remain up.

Teddy, a sensitive and understanding child, had known that she was feeling ill, and not only had he been as good as gold, but he had fussed over her in the way that once his father had done. For a six-year-old he was touchingly thoughtful, offering to fill the hot-water bottle she had kept at her feet on the sofa where she had spent yesterday and this morning; bringing her a glass of water, putting on the kettle for tea, even lighting the fire under her supervision. But in spite of the many small ways in which he tried, and succeeded, in assisting her, most of all by keeping so quiet, her head still throbbed and felt as if it would burst when she bent it downwards or moved her eyes quickly across the room.

By lunch time, Teddy had looked at her chalk-white face with two scarlet fever-spots on her cheekbones, seen her shivering hands and suggested he go round for 'Aunty Jane'. Susan had felt too weak and helpless to prevent him from worrying Jane; too concerned that if she were going to be really ill, Teddy might catch the germ from her.

After one look at her face, Jane had packed her off to bed and telephoned the doctor. Now here she was, forbidden by the doctor to move for at least three days and feeling so utterly ill, aching in every limb, that she had no wish to move. Teddy had gone to stay a few nights with Jane and Gareth. He had been very excited at the idea and although reluctant to leave her, had made her promise that she would send for him if she needed him, and disappeared happily enough with Jane, his small suitcase with his pyjamas and toothbrush proudly held in one hand.

"I'd come here and look after you and Teddy," Jane had offered, "but the doc thinks it best to have Teddy out of the house. Besides, Sue, I'm pretty hopeless at nursing and I'm not too proud to admit it. So I've arranged for my Mrs Mendall to pop round and 'do' for you. And I don't want a word of argument, because Gareth has insisted it's our expense as I am shirking my nursing duties as your friend."

Susan had tried to argue that Jane had taken good advantage of her throbbing head and general weakness.

It was wonderful to lie still, to know that in an hour or so Mrs Mendall would bring her a cup of tea and remake her bed; to know that she had nothing to do but give way to her illness and find what relief she could from resting like this in a darkened room, a little doped by the M & B tablets she had taken, warmed by the hot bottles in her bed so that she no longer shivered uncontrollably.

'What should I have done without Jane's help!' she thought. It was somehow so typical of Jane to sweep *her* worries away as if they did not exist. And yet, although she, Susan, would have taken someone else's child to care for, it took money to provide those other comforts . . . Mrs Mendall, the huge bunch of grapes on her bed-table, the hothouse roses on her window-sill.

"Those are from Gareth!" Jane had said, arranging the roses in their vase. "He doesn't know it yet but he'd want me to bring something from him. After all, *he* owes *you* something for cooking his meals last weekend!"

How far away last weekend seemed, although it was now only Wednesday. Jim had returned to London on Gareth's business train on Monday morning and she had not seen either of them since that jolly, irresponsible little dinner party. Jane, of course, had dropped in to see her, told her vaguely that Gareth had been "pretty fed up" about her little jaunt with Bim. But she went into greater detail about the jaunt itself. It had been obvious to Susan that there had been something in the way of a quarrel between Jane and Gareth but that Jane, so true to her nature, had brushed it aside and remembered only the pleasant part of the evening. Susan's heart had filled with pity for Gareth and, almost simultaneously, with an acute distaste for her emotions. It had seemed so wrong for her to sit quietly listening to Jane, appearing no doubt by her silence to approve of Jane's behaviour, or at any rate countenancing it, and yet in her heart feel bitterly towards her for not caring more for Gareth's feelings.

But then everything about her love for Gareth was wrong. She had tried so hard to reject the fact that she loved him; had lain awake all Saturday night, telling herself that the evening had been just a 'nice change' and yet knowing that it was so much more than that. For all her denials, it had been three hours of perfect and complete happiness . . . just to have Gareth under her roof, to see his slow smile; to hear his praise of her cooking, even of herself.

'Wrong! Wrong!' Susan fought against her heart. But the truth neither would nor could be denied. And her cheeks flushed with shame when she was forced to answer Jane's "Well, did you enjoy your evening, Sue?" with a casual nod of the head and a murmured "Very much indeed".

Sick in mind and spirit as well as body, Susan lay thinking of the impossible situation into which Fate had trapped her, and weakness led her for the first time into considering what her future could be, now that she no longer had the strength to deny her love. Tomorrow, perhaps, she would be able to tell herself again that her feelings for Gareth had been imagined, temporary, unfounded. But this afternoon she had to be honest with herself, having so little control left over her mind, doped and dazed as she was.

'If only I could leave here, go right away from him,' she thought. "And yet I can't do that. I couldn't afford to move house and I have no right to take Teddy away from school where he's doing so well. Children hate moves and Teddy is so happy here . . . happier than he's ever been since he grew up, having Gareth to hero-worship; to fill the empty place that should have been filled by poor Edward.'

Her mind turned wearily around the subject.

'If Jane and Gareth moved . . . and yet, why should they? Gareth loves his home and has made no mention ever of moving. And Jane . . . she might say she's bored, but neither has she made any mention of moving back to town or to a more lively place.'

'At least,' Susan comforted herself wanly, 'I am the only one involved. If Gareth returned my love . . .'

But the thought brought the colour racing to her cheeks and started her heart beating, her temples throbbing. Brought, too, that old feeling of guilt and shame as she remembered Jane to whom, once again, she was in debt. How Jane would hate' her if she knew the thoughts in her friend's mind; knew the fight that was going on inside her, the constant need there was to force Gareth from her mind or to force Jane back to it!

Mrs Mendall's arrival with a hot cup of tea gave Susan respite from her own company.

"Your young Teddy is getting along fine," she was told. "Ate a huge lunch and has just been up the town with Mrs Everett to help choose a television set. Mr Everett's going to give her one for Christmas. Won't it be a do? Mrs Everett says it's just like being at the pictures, only having them in your own parlour. Of course, Teddy's so excited about it he can't hardly contain himself. But he asked after his mum. There's not every lad would think so much of his mum as yours does of you, Mrs Parish. Real fond of you, he is!"

Tears started to Susan's eyes, tears of weakness, because after all, she was so lucky to have Teddy, whatever else life had denied her.

"There now, lovey, don't take on. Is your head worse?" the woman asked kindly, seeing Susan's tears.

Susan made an effort to smile, to shake her head.

"You're tired, dearie. I'll just puff up your pillows and you drink this down and go right to sleep. Best thing in the world for you. But all the same, better take your pills as the doctor ordered. Be on the safe side, that's my motto! There now, if there's nothing else you want, I'll pop along. I'll drop in later this evening to tuck you up; I've made up my bed in the spare room, if that's all right."

"Your bed!" Susan echoed, trying to understand.

"Well, yes, Mrs Parish. Doctor said you didn't oughta sleep alone. So Mrs Everett asked me if I would mind and it's no trouble to me. You've no objection, Mrs Parish?"

"Of . . . course not!" Susan said. "I just wasn't aware of the arrangements. It's very kind of you, Mrs Mendall."

'And kind of Jane to make all these arrangements for my comfort,' Susan thought. There was nothing now to worry about . . . nothing to do but lie back and give way to the pain in her head . . . to sleep . . .

How long she slept, Susan did not know. When she opened her eyes, the room was in darkness, save for the faint glow of the fire that had been going all day. The curtains had been drawn across the window and, still half-sleeping, Susan wondered dreamily who could have drawn them, for they had been open when Mrs Mendall left.

As her mind cleared a little from the drugged sleep, she knew without turning her head, that there was someone in the room. A moment's fear held her but was replaced by a strange awareness of friendliness, of someone sitting by her bed watching over her, protecting her.

Her heart started to beat, quicker, more quickly still until it raced with the thought that had sprung into her heart. She had been sleeping, dreaming of Gareth and now, perhaps still in her dreams, if she turned her head, she might see him there.

But her mind, gathering consciousness, told her that this could not be. It was someone who was breathing gently, quietly; who was sitting in perfect stillness believing her still asleep.

"Mrs Mendall?" she whispered.

"You're awake, Susan?"

Not Mrs Mendall's voice, nor any woman's, but a man's. A deep voice that she knew so well, that alone had the power to thrill through her body like an electric shock, to set her pulses throbbing.

She turned her head and allowed her eyes to receive his image. It was no dream . . . but Gareth, wearing one of his dark, town suits, a pleasant nondescript tie – clean white collar. How difficult it was to see in the darkness. His face was shadowed and his features indeterminate but for his eyes . . . such blue eyes.

"Gareth!" his name escaped her lips.

"Susan! I hope I didn't startle you. I came round to see how you were and found you asleep. I didn't like to wake you. I thought I'd wait a little while to see if there was anything I could do. I'm so sorry you're ill."

"It was very kind of you to come," Susan found the words with difficulty.

There was a moment's silence. He looked away from her towards the fire.

"It's nearly out!" he said at last. "I wanted to make it up but I thought the noise might wake you. I'll do it now."

"Really . . . please . . ." but her husky words did not reach him, for already he was leaning over the grate, adding a log or two, poking the embers into a blaze so that the room became filled with a soft, red glow.

"Would you like the light on?" he asked.

"Only if you would!" Susan said, for all her illness a sudden moment of vanity making her aware of her tumbled hair, her face which must be flushed and shiny with the fever, her lips colourless.

"The light might hurt your eyes," Gareth said considerately, as if in answer to her unspoken prayer. "Besides, it's nice like this. I nearly fell asleep myself it was so silent, so peaceful here."

"You . . . you've been here long?"

"Only about twenty minutes. How are you feeling?"

She knew suddenly that where he had been at ease while she slept, he was now feeling shy and awkward, that he wanted to go. Well, she would not keep him. She had so little that it was enough to know that he had been here, in her room, watching beside her bed for those most precious moments of time. To know that he was sorry for her illness.

"I'm better!" she lied. "What time is it?"

He stood at the foot of her bed; looked at his watch.

"About seven-thirty. I stopped off on my way back from the station."

"Won't your supper be ready?" Susan asked, trying to give him an opportunity to make his escape. Strangely sensitive now to his feelings, she knew that he longed to go. That he might soon wish he had never come. But he did not take advantage of the excuse she had given him.

"We seldom eat before eight. And I imagine if Jane's putting young Ted to bed, we shall be later still. Susan, isn't there anything I can get for you . . . do? Is the doctor coming again? Surely you shouldn't be here on your own!"

Susan closed her eyes to hide those hated tears of weakness that seemed to threaten her whenever her heart was touched. It was such sweet joy and such pain to know that Gareth was fond enough of her to be even a little worried!

"Mrs Mendall is coming back soon," she said with an effort. "I shall be quite all right, Gareth, really."

He took a sudden long stride towards the bed and leant over her, staring into her face.

"You don't *look* all right!" he said, his voice louder, firmer.

"And you sound awful. Please let me get you something. Or at least let me shake up your pillows."

She assented, but he could not know what it cost her to keep from trembling, as his arm went round her to help her forward, while with the other hand he shook up her pillows. Nor could he know how her heart was crying out for him in answer to the gentleness with which he smoothed the sheet and tucked her hot hand beneath the covers.

"I'm . . . fine . . . now!" she whispered, closing her eyes as if she might fall asleep again.

"Are you tired? Shall I go?" came Gareth's voice.

How great was this cross she had to bear! How great the temptation; the control she must exert not to cry out, 'Don't go, don't leave me, Gareth. I love you. I've loved you for two weeks and it's driving me out of my mind. You belong to Jane and yet my heart is yours, to break if you will. But don't go, don't leave me . . . ever.'

Caught in the whirlpool of her own emotions, Susan knew nothing of those that encompassed the man beside her. And Gareth in his turn, was swept along on a tide of feelings with which he felt powerless to cope. It seemed to him, standing hesitantly in this room, knowing that with one half of him he wanted to go, with the other half that he wanted to stay, that this very indecision had held him in thrall all day.

When Jane had telephoned him at the office to tell him Susan was ill, that Teddy would be staying and the arrangements she had made, he had not been unduly worried or concerned, only sympathetic with Susan for he knew how nasty flu could be. But as the day wore on, busy though he had been, he had found his mind turning back to her, wondering how she was, if perhaps the signs of flu were the prelude to something more serious. He had not told Jane (and as she seldom read the papers, she did not yet know) that there had been one or two outbreaks of infantile paralysis round the district. He had been unable to keep from worrying if these symptoms, so similar in the early stages to flu, might not be the case.

Jane, of course, he argued with himself, always exaggerated everything and she had given him to believe that Susan was really very ill. He had made the usual deductions and accepted the flu until those other thoughts beset him. There followed a strange, undecided half-hour where he toyed with the idea of ringing Jane or the doctor to make sure. Yet it had seemed so silly to do so. The local doctor, presumably no doubt as good as any other, had diagnosed flu so why disbelieve him? And why get het-up about little Susan Parish's illnesses at all? She was not his responsibility. All the same, the thought that she was no one's responsibility, that she had no man, no husband to look after her, did make a difference. And he had always liked her.

He decided to wait until he got back that evening and call on the doctor on his way home just to be certain and put his own mind at rest. But as his train had drawn into the station, he knew that he couldn't call at the doctor's. It would be an absurd thing to do. He would be having his evening surgery, and he would take an extremely poor view of having his diagnosis doubted.

Driving past the doctor's house, Gareth decided to go home and find out from Jane how Susan was. But again his mind had been changed. For Jane, he knew, was afraid of illness. She kept as far from any kind of infection as possible . . . and would not have gone round to see Susan again. It was a great mark of her affection for Susan that she had even offered to have Teddy, who might, who knew, carry a germ. This fear of Jane's annoyed him a little, even while he understood that some people were like that. Nevertheless, it had irritated him, too, for once when he had been ill, Jane wouldn't go near him for days, and he had been wretched and lonely with the nurse Jane had hired to do her duty!

He was almost home when he decided after all that he would do better to call and see Susan, if he were going to do so, before going home. Otherwise, Jane might try to stop him going in case *he* were to bring home a few germs.

Once more his mind had been in confusion. Why go to see Susan at all? And yet he had wanted to go.

In the end he had come, and in doing so had only thrown

himself into greater and deeper confusion. For some strange reason, as he had sat by her bedside, a little amused to find her asleep, worried at first, too, in case she were unconscious! . . . he had felt a deep current of understanding flow between them. Something about her face in repose touched him to sharp emotion. She looked so much younger, so utterly defenceless and innocent in her sleep. And yet none of the character was lost, for that lay in every line and bone of her delicate face. One long, slender hand lay in a kind of appeal pointing towards him, the palm uppermost as if she were asking something of him . . . something he alone could give her. Curiously impelled, he had lightly touched that palm, so burning hot, and instantly her fingers had closed around his own as if this were, indeed, what she had asked of him in her dreams.

The thought had disturbed him, shocked him a little, and he had gently withdrawn his fingers realizing suddenly that if she awoke, she might be angry to find him here, taking advantage of her loneliness to steal into her room and study her face, imagine her dreams. It was as if he had come to burgle her dreams rather than her house.

He had risen to leave and then, undecided again, reseated himself in the chair by her bed. He would wait a little longer to see if she awoke, if there was anything he could do.

His mind relaxed. Soon the noisy quiet of the room impelled itself upon him, and his body relaxed a tautness that so often lately seemed to grip him in sharp tension. Even his increasing desire to smoke of late had disappeared and watching the embers as they smouldered in the hearth, hearing his own and Susan's quiet breathing, he felt as if he had been hypnotized into a state of Yoga . . . of purely spiritual existence. He knew with a kind of hazy certainty that this was what his life in the past two years had lacked . . . this spiritual well-being; the ability to relax for a few moments in the day or night and find complete peace. Living with Jane was like living with an ever-live volcano. She was never still, never quiet, always wanting to be on the move, to talk, dance, run, laugh; and if he were silent, to replace his voice with the wireless, as if she were trying to drown her restlessness with noise. And how completely the noise had drowned his own peace . . . his own tranquillity! Even in her sleep, Jane was restless, flinging from one side to another, turning, sometimes talking in her dreams. Yet her sleep was as deep as this girl's lying so quietly, breathing so softly. It seemed as if even in sleep one retained one's basic nature. For it was Susan's nature to be calm, still, poised, as it was Jane's to be the opposite.

The thoughts floated through Gareth's mind like down blown gently in the breeze. There was no point in them, no conscious comparison. Yet the moment Susan awoke, it was as if he, too, had wakened. Awareness of the unconventionality of his visit made him shy and awkward. Susan's stilted reply to his inquiries recalled a sense of guilt for invading her privacy in such a way. And the memory of her fingers closing round his own in sleep, recalled the memory of that last time he had held her hand, when she had snatched it so quickly from his grasp, causing him to wonder, to ask himself if Susan were a little attracted to him.

It had been but a casual passing thought then but now it came back to him more deeply. And more deeply still, was aroused the same quick excitement that the thought gave him. Almost immediately he tried to turn his mind to the fire . . . her pillows . . . anything but to Susan herself, for he knew now that he had spent far too much time today in thinking about her. It was as if all the indecision of the day had been but the means to an end . . . that end being his visit to her tonight.

'Is that true?' Gareth asked himself. 'Did I just want to see Susan because two days have passed since I had supper here? Has Jim's infatuation for her of which, heaven help me, I had to hear in detail all the way to London, passed from him to me? Can it be that I resent his freedom to flirt with a girl . . . with Susan, when I am not free to do so? And yet why should I want to flirt with Susan? I don't want to. I don't want anything from her, I only wanted to see her . . . to see if she was better . . . to see if there was anything I could do.'

Perplexed, ill at ease, filled now with a restlessness that

matched Jane in her most accentuated moods, Gareth wished to go . . . to get away from whatever witch-like atmosphere there was in this room that was able to throw him so quickly from one weird state of mind to another. It was almost as if he no longer had a mind of his own.

He turned as if to leave and then, turning once more to say good-bye, he looked into Susan's eyes and felt that he was falling into two dark, mysterious pools of liquid light. He could not look away, could not move, only stand there as if paralysed, until at last the sound of her voice released him.

"Jane will be wondering what has happened to you, Gareth. I really think you should go now."

Jane! His wife. Jane, whom he had loved and desired above all things. Jane . . . blonde, beautiful enchanting fairy-like Jane.

But they were but words in his mind, words without true meaning . . . words without any truth left in them unless it was that Jane was his wife. For as he stumbled down the narrow staircase and out into the darkness, as he automatically pressed the starter of his car, and slipped into gear, he knew that Jane would never again enchant him, never again be desirable above all else, for his heart which he had offered to her so willingly, so truly, she had not wished to hold. And now it had been taken from him against his will.

He drove towards the home that was not a home, hardly seeing the road that led to it, seeing only the deep, dark eyes and white face of the girl who now held his heart.

'No!' he thought. 'Oh, no! Not Susan. I love Jane. Jane is my wife. Oh, no, no, no!' It can't be true!

Six

Jane sat in the train that was taking her to London, her hands idly flicking the pages of a brightly illustrated magazine, but her mind busy with her own thoughts rather than with what she saw. The man who had got in at the last station had looked a little like Gareth from the back but his face, she noticed as he sat down, was quite different . . . not nearly so distinguished-looking, so handsome.

She was reminded for a moment with a renewed sense of surprise of the ease with which Gareth had given in to her this morning when she broached him about lunching in town with Bim today.

'Dear Garry!' she thought, affectionate towards him because he really *was* very understanding, *and* generous, and on the whole, awfully easy to manage compared with *some* of her friends' husbands. Just take this morning, for instance. She had expected a rumpus and after a few preliminary inquiries, he had given in without a word or look of disapproval. If she didn't know him so well, she might almost have thought him indifferent. But that was one thing she could always be sure of . . . that Gareth loved her. He always had done so and there was no reason to suppose he'd ever change. After all, *she* hadn't changed and she doubted if she ever would be much different until she got older and began to lose her looks. And that was one of the advantages to marrying an older man. By the time *she* was forty, Garry would be almost an old man . . . nearly sixty, in fact! So he'd be past caring if she had a few wrinkles or grey hairs.

On the whole, she'd arranged her life very well and today she felt happy and contented with her home, her marriage and her husband. It never occurred to Jane that her good spirits were not attributable to these causes at all but to the fact that she had got her own way and had in front of her an afternoon away from home, husband and marriage. But then Jane's thoughts never went below the surface and for the time being, it sufficed that Gareth had consented to her wish to lunch with Bim again without a single difficult moment.

Of course, Jane remembered in self-appreciation, she had promised to be back in time for tea and not repeat her performance of last time, so really, there was no reason why Garry should have been difficult. All the same, she *had* expected opposition and although she had accepted Bim's invitation on the spot when he telephoned her, she hadn't been sure she could get away until she broached the subject to her husband. It wouldn't really have been worth the effort, she told herself now, if Garry had decided to make a scene about it. But he hadn't done so . . . just raised one eyebrow quizzically and said,

"Oh! Bartholomew Ignatious Mathews. *I've* no objection if you wish to go, Jane. I suppose you won't be . . . late?"

Then she had promised to be back in time for tea and he had shrugged his shoulders and the matter had been forgotten, she imagined, until he left for the station when he had given her the usual hurried peck on her cheek, told her to "have a good time" and disappeared out to the garage.

Everything had worked out very smoothly, Jane decided, flicking another page of her magazine and crossing one slim nylon-clad leg over the other. She noticed the young man who was not-so-like-Gareth-after-all glance her way and look quickly down at his paper, and she smiled contentedly. She knew from that one hurried glance that he thought her attractive and her vanity was lulled to further good feeling. Not that she was in the least interested in him, or would contemplate giving him more than a cool, imperious glance. In fact, she couldn't be bothered with him now that he had noticed her.

If Bim had suggested this luncheon yesterday, things might not have been quite so easy. She still had Teddy then and it would have been difficult to arrange somebody to look after him with Mrs Mendall still 'doing' for Sue. But Sue was so much better that the doctor had said she might get up a little today, and Teddy could safely go home provided he gargled three times a day and didn't go too near Susan.

In a way, the house would seem quiet without Teddy and yet in other ways, Jane had been thankful he had gone home. For one thing it left her free for her lunch today. That was the trouble with kids! she told herself. They were such a tie. Of course, one could always have a Nanny, but then why have kids in the first place? Either you liked them enough to look after them yourself or else you had a Nanny and never saw them. There really didn't seem much point in having children. They were an expense, a nuisance, and as for the time before they were born . . . when Jane thought of that, she wondered why women ever had children at all. And yet Sue was always saying she wished she had had more, and Jane believed she meant it.

'We've different natures, that's all,' she thought vaguely. 'Look at her patience with Teddy! And the time she spends knitting, mending, washing and cooking for him. I'd never be able to do those things. Perhaps it's a phase I'll come to when I'm a bit older. Garry will just have to wait until then. Anyway, he's got Ted to amuse him for the time being and the way he dotes on the child and Ted on him, I can't see he needs any of his own.'

It occurred to Jane suddenly that there were advantages to their move to the country. She'd not thought of it before, but since Garry had had Ted knocking around the place lately, he'd not brought up that everlasting subject of her having a baby. It was just possible that he'd come round to her way of thinking . . . or at any rate, decided Ted was enough to flatter his masculine vanity, or whatever reason made men want to become fathers. He could show off all he wanted to the boy and teach him all the games and whatever else he chose. That's one thing Garry couldn't tax her with . . . she never tried to spoil things for him. Some women might have been jealous of the time he spent with Ted. But she wasn't. She had encouraged the friendship.

'We're really a very happily married couple!' Jane decided, and then forgot Gareth and her home in the next instant, for the train was drawing into the station and the young man was holding the door open for her to step on to the platform.

Half an hour later, Jane met Bim in the cocktail bar of the ultra-modern new restaurant near Piccadilly which was attracting so many foreign tourists in spite of the high charges.

Bim was so typical of the average young American who invaded Europe during the war, that even in civilian clothes his nationality was recognizable at a glance. He had the tall, loose-knit frame, brown healthy features and snub nose that seem to characterize American youth. His hazel eyes, rather small for good looks but friendly and harmless, gazed at Jane and the world in general in natural *bonhomie*. It took a great deal to ruffle Bim or destroy his innate good humour. Even his loose-fitting American tailored clothes seemed to hang comfortably on his body as if pleased with their lot, and he with them. Only his tie, brilliantly zigzagged with red and yellow stripes, jolted him out of the indistinguishable mêlée of young men, chiefly foreigners, who crowded round the bar.

He greeted Jane with elaborate good manners, handed her a small cellophane box containing an orchid spray, as if this were his most regular of routines for a lunch date, which it was, and scrambled over to the bar to order her a drink.

Jane, a little intoxicated by the mass of people moving about her, by the many admiring glances thrown her way, and the general high spirits that invaded the noisy, over-crowded room, felt that she was at last back once more in her rightful *milieu*. This was life! And instead of pining in boredom in an old backwater of a country village, she was once more part of the eager, rushing, laughing throng. It was as much of a tonic to her as was the champagne cocktail which Bim handed to her; as was the faint amused whistle that came from him when he surveyed her from head to toe.

"I'm a wolf! I warn you, Jane!" he said in his teasing, slow drawl. "In that green outfit, you're a hum-dinger. If you weren't pri-mar-ily a married woman and the one-time wife of my best friend, I'd make such a pass at you it would knock out London along with you, honey! *I'll* say you're pretty!"

Jane dimpled and laughed up at him through her lashes. Bim said such funny, amusing things. In a way he meant them and yet one knew one was perfectly safe with Bim. In fact, Ham had once said Bim was the only man other than himself with whom he'd trust her. Although Bim paid her compliments and held her tightly when he danced cheek to cheek with her, or squeezed her hand beneath the table, he never once tried to be really familiar . . . would never give Gareth cause for real jealousy. Of course, Gareth, being English, would probably be stuffy about the cheek to cheek dancing and hand-holding, but he needn't have been. To Bim it didn't mean anything and to her it was just a lot of fun.

"I always enjoy myself with you, Bim," she said. "It's such *fun*!"

"Sure is, honey. Why, I recall the time just after Ham was posted to Italy we went to the Hammersmith Palais . . . remember? Guess we danced our feet raw that night . . . and *laugh*! That must have been . . . let me see, I've been in civvies five years . . . all of six years ago."

"Nearly seven since . . . since Ham was killed," Jane said, her eyes growing serious. "You know, Bim, I've often wondered what *did* happen to him. You . . . never heard, I suppose?"

"No, never did. Just one of those things, I guess. There were hundreds like him. Identification was pretty difficult, I guess. It hit you pretty badly, didn't it, kid?"

Jane nodded, her hair falling in a cloud over her face as she stared down at her hands.

"For ages I wouldn't admit it had happened . . . couldn't believe it *was* true. He was only missing and that meant I could hope. Even after he was presumed killed, I kept thinking he'd turn up somehow, somewhere. I never believed it . . . until the war ended. I suppose I kept thinking at the back of my mind that he might have been taken prisoner, lost his memory, something of that sort; that he'd turn up when it was all over. Finally, when I did know it was useless, the shock was pretty bad. But one gets over these things. At least, I suppose one gets over the worst of them. At any rate, I married again in spite of what I said to you just after it had happened. Remember?"

"Sure! And Ham would have wanted you to, just as I told you then. You're happy, aren't you, Jane?"

Jane looked up into Bim's anxious face and smiled.

"On the whole, taking the good and the bad, I should say I am happy, Bim. I get pretty bored sometimes but that's just me, I expect. I like people around and lots of friends and Gareth is the retiring settling-down type. But we compromise and have a bit of each. He's very devoted to me and very generous."

"Then I'm glad, honey. Now, what say to some lunch?"

"I'm as hungry as a horse," Jane told him laughing.

Arm in arm they went through to the restaurant and sat down to their meal.

At about the same time, Susan and Teddy were sitting down to the simple meal Mrs Mendall had cooked for them. Teddy ate ravenously but Susan had no appetite and Mrs Mendall cleared away her plate almost untouched.

"You should try and eat, dearie, to get your strength back," she said.

Teddy looked at his mother with a worried frown.

"Aren't you feeling well again, Mummy?"

Susan forced a smile to her face.

"I'm much better now, darling," she told him. "There isn't a thing to worry about any more. The doctor says I can go back to work next week and you're to go back to school on Monday."

"But I don't think I want to go back, Mummy," her small son said, looking at her seriously from dark brown eyes. "I think I'd rather stay home and look after you."

"Well, that's sweet of you, Poppet, and I'd love to have you home," Susan said smiling. "All the same, you've got to go to school if you want to learn things, haven't you? And you've got to learn things if you want to be an engine driver."

"Oh, but I don't want to be an engine driver any more," Teddy corrected her. "I'm going to be a big business man, like Uncle Gareth."

Susan felt her heart miss a beat. Just the sound of Gareth's name was enough now to set her heart racing. With an effort she said calmly, "Well, all the more reason to go to school and study hard. Men like . . . like your Uncle Gareth have to be very clever to be business men."

"Uncle Gareth makes lots of money, doesn't he, Mummy?"

Susan nodded.

"More than you make?"

"Oh, yes! Lots more."

"Then he's quite rich, isn't he, Mummy? I'm going to be a rich man, too. Then I can buy things for you. I'm going to buy you a beautiful blue bath like the one Aunty Jane has . . . and a car, too . . . and . . ." he broke off as he recalled the reason for his having started this conversation. "All the same, I don't think I'll go back to school, Mummy. I'm going to get a job instead and earn some money *now*. Then I needn't wait to grow up before I can buy you things."

Susan looked at her small son with a sudden rush of love for him. Had it not been for the doctor's caution, she would have gone round the table and hugged him.

"My darling, it's very kind of you to suggest such a thing, but I'm afraid you couldn't earn any money *just* yet. Six really isn't old enough, you know."

"But it is, Mummy," Teddy cried, his face flushed with excitement. "Aunty Jane told me that boys in America earn money when they're six. They run messages for people and take the papers round and things like that. So I could be a messenger boy, couldn't I?"

Susan felt too weak after her five day's attack of flu to try to explain the laws governing age limits for working in England. When she answered Teddy's questions, as a rule she tried to tell him as much of the truth as he would understand. But she didn't feel well enough to cope with the subject, one about which she knew very little anyway. So she said, "Don't think I'm not happy because you want to earn money for me, Ted, darling, but I'd really rather you went to school and grew up a learned wise man like Uncle Gareth. It would please me far more than having a . . . a blue bath, or a car. Really it would!"

Teddy looked at her doubtfully.

"Well, if you're *sure*," he said. "But I can't think how. I'm just splitting to have a car . . . a long, low sporting sort of one, like Uncle Gareth's Triumph. Look, I've got a picture of one on a cigarette card. And, Mummy, Uncle Gareth says he'll teach me to drive it when I'm much bigger. Oh, I do wish boys grew up quicklier!" And he gave a deep sigh.

"More quickly, Teddy," Susan corrected automatically, but in her heart she was thinking, 'And I wish you could grow up more slowly, Teddy. It seems so short a while since you were a baby. And all too soon you will be a man with your own life to lead. Then I shall be alone . . . without even you, my precious!'

It was strange how quickly years passed and yet how slowly the moments, the hours of the days. Lying in bed, she had watched the clock, hoping that Gareth might come to see her again; hoping every time the big hand passed the little one that this hour would bring the sound of his voice, his footstep on the stair. She both dreaded the thought of seeing him again . . . of the fight to keep her emotions controlled and hidden from him . . . yet longed desperately with a tearing ache in her heart, for him to come.

But he had not come again. Just once . . . and not again. Mrs Mendall had brought a note from Jane saying the doctor had advised both her and Garry to keep away for Teddy's sake, and although Ted's health came before everything, she would have been content just to hear Gareth's voice outside her door.

'I can't stand much more of this,' she thought, as she watched Teddy eating his pudding, leaving her own untouched. 'I *must* pull myself together. The tension is too great for anyone to bear. I must face up to the fact that I shall see him sometimes . . .

occasionally when he drops in with Jane . . . as he passes the house to or from the station.'

At least she had that glimpse of him every day . . . the dark blur near the steering wheel as he flashed by. Perhaps if he drove more slowly, turned to wave a hand . . . but he never turned . . . always seemed to gather speed as he passed the house.

It never occurred to Susan, lost in the depths of her own disappointment and unhappiness, in the well of her own longing, that Gareth was purposefully avoiding her; that, after the terrible moment of revelation when he had known he was in love with her, he had determined to tear that love out of his heart, never even so much as think of her again. He did not dare to and yet could not prevent his thoughts from finding their own way to her image, to the memory of her voice, her hand in his, her dark eyes staring at him as if asking him, begging him to help her.

Lying sleepless in his turn, in his dressing-room, he had fought against the truth, hating himself as much as Susan had at first despised herself for a love that could not be the fault of either one of them. Time and again Gareth forced himself to think of Jane . . . of his wife. Tried to convince himself that she loved him, needed him, that he was not free to love another woman. And coldly, logically, his brain fought in hand with his heart against all the natural loyalty and faithfulness in his nature; made him realize once again that Jane was 'fond of him' but did not know the meaning of the word love as he now knew it, as a woman of Susan's calibre would suffer by it. Jane, cried his heart and his mind, had never really demanded much of him; wanted only what his money and a weak will could give her . . . a good time and her own way. Then she could be happy and for the most part was so until, still thinking himself in love with her, he had struggled again to possess a part of her that did not exist; to create in her a will for the children he so longed for.

And so his mind came complete circle once more to Susan. He felt trapped by his very proximity to her. It would be so hard to avoid her as he knew he must, so utterly impossible to forget her with her son forever in his company. And not even for Jane would he cold-shoulder the boy who depended on him for so much of late; who, he knew without conceit, hero-worshipped him. No child should suffer through his weakness, Gareth cried. With some inner strength which he could and would muster, he would fight his love for Susan even while he continued to love her child.

When he passed Susan's house that next morning, he had driven like a criminal, slinking past as if he were guilty of some crime. He *felt* guilty. For to a man of Gareth's intrinsic integrity, his marriage vows were sacred and whatever Jane's nature, whatever her feelings for him, he had married her for better or for worse as she had given her troth to him. That his heart should play him false, make him even in thought false to those vows, gave him a feeling of guilt that was deeper than that other pain.

And he, like Susan, suffered alone. He, too, had to fight his own battles, telling no one, fighting even himself. It cost him as much effort to keep from stopping at Susan's door when he passed it in the evenings, as it had cost Susan to keep from calling out to him as he went by.

And neither knew, as yet, of the other's love. Gareth might suspect that Susan was not indifferent to him, that there had been a look in her eyes which he would have understood if he had known he loved her then. But each shied from such fancies. It was enough that they must fight their own battles without putting further temptation in their way.

And while they suffered, Jane, on whose account they underwent such private misery, laughed and sang around the house, sewed a button on Gareth's shirt, sent fresh fruit round to Sue; happy enough in anticipation of her lunch date and feeling truly fond of them both.

But this very moment, they had been forgotten. Bim had been telling her a remarkably interesting story, and as the food was as excellent as his company, Jane was very much enjoying her lunch.

"So you see," Bim was saying, "what sort of a woman she was.

Now take yourself, Jane, I reckon you've never hurt a soul in your life. You got a real nice nature . . . always happy, always bringing sunshine into other people's lives with your smiles."

"Perhaps you just don't know me very well, Bim dear," Jane said dimpling. "I can be pretty nasty sometimes. I get moods . . . horrible depressed ones and work them off on poor old Garry."

Bim laughed disbelievingly.

"Sure I know you very well, honey. Have you forgotten those two years you were married to my best friend? And you haven't changed one darned tootin' since then, unless to grow prettier. You're a swell girl, Jane, and I never blamed Ham for gettin' hitched up to you. Swore he never would marry, you know. We used to knock around college together and although he had plenty of girlfriends, there was never anyone serious until you happened along. I'm kinda glad he married, though at the time I wondered if it would work out. At least he had two years' wonderful fun before . . . well, before he had to get himself killed."

"Why didn't you think it would work out, Bim?" Jane asked with unusual seriousness.

Bim waved his hands vaguely as if they would help him to find the words which usually came so easily and glibly to his lips.

"Ham was a great guy, Jane. *You* know how much I liked him. We got along swell together. But he was an odd guy in a lot of ways. Not the settling-down type. He'd get a new craze every week, and it would be the only thing in life he could talk about, and next thing he'd forgotten it and something else had taken its place. I guess I was a little afraid he might treat his marriage in the same way. I knew he loved you all right, but I wasn't sure how long it would last. But I found out that you'd charmed him pretty thoroughly. I guess you were one of the few girls who could have kept him steady."

"I loved him!" Jane said, with a simplicity unusual to her.

"Sure you did. He was a lovable guy. But he had his faults, honey, as I guess you found out. Never could stop at one thing for long. Beats me how he ever stuck army life. Too much routine and discipline. But he did stick it and more hero he for closing the chapter the way he did. You could be proud of him, Jane."

"I always was!" Jane said. "It's funny how easy it is to talk about him to you, Bim. I used to find it difficult to mention his name but it isn't any more. Perhaps it's true that time cures most things. I sometimes wonder what I'd do if Ham were here now and I had to choose between him and Garry. I'm really fond of Gareth and I've been married to him so much longer than I was married to Ham. Yet it wouldn't be easy to choose. I loved Ham."

"No use thinking about such things, honey. You stay happy with that guy of yours. Ham would want it that way and I'm sure glad it's worked out right for you. Now let's stop being serious and have ourselves a good time. How long can you stay?"

"I really ought to be back by tea time. I promised Garry I wouldn't stay late. He was pretty fed up about our last jaunt," Jane said ruefully.

"Hey, I hope he's not jealous . . . *of me!*" Bim laughed. "He ought to know I'm not the home-breaking type. Didn't you tell him, Jane?"

Jane joined in his laughter.

"Perhaps it's good for him to be a little jealous, but I think he just felt neglected. I left him alone in the house with my brother and they had to go begging a meal from my girlfriend! I really must get back early this evening, Bim."

"Surely it's early enough to be home by the time he gets back? Can't you stay on until then? We could go dancing at that little club we went to last time. They open after lunch. Gee, honey, say the word and we'll have ourselves one whale of a time before you go back to the kitchen stove! Is it yes?"

"Yes!" said Jane. For after all, what point was there in getting home *before* Gareth and sitting around twiddling her thumbs. He'd probably not taken any notice of her promise to be back for tea and as it wasn't a Friday night, *he* wouldn't be early. "Yes, let's go dancing!" she said. "It sounds such fun. And we'll try that Samba again."

It was just her bad luck that, on leaving the club, they couldn't get a taxi for ten minutes (in spite of Bim, who like most Americans, seemed to wangle most things) . . . just bad luck that those ten minutes caused her to miss that all-important train.

Seven

When Gareth had first returned to his empty house, the fire unlit, no supper prepared for him, he had felt a moment's acute anger against his young wife. Storming through the empty rooms, banging doors behind him, certain by the very silence of the place that she had not returned home, irritation mounted steadily through him until he felt that if she appeared at that moment, he could willingly have put her over his knee and spanked her.

But Jane did not appear, and Gareth's anger died away as he sat in the armchair by the kindling fire and thought over the whole question of his marriage.

It seemed impossible that only a few weeks ago he should have felt content with his lot, prepared to accept Jane for what she was without facing up to his inner dissatisfaction; that he had still believed himself in love with her and certainly hoped that things would improve between them. He had even, hard though it was now to imagine, been convinced that Jane loved him . . . at any rate as much as she was capable of loving anyone.

And now, quite suddenly, his whole world had turned upside down. It was not enough that he should have discovered through his love for Susan, his admiration for her as a woman of character and deep understanding, his 'closeness of spirit' with her, that what he had felt all these years for Jane was a mere physical passion; a desire to make her his own because she had until his marriage, so constantly eluded him. When first he had, set eyes on her, a young, impressionable, serious-minded man of twenty-six, Jane had been but a schoolgirl. He had known that he wanted to make her his wife once she was old enough for marriage. He had watched her grow up, turning slowly into the slight, indescribably pretty woman that her girlhood had promised, and then the outbreak of the war had temporarily put marriage from his mind.

When next he had seen Jane, she had married her young American and he had felt hopelessly frustrated and wretched that he had allowed her, through his own fault, to slip away from him. Man of honour that he was, he had tried to put the memory of Jane from his mind; to banish the thought of all women. A posting overseas had made this not only easier but inevitable. So full had been his life in the army, so eventful, that he had had time to think of little else.

When he was wounded and sent home, he heard through his family that Jane's husband was missing. Lying in severe pain in hospital, with little else to do but think, he had remembered Jane again and all he had felt for her; had let his imagination whip him into fresh longing for her. Her very daintiness, her delicate, blond femininity came to represent everything that could contrast with his hard, bachelor, masculine life in the army. It seemed to him that Jane alone had the power to charm away those horrible interludes of battle, the ugliness, the brutality he had witnessed, the pain he had been through.

It was but a step from his state of mind to his longing that Jane might once more be free for him to win for his bride.

But he made no move to find her while her husband might still be alive. It was chance that had brought them together – when he had been posted to the War Office. Then Gareth had been far too human to wish to alter destiny. He had taken Jane out, let her pour out her unhappiness and concern for her husband's safety, comforted her and had a great pity and longing to protect her; adding to the hold she already had on his heart.

Jane would never know with what reserves of control, with what patience he had endured those final years of the war; how he had longed to hold her, to kiss her, to tell her of his love. But his patience had served him well, for in the end, when Jane had abandoned hope, she turned to him to help her forget, to start a new life. And he had thought himself the luckiest and certainly the happiest man in the world.

How far had he come since then! The novelty of first possession had worn thin, and now that he no longer felt the same instantaneous stirrings of desire whenever Jane looked at him through her lashes, touched his hand or lightly kissed his cheek, what was left? No common ground of interest, no intellectual life, no children; there was nothing to hold them together but their feelings towards each other. He had had to face up to the fact lately that Jane was almost indifferent to him; that his lovemaking held little excitement for her, small interest. Tonight alone proved that she now took him and his love for her completely for granted, and took advantage of his generosity and constant desire to please her to break her promises so ardently made and so quickly forgotten; to forget just as easily and quickly when something more amusing was in the offing, that as his wife it was her duty to see he had a warm home and a meal to return to . . .

It was a bitter pill to swallow but made easier by the fact that he himself was not free from guilt. The knowledge of his love for Susan lay heavily on his heart, and he felt that he could hold no blame against his young wife for her lack of affection, when in his own heart he loved another woman.

'But I cannot help my love,' Gareth told himself. 'I did not wish to love Susan, to feel so hopelessly drawn to her that it is all I can do not to go to her. I wanted to go on loving Jane, to give her the care and understanding I promised her. And Jane, if she ever really loved me, has withdrawn her heart from me for no better reason than her own pleasure. It is not that she loves anyone else . . . only herself . . .'

Beautiful, childish, selfish Jane! And now he had not even his former love for her to help him forgive or, at least, accept her disdain, her indifference . . . only his own guilt, that would force him to forgive her everything; to fight hard for both of them to put their marriage back on its feet.

But Gareth, flesh and blood as he was, could not for all his sense of integrity, prevent the thoughts that sprang to his mind.

For what reason did he desire to put their marriage to rights? If Jane did not care any more for him, why not let her go? Why sacrifice Susan's happiness, his own, possibly even Jane's ultimately, for a principle, a vow?

But his mind shied away from the thought of divorce. And Jane was happy enough. It would hurt her vanity, if not her heart, to discover Gareth no longer wanted her. Would hurt her more that her husband and her own friend . . .

'Susan may not care for me. I'm accepting her love as if it were a fact instead of supposition,' Gareth corrected his train of thought. 'And do I really want her to love me? I would rather that she did not if she must suffer as I am doing! Oh, Susan, Susan, how queer the world is that I should love you of whom I know so little except through your son? How incomprehensible is this 'loving' around which we human beings build our lives! Is it just a state of mind, a whim, or is it, as I believe, the inexplicable affinity between a man and a woman who were meant for one another, put here on this earth to find their way together as man and wife?'

But to believe this was to believe in Fate, and Gareth could not understand why Fate would arrange for such circumstances to surround Susan and himself. But for Jane, for a sudden whim to buy this house, he might never have met Susan at all. Cruel, indeed, if Fate had chosen that he should be married before he met his true love; *the wife he should have had!*

It was in this bewildered, thoughtful state of mind that Jane found him when she arrived home two hours later. She had crept into the house softly, afraid of the scene which she knew all too well she deserved and fully anticipated. She had resolved, as she fretted impatiently in the slow train, to try to charm Gareth out of his annoyance, and it upset her balance when he greeted her with no more than a quiet, "Is that you, Jane?"

Relieved but puzzled, Jane ran across the room to him and knelt by his chair, putting her small gloved hands on his arms, looking tentatively up into his face.

"Oh, Garry, darling! Can you ever forgive me? I didn't mean to be late but I missed the train by a few minutes. That's gospel truth. I've been fretting around that cold station waiting for the next train for a whole half-hour. Honestly, sweetie, I meant to be back on your train. I am sorry!"

Gareth looked down at the fair head, into the large anxious blue eyes and knew that she spoke the truth; that, like a child who had meant to be good but had nevertheless been naughty. He was unable to feel angry with her, only more hopeless, more bewildered. For he felt now a strange pity for her which was as unpremeditated as it was unpredictable.

"That's all right, Jane. I thought something of the sort had happened," he said briefly.

She gave her quick, flashing smile and nestled up to him more confidently.

"Then you forgive me, Ga-Ga?" using her private pet name for him, which once had amused him but which now he could feel was only a little stupid, undignified.

"Did you have a good time?" he asked.

"Well, yes, I did. Bim's such good fun. We talked about you, you know, darling. Bim thinks I'm lucky to be married to you and to be so happy. He thinks you sound awfully nice."

Gareth looked at Jane's pretty, smiling face and heard himself saying, "You . . . are happy with me, Jane? Really happy?"

Jane's eyes rounded in surprise.

"But of course I am, darling. You haven't been thinking silly things, have you? Good heavens, Bim's an old friend. He'd never try to make love to me and anyway, I wouldn't want him to. You know I love you, Garry darling, and of course I'm happy with you. I'd tell you quick enough if I wasn't!"

'She means every word of it,' Gareth thought. 'Jane is quite content with her lot. It is I who am discontented.'

Noting his silence, his unusually serious expression, Jane looked at him more closely, noted the lines beneath his eyes, saw suddenly that he looked tired, older.

"Is anything *wrong*, Garry? I mean, you're not ill, or anything?"

"No, of course not," Gareth said, trying to pull himself together, to appear normal.

"Then you're not worrying about anything? It's nothing I've done is it? You're upset because I'm late! I am a horrible girl. But I honestly didn't mean to be late, honestly, I didn't!"

"I know that, Jane. I suppose I was worrying a little . . . about you, but not for the reason you think. It's just that . . . lately we don't seem to have been hitting it off quite so well together. I've felt . . . that you were growing a little . . . well, dissatisfied with your life down here . . . with me."

Jane's mouth curved into a pout.

"Not with you, Garry darling, but perhaps I have been a bit bored sometimes. There isn't anything to *do* down here, is there? We had much more fun together when we lived in London, going to shows and dancing and lunching together and things." She waved her hand vaguely round the room. "It's so quiet here when you're away, Garry. Sometimes I feel I'll pop if something exciting doesn't happen. That's why I've been lunching with Bim. I'd rather lunch with you, but you haven't suggested it and I know you're pretty busy."

Gareth nodded his head.

"Then you still . . . you are still glad . . . you married me, Jane?"

"But of *course I am*, sweetie!" Jane cried. She jumped to her feet and curled up on his lap, winding her arms round his neck. "You're just wonderful to me and I'm a selfish pig. Yes, I am. I always want everything my way. Just fancy, you've been worrying all this time and I never suspected. You are a silly old thing!"

She rested her cheek against his and Gareth closed his eyes because he felt doubly guilty now – guilty for the love he bore Susan, guilty because of the complete lack of response to his own wife. And Jane was being her most charming, her most endearing self.

"We'll have to do something about it!" The words came unbidden from his lips.

"About what?" Jane asked, her voice warm, contented, cosy.

"Perhaps we should move back to London!" Gareth said slowly as the idea formed in his mind.

"Back to London!" Jane cried, sitting bolt upright, her eyes sparkling, her face glowing. "Oh, Garry! What a perfectly perfect idea! I thought about it myself but I never imagined you'd leave your garden . . . and what about Teddy? You know you'd miss him."

"Yes, yes I would!" Gareth said, thinking, 'and he'd miss me. He'd be terribly hurt but I must put my duty to Jane before my affection for him.' He bit his lip, staring into the fire, and added gently, "Perhaps we could replace him, Jane? Don't you think you might have changed your views a little about . . . children . . . now you're so fond of Ted? I think it's time we considered the idea more seriously."

Jane gave a deep sigh. She had feared the moment that she mentioned Ted that Gareth might bring up this subject. The smile left her face and once more her lips pouted and her beautiful eyes grew sulky.

"I can't see what all the hurry is about, Gareth. I'm young yet and I want to have a good time before I settle down and start getting old and frumpy and matronly."

"Susan isn't any of those things!" came unwillingly from Gareth's lips.

"Oh, Susan! Well, she's different. Besides, she always wanted children. She's always saying so. I'm not like her. I just don't like babies. I've told you often and often, Gareth, that they actually revolt me when they're new-born. It's so silly to bother about kids yet. We've loads of time."

"Perhaps you have, Jane. But I don't want to be too old a father to my children."

But he knew it was hopeless, that it didn't really matter any more. It wasn't Jane's children he wanted now. He had only brought up the subject because he had had a moment's hope that it might help to save their marriage, bring them close once more.

Ignoring his last remark, Jane brought the conversation back to the subject of a possible return to London.

"Did you mean what you said? That we can go back?" she asked.

"If you really want to go, yes!" Gareth said.

"And *you* don't mind?" Jane asked with a fleeting moment of conscience.

"No, I'd be quite . . . quite pleased to go!" Gareth said. For he knew now that this was the only solution. He could not go on living almost next door to Susan. He had not sufficient strength of character to continue to avoid seeing her. In London perhaps he would forget her. At least temptation would be out of the way. And Ted could come up to stay with them. He'd have to see the little chap sometimes. He'd get news of Susan, too, that way.

"Oh, *Garry*, darling! I'm so excited!" Jane cried, dancing round the room now. "I never realized how much I wanted to go until you suggested it. Of course, I shall miss Sue, but she'll have to come and stay, and we could always stay with her for a weekend. I'm going to ring her up, Gareth, this minute and tell her the news. I don't expect she'll be pleased but I just must tell someone or I'll burst. It's definite, isn't it, Garry? You won't change your mind and disappoint me?"

"No, I won't change my mind," Gareth said quietly. "But I shouldn't tell Susan just yet. She's been ill, you know, and I'm sure the news would upset her. She's . . . fond of you, Jane."

"Oh, well, perhaps you're right. I'll tell her tomorrow," Jane said, generously pleased to give way in all things to Gareth at this moment. "We'll have supper. You must be starving. I'll go and find something to cook."

"I'm not very hungry!" Gareth said, but Jane had already danced out of the room and did not hear him speak. As the door banged behind her, Gareth's head went down to his hands as he realized what it would cost him to keep his word. He was putting a barrier of distance between himself and the woman he loved, and if he could live up to his intentions, he might never see her again.

When Susan heard Jane's 'marvellous piece of news' the following afternoon, it was not of herself that she thought, although Jane's words had been shock enough, but of her son. Teddy, who had been busy with his interminable jigsaws on the sitting-room floor, gave a sharp cry and jumped to his feet, staring at Jane with a face that had gone chalk-white.

"You're not really going, are you, Aunty Jane? It's just a joke, isn't it?"

Susan put her arm round his shoulders but he twisted away from her back to Jane.

"*Is it true?*" he asked.

Jane looked at Susan, uncomfortably put out by the child's obvious distress.

"I'm afraid so, Ted. But you must come and stay with us often."

He ignored her last remark.

"Then . . . Uncle Gareth's . . . going . . . too?"

"Yes, darling," Susan said gently, feeling his own pain in her heart, suffering for them both.

"But he can't go. He can't!" Teddy cried, his voice rising excitedly. "He wouldn't want to go. He said he loved it down here and he'd never leave his garden . . . he said . . ."

"We have to go for lots of reasons," Jane broke in, wishing now she had telephoned Susan rather than having to face this difficult scene. She had never imagined Teddy would take it quite like this.

Susan caught her eye and motioned Jane to the door. It was with relief that Jane left them. Susan would cope with Ted, she reassured herself as she walked slowly home, annoyed that some of her own excitement had evaporated and that she was now feeling a little depressed. It just went to show how kids could spoil things, she thought crossly. Oh, well!

Susan took Teddy on her knee where, contrary to his independent behaviour of late, he buried his face against her, sobbing as if his heart would break.

"Don't, my darling. Don't cry. You shall go and see Uncle Gareth often. I promise you shall. He'll want to see you, I know. I expect he's very upset right this minute because he has to leave you behind."

"Then why's he going?" came Ted's muffled voice. "He didn't ought to leave me. We were best friends . . . and . . . and I love him!"

Susan felt now more than ever before how much this son of hers was really part of her. His pain was her own suffering, his cry, the cry of her own heart.

"I know, darling. I . . . I love him, too. But Uncle Gareth isn't your daddy, you know. He isn't even your uncle really. And he has Aunty Jane to look after. He must take care of her, mustn't he?"

"I hate Aunty Jane. I hate her!" Ted wept furiously with a child's instinct for the truth. "She's making him go. I know it's her. Uncle Gareth wouldn't want to go. He said so, often and often."

Susan let him cry, wishing that she, too, could give way to tears and perhaps find some relief. Tenderly she stroked his head, wiping his tears away with her handkerchief.

'He'll get over it,' she told herself. 'Children forget. He'll be wretched for a little while and then someone else will take Gareth's place. But for me there will never be anyone else. I have only loved twice in my lifetime and I will never love again. Edward was my girlhood's love, Gareth I love as a woman, and my love for him will go on through the years until I'm old, old, too old to feel anything. Then, maybe, I, too, shall forget.'

But even now she forgot him within the next instant. Upset no doubt by an excess of emotion, Teddy chose that psychological moment suddenly to be very sick.

Tucked up in bed, sleeping later on from weakness and exhaustion, Teddy lay in the land of dreams. Feeling weak and tired herself, Susan lay on the sofa, her head back against the cushions, thinking, remembering again. She was not worried about Teddy. Often in his short childhood he was ill after too much excitement and she never suspected his illness might be attributable to other causes. So she worried, not over him, now, but over herself, over Gareth. With that uncanny child's instinct, her son had guessed at what she felt sure to be the truth . . . *Gareth did not want to go.* He loved his home, his garden, his country life. He had never really been a man who cared for town life. It was Jane who had been bored down here . . . Jane, no doubt, who had persuaded him to move, for all she had told Susan it was Gareth's suggestion. It had been too sudden a decision for Gareth to have made it. The whole affair was too hurried, for already Jane had spoken of a flat they had in mind which the agent had told her about only this morning. Gareth was to see it at lunch time and if it were as ideal as it sounded, they would put their own house up for auction next week and move almost immediately.

None of these arrangements sounded like Gareth who was, in many ways, a slow-moving person. He would turn over in his mind advantages and disadvantages, think carefully and exactly and only then make his decision.

For the most part, Susan was right in this surmise. But sometimes men of Gareth's nature could be swept into sudden impulsive decisions . . . perhaps truer to say goaded into them. But Susan knew nothing of the reasons behind this one and gave Jane the credit, if any.

And she could almost be glad, even while her heart ached with the knowledge that soon Gareth would go out of her life and she might never see him again. Indeed, would endeavour to avoid seeing him again. It could only hurt her to see all that she herself could never have; only tear her heart to see him, a little lonely, a little tired with Jane so indifferent to his needs, his comforts, his peace of mind, while she ran after her own.

"Oh, Gareth!" she whispered as she went slowly up to bed. "If you were mine! If only you were mine!"

She must have been sleeping some hours when Ted's voice,

calling to her, roused her from her dreams. Slipping a dressing-gown over her shoulders, she hurried through to his room and found that he had woken and been sick again. His face was flushed a bright red and he was crying weakly.

"My head hurts, Mummy. Oh, it does hurt!"

"Darling, where, show me where?" Susan cried anxiously, but he only passed his hand helplessly over his face and head and moaned again. "It aches. It does ache so."

"Oh, sweetheart, I'm afraid you've got my flu," she said as she busied herself in the room, clearing up, bringing a basin of water to wash his face and hands. They were burning hot and she knew with a sudden catch at her heart that he was feverish. Hurriedly she took his temperature and was aghast to find it just over the 103 degree mark. He cried for a glass of water and she gave it to him together with one of her 'M & B' tablets and sat down by his bed, placing her cool hand on his forehead while he tossed and turned and cried a little. His voice became more incoherent until at last she felt sure he slept. But as she turned to go, she noticed that the clean pyjamas she had put on him were soaked in perspiration and a sudden fear caught at her heart. Was Ted going to be really ill? She bent over him, feeling his forehead, which seemed to her to be hotter than ever. She slipped the thermometer beneath his arm, but he did not stir. When she removed it, it was up to 104, and in sudden panic she bent to wake him, afraid that perhaps he was not sleeping but unconscious. He moaned a little but did not open his eyes and the breath caught in Susan's throat. She bit her lip frantically, trying to remain calm, to think what to do. She must get the doctor, but it cost her all of her strength of mind to leave Ted for the few minutes it took to run downstairs and telephone.

The minutes before she heard the doctor's car stop outside her door were interminable. When at last he arrived, she felt so weak with anxiety that the tears started to her lids.

"Thank God you've come. I'm so worried, Doctor!" she said.

The doctor, a Scot by the name of McMillan, was a pleasant, round-faced, kindly man. For all his brusqueness and seeming severity with his patients, he was immensely popular and rightly taken to be clever at his job. He put a hand on Susan's arm and just that touch steadied her. Then he bent over the boy.

When he had finished his examination, during which Ted had still not stirred, he turned to Susan and again put his hand on her arm. There was a look in his eyes that she had half expected but dreaded to see.

"Then . . . it's serious?"

"I'm afraid so, lassie. But you'll have to be strong . . . for both your sakes. Can I count on you?"

"I'll keep calm, Doctor. But I must know. What is it?"

"Then you don't know? I thought, maybe, you'd have guessed with the outbreak there's been lately."

"Outbreak?" Susan repeated, her face chalk white. "Of what?"

"I'm afraid it's infantile paralysis, Mrs Parish. I may be wrong, but that pain in his head you spoke of . . . and the other symptoms. We'll know more tomorrow."

"Doctor . . . he won't . . . there isn't any real . . . danger?"

"I canna say as yet. But you must bear up, Mrs Parish. You've been ill yourself and you'll need all your strength. There's always hope, me dear. Meanwhile I'll have to try to get him to hospital. Have you a phone I could use?"

Eight

Sitting by Teddy's bedside, holding one hot, damp little hand in her own, Susan felt dazed by shock and fatigue. Downstairs she heard the doctor's burred Scottish accent as he spoke to one hospital after another, each time his voice getting a little louder, a little angrier.

"But I tell you man, that's ridiculous. A child's life may be at stake and next week won't do. This is an emergency . . . Yes, I know . . . but . . . very well, then."

And then finally, "Of course he can't go that distance. Thirty miles in an ambulance at this stage would be fatal . . . yes, fatal."

She bit her lip to control the trembling. Every nerve in her body was taut as she heard the heavy footsteps coming upstairs. The doctor was breathing quickly and Susan noted absently that he, too, was having to make an effort to keep his emotions under control, only with him it was anger, with herself, fear.

"I'm very sorry indeed, Mrs Parish, but I'm not getting along too well. It seems as if the local isolation hospital is full and the next nearest to here has been closed through lack of staff. There's a bed for the lad in St Margaret's Hospital thirty miles away, but I will na' countenance such a move. If it can be arranged, he'll have to be nursed here. It's the only thing to do."

"I'll nurse him, Doctor!" Susan cried. "I've had a little training. I'll take better care of him than anyone else. Only tell me what to do."

"Ach lass, you're no fit to take it on. And I'm suspicious now as to this dose of influenza you've had. It's possible you've had the other germ but your general good health was such that it kept it under control. That's possible, you know. A lot of people have had the disease without knowing it. Now the boy's not been near you for three days, but I take it he was in contact with you before you retired to your bed and you could have passed it on to him. Now, don't take on so, my girl. It isna your fault. And I'm only guessing. But if it's true, then you've been sicker than we thought and you'll need to convalesce. We must get a trained nurse for your lad."

"I have a little money saved. It's not much, but I want him to have every care, every possible necessity," Susan cried.

"We'll try to see that it doesna cost you a thing, Mrs Parish. We'll see if we can get a nurse under this health scheme of ours. Now don't worry. I'll make up some of my own prescriptions for the boy and give him an injection now before I go. Have you a neighbour or anyone who could come along for the stuff?"

"I'll find someone!" Susan said. And her mind went to Jane. She was too frantic with worry to think of the time. That it was three in the morning did not deter her from ringing Jane as soon as the doctor had gone.

But it was Gareth's voice who answered her, a deep, calm voice, a little husky with sleep.

"Oh, Gareth, it's you!" Susan heard herself saying stupidly. "I'm so sorry for ringing like this . . . so early . . . but I'm desperate. Teddy's ill. The doctor has just been and he thinks it's . . . it's . . ." her voice broke suddenly and the horrible words would not come.

"Susan, Susan are you still there?" came Gareth's voice, fully awake now and loud with concern. "What are you trying to say?"

With a great effort, Susan pulled herself together. Her voice sounded thin and horribly near to tears, as she repeated the doctor's suspicions.

"I thought Jane might go up for the medicine for me," she ended weakly.

"I'll go myself," Gareth's voice came firmly, reassuringly. "Now don't worry too much, Susan. It may not be . . . the worst. I'll go straight up to the doctor's now. I should be with you in fifteen minutes. Will you be all right until I come?"

"Yes . . . and thank you, Gareth!" Susan said. "I'm sorry . . . to make such a fuss, but . . ."

"You go straight back to Teddy!" Gareth said. "And *try not to worry, Susan* . . . Oh, and Susan?"

"Yes, Gareth?"

"If he can understand, give him my love."

Then he was gone.

It was greatly comforting to Susan as she sat once more with Ted, listening to his harsh, uneven breathing, to hear Gareth's car go roaring past the house up the hill . . . to know that soon he would be here himself. She needed him so desperately, someone to turn to, to take control. For the first time since Edward's death, she felt unable to cope on her own. Knew that after all she was not so independent when it came to a real emergency. She had found a way to work and support and educate her son, to make a life for them both, but when faced with losing the one person she loved most in the world, she was weaker than ever in her life before.

Gareth did not return for half an hour, but when at last he came, he was wonderfully reassuring.

"The doctor said I wasn't to come past the front door," he said quietly, following her into the sitting-room. "But that's just too bad. How is he, Susan? The doctor will be down again in an hour or two. I want you to promise me you won't try to argue with me if I tell you what I have arranged?"

Staring at him, drawing renewed strength and courage from his calmness, his dearness, Susan knew that she could argue with nothing that was for Ted's good if Gareth wished it.

"I've arranged for a private nurse to come down from London. She'll be on her way now. And with Doctor McMillan's approval, I've called in a specialist. Now I know you can't possibly afford these things, Susan, but I feel I must do for Teddy all that I can. The fact that I . . . I love him must give me some right to offer a little help. If it will make you feel better, I suggest I become a belated godfather. But if anything happened to him . . . well, let's not think of such a thing. I just want to be certain that nothing will."

"Gareth, I can't let you do this. You don't understand!" Susan cried desperately.

Gareth looked down at her flushed, desperate face and knew that he loved her at this moment more surely than he had ever loved her before.

"It's done, Susan!" he said quietly. "And you promised not to argue if it was for Ted's welfare. He must have every possible chance. Who provides the wherewithal hardly matters."

"But it does, it does!" Susan cried. "I just can't accept these things from you, Gareth."

He looked at her steadily for a moment and then said very quietly, "Do you remember, Susan, a poem, written by someone in the RAF? Perhaps a friend of your husband's. It was about a man called Johnnie. I'll quote it for you. The last verse goes something like this:

> 'Better by far
> For Johnnie the bright star,
> To keep your head
> And see his children fed.'

"Remember it, Susan? Well, you've managed to support Teddy, but it's the privilege of those of us who were more fortunate than your husband, to give what extra little help we can to his child."

There was a long moment of silence, and then Susan lifted her head and said with a simplicity that went straight to the heart of the man who loved her, "Thank you, Gareth. I'll accept your help."

"Then I'll be going home, if there's nothing I can do," Gareth said, knowing that if he stayed longer he would have to take Susan in his arms, to hold her close and pour from his heart to hers the longing within him to cherish, protect and comfort her.

"You've done so much already," Susan murmured. "I'm so very grateful."

And then he was gone and she was alone once more.

The dawn had broken and the grey sky outside was heavy once more with rain when the doctor's car drew up outside Susan's cottage. With him came the trained nurse whom Gareth had insisted upon for Teddy's sake.

The next hour passed in a great haze of activity and weariness for Susan. By the end of it, Teddy had been moved into the large spare room, which had been transformed. Everywhere was the stinging, fresh smell of antiseptic. A white sheet served as a counterpane in place of the blue eiderdown on his bed. A table with bottles, syringes, pills, every medical appliance, it seemed to Susan, stood in the centre of the room. And by Teddy's hot, fever-burned face sat Nurse Atkinson, prim, efficient, competent in her white starched apron, cuffs and cap.

"Ring me immediately there's a change," the doctor said to her, and to Susan, "Straight to bed now, Mrs Parish. You'll need all the sleep you can get if you're going to relieve Nurse Atkinson for her sleep this afternoon. Nurse will wake you if anything happens."

Susan was just helping him into his coat when there was a knock on the front door and in walked Gareth. There was a strained, angry look on his face.

"You shouldn't be here, Mr Everett," the doctor greeted him. "The house is out-of-bounds now to everyone. I shall be notifying the authorities today. We don't want you catching any germs."

"My wife considers I'm already a possible contact," Gareth said coldly. "She feels it would be better if I don't stay in the house."

There was a tight, angry line about his mouth that only Susan noticed. Could Jane really have turned Gareth out of his own home?

"Well, she's quite right, of course," said Dr McMillan. "You could be a contact if you disobeyed my orders and came right indoors this morning."

"I did!" Gareth said briefly. "In any case, Teddy has been at our house, so I presumed if either my wife or myself were going to catch anything we'd already have done so. But she doesn't quite see it that way. I just thought I'd let you know, Susan, that I shall be staying at the hotel from now on should you wish to contact me for anything."

"You'll be doing no such thing, man," said Dr McMillan. "You and your wife are both in quarantine for the next three weeks. Mrs Everett will have to take the risk of having you back, I'm afraid. I can't have you spreading infection around hotels and such-like."

"Gareth, you . . . could stay here!" Susan suggested tentatively. "Nurse Atkinson has Teddy's little room . . . she insisted on it, but you could have the lean-to in the sitting-room."

"I couldn't trouble you to that extent," Gareth said, but in his mind he thought, "If Jane's so frightened of illness that she can literally bar the door of my own home against me, then this is her fault. I have no alternative but to stay here. It's that or else go home. And that I will not do."

"It wouldn't be a trouble, really, Gareth. I know Jane is . . . a little afraid of . . . catching things. This whole business is my fault and it's the least I can do."

"So that's fixed, then," said Dr McMillan to Gareth, "for I canna see, man, what alternative you have. Besides, Mrs Parish is a guid cook, I'm told, and you'll be comfortable enough. Well, I'll be off for the time being and unless Nurse rings me, I should be down with Mr Amery as soon as he arrives. I've heard of him often, Mr Everett, and admire his work a great deal. It will be a privilege to meet him. Guid-day to you both."

And he breezed out of the house.

Gareth and Susan stood awkwardly in the hall, looking at each other and away again, trying to find words that would not betray what lay in each of their hearts.

"Susan, I really don't want to impose on your kindness," Gareth said at last.

"I'm glad to be able to repay some of your goodness to me, Gareth," Susan said from her heart.

There was another long silence during which time Gareth looked at Susan's dark head, bent a little as she stared down at her hands. He noticed her hands were trembling and he had seen the pallor of her face, the violet shadows under her eyes when first he saw her this morning. She was tired, deathly tired and near to breaking-point. He knew, quite suddenly, that she was having a fight to keep herself in control, and could not prevent the thought that raced into his mind . . . could it be possible that Susan was feeling as he did at this minute . . . ?

With a great rush of angry, tumultuous emotion, Gareth took a step towards her, placing his hands on her shoulders, feeling them tremble beneath his grip. His voice was low, husky, barely audible when he commanded her, "Susan, look at me!"

Slowly, very slowly, she raised her head and he could see her eyes, tear-filled and dark with pain.

"My darling, don't be worried. It will come right. I know it will. Teddy is a strong boy and years of good health will stand him in good stead. You must be brave, you know."

His sympathy broke the last vestige of control. Her head went down on his shoulder and the tension gave way to sobs that shook her tall, slight body. As his arms went round her, drawing her closer and closer to him, she heard him repeat the endearment she had been afraid she might only have imagined. "Susan, my darling, my very dearest. I love you so. I never meant to tell you. I have no right, but I can't help it, my own dear, sweet Susan. It breaks my heart to hear you cry. Hush, darling, hush. Please, please don't cry."

As she clung to him, her mind reeling, Susan thought with almost hysterical amusement that it was indeed a strange world where this day had been chosen from thousands of others to be the advent of such opposite ends of emotion . . . the deepest, most dreaded fears for her son's life . . . the great unbelievable tribute that Gareth offered her when he declared his love.

There was no room now in her weariness, her desperate fatigue, to remember anything but these two emotions. There remained no one in the world but Gareth and Teddy . . . no duty but to them, no love but *for* them.

"Gareth, help me, help me!" she whispered. "I need you so. I love you so."

Then only did he put his hand tenderly beneath her chin, turning her tear-wet face to his, looking down . . . drowning in the depths of those dark pools that were her eyes. Wonder caught in his throat at her beauty . . . at the great fount of love that welled up in him in answer to her appeal; wonder, too, that she could love him . . . the man who had not been able to awaken love in his own wife.

But for this one moment of time, he could not and would not think of Jane . . . Jane, who was too afraid of illness to care what happened to him, nor how much she hurt his feelings. He never again wished to hear those words of hers, or see the look of horror on her face, when he had told her, as she sat stiffly in the large double bed, that he had just come from Susan's . . . that Teddy had infantile paralysis.

"Don't come near me!" she had shouted at him. "Get out of my room at once, Gareth. I don't want to catch anything. You'd no right to go into that house . . . go near them. You can't stay here now. You'll have to go away. Oh, God, why ever did we have Susan's kid here. To think we might already have caught something . . ."

No thought for Teddy, for Susan, for himself . . . only for *Jane* herself. In disgust he had turned and left her, left the house with only a small suitcase of things. No, least of all could he bear to think of Jane.

"Susan, we'll pull him through, together!" he said as his arms tightened about her. "He'll be all right soon. And in the meantime, have courage, my darling. I know you have so much already. Afterwards . . ."

Yes, afterwards would come the reckoning. Time enough then to remember duty, honour, his hopeless marriage.

"I love you, Susan!" he said again, and bent his head to hers. The last vestige of strength left Susan as she clung to him, and when his lips touched hers, she returned his kisses with all the unleashed passion and longing which she had so long controlled. Her senses reeled in the ardour of his passion, the despair of her own. For as her heart and body wakened to his touch, she knew all too well that they would never sleep again. This love and need for him would be alive in her now for as long as she lived. And for that eternity of lifetime she could never be his . . . never claim him for her own.

A sob escaped her lips and instantly he relaxed his hold of her; led her gently towards the sofa where she lay, weary and exhausted against the cushions. He knelt beside her, her hand held tightly in his own, his eyes anxious, watching her face.

"Gareth, I never knew . . . I never thought you loved me. I wanted you to and yet I dreaded that this might happen. I thought I might get over my need for you as long as *you* did not need *me*. Then this morning . . . the shock of Teddy . . . my heart went straight to you, calling for you. I could not help myself."

"There is no blame that is yours, Susan, my dear heart," Gareth cried vehemently. "Neither at my door for the love that is in my very soul for you. That I cannot help . . . only fight against it to the best of my ability. That is why I was going away. To try to forget you . . . to start my life over again."

"I never guessed . . ." Susan whispered.

"Nor I . . . that you loved me," said Gareth. "But I suppose deep down inside me I hoped. That is why even love is selfish . . . it demands something always in return. Without that it cannot flourish . . . for a little while, perhaps, but not forever. With part of me, I hoped you did not care. I could never wish you to suffer for my sake, Susan, and yet even now I am contributing to your future pain while I do the same for myself. But I, too, can be weak and just now . . . I doubt if any man could have kept back the words I spoke to you if he loved you as I do. It was beyond control, honour, beyond anything, Susan. Can you understand?"

"Oh, Gareth, of course I do. I, too, have suffered dreadful pangs of conscience. Jane is my friend. And you are a married man. I have always believed that the worst thing any woman could do to another was to come between husband and wife. I swore to myself I never would."

"Nor have you, my own dear heart," Gareth cried. "It was no words of yours, no action of yours that brought us together; that first made me realize I loved you. I will never speak of this again but now we have got this far, I must tell you. For months now Jane and I have not been getting along too well. She has been reasonably happy but she does not really love me . . . she never will. It is not in her nature to love as we do and I do not blame her for it. I blame myself for forcing her to marry me against her better judgment, because that is what I did. I took advantage of the fact that she needed someone to help her forget her American husband; to start life again. She may not altogether have known it then . . . or now . . . but she married me on the rebound from her unhappy state of mind. I must have realized she did not love me but I would not listen to the truth. I thought I might win a way to her heart . . . that she would grow to care for me the way I was so certain I cared for her. It may seem dreadful to talk of her to you this way, Susan, but I have thought about it so much lately and it is still confused in my mind. I feel you will understand and forgive my disloyalty."

"I understand, Gareth. I . . . I have suspected that things weren't altogether right between you from the way Jane talked. She is not . . . very reticent about . . . her private life."

"Or anything!" Gareth agreed with a wry smile. "Oh, it's a hopeless state of affairs, Susan. I'm so much older than her and I am wholly responsible. But circumstances were such that I wanted to get married, have a home life, a wife, children, and I met Jane again. I had known her when she was still a child, before she married her American. I let myself fall in love all over again. Her very reluctance to have me around only served to increase my wish to marry her. She was utterly indifferent to me . . . as a man, and needed me only as a friend, for she still hoped, then, that her Hamilton might return. When the war ended and she knew it was hopeless, she agreed to marry me. It was no real foundation for marriage but I refused to admit this was so. She seemed happy enough with me . . . seemed at first even to care for me . . . love me. But that was never true. She has been happy . . . still is, I think, because she demands so little of the more serious things of life. If she has an attractive environment, plenty of friends, a good time, what she calls 'fun', it is enough to satisfy her. All these things any man with a little money could give her and only lately have I faced that fact. Then we came here. I met you but was a little shy of you, my darling. You seemed so remote, so cool, so self-assured. I suspected a sophistication which isn't there."

He smiled down at her with great tenderness and continued, "Then your son stepped in. Your name was seldom off his lips and every word showed his love, his respect for you; every sentence he spoke told me a little more of your courage, your wisdom, your sweetness. It was Ted who sowed the seeds of love in my heart, Susan, for I grew to love you through his eyes. But I did not know it until the other night . . . that first day you were ill. I had worried so all day about you without reasoning out my concern. When I came up to your room to see you, you were asleep. You looked so lovely, my dearest, so much in need of someone to love and protect you, so defenceless as you slept. I touched your hand and your fingers closed round mine as if they belonged there. I *felt* that they belonged. Even then I tried to recall my position . . . tried to remember I was a married man, that I had no right to love any woman. But it was too late. You had already captured my heart and I fled from your house as if the devil were behind me . . . And I meant to flee even farther, my Susan. I had hoped by next week to be away from here, in London. But for a stroke of ill fortune, this would never, never have happened."

"I first loved you after the dance . . ." Susan in her turn confessed all that was in her heart. She, too, felt that this short hour was stolen from time itself and as soon they must return to life, to sanity, she might never have a chance again to open her heart to him, poor unhappy Gareth. *There might never be another chance.* "When you held my hand . . . I knew. I hated myself for it, fought against it, but after all it has been too strong for me. Perhaps if you had not returned just now . . . but it has happened, and whatever it may cost me, I cannot be sorry in my heart, Gareth. I shall always be able to treasure the fact that you loved me. It will be something to live for . . . that memory."

"Oh, Susan . . . how final those words sound, and yet I know you are right. I cannot stay here now for if I do, I should never leave again. And it is not in either of our natures to find happiness through another's misfortune. As long as Jane is content to stay with me, I must look after her, care for her, try to make a success of our marriage. She will never know of this from my lips, through any action of mine. But it is hard to let you go, my dearest one . . . so hard that I do not know how I can leave you."

"Where will you go, Gareth?" Susan whispered, her dark eyes never leaving his face, following the contours as if she would etch them on her memory forever. He looked so tired, so hopeless, so defeated!

"Home!" Gareth said briefly. "Jane must accept that. I will not go near her but I shall return to the house. As soon as I'm out of quarantine, we'll leave for London. Oh, Susan, Susan, if only you knew how utterly beautiful you are, how much it will break my heart leaving you when you need me most."

"I'll manage . . . somehow . . ." Susan cried, clinging to him now, for soon . . . so soon . . . he would be gone. "Always remember I love you, Gareth, that I honour you, respect you. Don't let anything destroy your own self-respect. It is not you who have failed Jane, my darling, for no one can force love where it does not exist. And Jane . . . maybe she will change . . . grow up a little, give you the love and care you need. I shall pray that it will be so."

Her understanding, her sympathy, her wisdom . . . everything about her seemed so doubly precious to him now that he must leave her. Only human, he could wish for a moment that he had never declared himself and his love . . . for then it might have been possible for him to stay beneath her roof; see more of her, help her through this crisis of Ted's illness. But now it was quite impossible. Though neither might mention it again, it would always be between them. He could never look into her eyes again without regretting . . . desiring . . . loving . . . and such emotions were made by the circumstances of his marriage as dishonourable and unwelcome to himself as to the woman he loved. This very love he had for her and the great prize that he felt he had received through her love for him must never be sullied by dishonour.

"I'm going now, Susan. I may not see you again, but I shall love you . . . always!"

Her strength went then and it was he who had to be strong for both of them as she clung to him. He, who with understanding and wisdom, forbore to kiss her except once, gently, as he might have kissed a child. And indeed, passion was beyond either of them in this moment's agony of their parting.

He had not the heart to prolong that misery. With one last, long desperate glance at her face, which was pale, yet infinitely beautiful to him, he turned quickly on his heel and left the room.

But the Fates, perhaps favouring love rather than honour, had decreed that this parting should not be. As Gareth was leaving the house, Nurse Atkinson came hurrying downstairs.

"The little boy is calling for his Uncle Gareth," she told Susan. "I think if it's possible he should be sent for. The child is so restless and it might calm him, to have his way."

With one swift, frightened glance at the nurse's serious face, Susan ran to the door and flung it open.

"Gareth, Gareth!" she called. "Come back, quickly. It's Teddy. He's calling for you."

He heard her voice and without hesitation, turned round and went quickly back into the house.

Nine

For Susan, time no longer had any meaning. Days merged with nights and the hours had ceased to exist other than for the routine in the sickroom. And Teddy, who was her very life, part of her flesh and blood, was breathing with deep, ghastly intakes of air with the aid of an iron lung.

She haunted his room, sitting for hours beside the table which held that monstrous-looking but so very precious miracle. Try as she might, she could not prevent the dragging fear in her heart that if it broke down . . . her son's frail hold on life would be broken. There was nothing visible of his little body, only his head through the aperture. Sometimes his eyes opened and met her gaze, but he did not seem to know her. It was Gareth's face which brought him apparent comfort, and only then would his eyes close once more as if he could sleep in peace.

The footsteps came and went. There was seldom any sound in the room but the pump, the loud, artificial breathing of the lung. Hour upon hour, Susan watched it inflate, deflate, inflate, deflate. Her own breathing seemed to keep time with it, slow down to that monotonous heart-breaking sound.

Sometimes Gareth would come and drag her forcibly away for a meal, a few hours' sleep. Sometimes Nurse Atkinson would say a word to her, encouraging her to keep up her hope, to relax her vigil for her own sake. The doctor, too, had begun to worry seriously about her. The shadows beneath her eyes were purple and great lines of fatigue were etched on her face, which was deathly pale. But she hardly heard the advice he or the nurse gave her, and only Gareth, moving quietly to her side could persuade her with a softly spoken word to leave the room.

Gareth! What a tower of strength he had been! With what understanding and sympathy and sound common sense he had helped her through the worst of the crisis. And he spared no money. It was he who had arranged for the electrician to run a special cable to the cottage from which the electric pump could work; he who saw to it that not a second's time was lost and the work completed even before the lung arrived. It was Gareth, too, who, with Mrs Mendall, saw that the meals were bought, cooked and paid for; for he alone realized what agony of mind it cost Susan to leave her son's bedside even for a minute. At first she had fought to continue her household duties herself, but Gareth had been so worried about her own health that he had succeeded in persuading her to let him re-engage Mrs Mendall. Susan, knowing that she was already so greatly in his debt financially and otherwise, had to see the force of his argument that a little more would make no difference. And she argued with herself that it was for Teddy he was doing these things . . . not for her. He knew without her having to say so that she could not accept so much from him for herself. Nor would he have attempted to do so, for he respected her pride and independence.

Of Jane he saw nothing, although he had telephoned her that first day to explain that he was remaining at Susan's house, as Teddy was calling constantly for him and the doctor felt it to be for the best. Jane had not demurred. Secretly, she had been relieved that Gareth was settled comfortably (as she thoughtlessly imagined) in Susan's house, where domestic routine prevailed. She could not, nor had any wish to, envisage the cottage as it might be, with doctors, nurses, and the hateful smell of disinfectant that terrified her in places that housed the sick.

She watched her own health with enormous anxiety, gargled often and spent a day in bed to be on the safe side. But the quiet of the house bored her, and by evening she had telephoned Jim asking him to come and stay with her while Gareth was away.

It did cross her mind that she might in her turn be subjecting

Jim to possible infection, that the doctor had placed her house "out of bounds", but she conveniently put her own brother in a separate class from ordinary people and begged him to come and console her.

Jim, although he was due for a fortnight's holiday and could get away if he chose, felt that with Gareth, too, absent, he should remain where he could get to work easily. But against such arguments there was Jane's pleading (he had always been inclined to spoil his young sister) and the thought that he might see something more of Susan, perhaps even be of use to her in some way.

So it was Susan who unwittingly tipped the scale in favour of his coming, and having arranged two weeks' holiday, he travelled down to the country next day. Jane greeted him with open arms and shed a tear or two of relief.

"I just can't stand being by myself, Jimmy," she cried, kissing him warmly. "And Gareth's so busy round at Susan's I never see him."

"Don't you go round?" Jim asked artlessly.

Jane gave a little exclamation of horror.

"Goodness, I wouldn't dare, Jim. That would be asking for trouble and I'm frightened enough as it is."

Jim gave her a quick look. He could not prevent the thought that flashed through his mind . . . that if it had been Jane who was ill, Susan would have risked any infection to help her. *She* would not have been afraid.

But there were excuses for Jane. She had always had this morbid horror of illness and it was a kind of "phobia" now. She looked pale and miserable and he could feel sorry for her.

"Well, let's find something on the wireless to cheer us up," he changed the conversation. "And something good for lunch, too, Jane. I shall expect undivided attention."

Jane dimpled at him and gave him a sisterly hug.

"So long as you'll stay with me, I'll do anything you want, Jimmy boy," she said, and danced off into the kitchen.

While she was preparing lunch, Jim took the opportunity to

telephone Susan, but it was Gareth who answered him. He felt a quick, unexpected moment of jealousy, and it deepened as Gareth said, "Unless it's important, Jim, I don't want to disturb her. She's having a few hours' sleep and she needs it so badly."

It was annoying to think that Gareth, who had no right to do so, was protecting Susan, helping her, looking after things for her. It was one of the reasons he, Jim, had come down . . . in order to do so.

"I thought perhaps I might be of help in some way," he said, realizing that he sounded rather stupid and his voice became slightly aggressive.

"Thanks very much, old man, but everything's pretty much under control. The doctor seems to think the worst is over. Ted's still in danger, of course, but it's not so great now. By tomorrow he may have turned the corner. I'll tell Susan you rang as soon as she wakes."

There was nothing left but for Jim to ring off.

"Everything okay at home?" Gareth asked into the silence.

"Oh, fine! Jane's pretty scared about the whole thing but she's chirping up now she has some company. You really ought to come home and look after her yourself, Gareth."

Jim could not see the angry colour which spread over Gareth's face, anger that was partly with Jim for telling him what to do, and partly guilt because of the way he felt about Susan.

"Jane specifically asked that I should stay away," he said briefly. "Otherwise I wouldn't have come here. As it is, I have to now as I'm not allowed out to spread the infection."

"I suppose that means I won't be allowed near the place!" Jim said awkwardly. "Oh, well, if there's nothing I can do anyway, there's not much point trying to fight my way in. I mustn't keep you, Gareth. You sound busy and occupied. See you some time I suppose," and he rang off.

He had not meant to sound so bitter, so sarcastic, but his tone was well marked by Gareth who stood by the telephone, looking down at it, and a slow wave of unhappiness stole over him. In many ways, Jim was right. His own place was at home with Jane.

That state of affairs was not his fault, but would he have done much differently if Jane had been willing to have him home? Would he go if she rang him up now and asked him to go back? He had known such great happiness these last few days in just being able to help Susan, to know that she depended on him, needed him. It would take an inhuman amount of will power to leave her now while she still needed him.

'But!' Gareth told himself bitterly, 'and a big "*but*", too – what right have I to let Susan become dependent on me . . . even at this time? It should be some young man like Jim to whom she could turn, someone who has the right to love her. Then, when she is herself again, she could turn to him and open her arms to receive that love, return it.'

The thought was so unbearable to him, that he put his hands over his eyes, as if by doing so, he might destroy the picture of Susan in Jim's arms, loving him, needing him. He, in his turn, would know such jealousy that he could not stand it. And if it should come to pass he would have no right to be jealous, or angry, or hurt. He had no right, as it was, to stand between her and Jim. Instinct told him that Jim was more than a little attached to Susan. Their friendship was too new for love, but it could ripen, develop, if given a chance. By loving him, Gareth, Susan was missing that chance. But for him, she might turn to Jim, who would be free to marry her, to take care of her always.

'I could not endure it for myself,' Gareth soliloquized. 'And yet for Susan's sake . . . and Ted's . . . they are so alone and need someone to take care of them. Oh, if only I had the right!'

But he turned his thoughts quickly away from this treacherous reflection. He was even a little shocked to think that the crisis of these last few days had so weakened his earlier determination never even to admit his love for Susan, as to make such regrets possible. And he hated himself for his weakness.

'If I had gone to London . . . never seen Susan or Ted again,' he thought, 'maybe then it would have been different!' But now it had gone so much too far, too deep, to be forgotten without a struggle which would need every bit of his strength and determination, every ounce of effort. Jane's recent behaviour hardly gave him the assistance and encouragement he needed from her and yet he could not find it in his heart to blame her. She knew nothing of his inner tumult, his struggle to put his love for Susan out of his life. He had no right to expect her help, no right, even to expect her love, which alone would have made everything more simple. As it was, he could not prevent the nagging thought that all his suffering, his denial (and Susan's) were perhaps in vain. For it would indeed be useless if Jane was indifferent as to whether he loved her or not, as to the outcome of their marriage.

It was only Gareth's common sense that told him Jane would not wish a divorce. Indifferent though she might be to him in her casual, unthinking way, she was nevertheless fond of him, and on the whole, happy in the life she led with him. And until such time as she wished herself free, Gareth could not and would not break up that existence. Even had he been able to do so without conscience, neither he nor Susan could build their own happiness on such shifting sands. He respected Susan too deeply even to contemplate such an idea; knew that Susan would never expect even so much as an explanation from him on the subject of his marriage. Susan, at least, understood without words the fight that was going on inside him; the fight that was for his own honour, for Jane's happiness which was his duty, but was against every instinct of his heart.

It was strange to think how their love for each other had grown and developed without a further word on the subject. They had both been far too concerned for Teddy to think of themselves, and yet a spoken word, a slight gesture, a brief touch . . . were all enough to draw them closer. Susan's barriers had gone down as anxiety and her fatigue further drained her strength. But she had known she could rely on Gareth not to take advantage of this fact and he had not let her trust in him be misplaced. At times it had taken more effort than Susan would ever know for him not to take her in his arms, to kiss those beautiful shadowed eyes, to bring the colour back into those pale cheeks. He longed to offer her the comfort of his love and yet shrank from placing that added burden of guilt upon them.

All that was left for him to do (which no single person could have misconstrued) was to take a little of the work off her shoulders; to persuade her to take the rest she needed so badly, and to be there whenever Teddy called for him.

It was Teddy, Gareth reflected, who had made everything so much more complicated. The boy called for Gareth more often than he called for his mother. And when Susan explained that Teddy had only just that day learned of his impending departure, and had been terribly upset and shaken by the news, Gareth understood that only his bodily appearance could give the child the reassurance he demanded. Even in his delirium and moments of semi-consciousness, Ted worried lest Gareth should go away, might even have gone . . . without him. He would call his name ceaselessly until Gareth reappeared, then his eyes smiled if he were awake, or his body would relax, and he slept – all anxiety removed for a little while.

It had touched Gareth deeply to learn how much Susan's boy cared for him. He had himself become very devoted to Ted, but it also worried him as it worried Susan. Neither had realized quite how deep-rooted Ted's love for Gareth had grown; how dependent he had become upon him. In itself this was not a good thing and under the circumstances, one of the worst that could have happened. If Gareth were to leave now – the doctor warned him – it would set the child back, retard his recovery. And that recovery was still in doubt. Although his life was no longer in acute danger, it would not be known for some weeks if the paralysis had affected any part of his body, or how permanent any effect might be. Loving Ted, loving Susan, how could Gareth drag himself away from them both, leaving them to fight out these battles and anxieties alone? And yet, do so he *must*. As soon as possible he must return to his own home and make arrangements to move up to town without further delay. Unless he did so soon, he feared what might otherwise happen to his good intentions. He was, after all, only human, and every day the parting, or thought of parting, became more impossible to contemplate.

'I must leave her in Jim's care!' Gareth thought with a heavy heart. 'Jim wants to help her and if I am not here, he can do so ... can step into my shoes – in her heart and Ted's. And the sooner, the better.'

Having accepted this decision as being the right one, Gareth set his mind to working out a way in which he could carry it out. While Jane would not have him at home, there seemed no alternative, and yet Jane was his wife and he had every right to insist on returning to her.

In this moment of honesty, Gareth knew that it was only because he had not *wished* to return that he had not done so. It had served as an excuse, leaving him free to do as he wished. But that moment of weakness had passed now and he knew with a painful certainty that he must return to his own home, to his wife, tomorrow. This evening he would tell Susan and tomorrow he would go. And as it would be a week or two before they would be ready to move to London, he would be at hand to see Teddy if it were really necessary. This he would and must do. But he and Susan would try to arrange that they did not meet each other ... or if they did, never alone.

"Pray God I shall have the strength to carry out my plan," Gareth cried. "Help me to do the right thing for us all."

But it was not to be made easy for him. Later that evening when supper was finished and Susan had left Teddy's room for a few minutes, Gareth managed to persuade her to follow him into the sitting-room. Silently, she obeyed him when he told her to sit down, half wondering what it was he wished to say, for it had not occurred to her that it might be anything serious.

She looked thin, tired to the point of exhaustion, and staring down at her upturned face, Gareth felt himself weaken but fought against it. It seemed too cruel to upset her further, worry her at this time, and yet for her sake, as much as for his own and Jane's, he *must* do so.

Quietly, he sat down beside her and looked away into the blazing fire in the hearth.

"I'm going . . . home . . . tomorrow," he said at last. "I wanted you to know. I think it is best . . . for all of us."

Susan's dark eyes widened and she drew in her breath sharply.

"But Gareth . . . I . . . you . . ." but she broke off, unable to appeal to him not to leave her when she needed him so much, because she knew so well that this right was not hers. But for Teddy she must and could appeal. Gareth anticipated her question.

"I'll come and see the boy, of course. We won't be leaving for a few weeks yet. By then, he'll be out of all danger. But I can't stay on here, Susan. You know that I want to but I cannot do so, darling. It isn't fair to you . . . or to . . . Jane. I know you want me to do the right thing and will understand what it costs me to do it."

Susan was silent for a moment, her gaze fastened on Gareth's thin, unhappy face. During the past few days, her consciousness of him had been only half real, so fully had her mind been taken up with her small son. But it had been there. She had known, somewhere deep within her, that Gareth was within call, ready to speak to her, touch her hand, help, advise, comfort her. His presence had meant so much because it had been so completely selfless, giving everything, demanding nothing. In this unobtrusive way he had become doubly dear to her, doubly necessary and it was not until he spoke those fatal words a few moments ago that she had allowed herself to imagine what life would be like to live once more without him. For this moment, even Teddy was forgotten as her heart filled with the knowledge of her love for Gareth and dependence upon him. She had not thought to lose him yet awhile, had not had time to admit the uncertainty of their daily meetings. It had been sufficient after Teddy had called him back from that earlier hour of departure, to know he was here, in the house, near to her.

Now it seemed suddenly as if she had wasted those all-too-precious and never to-be-repeated moments. So greatly had her concern for Ted's life taken up every thought, directed every action, every word, that that physical unawareness of him had alone made it possible for them to continue until now. Was it possible, too, that Gareth's mind and body, which had not been harassed to quite the same extent as her own, had been more fully aware of her than hers had been of him? The thought that he might imagine she was not so deeply in love with him as he was with her, caused her to speak impulsively, rashly.

"Gareth, my dearest, I do understand. Even if I did not I should accept your decision as the right one. But I do know. We spoke of it before and neither of us wishes it otherwise. But my heart does not understand. It tells me only that I love you more than anyone on earth, that I shall always love you, always need you; that it wants nothing more than to devote the rest of life to loving you, making you happy. That heart belongs to you for always, Gareth, and although I cannot offer it to you, it is nevertheless yours."

Gareth took her hand in his own, held it so tightly that it seemed to throb against his palm. Her words were like strong wine, bringing a swift rise of emotion that he must fight hard to keep under control if they were not both to lose their heads. He loved her so much, so painfully, that this second parting (of his own making) would become a real agony of body and mind.

"Susan, forgive me for everything! I shall hate myself always for having made you unhappy. If only . . ."

Susan lay her fingers against his lips, preventing the words she knew he would regret later.

"Hush, darling, I know!" she whispered.

He pressed his lips against her hand, held it for a moment against his cheek. It was all that he dared to do, for any closer contact would endanger the very reason for their parting.

"There's nothing . . . nothing we can say to each other," Susan said brokenly. "But we both wish it this way, since to have it otherwise at the beginning was beyond our control. I shall try to start my life again without you, Gareth, and this will be easier if I know *you* will find happiness. Promise me that you will try to forget me; that you will do everything in your power to make things right in your marriage again. I want it to be so. Only that can give this parting sense, reason. If it should not be so and you are unhappy, then others will be so too, and this sacrifice of our love will be futile."

Gareth bit his lip, drew in his breath sharply.

"I promise to try, Susan, but it is not going to be easy. I, too, want you to promise me that you will forget all this. I should be happier if I heard that you had someone else to care for you, look after you, love you. You should not live alone always, my darling. You are far too beautiful, too lovely a person to waste yourself in isolation. You have so much to give to a man . . . peace, contentment, understanding, companionship . . . as well as beauty. If someone should come along Susan . . . someone of whom you could be fond, marry again, my darling, for Ted's sake as much as for your own."

"Never, never that, Gareth. I cannot promise!" Susan cried passionately. "No man could do . . . after this."

It cost Gareth a great deal to continue his persuasion. Even the thought of her marrying some other man distressed him beyond belief. But he truly believed that with her life before her, she would be happier if she remarried. Susan was not the type of woman who should live alone for long. She was made to be a wife, a mother, to give and receive love.

"There are so many different ways of loving people, Susan, my dearest one," he said with determination. "You loved your husband in a different way. You will love again, my dear. When that happens, don't think of what might have been between *us*. If you did so, I should never know a moment's peace for being the cause of wasting your life, perhaps even denying Ted the happiness a father can give him. Tell me, at least, that you won't let any memory of me affect your decision."

"How can I say that, Gareth, *how can I?* It does not seem possible to me that I could ever fall in love again. Nor would it be fair to marry a man if I did not care for him with all my heart."

"Time will help!" Gareth said. "Soon all this will become just a memory. I should wish it to be a happy memory. Then other things will become more important than that which is so important to us now. It happened so suddenly and must end so soon after it has begun. These few weeks must not be allowed to affect all the many years that you have yet to live."

He turned towards her, looking down into her dark eyes, seeing only the pain and suffering reflected from his own eyes. He longed with every nerve in his body to take her into his arms, to kiss away those lines beneath those beautiful eyes, to pour out the love for her that overflowed his heart. But he dared not touch her, and waited in wretched silence for her to tell him she must return to Ted's side.

But Susan, although she was remembering Ted again, had not the strength nor the will to leave Gareth just yet. There was so much left unsaid . . . so much perhaps *better* unsaid, yet which hung between them like a tautened rope, dragging them towards one another, pulling on their hearts until it seemed that the tension must give way. There were no tears in her to shed, to relieve the tight ache in her heart, her head, her body . . . only a dull uncertain misery that fogged her mind, her will and clear thinking.

'This cannot be true!' she thought. 'I am in a nightmare with no will-power left to make a move. If Gareth were to leave this room now, I could not lift a hand to stop him. I am like a dead person. I shall be like a crippled person when he is gone. Oh, Gareth, Gareth, I love you so much. My son loves you. *Our* children would have loved you. It could all have been so wonderful, so utterly perfect if you had been free. But there is Jane . . . Jane who I should hate if I did not know her so well. Lucky Jane, who will never know the heights of happiness in loving someone this way, and yet who need never know the depths of misery that this loving can bring. Only be kind to him, Jane. Love him as much as it is in your power to love anyone. Look after him and make him happy. That is all I ask of you. But do not be indifferent to him. He needs love . . . your love, as it cannot be mine. If you will not take care of him for yourself, then do so for me, for my happiness depends on his . . . on yours.'

Susan turned once more to Gareth and when she spoke, her voice was barely above a whisper.

"When . . . when will you go, Gareth?"

"Tomorrow . . . first thing. I won't say good-bye. Only now I will say God bless you, my heart, both you and Teddy."

It was Gareth's way of saying good-bye now. Susan knew it, heard the dreadful finality of his words, and what little courage she had left, ebbed slowly away. She stared at him with a hopelessness, a defencelessness which caught at his heart strings, for her pain was his own, the mirror of his heart.

With one last look at her, deep into those dark eyes, at the cropped dark hair that seemed moulded to her head, at the fine, beautifully shaped mouth, as if this indeed was the last time he might ever see her, he rose swiftly to his feet, and despite the little cry that sprang involuntarily from her lips, walked purposefully and with determination from the room.

As the door closed quietly behind him, Susan's trembling hands went to her face and her eyes closed. She fell back against the cushions. For she knew that although she might see him again, it must be only as a stranger and never again must she see him through her love's eyes, nor see the love shining for her in his.

"You will love again," Gareth had told her, but she could not wish it. Love brought too much suffering, too much pain in its wake. She wanted no more of it . . . would deny any calls it might make on her heart in future.

"Love! Love!" she repeated bitterly. "May it leave my heart alone so that I can find peace again."

Ten

Gareth pushed open the front door of his home and the very familiarity of the hall, the smell of Jane's perfume faintly stirring his nostrils, seemed queerly accentuated. It was all just exactly the same and yet somehow it seemed different, as if he were really seeing it for the first time. He stood in silence, hearing the faint murmur of voices and laughter from the sitting-room but not yet ready to go towards them.

The hall clock ticked the seconds away. In one corner stood his umbrella, neatly rolled, and above it his blue city coat and felt hat. On a chair beside them, Jane's garden coat lay sprawled untidily across the seat, with a canary-yellow scarf curling over it. Her yellow gloves lay some distance apart on the floor where she must have flung them, hoping to reach the chair but missing. He stooped automatically to pick them up and hung her coat on the hook beside his own.

Once, not so long ago, the sight of Jane's clothes, so tiny and feminine alongside his own heavy masculine clothes had moved him to an odd tenderness . . . much the same emotion, perhaps, as people felt about children's little shoes beside a grown-up's full-sized ones. There was something pathetic and appealing about them by their very contrast, and Jane's smallness used to rouse just this feeling of protectiveness in Gareth.

Now he saw only his coat and hers, both meaningless. It was an old coat that Jane wore only in the garden and because of its age, seemed to retain a little of her shape. If he were to go yet closer to it, he knew that it, too, would have the faint scent of Arpège . . . the perfume which in his mind belonged exclusively to Jane. Once he had told her it was perfect for *her* . . . dainty, fresh, provocative . . . and never yet had he failed to put a bottle of it in her Christmas stocking, or with some more extravagant birthday present, hiding it in unlikely places . . . inside a new handbag, tucked away in the corner of a new dressing-case. Jane loved the fun of 'looking for it' and he had been happy to see her sparkling, laughing face when she discovered it, running to him to drop a quick kiss on his cheek and cry, "Oh, darling, you didn't forget!"

Would these moments when she had seemed so close to him, so near and dear to him, return once more? Would time help him to forget that other perfume, the fragrant, barely decipherable smell of garden lavender that came from the soap Susan used? It was so simple beside Jane's more exotic scent that had cost her or him far more than Susan could afford to spend on herself; so redolent of Susan herself by virtue of its naturalness; its remote, elusive quality that was part of her charm. It was as if the thought of lavender growing in a quiet, sunny garden must also mean the thought of Susan moving gracefully and quietly through it, children clustered round her skirts, her eyes serene and smiling as the sun shone on the flowers.

'Perhaps after all, I am just an old-fashioned romantic!' Gareth told himself what Jane had so often told him. 'And yet how many men at heart are different? How many of them whose wives wear smart, fashionable clothes, paint their nails scarlet, drink as a man would, and lead their bright, brittle empty lives . . . ? How many men do not wish deep in their hearts for a woman who lives only for her husband, her children, her home, her garden; a woman who would bring peace and softness into the hardness of modern life; who would in their inner fulfilment, complete a man's life?'

"You think men want a dowdy, homely sort of wife? Never!" he could hear Jane's comment to his unspoken thoughts. And yet Susan was never dowdy, never homely in the dull, stuffy way the words indicated. And however inferior her wardrobe was beside that of Jane's, yet Gareth had never, as far as he could remember, seen Susan look anything but tall, slender, cool and beautiful.

With a little gesture of distaste, Gareth realized that he was letting his thoughts behave in a way that was repulsive to him, comparing the girl he loved with the woman he had married. It was, in a fashion, disloyal to them both and he must go through with his efforts to make his break from Susan complete and permanent. The first step he had taken when he left her house this morning. The next must be to refuse to allow any thoughts of her to enter his conscious mind. The immediate one, to go into the sitting-room and tell his wife he had come home and face her disapproval.

His mouth set in a hard, determined line, Gareth walked forward and opened the sitting-room door.

There was a large bright fire burning in the hearth. Jim sat in the big armchair with his feet stretched out to the blaze. Jane lay curled in her customary feline position against a pile of cushions on the settee facing him. Somewhere in the background there was a programme of dance music on the wireless and the atmosphere was cheerful, inconsequent, welcoming. In contrast to the dim light, the hospital-like quietness of the house he had just left, this seemed another world, brighter, noisier, more brittle. The music jarred against his nerves which were still raw from the effort of his parting from Susan.

Jane and Jim had turned to look at him with surprise. He felt stupid, standing there in the doorway saying nothing. Yet for a moment, he could find nothing whatever to say. Then Jim got to his feet and giving Gareth a curious stare, said enigmatically, "So the wanderer returns!"

Jane uncurled her feet and studied her husband curiously. How tired and depressed he looked! It was pretty obvious that he had been moping and miserable away from home; that he had come back because he couldn't stand being parted from her any longer. The thought pleased her and yet she was angry with him, too. He ought not to have returned until the end of the quarantine. It wasn't fair of him to put *her* in this awkward position.

After all, in a way it was Gareth's home, or at any rate, his as much as hers, and she couldn't refuse him entrance. Anyway, she wasn't quite sure that she wanted to do so now. The first shock of the mere mention of the words "infantile paralysis" had worn off and now that she didn't appear to be going to catch anything, the fuss she had made seemed a little unnecessary. But she wouldn't let Garry know that just yet. Meantime, it was rather nice to see he hadn't been too happy without her! She had missed him, too, in lots of ways. No one to pet and spoil her, because Jim certainly didn't! He was far too brotherly to run round after her the way Gareth always did. And much less easy to manage. He was almost surly if she didn't get his meals just when he wanted them, or sew a button on or tidy his room. In fact, Jim hadn't been the good company he usually was. He had just moped around the place trying to find something to do and yet turning down every suggestion she made. Secretly, Jane had wondered if Jim was fretting because he hadn't seen Susan. She was pretty certain from all sorts of signs, such as the number of times he brought Susan's name into the conversation, that Jim was half-way to being in love with Susan. And he'd frankly admitted that he didn't approve of Gareth being there.

"You're not jealous of Garry!" Jane had laughed at him, both amazed at the idea and amused. "My poor dear brother, you must have got it badly! Why, Gareth never looks at any other woman, and as for Susan . . . I don't think he even likes her very much."

"Don't you be so cocksure, my girl!" Jim had grunted. But Jane had only laughed at him again. Who ever heard such an inane idea! But then, Jim didn't know Gareth, or Susan, come to that, as well as she did. It was obviously a case of jealousy, and Jane felt sorry for Jim when she wasn't feeling sorry for herself, because she was so soon bored by Jim's company. Tied to the house and with not even Gareth around, life had been dull to the point where she could have screamed.

She gave her husband a quick look from beneath her lashes.

"Of course, it's lovely to see you, Garry, but ought you to be here? I mean, I should have thought I'd made it pretty clear how I felt about the whole thing."

Gareth stared at his young wife, noting absently that she looked as pretty as a picture from *Vogue* in her emerald-green corduroy slacks, her canary-yellow angora twin set which he had always considered suited her and called "that fluffy yellow thing". There was a yellow ribbon in the fair hair which curled round her small, pointed face and down to her shoulders. Against the bright yellow of her cardigan, her hair looked almost white. Had he not known her age, he would have said at this minute that she was sixteen, seventeen. The harsh words that had risen to his lips died away, leaving in their place a strange hopelessness. He was utterly defenceless against this youthfulness that was so much a part of Jane, the woman. To speak to her harshly was like speaking to a child who one knew all the time had known no better. And her only misdeed had been her fear of illness, which he knew to be a relic from her childhood.

"I felt I should not impose on Susan's hospitality any longer," he said, thinking as he heard his own words how stiff and pompous they must sound to Jane, to Jim. "I'll keep out of your way, Jane, and try not to pass anything to you. I don't honestly think there's much danger. People of our age are not usually prone to this particular disease."

"That's exactly what I think!" Jim said unexpectedly. "As a matter of fact, I think Jane's made far too much fuss about the whole thing. It was a mean trick turning you out of your own home, anyway."

Gareth did not quite know how to take this championing of his cause, nor sure that he wanted it. He wondered how much of it was due to selfish motives . . . that Jim, in his turn, might wish to see Susan without any "fuss" from Jane.

"Well, really, Jim!" Jane was saying, "you can't pretend it isn't catching. Or very serious if one did get it. And people of our age do get it, Gareth. I've heard of lots of cases."

"I'm not denying it," Gareth said calmly. "But all the same, I've come home. I'll use my study until the 'danger' is past and of course, my dressing-room. Mrs Mendall can bring a tray to me in my study at meal times."

It was a reasonable suggestion but did not quite fit in with Jane's idea on the subject. She really was pleased to have Gareth home but only if she had the pleasure of his company.

"Oh, bother the old disease!" she cried, jumping to her feet and running across to Gareth with one of her typical, impulsive changes of mood. "I'll take a chance, darling. Now come and sit down by the fire and get warm. You look half dead!"

She linked her arm through his and dragged him into the room, over to the settee where she curled up beside him, her fingers intertwining with his own, her eyes looking provocatively into his grey-blue ones.

"I'd almost forgotten what a handsome man I married!" she said impishly.

Jim gave a snort that might have meant anything.

"If you're going all 'lovely-dovey', I'm off for a walk," he said. "Clearly I'm not wanted."

"No, you're not!" Jane flung after her brother's departing figure. "Go and see how Susan is and don't come back till lunch time. I want my Garry all to myself!"

"Only a few weeks!" a voice cried in Gareth's heart. "Only those few short weeks ago and I should have been so happy. This is the way I longed so often for Jane to be . . . longed for it and so seldom had it. Now, when I can feel only the same indifference that Jane had for me, it is too late!"

But Jane remained unaware of this inner despair, this silent cry against the Fates. She leant her fair head against Gareth's shoulder and said, "I *have* missed you, Garry darling. I was an awful pig to push you out the way I did. But you know how frightened I get and I never stopped to think. Were you awfully cross with your Jane?"

"Not exactly cross!" Gareth said with difficulty. He could not bring himself to make the gesture of putting his arms about her. They lay stiffly, unresponsively by his sides.

"Hurt, then, sweetie? Well, I'm truly sorry. I've suffered just as much as you have by my own selfishness. But it's taught me a lesson, Gareth. I've really missed you and I'm glad you're home. Now smile at me, darling, and stop looking so horribly miserable. I didn't stop loving you just because you weren't here, you know."

"No, I know, Jane!" Gareth said. "I understand . . . I'm not hurt or . . . angry . . . any more. Just rather tired. Things have been pretty hectic round there and I feel a bit done in. I've been worried, too, about Ted."

"Oh, sweetie, of course! I know how much you love the kid and I'm sure there must have been lots for you to do. Susan must be very grateful for everything. I want you to know, Garry darling, that I thoroughly approve of all the money you must have spent. It seems a shame that poor old Sue has to pinch and scrape along, just because she has a kid and no nice husband to provide for her. We've plenty, haven't we, darling . . . to spare, I mean?"

Jane's generosity brought her nearer again to Gareth's heart than anything else she might have done or said. It was, perhaps, the nicest trait in her character and, even while it hurt him to be reminded of his own duplicity, he was glad that Jane had spoken of it. For he would have done just the same for Teddy even had he disliked Susan, or for any friend similarly placed.

He took Jane's hand in his own and pressed it gently.

"I felt sure you would approve, Jane, dear," he said sincerely. "And I know Susan will be grateful when she can think of such things. As to our having 'plenty to spare' as you put it, we're not all that rich, you know. Just comfortably off, I think you'd call it."

Jane giggled.

"Well, I don't understand much about things like finance but it seems to me we are fairly rich. We must have spent a fortune on this house. I'm sure Susan thinks so, anyway, because you could tell she was very impressed. That's one of the good things about money, impressing people . . . that, and being able to help them, don't you agree, Garry?"

Gareth could not agree that he cared for "putting on a show", but Jane's admission was so frank, so completely natural coming from her, that he could not find it in his heart to reprove her. In any case, the giving was as important to her as her childish desire to impress.

He nodded his head absently in a way that Jane took to mean assent. She gave a contented little sigh and said dreamily, "Garry, what plans have we made about moving . . . to London, I mean? Did we lose the flat?"

"No, the owners very kindly gave me three weeks to think it over. You . . . still . . . want to go?"

"Oh, yes indeed, Garry!" Jane cried. "You're not going back on all you said, are you?"

Gareth bit his lip.

"No, I think I'd like to get away as much as you, Jane. I know you've not been particularly happy down here and . . . well, we've rather drifted apart lately, haven't we?"

Jane gave him a quick look through her lashes. Garry was in a serious mood, but that was only to be expected in some ways. If he'd been missing her a great deal while he was at Sue's, he'd only naturally be in a romantic frame of mind now. And it was perfectly true that she had been a little bit crotchety with him sometimes.

"We see so little of each other down here," she complained. "I'm sure it will be different when we're back in London. There's lots and lots of interesting things we can do together . . . just like we used to do, remember? I could lunch with you every day at that little restaurant we liked, or there's the new club Bim took me to. That's just heaps of fun, Garry. I'll get Bim to make you a member."

Her eyes sparkled, her face took on a new glow as she warmed to the thought of the "fun" they'd have.

"We'll give a really super house-party as soon as we're in," she went on, blind to Gareth's stricken, unhappy face. "That will show all the old crowd we're back in circulation. After that, I know we'll have invitations for every night of the week. I think we're a popular couple – as far as married couples ever are!" she added with a little laugh. "You're so tall and handsome and distinguished. All the women are nuts about you, and the men like me because I keep them amused. Oh, we'll get asked out a lot, I know, and have real fun again."

The picture Jane painted was all too vivid in Gareth's mind, as he contemplated his wife's ideas for their future. They were so very remote from his own that he felt frightened by the dissimilarity. Those were the pastimes that would keep Jane happy. Either he must follow the path she chose or else she would become petulant, bored, indifferent again. And he had set himself the task of making her happy. That was the one reason for his breaking his own and Susan's hearts.

Nevertheless, it was not in Gareth's nature to be the kind of husband who trailed around after his wife, slowly losing his individuality, his own interests in life, his own will. Somehow, they must arrive at a compromise which Jane would accept.

"I'm not sure that I want to be out on the razzle every night, Jane," he said, quietly but firmly. "It would be fun, sometimes, to be on our own . . . just the two of us in our home . . ."

But now the words were spoken, he knew that this was not what he wanted any more . . . only what he had once wished for himself and Jane. Because he could not yet revive any deep feeling of love for her . . . because his heart demanded Susan to complete the picture of home life . . . he no longer wanted solitude. Perhaps, after all, it would be easier to follow Jane's lead. It cured her inner restlessness. It might even cure his.

"Well, I didn't exactly mean *every* night, Garry darling," Jane was saying. "Naturally I want you all to myself sometimes. But we've no reason to sit at home twiddling our thumbs, have we? We'll go dancing together, just the two of us, as we used to do. You'd like that, wouldn't you?"

"But you never enjoyed it, Jane!" Gareth cried silently. "You were bored, said I couldn't dance the way you like to do, that I was 'stuffy' because I wouldn't ask the band for all your favourite tunes."

But this was not the memory that had crossed Jane's mind.

She had seen herself entering a room, feminine, exquisitely dressed, tiny beside Gareth's tall figure, perhaps leaning a little on his arm. She saw heads turning to watch their entrance, women remarking to one another about that "handsome couple", about her clothes, the white fur that would slip a little off one bare shoulder, and Gareth discussing the wine list with the head waiter who bowed to him because he knew all about good food and drink and was so obviously a gentleman and rich. She saw, too, the faces watching her as she danced in Gareth's arms, knew that people envied her when he smiled down at her, knew the men would be wishing themselves in Gareth's shoes as she turned her face a little sideways as she talked to him, smiled up at him.

The admiration would be like wine, exciting, intoxicating. But she had forgotten how, like wine, the feeling wore off and she became bored, restless again, annoyed with Gareth because he wouldn't "swing it" just a little, because he wouldn't dance cheek-to-cheek as Ham used to, as all the Americans did, because it was all so sedate . . . and dull.

"If Ted's out of the fog we should be able to go in a week or two," Gareth was saying. "Naturally, I don't want to leave until I'm certain he won't be set back by my absence. He keeps calling for me, you know."

"You've really let him get far too fond of you," Jane said. "It wasn't fair on the kid when you might have left any time. He looked pretty shattered the day I told Sue we were going. I thought then that he wasn't taking it too well. Seems a shame he hasn't someone else around the place to hero-worship . . . an uncle or something. Though the best possible thing would be for Sue to marry again. I've told her so often, but then there really isn't anyone round about whom she might meet and get fond of. There's Jim, of course."

Jane warmed to her subject. It would be fun in lots of ways if Jim and Sue were to fall in love and get married. She, herself could be matron of honour and Teddy a page boy.

"Of course, if they did get married, Sue and I would be sisters-in-law," she said with a laugh. "I wonder if anything will come of it. I'm sure Jim's smitten, but I'm not so certain about Sue. What do you think, Gareth?"

"I'm . . . not . . . in a position to say . . ." Gareth said awkwardly, the conversation having become intolerable to him. But there was no way to avoid it without Jane's suspicions being aroused. For one moment, Gareth wondered what Jane would do if he told her the truth . . . said to her now, "I can't bear to think of Susan marrying your brother because I am in love with her myself, because the thought of her married to anyone at all is torture to me." He felt Jane would imagine he was joking and tell him not to be silly.

"But you must have got to know something about Sue while you've been staying there," Jane was persisting. "Did she ever mention Jim?"

"Once or twice."

"In *that* sort of way?"

"I don't think so . . . I can't remember. I really don't know. These things have to work themselves out. There's no use you trying to plan for other people."

"Well, not plan, exactly, but I can help things along," Jane said, refusing to be put off. She looked at Gareth closely. "I'm sure you know far more than you'll say," she teased him. "I think Sue must have confided in you and made you promise not to tell anyone. Did she?"

She was surprised and amazed to see the colour rush to his face, leave it quickly with a white, stricken look.

"Gareth, she *did* say something!" Jane cried triumphantly. "I knew it all along. Surely you can tell me about it? After all, Sue is my friend."

She waited hopefully for him to speak, but Gareth remained silent.

"Oh, well, I shall ask her myself!" Jane tossed her head.

Gareth gave her a quick, anxious look.

"I wouldn't, Jane. You know what Susan is like. If she wants to confide in you, she will. But I shouldn't worry her now with any awkward questions. She has enough on her mind as it is."

"Then you *do* know something!" Jane laughed. "What a lark! I'll bet you didn't know what to say when she poured out her heart to you. Though I suppose you are a very understanding sort of person in some ways . . . the quiet, thoughtful type. As a matter of fact, you and Susan are rather alike in some ways. But maybe that's why she confides in you. She thinks you'll understand."

"I haven't admitted Susan has confided in me," Gareth said. "And really, Jane, I can't see that it's anyone else's business but hers. So let's drop the subject."

"Oh, all right, stuffy!" Jane said, pouting, but her eyes were still sparkling with laughter. "Jim will tell me if anything's up. He'd be so thrilled if Susan did say she liked him that he'd have to tell someone, so I shall know pretty soon, anyway."

'Don't keep on about it, Jane,' Gareth begged her in his mind. 'Can't you see that it is more than I can bear? I don't want to think of her, to hear her name, to be torn with jealousy in case she and Jim . . . oh, God, help me to bear all this.'

He passed his hand wearily across his forehead and Jane, noticing the gesture, looked at him anxiously.

"Darling, you're not well! I knew you weren't when you came home. And I've been talking my head off when all the time you've got a splitting headache. Now you go right up to bed, sweetie, and have a rest before lunch."

"I think I will!" Gareth said, glad of this opportunity to escape. "I am a bit tired."

Jane fussed round him until he was laying on the bed in his dressing-room, his eyes closed. Then with a quick kiss on the top of his head, she tiptoed out of the room and at last he was alone.

Only when Jane was once more curled up on the sofa with a box of chocolates and a magazine, did it occur to her that there might be a more serious reason for Gareth's pale, exhausted face and dark-rimmed eyes, than just fatigue. *Perhaps he was sickening for something!*

The idea drained all the colour away from her own face and

shock robbed her for a moment of thought. If Gareth were to go down now with infantile paralysis, she thought with horror, she too, might get it. She had just kissed him. She had been sitting right here next to him, breathing in the germs . . .

In desperate haste, she jumped to her feet and rushed along to the bathroom and gargled furiously. Then she rushed to the telephone and dialled Dr McMillan's number. Her voice shook a little as she spoke to him.

"It's my husband, Dr McMillan. He isn't very well and he's gone to bed. He says he's just tired but I think it might be something worse. He looks dreadful! Under the circumstances, don't you think it might be best to look in on him . . . just in case . . . ?"

"I'm terribly busy, Mrs Everett, but I'll look in after I've seen young Ted, or just before, if you prefer. About twelve o'clock."

Jane went back to the sitting-room and looked at her watch. Only just eleven. That meant an hour to wait . . . an hour that for her would be mental torture . . . one whole hour before her mind could be put at rest . . . before she could be sure.

Eleven

"Jim, do tell me what is making you smile in that peculiar way!"

Jim looked at the slim, neat figure Susan presented as she reclined in the deck-chair beside him. In her long, slender hands was a piece of embroidery, for when she was not actually busy around the house there was always something in her hands, and Jim had noticed she was never without her sewing or knitting. It was as if her hands were too restless to remain still even when her body was in repose.

She looked very beautiful . . . much thinner than when he had first met her last winter, but then she had not seemed to put on the weight she had lost when Teddy was so ill. Nevertheless, it added to her beauty, making even bigger those large, mysterious dark eyes, accentuating the gentle curve of her lips.

He brought his mind back from the present to the thought which had made him smile.

"I suppose it wasn't funny at all!" he told her, his eyes still smiling nevertheless. "I was recalling that day when Jane thought Gareth had got infantile paralysis . . . her face when I got back from your house and the expression on it."

"It doesn't sound funny," Susan said. "I never knew about Gareth. Tell me."

"I know it wasn't funny . . . or wouldn't have been had it turned out to be true. But Jane always did have a fit if there was any hint of illness about. Gareth was pretty fagged out, I think, and retired to his bed for a rest. Jane got rattled and telephoned Dr McMillan. I don't think he ever suspected Gareth was sickening for Teddy's troubles but he told Jane to keep him in bed for a day to be on the safe side. The doctor had just left when I turned up and Jane was almost in hysterics because the doc had told *her* to take in his meals and look after him. I think she'd have given me a million pounds when I offered to be the go-between. She's a funny kid."

"Gareth wasn't really ill?" Susan asked carefully.

"Oh, lord, no! Just tired as far as I can gather. But then he nearly always is that way. It's the rackety life he leads. I can't think how he can enjoy it, myself. I always thought Gareth was more the stay-at-home type."

He was watching Susan's face, but her head was bent over her sewing and she made no comment.

"Jane's overdoing it, too," Jim went on. "She looked pretty exhausted last time I saw her. She and Gareth had been to some party or other and hadn't got to bed until four next morning. Personally, I've grown out of that stage myself. Used to think it was clever to stay up until dawn broke over the city! Now I'm ready for my bed by midnight. Must be getting old."

"Jim! What a thing to say. Why, you're only a few months older than I am," Susan said, smiling at him.

"That's right!" Jim admitted. "And I'm glad of those few months. I'm certain women prefer men to be older than themselves . . . Susan, when are you going to take my idea seriously?" The words were lightly spoken, but there was a glint of seriousness in his eyes which Susan could not help noticing. Until now she had been able to tease Jim out of these moments of sentiment. She had known for some time that he was in love with her. The signs were so unmistakable . . . the phone calls, letters, excuses to visit her and Ted, to do things for them. Lately she had seen him nearly every weekend.

It was not that she disliked Jim. He was wonderful company and she valued his friendship, coming as it did just when she most needed it. After Gareth and Jane had left, she had picked up the old threads of her life – a life which included only Teddy and herself; but she was no longer satisfied, no longer content just to dream through the days. There were far too many memories of Gareth for her to retrieve that peace of mind. Teddy, Mrs Mendall, someone in the village, had but to mention his name for her heart to accelerate, for the colour to come to her cheeks. Her parting from him was still a deep, raw wound which even the passage of time seemed not to have alleviated. Six months now since Teddy's illness, which to her would always be associated with her discovery of her love for Gareth . . . his for her. Teddy, mercifully, was well again with nothing but a slight stiffness in one arm, which Dr McMillan had promised her would wear off in time if she continued the massage and he made normal use of it. Those ghastly days of anxiety were in the distant past, tempered by time that had had no effect on her memories of Gareth.

They had not met again. Once or twice Jane had written or telephoned asking Susan to go to town, but she had found excuses to avoid doing so. Jane had finally suggested she and Gareth should spend a weekend at Susan's cottage but had later telephoned to say Gareth couldn't manage it after all. Susan had realized then that Gareth, too, was making excuses to avoid meeting her. Throughout those long days and sleepless nights, six months had done nothing to erase the memory of Gareth's face, his kisses, his arms around her.

And Jim had given her scraps of news about him from time to time which she had craved and yet dreaded, for always the sound of his name accentuated the ache in her heart.

When first she was certain that Jim loved her, she had not been sure what she should do about it. A decision had not been forced, for Jim made no attempt to propose to her and only alluded in a round-about fashion to his hopes for the future. She had, at first easily, and of late with more difficulty, managed either to turn the conversation, or else joke him into a more humorous frame of mind. But the time would come, she knew, when the words would be spoken and because she could never love Jim in that way, never marry him, she was afraid that it must mean the end of their friendship.

The idea which he wished her to consider seriously, was that of providing Ted with a father, and the necessary firm hand he now needed, for only naturally he had become a little spoiled since his illness. This suggestion had been put forward by Jim fairly frequently, but in a light-hearted vein which she parried by joking in her turn that Jim was the one who needed the firm hand.

Strangely enough, Teddy had completely transferred to Jim his erstwhile affection for and hero-worship of Gareth. Susan knew that children were notoriously fickle, but she had imagined Ted's love for Gareth had gone so very much deeper than transient emotion. But from the day Gareth and Jane had left for their new London home, Teddy had scarcely mentioned his name and had, moreover, turned any conversation in which Gareth's name was mentioned.

Once, Jane had written suggesting Ted go to stay with them for a few days. Susan had seen Gareth's love for Ted behind the suggestion and passed the idea on to Ted. But he had only shown a glimmer of interest, sufficient to inquire if she, too, had been invited and when learning that she was not going, shook his dark head and said he did not want to go either.

"But I thought you were so fond of your Uncle Gareth?" she had insisted, distressed because what she had expected to be a wonderful surprise for him had fallen flat.

"Well, I *was*!" was Ted's mumbled comment before he changed the subject.

She had not pressed further with the discussion, although it hurt her to think that her son no longer cared about the man she herself loved so hopelessly and so faithfully. But in a way she could understand that to a child, the present was more important than the past and Jim had paid Ted as much time and attention as Gareth had done in his different fashion. Where Gareth had taught, explained, discussed, listened, Jim acted. He would spend a wet afternoon on the sitting-room floor helping Ted run his new train, where Gareth would have explained how it worked, answering all Ted's innumerable questions. And when Ted tired of playing trains, Jim would take him for a long walk or organize a rat-hunt or a scouting trip. He was more elder brother than father, as Gareth had been, and Ted obviously loved this companionship. It had become 'Jim and me' where once it was 'Uncle Gareth and me'. And Jim's cheerful, amusing company had helped Ted over the long, tedious convalescence.

Susan knew that she came nearer to loving Jim when she thought of the attention he gave to her son, than ever she could from his attentions to herself, which were many. He never failed to pass some teasing but admiring compliment, to tell her how pretty she was looking, that he liked a new dress, a new hair-style.

Even now, at this very minute, he was saying, "You're the first woman I've met who could look beautiful even when she frowned! Susan, surely my suggestion doesn't need all this terrifying thought and consideration? Why don't you just accept things the way they are and be impulsive for once?"

Susan gave him a long look that was half compassionate, half borne of a very real affection for him. It seemed as if she could no longer pretend she knew nothing of what lay in Jim's mind.

"I'm not a very impulsive person, Jim," she said. "It's the nature of the girl, I suppose!"

Jim sighed.

"I know, and I wouldn't want you one scrap different Susan, except over this. You know, don't you, that I'm crazy to marry you? No, don't say anything just yet. Let me finish and then you can tear strips off me. I realize that you aren't in love with me. But that doesn't matter so much. I'm prepared to accept that fact and to live in hopes of something more. You see, Susan, I love you enough to want nothing more than to make you and Ted happy, to have the right to take care of you both, to know you belong to me."

"I must interrupt, Jim. I won't pretend I haven't known you felt this way. I hoped you might 'get over it' as the saying goes. You see, I feel rather deeply on the subject of marriage. It isn't an easy relationship, Jim, in a lot of ways. Even in the short while I was married to Edward and although we loved one another very much, there were little quarrels, a need to adjust ourselves. Only love can make these differences cease to matter; only a proportion of give and take *on each side*, can make the compromise possible, or fair. One person cannot do all the taking, none of the giving."

"I think I believe all you say to be true, Susan, but I don't agree that you would do none of the giving, for that is what you meant, wasn't it? Just being with you is enough to make me happy, and you give so much more than you know. Your very beauty is a gift. The quietness and peace of mind that you seem to impart is a very valuable gift. The right to share your life in itself is large enough a gift to me to make everything else worth while. And besides, I do honestly think you are fond of me, aren't you, Susan?"

"Oh, Jim, of course I am!" Susan cried warmly. "But even though I'm so fond of you and have an immense affection for you, that can't make it love."

"But your friendship and affection are two more of the gifts you mention!" Jim cried triumphantly. "I know I'm not much of a 'catch' for a girl and that I have an awful nerve even to hope you might give me the answer I so much want. But I suppose even I have certain advantages and since there's no one else to put my case, I shall have to risk your thinking me a vain idiot and tell you that I'm an easy-going fellow. I don't make outrageous requests for impossible things and for all I'm a bit hare-brained at times, I'm steady enough at heart and doing well at the office. I stand a good chance of becoming a junior director next year. I'm sure if my boss knew I was hoping to marry you on the strength of it, he'd say it was in the bag."

Susan bit her lip.

"Jim, dear, that side of it doesn't enter into the discussion. If I loved you I'd want to marry you whether you were a pauper or a millionaire. I don't think you overestimate yourself one little bit. You're a wonderful person and I admire and respect as well as like you. It's just that I do think love is necessary *on both sides*. You may think you didn't need it at first, but in time you would. I know you would. Look at some of the married couples you know."

"Gareth and Jane, I suppose!" Jim said gloomily, although Susan had not meant to do other than generalize. "I must admit I think Gareth is a bit fed up with Jane's behaviour. She never really loved him the way you mean and I guess he hasn't any illusions left. Not that she's gadding about with other men, but anyone can see it by the way she treats him. And that makes it sound worse than it is because she is fond of him in her way. But I don't honestly think she's ever loved anyone but herself! Not a very nice thing to say about your own sister but there it is. Unless she loved that American of hers. That's really the type of man she was suited to. He knocked her about a bit, you know . . . not physically, but she was never quite certain where she stood with him. One always had the feeling about him, that he was liable to dash off on some new venture and leave everything behind him. Definitely unreliable, I'd say. But Jane adored him. I dare say she married old Gareth on the rebound."

Once again there was no comment from Susan, for she could never discuss Gareth and Jane's relationship . . . never dared even to think of it. She hoped that Jim would not see her embarrassment, the colour that she knew to be in her cheeks.

But Jim was far more astute, perhaps made so by his love for her, than she had given him credit to be.

"You're in love with Gareth, aren't you, Susan?" he said suddenly, before she could anticipate and prepare herself against such a question. The colour deepened in her cheeks and her hands were trembling.

After a moment, she said, "What . . . an odd suggestion, Jim. Whatever gave you that idea?"

Her assumed surprise cut no ice with Jim, nor did she really hope it might have done.

"You can be honest with me, Susan. I think I've suspected it from the first, although I tried not to see it. I hoped, I suppose, that given a little time, you might get over it . . . that it might just be infatuation. It's still . . . there . . . isn't it?"

She could not lie about it, belittle it by untruths. She nodded her head.

"And I suppose Gareth feels the same way. I couldn't blame him. I don't see how any man could feel otherwise about you, Susan. It answers all the questions . . . why he never comes down here and why you never go up to see them. Why they left so hurriedly and all that. I take it Jane doesn't know?"

"There was nothing to know," Susan said, her voice barely audible.

"Except what she would have seen with her own eyes if she'd loved him herself," Jim said flatly. "But she can't see because she doesn't care enough about Gareth to study him closely. Just as well in the circumstances, I suppose. Oh, Susan, I think I'm sorry for you because I know what it's like to love someone without much hope. I can sympathize even while I'm horribly jealous. Can't you and Gareth . . . wouldn't you . . . I mean, since Jane . . .?" he broke off awkwardly.

"I think Jane does love Gareth in her way. Neither he nor I would like to be responsible for breaking up his marriage," Susan said quietly. "It was never even discussed between us. It's all over and done with, Jim. I dare say Gareth has forgotten about it and I'm trying hard to do so."

"But without a lot of success," Jim added, watching her face, now dead white and with sharp lines etched round her mouth. A deep compassion for her overcame him and he leaned over to her and took her hand in his warm clasp.

"I'm so sorry, Susan. It hurts me to see you unhappy. We won't discuss the subject again. Let's talk some more about us!"

She gave him a wan smile and said, "What more can we say about us, Jim? You must see now how out of the question it is."

"On the contrary, I see every hope," Jim argued. "Susan, *let me help you to forget, to fight it out*. Two are better than one as the saying goes and believe me, I'll fight hard! Seriously, Susan, it might help you. There'll be new ideas, a new life together. And you wouldn't have nearly so much time to think. It would make it even more impossible too, if you were no longer free, wouldn't it? At any rate, Gareth wouldn't spend his life wondering if he had done the right thing. He'd have no choice left."

It was an argument that hadn't crossed Susan's mind but she had not hitherto believed that Gareth might be unhappy ... seriously so, with Jane. The frank picture Jim had given her today, of the life Gareth and Jane were leading, had disturbed her a great deal, and until now she had never considered that Gareth's heart might still be torn by wondering if he had made the right decision. *It was the right one*, his duty, her own, and yet his heart must tell him differently, as did her own, if Jim were right in saying he still loved her. Could it be possible that her marriage to Jim might be what Gareth needed to help him settle down again? Might it help her, too, to overcome her wretchedness, her sleepless nights and that loss of her most prized peace of mind? And if the answer to all these questions were in the affirmative, would it be fair for her to marry Jim for these reasons?

"I suppose you are thinking it wouldn't be fair to marry me on those terms!" Jim said, reading her mind. But pressing home the advantage he saw he had gained, he added, "You're wrong, of course, Susan. It *would* be fair because I know the exact position, don't I? I'd be going into it with my eyes open. I should know and understand, and it doesn't alter my views in the slightest. Time would bring you closer to me, Susan, and our shared life. I wouldn't make any demands on you. You should dictate the terms. Only say you'll give me a chance, if not for your own sake and Ted's, then for mine. Give me a chance to win your love, to try to make you happy again."

For several minutes, which seemed an eternity to Jim, Susan remained silent, lost in thought. Then she looked up at him and said, "Give me time to think about it, Jim! I never imagined I might consider it so I haven't been thinking about it in the way you have. Don't rush me into anything. Be patient a little longer."

"Then I can hope?" Jim asked eagerly.

Again Susan bit her lip.

"I don't want to disappoint you, Jim. I can't give you hope until I consider the possibility . . . whether it can be right from all points of view. Give me a little while longer, a week or two, and we'll discuss it again."

"And that's a promise?" Jim persisted.

Susan nodded.

Jim gave a deep sigh.

"Well, I feel happier and more hopeful for all you won't give me much hope," he said. "I'll wait, Susan, as long as you ask. I'd wait for ever if I did not feel it was a dreadful waste of our lives!"

He was grinning at her in his charming, boyish fashion and as always, his humour brought a smile back to Susan's face.

"You're a dear, Jim!" she said warmly. "It's so nice to be made to smile, and I want to. I want to be happy in my life again."

"So you shall, if I die in the attempt," Jim stated. "And if I'm not the one in the end to achieve that happiness for you, I shall still be glad. You're made for living, for love and laughter, Susan. It's a terrible waste to deny yourself to the world, living out of it as you do down here."

His words brought back all too vividly the almost identical words that Gareth had spoken. Recalling them, she could remember also that he had said she should marry again. It was as if he were here now, trying to help her, to make her decision clearer. He *had hoped she would marry again*. At the time she had barely given thought to his remark. It had seemed so irrelevant when his arms were around her and her love for him the only emotion in her. But now, as she thought of it, it seemed indeed as if he had foreseen such an event and had wanted her to know that he, too, thought as Jim did, that it would be best for all of them, herself, Ted and maybe even for himself, too.

"Oh, Gareth!" her heart cried out her need for him. "I cannot do it. I belong to you . . . only to you!"

But always came the cold realization that she could not and never could belong to Gareth. Only divorce would make that possible and neither of them, even had they considered it in the dark recesses of their minds, had allowed the idea to form. Divorce was a common enough event these days but there were other factors involved besides their private principles. There was Jane to consider. Jane, who was Susan's friend before Susan had met Gareth. Jane, who in her casual, generous way had given her so much. Jane, who however indifferently, still loved Gareth after her fashion and had never contemplated making a new life for herself without him.

Even to think of Jane's pretty vivacious little face, was to put all thoughts of Gareth and herself out of the realms of possibility.

Gareth was in love with Jane once, Susan had told herself time and time again. He would love her again. And if she, Susan, were to marry Jim, this might make a proper reunion between husband and wife more possible, much easier.

Susan was seeing herself suddenly in a new light . . . as the kind of woman whom she had always despised . . . one who came between a man and his wife. She had never intentionally tried to do so but it seemed now as if inadvertently, this was exactly what she had been doing. Jim had thought Gareth still loved her, still longed for and needed her, wondered if he had done the right thing in trying to start life anew with Jane. He might always wonder while she, Susan, remained alone, if she were waiting for him to come to her. The very fact of her own faithfulness to him made his decision more difficult. It made her own acceptance of their parting harder, to learn that Gareth was unhappy, leading a life he did not care for, that he was tired, lonely. The knowledge of his need for her increased her own need of him. Had she known he was happy again with Jane, in love with her, she herself would have accepted the fact and her own adjustment to it been the easier. All this might equally well apply to Gareth in his consideration of *her*.

Susan looked across the lawn where Jim had joined Ted in a game of French cricket. His young, attractive face was bright with laughter and she heard her son's happy laugh in reply to some remark Jim had passed. Jim's fair curly head, far above the dark head of her son, looked appealing in its youthfulness. There was, she thought, something maternal in her fondness for Jim. No matter what his age, he would always have that same Peter Pan quality which was so much a part of his sister, Jane. And yet Jim was not really like Jane. He lacked most of her faults . . . was never selfish nor self-centred in the way that Jane could be.

"Perhaps I ought to dislike the physical resemblance that exists between him and Jane!" Susan mused. But she could feel no dislike, because strangely enough, in spite of all that had happened, she was still fond of Jane, had never felt that Jane was her "rival" or in any way felt antagonistic towards the woman who was married to the man she herself loved; for whose sake she and Gareth had both rejected their own happiness.

Nevertheless, if ever she should agree to marry Jim it must inevitably mean reopening the close ties of friendship with Jane and Gareth and this she certainly did not wish to do. Her heart was in no way under her control and she *dared* not see Gareth for fear that her resolutions might collapse. She was, after all, so weak! Love seemed to have robbed her of that immense self-control which had helped her so much in her battles with life. Now she knew all too well that for all her fine intentions, it would need an inhuman effort to prevent herself running to Gareth should he call her; giving herself into his care if he demanded it.

"I still love you, Gareth, my own dear heart!" she cried silently. "Time has not helped as you promised me it might. My heart is still yours . . . all yours. If I could but break from within the spell you have cast around me . . . find peace again!"

But Gareth could not help her. He must suffer alone as she was doing, and it were better that their paths should not cross again until they had armoured themselves against the treacherous longings of their hearts.

'Would I find it easier to forget if I married Jim?' Susan asked herself again and her hand passed wearily to her forehead as immediately came the thought, 'It would not be fair to Jim. I can never marry him. If he knew how hopelessly and irrevocably I love Gareth, he would know that there must be nothing left for him but my friendship. And friendship would not satisfy him for long . . . nor any man.'

A shaft of pity shot through her for Jim, who, like herself, loved without hope of future happiness. Pity, too, for herself, since she must resign herself once again to a life alone with few friends. Once it had seemed enough. Could it ever be again? Would those swift, tumultuous emotions that Gareth had reawakened so unintentionally ever fade away into insignificance? Would she ever hear his name without longing, without fear?

So deep in thought was Susan, that she did not hear the car stop outside her gate; did not hear the footsteps walking up the path; was unaware of her visitors until she heard Teddy's wild shriek of surprise and amazement, "Mummy, come quickly. It's Uncle Gareth . . . and Aunty Jane."

Slowly, her nerves tightening, steeling themselves against this newest assault on her heart, Susan turned her head and found herself looking into the quiet grey-blue of Gareth's eyes.

Twelve

The trees, the sky, the garden . . . all revolved crazily as the blood throbbed in her temples, and her heart beat its mad, wild welcome. Gareth, Gareth, *Gareth*! Her whole being seemed to resound with his name, to melt beneath his grave, sad, unhappy gaze.

"Hallo, Sue!" he said quietly, and his voice steadied her, gave her back a measure of self-control. The colour, bright in her cheeks, died slowly away leaving her white beneath the light tan. Beyond Gareth's shoulder, her eyes focused on Jane's small figure in a full-skirted cotton frock billowing about her brown legs as she laughed up at her brother. Jim's head was turned slightly towards Susan as if his mind were not on his sister's greeting but on Susan's meeting with Gareth. Susan knew that he wanted to come over to her but did not like to be too obvious about it. She wished he would come, and yet another part of her begged for a moment or two longer alone with Gareth; a moment to look once more at his face, to etch it on her memory; so see the look in his eyes, hear the deep, beloved voice speaking her name.

"Gareth!" she whispered.

His hand went towards her in a half gesture then dropped swiftly to his side. He seemed to stiffen and the lines about his mouth became deeper, harder.

"I had to come down to take a possible purchaser of the cottage for a good look round," he said, biting his lips, his eyes looking away from her to the trees, bright in their yellow-green summer foliage against the glittering blue of the sky. "Jane decided at the last minute to come down with me and, of course, she wanted to stop and see you although we haven't much time."

Susan knew that he was trying to explain that it was not his wish to be here; that this meeting was as painful for him as it was for her, as much a trial. She knew, too, that he still loved her, still longed to be near her even while he feared it. For him, as for her, this sight of the loved one was both an ache and a blessed moment, snatched from time to satisfy the parched thirst of their eyes for one another's faces.

For one long moment, they stood in silence, reading the pain and the longing and the love reflected from their eyes. Then a small, dark, curly-headed boy ran between them, clung to Gareth's arm as if he would never let go and cried, "Oh, Uncle Gareth. We *have* missed you. It seems such a dreadful long time."

'So he hasn't forgotten!' Susan thought. 'He only buried his love as I have tried to do.'

She saw Gareth's arms go round her son, lifting him into the air as if he had no weight. His voice was husky and full of deep tenderness as he said, "Ted! I've missed you, too. You have grown!"

Then suddenly, to Susan's surprise, Ted wriggled free of Gareth's arms. The bright flush of excitement that had been on his cheeks died away and was replaced by an expression of withdrawal that was strangely adult. His small body seemed to stiffen and he bit his lip once or twice as he did sometimes when he was not sure of himself. There was a hard look in his eyes when once more he turned to look at Gareth and said, "Uncle Jim's teaching me to play cricket. He says I'm jolly good. Uncle Jim and me do all sorts of things together. He's going to take me to Lord's this summer. He's promised. And Uncle Jim doesn't forget promises."

And he turned and walked abruptly away towards Jim and Jane, leaving Susan and Gareth alone once more in a constrained silence.

"I . . . I can't understand him," Susan said helplessly. "He was so obviously thrilled to see you, Gareth, and then . . ."

"Then he remembered!" Gareth broke in quietly, his voice full of pain. "I understand, Susan. He can't forgive me any more than I can forgive myself. But I didn't really let him down. He's too young to understand. Some day, perhaps, he will."

Susan had no time to try to reason Gareth's enigmatic remarks. Jim and Jane were walking towards them and automatically, Susan forced a smile to her face, her feet to walk a step or two towards them.

"Sue, *darling*!" Jane cried. "So you're the dark, mysterious woman who has seduced my poor young brother away from the bright lights of London! Darling, it's wonderful to see you. You look marvellous. A bit thin, but then we're all getting old and haggard, aren't we?"

"You look just the same, Jane dear!" Susan said, but as her eyes studied Jane's face, she knew that it wasn't true. There were dark shadows beneath Jane's bright, laughing eyes. She was pale, and the fresh pink-and-white complexion that had contributed so much to that little-girl youthfulness was now blotched with tiredness. Her voice, like her smile, was brittle. Only her eyes were unchanged. Jane was beginning to look, as she had said, haggard.

"This is a surprise," Susan said. "If I'd known you were coming, I'd have . . ."

". . . baked a cake!" Jane broke in giggling. "I know, darling, but we can't stay to tea. Garry is fussing like an old hen to get back to London and I had to drag him here. He gets daily more and more unsociable."

There was an edge to her voice which Gareth, too, must have noticed although he showed no sign of doing so.

"Anyway, now we are here at last," Jane went on, "I utterly refuse to budge an inch until I've had a good old gossip with you, Sue. So off you go, Gareth, and take Jim and Ted with you. We're going to be girls together for five minutes."

"Come on, old chap. We aren't wanted!" Jim said to Ted, who was standing silently beside him. "Let's go and show Uncle Gareth the thrush's nest while the girls gossip."

"It is nice to see you, Sue," Jane said, as the men moved away across the lawn. She settled herself down in one of the deck-chairs and curled her sandalled feet beneath her. "You know, you *are* thinner, Sue! You look frightfully Mona Lisa-ish, if you know what I mean. Tell me all the news."

"There isn't any!" Susan said, leaning back in the deck-chair and hating herself for the knowledge that she was listening with one ear for the sound of Gareth's voice. "Tell me about yourself. I hear from Jim you've been leading quite a jolly life in London."

"Jolly!" Jane gave a hard laugh. "Oh, well, I suppose one might call it that. But it's beginning to pall a bit. I wouldn't admit it to anyone else, but I'm really rather bored with it all. I don't know what's the matter with me, Sue. After about six months of the same thing I just get fed up with it and want something else. I suppose I'm spoilt."

"Perhaps it's just that you overdo it?" Susan suggested. "You go so hard at whatever you're doing. Just a little at a time is the way to enjoy things."

Jane gave a sigh. She was happy now that she could pour out her troubles to Susan.

"You're always so horribly sensible, Sue," she said affectionately. "And I know you're right but I just can't be different from 'me', can I? Tell me, darling, are you going to marry my devoted brother?"

Susan met Jane's curious look with a steady gaze.

"I don't think so, Jane. He has . . . asked me. But I don't feel able to accept. You see, although I'm very fond of him indeed, I don't love him."

"Love!" Jane said enigmatically. "Well, I don't know, Sue. You and I don't see eye to eye about those sorts of things. We never did. All the same, you can't remain faithful to a memory for ever."

"You mean Edward?" Susan asked. "It isn't that, Jane. Edward doesn't come into it."

"But you always said you could never fall in love again," Jane argued.

Susan bit her lip.

"Did I? Well, perhaps I was right. In any case, I wouldn't want to marry unless I was in love."

"Do you think it matters so much?" Jane asked. But she did not wait for an answer. "In any case, what is love, when you try to describe it? Life's so difficult, isn't it?"

There was something both lost and lonely in Jane's voice and remarks that immediately made Susan forget her own troubles and unhappiness. She put a hand impulsively on Jane's arm and said, "Aren't you finding life very easy, Jane?"

She was prepared for the flood of intimate confidences which followed, but not for the nature of those confidences which must affect her own life so closely.

"It's Garry!" Jane was saying. "I feel such a brute, Sue, but how can I help it? He knew I wasn't in love with him when we got married . . . at least, not the way I was in love with Ham. He said it didn't matter and that I'd grow to care. Well, it just hasn't worked out that way. It's a horrible thing to say about anyone but I'm tired of feeling a failure."

"Jane, you're no such thing. Gareth cannot have told you that."

"Oh, he never says anything nowadays, but I know I'm not what he hoped I would be . . . a nice domesticated wife and mother. I loathe babies, Sue, you know I've always told you I never wanted them. Gareth just can't understand it. He used to worry on about children, and now he never says a word, which is far worse. I won't give in to him and yet I feel beastly because I can't make myself do it. And all the other things . . . our life in town. He doesn't enjoy gadding around the way I do and either I go without him and feel guilty because I've left him alone at home, or I drag him along, too, and then feel guilty because I know he isn't enjoying himself. He tries. That's the whole trouble. He's always so kind and generous and self-sacrificing. His devotion gets on my nerves."

Jane must have seen something of the shock her words had caused Susan for she added, "Don't think I'm not fond of Garry, Sue. I am. If I weren't I'd have left him ages ago. In lots of ways we get along together wonderfully. And you know, Sue, I've been thinking a bit and I've come to the conclusion there's something wrong with me. I just don't seem able to be content with life. If I left Garry, it would be just the same . . . worse, probably, because I know I should miss him. And I've never met another man I'd rather be married to. It *is* old, isn't it?"

"Maybe you're just a restless person, Jane. Are you sure you aren't blinding yourself to the things that really matter? I know it sounds smug, probably, but in the end it's your home and your husband and children who keep life from getting stale. They are the *lasting* happiness. Perhaps Gareth sees a little farther than you do and realizes this. You may be a different person underneath, Jane . . . someone you don't know. You'd feel so different about your own children, and once you had a child, I'm certain everything else would sort itself out, too. Gareth would be . . . a wonderful father. He's so good with children. And then you'd be pleased you had the kind of husband who would stay at home with you and help to look after them."

Jane gave a sigh.

"I dare say that would be the solution to the problem of Gareth," she said. "But I can't pretend what I don't feel, Susan, and I cannot imagine wanting a baby. It would be a dreadful tie and I should be more bored than ever. I know I would."

"Then . . . you'll go on as you are?" Susan asked.

"I suppose so!" Jane said. "This is just a 'mood' and I'll be chirpy again tomorrow, no doubt. In fact, I'm feeling better already just for talking to you. Garry didn't want to come and was quite boorish about it. I thought you and he used to be such good friends."

Susan clenched her fists tightly at her sides.

"We are good friends, I think, Jane. I expect he's just busy and anxious to get home."

"I know, but you'd think he'd want to see Ted. I've come to the conclusion men are odd. I don't suppose I shall ever understand Gareth properly. Anyway, let's forget silly old me and talk about you. When are you coming up to see me?"

"One of these days," Susan said, knowing that it was not, could not be the truth. "I'm pretty tied with Teddy as you know, but perhaps in the school holidays," she ended vaguely.

"I want Gareth to take me abroad this summer," Jane said. "I'd like to go to America but he can't get away that long from business. So it'll probably be France or Italy. It's something to look forward to. Perhaps Jim will come along with us and recover from a broken heart!"

Susan smiled.

"I don't think Jim's heart will be broken, Jane. I hope not. He's been a wonderful friend and I should hate to have to end that friendship. I should miss him terribly."

Jane gave a little *moue* with her lips.

"I can't see why you don't marry him, Sue. After all, he knows the position, I presume. He'd be no worse off than Gareth when I agreed to marry him and better off in lots of ways. You'd be sure to make him a proud father."

"That wouldn't necessarily make him happy," Susan said.

And she thought, 'Any more than you have made Gareth happy.' But this thought was soon followed by another . . . that Gareth loved Jane and might again, if she made an effort to close the breach between them; if she would only have the children Gareth had always wanted. Their marriage could still be a success if only Jane were prepared to make it so by giving a little as well as taking.

'I cannot advise you, Jane,' she thought, seeing her friend's pretty, discontented face puckered like a small girl's when she was not having things all her own way. 'I am not in a position to offer you advice now. There is nothing I can do to help you except to stay out of your life . . . and Gareth's.'

Nothing, except perhaps to marry Jim. But would that make so much difference? Gareth had been playing his part well. Jane had said he was kind, considerate, devoted.

Was it possible that somewhere deep within her, Jane sensed that she had lost Gareth's love? She might still imagine it to be there, but did she feel instinctively that something was lost . . .

something necessary to her life for all she had valued it so lightly? Love was said to beget love. Might the lack of it beget the indifference that was growing in Jane for her home, her marriage, for Gareth?

"Here come the boys!" Jane said, interrupting Susan's thoughts and causing her heart to jump violently. She dared not turn her head for fear that Jim would see how quickly her glance went from him to Gareth . . . Jim, who knew what lay in her heart.

And loving her, Jim understood better than Susan realized, what this chance meeting with Gareth was costing her in effort to appear normal . . . not to betray her feelings. His first thought when he had seen Jane's small figure with Gareth towering beside her, had been for Susan. He had seen her head jerk round at Teddy's cry; had seen how her hands went to her breast in an unconscious gesture.

Pity, jealousy . . . both had swept over him in turn. For a brief moment too, he had hated Gareth. This man held Susan's heart in the palm of his hand, unwittingly, perhaps, but nevertheless he had no right to love her, to have her love. He already had a wife . . . Jim's own sister. That he should be the barrier between Susan and himself was for that instant quite intolerable.

Then, when he and Gareth left Jane and Susan to their "chat", he had known deep within him that whatever their personal problem, he liked Gareth, admired and respected him. He was one hundred per cent a man's man and Jim knew himself unable to credit Gareth with any baser motives. He knew that Gareth was a man of honour and that he had been as powerless as Susan to prevent himself from falling in love.

Now, as he saw Susan's dark head held rigidly forward as they walked towards her, there was no anger left in him . . . only pity for the four of them whose lives had become so hopelessly intermingled. He had a moment's blind impulse to put a hand on Gareth's shoulder, and say, "I understand, old chap. No one could help loving her. I don't blame you. She's worth ten of Jane!"

But he could, in fact, do nothing to help Gareth, who walked with a stiff, uneasy gait, his shoulders a little bent, his face grim and serious. And Teddy, who might have lightened the situation, was, for some reason of his own, behaving very strangely. He hung on to Jim's hand with quite unusual affection, answered Gareth's questions with surly, muttered replies, and now maintained a strict and curious silence.

Jane alone appeared at ease, reaching out to Gareth for a cigarette, chattering lightly about their old cottage.

Jim had thrown himself on the grass beside the deck-chairs but Gareth remained standing, his hands busy with his lighter, his eyes anywhere but on Susan who stared, in turn, at Ted.

"We ought to be pushing along, Jane," Gareth said, "We shall have to miss tea if we're to be home by six."

"Oh, blow the cocktail party!" Jane said lightly. "Let's stay and have tea with Sue! It's lovely here in the garden and it's bound to be hot and stuffy in town."

Jim saw Gareth's eyes go quickly to Susan's face, away again a second later.

"We'd be . . . putting Susan out . . . spoiling her tête-à-tête," he said, a note of teasing which Jim felt to be obviously forced.

"Stuff and nonsense!" Jane laughed. "Jim will have to lump it. Anyway, we don't want anything to eat, Sue."

"There's plenty . . . if you really will stay!" Susan had to put in, although she longed now for them to go. It was worse than agony to have Gareth so close . . . to know that this meeting was as painful for him as for her . . . that he, too, longed to be gone, to put as great a distance as possible between them since to stay meant a nearness that could never be near enough.

"Then that settles it," said Jane. "I'll help with the tea things."

"No, I'll manage," Susan cried, quickly jumping to her feet. "You stay and talk to Jim."

"Let Garry help you," Jane said to everyone's consternation but her own. "He can carry trays and things." And as he made no move, she added, "Go on, Gareth. You *are* getting lazy!"

"Really, I don't need any help," Susan said desperately, but

Jane had made up her mind for no particular reason and was determined not to be balked.

"Let him do some work, Sue. It's good for him!" she said, and Gareth had no alternative but to follow Susan to the house.

They stood in the kitchen on opposite sides of the table, neither able to find words that were casual; neither able to think clearly of anything but this isolation.

"I . . . I'll cut some bread and butter," Susan said at last. "If you could get the tray from the cupboard over there?"

"Susan!"

The sound of her name on his lips thrilled through her and she felt her heart beating faster, faster until it seemed she must suffocate with the wild emotion within her. Slowly she lifted her head and faced him across the room. His eyes, so wide, so deep-set and unhappy, stared into her dark ones. Desperately, he said, "I tried not to come. Jane would have it this way. You do . . . understand?"

She nodded her head but could not speak.

"Don't be unhappy!" Gareth said. "You look so pale and thin, Susan. I can't bear to think that I . . . that you . . ."

"That I still love you, Gareth?" Susan could not prevent the words from rushing to her lips.

The tension in his face gave way to a slow smile that was full of sweetness, glowing with a happiness he could not prevent.

"That is a tribute I treasure always in my heart," he said simply. "Oh, Susan, it has been so hard. I've tried . . . I am trying . . . but it is not easy. I think I could bear with it all more easily if only I knew that you were not unhappy. That, I think, is most difficult of all to contemplate when I am alone."

'Then it is true that it would be easier for him if I were really beyond his reach,' Susan thought. 'If I were married.'

"I'm not . . . unhappy, Gareth," she forced herself to the lie. "Sometimes, perhaps, when I remember. Today, when you are here. But you . . . were . . . right . . . when you said time would help. It is easier . . . now. I want you to know that. You see, although I . . . I love you . . . I find that I can love . . . others, too. Jim, for instance. I'm very fond of him. Perhaps in time, I shall . . ."

Gareth's hands were gripping the edge of the scrubbed, white wood table. Emotion drained away from him leaving him cold . . . without any thought but this one which Susan had just put into his head. Love had not after all made so deep a scar on her heart. Not for her, as for himself, those long, agonizing, wakeful nights remembering, longing, knowing that life held only emptiness without her. That she had loved him . . . still did to a lesser degree, he could not doubt. But already she was recovering from those wounds still so raw in his own heart. Already she was making plans for her future, plans which could not include himself.

'For her sake I'm glad it's so!' he told himself, but knew that later, when the first numbness of shock left him able to feel, to suffer once more, that the loss of her love would hurt him as deeply as an amputation. During these last months he had been unhappy enough. Heaven alone knew what mental torture he had undergone. He had truly done his best to make his marriage a success . . . to give Jane those things in life which, however artificial, still seemed to make her happy. He had tried, too, to rediscover his love for her, but had learnt that his heart was only made for one love to the exclusion of all others. While Susan was alive on this earth he could want no other woman, neither desire nor love another. But he had forced himself to do what he believed was his duty to his young wife. Never once had he let her suspect the truth. Never once had he given her the slightest cause for complaint against him. And although it was abominably difficult for a man of Gareth's honesty to dissimilate, pretend, he had managed to hide his agony of mind so successfully that Jane, his own wife, had noticed no change in him.

Throughout all this, Jane's superficiality had helped him. Also her indifference to him as a man, a lover, which had once so unnerved him. Now he could be glad of these traits in her character, for a deeper-thinking woman, a wife who truly loved her husband must inevitably have sensed that something was wrong. But Jane, lost in her own selfish search for pleasure, never noticed that she had lost the love of the man she had married.

Life had not been easy for Gareth, nor happy. He hated the artificiality of the life he led for Jane's sake. He was tired from endless late nights, weary to the heart of the friends, if one could call them so, who filled his leisure hours. He longed for a return to country life, to his garden and a real home, almost as much as he had longed for Susan's quiet, sweet ways and the peace she brought to him in her simple dignity. Only two things had sustained him through the ordeal of the past six months . . . his memories of her and his desire to do the right thing, because she wished it so as much as he did. His sacrifice was equal only to her own and they suffered it together for their mutual self-respect and honour. By virtue of the fact that she did not come to see him, Gareth had known that she dared not yet trust herself to do so any more than he could trust himself to see her. The knowledge that she still loved him had been bitter-sweet. It both hurt him to know she suffered and yet comforted him beyond measure to know that somewhere she was thinking of him, longing for him as he longed for her.

And now he must forget that last comfort. He could find excuses for her so easily. She was young, beautiful, utterly desirable and, as he had once told her, far too lovely to waste her life living in the past. She had a future to live for, a son to care for and with that innate common sense and wisdom, she was putting her love for him behind her in the past where it belonged and looking once more to the future.

Without looking at her, for he could not trust himself to keep the pain, the deep misery from his eyes, Gareth said in a low voice, "I'm sure you're doing the right thing, Susan. Ted needs a father and you . . . I wish you every good fortune, my dear."

Susan looked at the bowed head, at the long, beautiful hands gripping the table edge, heard the husky, uncertain note in his voice and felt her resolve melting slowly, inexorably within her. She fought desperately against the desire to go to him, to put her arms round him and look deep into his eyes; to tell him that she loved *him*, only him, and would to eternity. For it was clear to her, who could read him so easily with the eyes of love, that she had shocked him by withdrawing the love she had declared to him so many months ago, shocked him as she in turn would have felt shattered had she learned from him that he no longer cared.

'It is for his sake, his peace of mind I'm doing it,' she reminded herself fiercely. 'Don't weaken. Be strong for his sake as much as for your own.'

"Thank you, Gareth!" she heard her own voice, cool, calm, devoid of any emotion. And because she knew that next time she spoke it must be from her heart . . . of all that lay hidden now within it, she hurriedly turned away from him, laid the tea tray and thrust it into his hands.

"Shall I take this out?" Gareth asked, lifting his head now to look once more into those dark, unfathomable eyes. But Susan glanced swiftly away, nodding her head, and did not raise it again until his footsteps had died away as he crossed the hall and stepped out on to the lawn.

Only then did she look up once more, her eyes darting to the window where they fastened eagerly, desperately, on Gareth's tall figure walking away from her. She took a quick step towards him, a hand raised as if she wished to call him back. Then the hand dropped to her side and her shoulders stooped. Slowly the tears ran unheeded down her cheeks, and it was thus that Jim found her. She had not heard him come into the room, had not been aware of his footsteps across the kitchen floor as he came up softly behind her. He heard the strangled sob that came from her throat and gently, tenderly, his arm went round her.

"Susan, darling, don't!"

She turned to him then, grateful for the strength of his arms as they supported her, grateful for the understanding he was offering her.

"Oh, Jim!" she whispered, all her unhappiness in her voice plain for him to hear.

"I came to see if there was anything I could do to help," Jim said simply. And with a half smile, he added, "It seems I've chosen an opportune moment."

Her head went down on his shoulder and the tears fell more easily as the control she had exercised in Gareth's presence was lost now beyond recall.

"I've sent him away, Jim," she whispered. "For always. He thinks I don't love him any more. I told him . . . oh, Jim! . . . I told him I was probably going to marry *you*!"

Thirteen

For one long, delirious moment, Jim allowed the exultation of hope to sweep through him.

'Now she will be mine!' he thought. 'Gareth will never worry her again. She will marry me now!'

That she did not love him he was left in no doubt! But he had youth on his side, time to wait, time to win her love over to himself. There was all the time in the world for things to come right between them. Married to her, he would have every chance to make her happy, help her to forget the past. She had got over her first loss of Teddy's father. She must, in time, get over Gareth. His own love for her would break down the obstacles to his happiness.

And then, for the first time in his life, Jim knew that his own happiness was not as important as another's. With realization coming like a splash of cold water to cool his ardour, his newly realized hopes, Jim discovered that his love for Susan had given him a new personality, an unselfish wish to put himself and his wishes second to hers even if it meant the loss of all that he had been hoping for these last months. It seemed suddenly unbelievably stupid for Susan and Gareth to suffer as deeply as they were doing for the sake of one person, his sister, who was not worth a quarter of either of them.

Jane, for all she was his sister, was selfish and self-centred. She took everything from life, gave nothing but the things she no longer had use for. Other people's feelings were trodden under her heel if it suited her mood, her desires. She had never really tried to make Gareth happy; had never really loved him if, indeed, she were capable of loving anyone but herself. He could himself love Jane because she was his sister, but had she been unrelated to him, he might have found it in his heart to dislike her. Her prettiness, her charm, her little-girl ways, had turned her into a parasite, for now she lived on other people, depending on them to think for her, amuse her, order her life. And they were willing because she graced their parties with her smiles, her inconsequential chatter, her whims.

And it was for Jane's sake that Gareth and Susan, two such fine, decent people, were to remain without one another for the rest of their lives.

He looked down at the dark, sleek head on his shoulder and tenderness replaced the passionate desire to possess her that so often held his heart in sway.

"My dearest Sue!" he said softly. "I'm greatly honoured by what you have said but I'm not going to allow you to throw your life away. I am withdrawing my proposal . . . all my proposals. I no longer want you to marry me nor anyone but the man you love."

"But that isn't possible, Jim!" Susan cried painfully. "Can't you understand it is over . . . all over!"

"Somehow I don't think so," Jim said smoothly. "I think it will come right in the end for you both. Trust me, Susan. Don't ask me how or why. I think it might come right. If it doesn't, have I your permission to renew my proposal . . . to accept yours?"

His words brought the glimmer of a smile to her tear-wet face as she raised it to look at him.

"I don't understand, Jim. And I dare not hope. We have just finished things for good and all. Gareth believes I no longer love him. It will be easier now for him to settle down with Jane and forget me."

"I wouldn't say you were very easy to forget, Susan," Jim said wryly, "although I am not doubting Gareth's efforts to do so. But we won't talk any more about it now. You must call on your feminine box of magic to remove all traces of those tears, Susan, and come out to tea. Gareth and Jane will be wondering what's up."

She clung to him then like an anxious child.

"I can't go out there, Jim. I can't! I don't want to see him . . . don't want either of them to see me."

"You'll have to, Susan, unless you want me to make some excuse; say you aren't well. Jane might believe it but Gareth won't. Summon up a little of that courage of yours. I'll help you to face them both."

"My eyes . . . !" Susan murmured, and for answer, Jim placed his hand gently beneath her chin and forced her to meet his gaze.

"They are more beautiful than ever!" he said, then releasing her quickly, he told her to hurry up and bathe her face while he waited for her to rejoin him.

Three minutes later, Susan came down from her bedroom, her face freshly made up and showing almost no trace of the tears she had shed. Jim gave her an encouraging nod of approval and with plates in each hand, they walked side by side down to the lawn where Gareth was seated with his wife.

And Jim, true to his promise, made conversation easy by his light, amusing chatter, keeping Jane laughing, forcing Susan to smile at his ludicrous jokes. Never once did he allow an opportunity for Gareth and Susan to be alone, nor have to speak more than a word or two to one another. Pretence, this once, was made easy for them and after it was all over and Gareth and Jane had gone, Susan's thanks to Jim came sincerely from her heart.

"Don't thank me yet. I've only just begun to help you," was Jim's enigmatic reply; one which Susan failed to understand. But she was too tired to worry about it further. The strain of the afternoon had been exhausting and now her head throbbed in tune with her heart.

"I'll go and lie down for a little while," she said. "Will you keep an eye on Ted for me?"

Jim stood in silence, watching her until she had disappeared up the stairs, and then turned slowly and went back into the garden to find her son.

Two days later Jim sat in his sister's sitting-room and tried to wait patiently for her to keep this appointment with him. A smart, young French maid had opened the door to him and given him a coquettish glance from her bright almond-shaped eyes, but Jim had felt immune for once to the charms of a pretty girl. His mind was too full of Susan and the mission which had brought him here.

He sat on the pink and lime-green candy-striped *chaise longue* and studied the room, wishing at the same time that there was one comfortable chair to sit on. But the comfort of the room had been sacrificed to elegance and it was obvious even to Jim's inexperienced eyes that his sister's flat had been furnished with every regard to style and none at all to expense!

The walls were papered in the same green as the stripe in the material that covered the stiff-backed chairs and draped in folds round the huge windows. Had it not been for the magnificent view over London's rooftops, Jim would have believed himself in some fantastic aquarium.

Perhaps the odd yellow tone of the green saved it from the deep-sea effect, as well as the candy-pink stripes; gave it more the impression of a page on home designing in one of the ultra smart magazines. Whatever the result, Jim thought wryly, comfort was not in it. He found his gaze attracted to the furnishings and he was unable to concentrate on the newspaper he had picked up to pass the time until Jane returned.

Gradually, as the minutes ticked themselves into oblivion, the silence in this disturbing room grated on Jim's nerves as much as did Jane's unpunctuality. He did not particularly like this mission he had chosen to come on, but now he was here, he wanted to get it over as quickly as possible.

His eyes wandered yet again to the white and gold ornate clock that stood on the marble mantelshelf. A quarter past three and Jane had agreed to meet him at two-thirty. Really, he decided, it was the limit! Had he not determined to go through with his plans, he would have got up and left.

Then he heard a key turn in the lock of the front door, heard Jane's bright little voice calling to the maid, and a few minutes later, she tripped into the room on four-inch heels, dropping the parcels she carried on to the floor at her feet as she ran forward to kiss him.

He returned the kiss somewhat stiffly, but Jane did not appear to notice.

"I'm frantically apologetic, Jim!" she said, laughing and dimpling at him. "But honestly, darling, I did *mean* to be back in time. I just meant to buy a new hat and got caught up in the model gown department. I've bought the most . . . oh, Marie, pick up those parcels and get some tea, will you?" she ordered the French maid, who stood patient and immovable behind her, her eyes on Jim rather than on her mistress.

Jane turned once more to Jim and hurried on, "I hope you don't mind having tea a little early but I'm dying of thirst! I think it was the gin I had before lunch. Horrible stuff really. Don't know why I drink it!"

She flung herself into one of the chairs, and somehow or another managed to curl herself up on the hard seat with every appearance of comfort.

"Well, darling, tell me all the news," she said, giving her attention to her brother.

Jim lit the cigarette he held and took a deep breath. It was going to be more difficult than he had anticipated. Somehow, Jane's cheerfulness, her light-heartedness and that incredibly youthful air made it so difficult for him to hurt her.

"You look very pretty, Jane," he said evasively, glancing at the immaculate, white linen suit she wore, with the cherry silk scarf at her throat matching the bright lipstick and fingernails. The sheerest of sheer nylon stockings clad her small, dainty legs and the high-heeled sandals that had dropped where she had kicked them made that queer contrast so often noticeable in Jane . . . sophistication and immaturity. With the long fair curls dancing on her shoulders and her piquante little face lightly tanned by the sun, she might have been sixteen dressed up as twenty-six.

"I bought this suit last week," she said, seeing his glance. "It's the very devil to keep clean in town but I like it. You look very nice yourself, Jimmy!"

"I don't feel very nice," Jim said quietly. "You see, I've come on rather a difficult errand. I'm afraid you won't altogether like what I've got to say but I must say it. I think someone must say it and no one else can."

Jane's smile vanished and a slight frown took its place.

"I hope you aren't going to start 'jawing' me," she said, using the old childhood name for "a good talking to". "I can't think I've done anything very wrong, anyway."

"It isn't your fault at all, Jane," Jim said quickly. "In a way it hasn't anything to do with you . . . the blame, I mean. Not that anyone is to blame," he stumbled on, unable to stop now he had started. "But these things happen, Jane, and that's all there is to it."

"I haven't the slightest notion what you are talking about," Jane said in a cool, amused voice. For one moment Jim wondered if she were being purposefully obtuse and then rejected the idea.

"It's about . . . Susan," he began again, but Jane broke in, "Jim, I know what you're trying to say. You're going to marry Susan. I'm *so* glad. Why, by the look on your face I thought you'd come with bad news. Did you think I mightn't approve of the match, sweetie?"

Jim bit his lip. This was even harder than he had imagined possible.

"No, I'm not going to marry Susan," he said awkwardly. "You see, she's in love with someone else, Jane. I hardly know how to say this, but the fact of the matter is she's in love with . . . Gareth."

He broke off, waiting for Jane to speak, but as if this silence had been her cue, the French maid opened the door and came in with the tea tray. When she had poured out the tea in delicate china cups and passed Jim the sandwiches which he refused, Jane dismissed her and again silence fell between them. Jim looked at his sister's face but for once it was completely expressionless. She said, "Well?"

"That's only half the trouble, Jane," Jim forced himself to

continue. "Naturally she did everything within her power to prevent herself believing it was true. She fought against it but without any success. It was . . . the real thing, Jane. It always will be, I think."

He paused again but Jane made no move to speak. Jim went on, "Then Susan discovered that . . . that Gareth felt the same way about her. Oh, I know this must be a horrible shock to you, Jane, but I had to say it. You see, I've known for ages that you aren't really in love with Gareth yourself. Otherwise, naturally, I'd have kept my mouth shut. But you don't love him, do you?"

Jane gave a short, hard laugh.

"I really don't see that *that* is your business, Jim. Go on!"

"Well, there isn't much more to say, Jane. Of course, they decided to do the decent thing and leave things as they were. For six months, ever since you left the country to come to London, Gareth and Susan have been fighting to carry on their lives as if nothing had happened. But it was hopeless. Susan even went so far as to tell Gareth she was going to marry me because she thought it might help him to . . . to feel as he used to do about you. They have both put themselves and their happiness right out of the picture, Jane, for your sake, believing that you love Gareth. Since that isn't so, I felt that if I came to you and explained, you would do the decent thing and set Gareth free. You will, Jane, won't you? Gareth would see that you didn't suffer by it. And I'll make it up to you in any way I can. We'll take that trip round the world you've always wanted . . . you and I together. I shall be giving up Susan, you know, so we'll both be in the same boat. You will do this, won't you, Jane? For their sakes?"

It was said now . . . all he had wanted to say. Relief flooded through him and he raised his eyes to his sister's face. The expression he saw there shocked him into immobility. There was a cold, determined light in her eyes and her prettily curved mouth was set in a hard thin line. Her voice was as hard and brittle as her laugh had been.

"So!" she said. "My noble brother has to let the cat out of the bag for the sake of the woman he so ardently loves. He will give up his lady-love in a glory of self-sacrifice and expects me to do likewise. Well, my dear boy, it's time you took the rose-coloured spectacles off your nose. This wonderful surprise you have churned up for me isn't a surprise at all. It so happens that I have known about Gareth and Susan for months . . . yes, months!"

"You . . . you've known . . . all along?" Jim gasped.

"Certainly!" Jane said sharply. "The night Gareth was so 'ill' and I was worried out of my wits because I thought he was catching Ted's germs, he slept in his dressing-room, you'll remember. In the night he called out. I went to his door to see if he wanted anything. He was talking in his sleep. So you see, their precious secret wasn't a secret at all."

Jim stared at his sister aghast.

"You've known . . . and done nothing about it?"

Jane tossed her head and the curls danced again on her shoulders.

"And why should I do anything? Gareth is my husband, mine, do you understand? Whether I happen to be in love with him or not is hardly relevant. He's married to me and he'll stay married to me. Why should I ruin my life just because he gets an attack of calf love for Susan! As for Sue, I certainly see no reason why I should hand my husband over to her. I don't owe her anything. It wasn't my fault she fell in love with my husband. I'm sorry for her . . . I pity her, but that's as far as it goes. Personally, I think she's a fool if she's eating her heart out for him. But that's her affair. Besides, she has you to fall back on. You're apparently so much in love, I'm sure you're fool enough to pick up the bits."

Jim's face was white and his hands shaking as he stood up.

"I never thought . . . never knew you were like this, Jane," he said. "I could understand you if you were putting your case on moral grounds. A lot of people dislike the idea of divorce . . . believe their marriage vows are sacred and that sort of thing. That I can understand and in some ways agree with. But that isn't your point. You don't want Gareth yourself . . . you have all but admitted it. But you'd die rather than let anyone else have him so long as he is of use to you. You're hard, Jane, hard as nails and utterly egotistical. And worst of all, I think you're without feeling. You'll chain a man to you for life, a man who doesn't love you, for no better reason than that you don't want anyone else to have him. But you'd throw him over if it suited you, wouldn't you? *Wouldn't you?*"

"Maybe!" Jane said casually. "But it doesn't suit me right now. I'm not in love with anyone. I have no intention of falling in love with anyone. My life with Gareth suits me perfectly well, thank you, and I have no desire to alter it."

"It suits you because he gives in to you all the time!" Jim was almost shouting. "You take everything and give nothing in return."

"He only gives in because he has a bad conscience," Jane said. "He owes it to me in a way."

"Gareth can have nothing on his conscience," Jim said. "You may try and deny that, Jane, but you cannot believe in your heart that Gareth has anything to reproach himself with."

"If you mean do I think he has been unfaithful to me, then I'll admit that I don't!" Jane said. "I don't think he has the nerve. If I'd been in his shoes . . ."

"I don't want to hear any more, Jane," Jim said. He paused as he walked towards the door. "But before I go, you're going to hear one thing from me. I came here today to try to help everyone. I felt sorry for you and wanted to do everything I could for you. You were my sister, I told myself, and I had always been deeply fond of you, Jane, for all your faults. But now I am denying that relationship. I hope I never have to see you again. Good-bye!"

And he turned and walked out of the room.

The door slammed behind him before Jane moved. Then she jumped out of her chair and walked over to the window, staring out over the rooftops; her eyes usually so full of laughter, dark with inner thoughts.

It was all very well for Jim to go off in a huff, she considered. He'd make it up, of course. When they were children and had quarrelled, they always made it up after they had cooled down. Mostly she had made the first move because, she supposed now with a rueful smile, it was usually her fault. But then she couldn't help wanting things and at least she didn't go round wanting other people's. Jim was in love with Susan, so, of course, he was on her side. But the law would be on Jane's.

This gave her small consolation, for she knew that it would never come to a court of law. Gareth was far too decent ever to be the first to break up their marriage. That was one side of Gareth she could always rely on. Duty first and pleasure second. This trait in his character hadn't always appealed so much to her, particularly if it meant his idea of their duty before her own suggestion for their pleasure. Nevertheless, she could feel quite safe in that direction now. The very fact that Gareth had kept his feelings to himself, showed her that he had no intention of leaving her for Susan.

Susan, too, was utterly reliable. She was rather like Gareth in that way. She'd never try to take Gareth from her. She was utterly trustworthy.

'It's funny, but I still like Sue!' Jane thought. 'I suppose I ought to hate her but I don't. I was pleased to see her last week. In lots of ways I miss her friendship.'

It did not occur to Jane that she could still like Susan because she had robbed her of nothing that she wanted . . . only of Gareth's love and Jane knew in her heart of hearts that she had been amused by, flattered by, but never really desirous of Gareth's devotion. Everything else he gave her, yes! The attention, the position both social and financial, the security and, no doubt in the first year or so, the balm to that wound which the loss of Ham had occasioned.

'I really did love Ham!' Jane thought. 'I used to give in to him all the time . . . wanted to. I suppose that is real love . . . the wish to make others happy rather than oneself. I'd have gone to the ends of the world for Ham . . . even given him up if I thought it was for his good.'

But the memory of Ham was not what she needed to regain her

good spirits. She hated quarrelling with Jim . . . being made to feel she was in the wrong. It was hateful of him to side against her, anyway, she told herself, whipping up some indignation. As his sister, she was at least entitled to some consideration. And he ought to be grateful to her, too. If Gareth were out of Susan's reach, then Susan would almost certainly end up married to Jim. And since she, Jane, had no intention of setting Garry free, then she was virtually helping Jim's cause.

'Then he'll come and thank me!' Jane thought with satisfaction. 'And be sorry he was so horrible today. I'm feeling miserable now and it'll be Jim's fault if Garry suffers for it. I certainly don't want to stay home tonight. That's certain. I should die of boredom with nothing but these horrible thoughts and Gareth's gloomy face for company. I'll book a couple of seats for that new play at the Lyric. That'll cheer us both up. Garry can have his night at home tomorrow instead.'

Already Jane was feeling happier as she hurried to the telephone to book the seats. She sent Marie round to the theatre to collect the tickets. And by the time Gareth, tired from a busy day at the office and a shareholders' conference, returned to his home, his wife was already dressed to go out and he could not bring himself to erase the happy anticipation that shone on her radiant, expectant, appealing little face.

While Gareth changed, Jane chattered to him gaily across the hall between his dressing-room and her own pink and silver bedroom. She mentioned vaguely Jim's visit.

"What did he want?" Gareth asked, for Jim did not often come to their flat . . . had not been for some months, in fact.

"Oh, I don't know!" Jane said evasively. "He was in rather a gloomy mood. Mooning about Susan, I expect."

Gareth made no reply although the sound of Susan's name had quickened his interest in his wife's remarks, caused his heart to miss a beat. Every day now he anticipated and yet dreaded the announcement of Jim's engagement to Susan.

"Seems she is in love with someone else," he heard Jane's bright voice. "But it's a married man so there's no hope there I imagine. She's bound to marry Jim in the end, I should think. Gareth, I wonder who the married man is!"

Again Gareth's heart missed a beat. His hands shook as he tried to fix his bow tie. Could Jane know the truth?

"Didn't Jim tell you?" he forced himself to ask casually.

"No!" Jane lied. "Oh, well, Sue's not our problem any more. Come on, darling, or we'll be late."

She walked through to the sitting-room, throwing open a door and immediately a cocktail bar, cleverly constructed out of an old cupboard was revealed by a concealed strip-lighting.

She mixed herself a strong drink and tossed it back with a contented smile.

That little conversation with Gareth had proved her point. He had no intention of making a move. Susan wouldn't, she was sure. So there was no further need to worry that her life might be disorganized after all. She might not love Gareth but she could appreciate his value as a husband. Not every man would treat her so considerately, give her so much, sacrifice his own pleasures so that she might enjoy hers. And in spite of his weakness in giving in to her so much, he was not really a weak man, a man to be despised. He was strong, mentally and physically, and attractive, too. More so than ever now she knew some other woman loved him.

'I'm not jealous!' she thought. 'But I think I'll make him fall in love with me again. I can if I choose . . . And it might be rather fun.'

As Gareth came into the room, she ran to him and kissed him provocatively on the mouth.

"*Darling!*" she murmured. "Let's not go to the theatre after all. Let's stay home together like you said . . . just the two of us . . . you and your Jane?"

Fourteen

Teddy wandered round the garden jingling two sixpences together so that they made a rich, clinking kind of noise and gave him the feeling that he had but to display them in his rather hot, sticky palm to be able to buy anything in the world he wanted.

Not, he reminded himself carefully, that he was going to spend his money on himself. But it was lots of fun thinking of all the things he could buy . . . if he wanted to. A new Dinky toy, or maybe a jigsaw like the one in the library, or a new carriage to hook on to his train. Two sixpences, he reflected, might also buy a penknife which he wanted more than anything else at the moment. On the other hand it would be fun to buy ice-cream. And today was just the sort of hot day when a boy felt like an ice.

"I think I'd like an ice more'n anyfing!" he said aloud, but he knew it wasn't true. The very most of all, he wanted to buy something *special* for Mummy's birthday tomorrow.

Ted sat down on the grass and hunched up his knees and leant his chin on them. It was odd, he thought, but he couldn't remember Mummy having had a birthday before. *He* had them, of course, heaps of times . . . six of them anyway! He'd never thought about Mummy having one until Uncle Jim teased her into admitting that her birthday was the day after tomorrow. That had happened last Sunday when Uncle Jim was visiting them for the day.

"I'm much too old to celebrate my birthday!" Mummy had said, smiling.

"I guess twenty-six is pretty old!" Uncle Jim had answered, his face very serious.

"My mummy isn't old. Twenty-six isn't a bit old!" Teddy had defended his adored mother, but strangely enough she and Uncle Jim had burst out laughing, as if he'd said something funny. One never really knew why grown-ups did things. Most times they made sense when it was people like Mummy and Uncle Jim, but even they could be incomprehensible at times.

When Mummy was getting the tea ready, Uncle Jim had given Teddy one of the two sixpences he now held . . . to help buy Mummy a little present for her birthday. Uncle Jim was going to give her a present, too, but it was a secret and he wouldn't tell Ted, not even though he tried his hardest to make him.

He'd asked Uncle Jim what to buy Mummy but Uncle Jim didn't seem to have any of his usual good ideas that day.

"You choose something *you* know she'd like, Ted," he had answered. "It'll mean much more to her if you think of it."

Well, he'd thought and thought and thought. A whole shilling, for he had his Saturday sixpence to add to Uncle Jim's, ought to buy something pretty smashing but he just couldn't think what. Jenny, Mrs Mendall's little girl, said her mum liked bath salts 'cos they smelt ever so nice. But Teddy decided in the end that Mummy didn't need anything to make her smell nice because she always did, anyway. He'd thought of a jigsaw but then remembered she was a grown-up and probably wouldn't want a toy after all, though she liked helping him do his puzzles. He thought of a diary but she'd been given one at Christmas and besides, July was rather far on in the year to start a new diary.

"I wish I could think of something *special!*" Teddy worried. One shilling was a lot of money and ought not to be spent on any old thing and anyway, this was going to be an extra Special Occasion because Uncle Jim said so and birthdays always were in any case.

'If only I knew what she wanted most in the world!' Ted thought. He might, of course, ask her, but then it wouldn't be a surprise and she didn't even know he was going to buy her anything.

Restlessly, Teddy got up from the lawn and wandered into the house.

"Isn't it nearly lunch time, Mrs Mendall?" he asked.

"Not for an hour yet, son," she told him. "Your mum said half past twelve lunch and half past twelve lunch it will be. You can have a biscuit if you want."

Ted took the biscuit and ate it on the way up to his bedroom. He had to pass Susan's bedroom to reach his own and her door stood open. Unthinkingly, he wandered inside, staring round the room and realizing by virtue of her absence that he wasn't enjoying today very much after all. When Mummy had first decided to go to London to do some shopping, she had said she would take him, too, as she would be buying new school clothes for him. But yesterday had been scorching hot with the temperature in the eighties, and Susan had suggested Ted might prefer to stay home instead of tagging behind her along the dusty pavements.

"You're old enough to stay here on your own, Ted," she had said, "and I can arrange for Mrs Mendall to come in and get your lunch and tea, too, if I'm not back by four. Wouldn't you rather stay, darling?"

He had chosen to stay, partly because he hated being in London when it was hot, because he hated shopping, too, and mostly because he thought it would be fun to be all alone all day. It made him feel very grown up to think that Mummy trusted him.

And when he had waved good-bye to her this morning he had been terribly excited and pleased. Now he stood in her bedroom and knew that he was missing her. It was funny, really, because often when she was here he, himself, would be out all day playing, only coming in for meals, and would hardly see her at all until bedtime. He realized subconsciously that he had been content just to know she was there when he wanted her. And now she wasn't there. Her cotton frock lay on the chair beside the bed, looking empty and thin and although it was part of her, its softly drooping lines depressed him.

He went to her dressing-table and fingered her hair-brush and sniffed at her face powder. It gave him an idea suddenly that he might find something in her room which would help him decide on her birthday present. Face powder . . . but the box was nearly full . . . a hair-brush, but hers looked as good as new . . . a handkerchief, maybe, but who'd want a beastly handkerchief for a birthday present, 'cos he wouldn't.

Then he saw the diary . . . the very one he had been thinking about that had been in her Christmas stocking.

"Just as well I didn't buy another one," he told himself with a satisfied grin as he flicked over the page to see if she had been writing in it the way she had said she would. Ted had written inside the diary that it was from Father Christmas, but he wasn't sure that she hadn't recognized his handwriting, which didn't look much like an old man's. He was glad to see the writing . . . her writing on the neat little lines, because it showed she had really wanted the diary and hadn't just said she used it to please him.

As the pages turned, a name caught his eye . . . he could read that name easily without spelling it out slowly because he'd chosen it once last year for composition class. They had been asked to write an essay on what was their favourite name and why. He'd chosen Uncle Gareth, of course; because it had seemed a wonderful name for a wonderful person. He had said so in his essay and written the name lots of times.

He held open the page and tried to read what Mummy had written. Her writing was tiny and difficult when he was used to big printed letters and he had to spell them out. He couldn't read them all.

"Oh, Gareth, I have been so . . . all day. If only you were here to com . . . me. More than any . . . thing in the world I long to see you . . . to have just one whole day in . . . to tell you what lies in my . . ."

There were many words he couldn't fathom, but what he had read made sense . . . triumphant, glorious sense. Here, after all, was the answer to his problem. He had wanted to give Susan what she herself most wanted in the whole world, for her birthday. And now he knew. It wasn't something he could buy, but he could still get it for her. He could write a letter to Uncle Gareth and tell him to come down tomorrow for the whole day . . . It seemed almost as if Mummy had left the diary for him to read, so that he would be sure to know what she wanted.

His face flushed with excitement, Teddy raced downstairs and into the kitchen.

"If I post a letter to London, will it be sure to get there by tomorrow?" he asked Mrs Mendall.

"I wouldn't like to say as how it would be *certain*, ducks!" she said. "Perhaps by the second post for sure."

Ted's face fell.

"But that wouldn't be soon enough!" he cried. "Not even if I write it this minute and post it?"

"Well, maybe!" said Mrs Mendall, rolling out the pastry. "But I wouldn't promise, mind! Now run along into the garden in that nice sunshine."

His hopes dashed to the ground, Ted walked slowly into the garden once more. He could write to Uncle Gareth, but he couldn't be sure of reaching him in time and if Uncle Gareth was busy at the office he would want some warning anyway to get away for certain.

New hopes came and were cast aside . . . the village telephone, but he didn't know Uncle Gareth's telephone number. Uncle Jim, who might pass a message, but Ted didn't know his number either. He only knew Uncle Gareth's address because it was on a change of address card Aunty Jane had sent when they went to London, which he had seen in one of the pigeon-holes in Mummy's desk.

Lunch time came, but his appetite was gone and Mrs Mendall, looking at his frowning face, hesitated about leaving him. With an effort, Ted assured her he would be quite all right until tea time and finally the woman left and Ted tried once more to think of a solution to his problem. Quite suddenly, it came to him.

Only that very morning he had heard Mummy and Mrs Mendall discussing the Green Line bus service.

"It's by far the cheapest way," Mummy had said. "Only three and eightpence return. And they go as far as Marble Arch."

"Fancy now!" Mrs Mendall had answered. "Perhaps I'll go for a day and take Jenny to the Zoo to see Brumas."

Three and eightpence. And he had one shilling. For another two shillings and eightpence he could go up to London and walk from the Marble Arch, whatever that was, to Aunty Jane's. You could always ask a policeman to help you to find the way if you got lost. Mummy had told him so often.

Two shillings and eightpence between him and success. And he knew where he could find it . . . in his money box. If you shook and rattled it the pennies sometimes came out of the slot. And it was nearly full!

Teddy rushed upstairs, his dark hair sticking to his hot little face and for fifteen minutes he rattled furiously at his savings. One by one the pennies came.

Trembling with excitement, Ted rushed into his room and put on the clean shirt Mummy had ironed specially for him when they still thought he would go to London with her. The new grey flannel shorts which were his best replaced his khaki drill ones. Clean white socks and his best brown sandals. He was ready . . . except for a quick splash in the bathroom at his hands and face.

Ten minutes later, he was running up the lane towards the bus stop and as luck would have it, a Green Line bus saying "LONDON" on it turned the corner and pulled up as he got there. He scrambled on board and made his way to the back of the bus where he could look out of the back window.

After a little while, the conductor came and asked him where he was going.

"London . . . and I'm returning tonight!" Teddy said importantly.

The conductor studied the little boy for a moment or two, looking from the bright, unworried face to the small pieces of silver and the coppers displayed in his clean palm. It crossed his mind that the kid was a bit young to be travelling alone . . . one had to look out for kids running away these days . . . getting up to mischief.

"Your mummy know you're going to London?" he asked carefully.

"She's already up there!" Teddy said brightly. "I'm going up to have tea with my Uncle Gareth and my Aunt Jane."

Ted's prompt and obviously truthful answers reassured the conductor and a further glance at Ted's neat appearance and cleanness, unusual enough for a small boy who was "up to something", convinced him that all was well.

He punched a ticket and selected two and a penny from Ted's palm.

"Isn't it three and eightpence?" Ted asked anxiously. "I'm going to the Marble Arch, you know . . . all the way."

"That's right, chum, but you're half-price!" the conductor said and with a friendly smile, left Ted alone to meditate on his good fortune. For it had occurred to him suddenly that Mrs Mendall said London was ever such a big place and miles and miles from one end to another. Maybe Uncle Gareth's house was a long way from the Arch and it would be pretty hot for walking. Now he could afford a bus ride, too.

Relieved, excited, contented, feeling very important, Ted gave himself up to full enjoyment of the journey. He played at counting number plates on cars for a while, then at seeing how many tractors were in the fields they passed so swiftly. The hour and a half before they came to the outskirts of London passed in no time at all. One of the grown-ups sitting in front of him gave him several sweets . . . another passed him a magazine to look at. And suddenly, just when he was getting tired of the bus ride, the conductor called out in a loud voice, "Marble Arch. Here you are, son!"

And he was climbing out on to the pavement amongst the jostling crowds of people.

Keeping his head, Ted remained quite still while he searched in his trouser pocket for the piece of paper on which he had copied out Aunty Jane's address. Having found it, he held it tightly in one hand while he went off in search of a policeman. There didn't seem to be many about, but at last he did find one and very politely he asked his way, showing the written address.

"I'm going to tea with my Uncle Gareth and my Aunty Jane," he said. "But if it's very far I'll go by bus."

"Does your mother know what you're doing?" the policeman asked the small boy.

Ted gave him a beaming, conspiratorial smile, and shook his head.

"No! It's a secret for her birthday. She's in London for the day, too, but she doesn't know I've come. I'm going to Uncle Gareth's."

The policeman was not quite so convinced that all was well as had been the bus conductor, but the address on the scrap of paper was a good one . . . an expensive block of flats and not very far away. Nevertheless, he felt a six-year-old should not be wandering around London alone and he hailed a passing taxi.

"Take the boy to this address," he told the driver, giving him the now hot and crumpled piece of paper. "They'll pay there. Make sure he's handed over to someone who knows him. Don't want you to get lost in London Town, do we, lad?" he added, turning to Ted.

Teddy gave him another bright smile.

"It's very kind of you," he said in his best manner. "My mother said policeman never let you get lost. I'll tell her you helped me."

But in the taxi he remembered he couldn't keep this promise after all as his trip to London would have to be a secret . . . anyway until after the birthday.

It was long past his tea time when at last Ted and the taxi-driver were taken up in the lift by the hall porter on the last lap of his journey to Uncle Gareth, but Ted was unaware of time, for the sun still shone brightly and the time had passed magically quickly and with no troubles to spoil his plans.

Outside the door of the flat, the taxi-driver rang the bell. Marie, Jane's French maid, opened it and gave a little gasp of surprise.

"Mrs Everett's home?" the taxi-driver asked firmly.

Marie nodded.

"Here we are then, son!" said the man to Ted. And to Marie, "That'll be two shillings, please, for my fare."

Marie recovered herself sufficiently to ask the driver and Ted to wait while she went for her mistress.

Ted waited anxiously and impatiently until Marie returned at last with his Aunt Jane, whom at first he hardly recognized for she looked so different. But it *was* Aunty Jane, for she swept down on him and gave him a big, friendly kiss.

"What on earth are you doing here, Teddy?" she cried. "I must say, I never expected *you* to my cocktail party! Now, what's all this about a taxi?"

Ted watched her a little nervously while she paid the taxi-driver. She had on some very tight black thing and her hair, which used to curl round her shoulders like a little girl's, was now swept high on top of her head. Bright jewels flashed round her neck and on her fingers with the long tapering red nails. She looked very strange . . . and much older . . . hardly the same person who had come in a cotton frock and sandals to tea last week.

"Now, tell me all about it, Ted," she said, turning back to him and dismissing Marie with a wave of her hand. "Does Susan know you're here . . . Mummy, I mean?"

"Oh, no, it's a surprise!" Teddy said. "It's a secret, Aunty Jane. I've come to see Uncle Gareth!"

"Gareth!" Jane echoed. "Oh, well, he's somewhere around, though I must say I can't understand what this is all about. However, since you're here you'd better join the party!"

Obediently, Ted followed behind her, wondering how she could walk on top of those high, wobbly heels. He was so intent on them that he was quite unprepared for the noise that burst from the room as Jane opened the door where her cocktail party was in full swing. His mouth fell open and he reached for Jane's hand.

"Folks, meet my youngest admirer!" Jane was saying in a high voice full of laughter. "Couldn't bear to miss my party, could you, Teddy?"

Teddy bit his lip.

"I really came to see Uncle Gareth!" he said. Jane's angry tweak at his hand was unnecessary, for the women guests were now crowding round them and all talking at the tops of their voices.

"Darling, what an absolute poppet!"

"My dear, wherever did you find him?"

"Have you come for champagne pop or just ginger pop, sonny?"

"Jane, trust you, darling, to find something out of the ordinary. That's one thing about your parties . . . there's always a novelty!"

"Let's take him to the bar and get him a drink!"

"But what ge-orgeous eyes he has!"

Ted stared from one to another of the bright, laughing, painted faces that stared down at him and he felt suddenly as if he were in a nightmare . . . as if he were being slowly suffocated by the people pressing in on him from all sides. He clung more fiercely to Jane's hand, determined not to show his fear.

He tried once more to tell her he wanted Uncle Gareth but she wasn't listening and he felt himself being dragged across the floor towards something she called "the bar". Next he felt himself being lifted on to a big stool and a large fizzy drink was placed in his hand. It had a lump of ice floating in it and looked like lemonade. Ted knew suddenly that he was thirsty and he drank it gratefully in one or two quick gulps. Around him the faces cracked into laughter and the red mouths like letter-boxes opened and blared forth more laughter.

"Down it in one! There's the boy!"

"Jane, he's a character. What a dream of a child!"

"Do tell us about him, darling!"

"I came to see . . ." Ted began, but Jane gave him a quick,

fierce look that jerked him into silence. He watched her fascinated and afraid and slowly her face began to swim around his own... all the faces began to go round and round in circles. The laughter became a buzzing and he felt that at any moment he would fall off the chair.

Then, suddenly, he was jolted back to enough of his senses to realize that he had just heard Uncle Gareth's voice. Now, strangely, there wasn't a sound in the room. None of the whirling ladies were talking. Only Uncle Gareth's voice... cross, loud, and somewhere, his face, blurred and unrecognizable.

"What have you given him to drink, will you answer me?"

"Only champagne, Gareth. Honestly, he only had a teeny sip. He was thirsty!"

'I'm going to fall now!' Ted thought, but as he felt himself falling forwards, two strong arms went round him lifting him, carrying him and miraculously a cool draught of air blew on to his face. He knew he was being carried downstairs, knew by the sudden warmth that the sun was on his face. He was sure, too, that he was in a car, for he heard the engine start, felt the jolt as the gear slipped. And then he fell asleep.

Ted was still asleep when Gareth came out of the suburbs into the less crowded main road that headed towards the open country. He had time and opportunity, now, to glance down at the boy's flushed face where the long, dark lashes curled softly over his cheeks in sleep. Anger, white hot, coursed through him once more. This was one action in Jane's life with him that he would never, could never forgive... to give a child of Ted's age an intoxicating drink... enough to make him... Gareth bit off the words, hating to say them even to himself. He had no idea yet why Ted was in the flat, had learned nothing from Jane or her guests. He felt some slight satisfaction in the thought that at least he had broken up that party successfully. It had been clear enough to everyone that he was in a terrible rage and as he had carried Ted out of the room, he had heard the first feeble voice suggesting into the silence he had created that it was time to make a move.

He had taken the child out of the flat, out of the building, with only one idea in mind, to get him home. Only after he had been driving for ten minutes had he realized that Susan might be in London for the day and searching now for Ted . . . for surely she could not realize that Ted was with Jane at a cocktail party?

Impulsively, he had stopped the car at a call box and telephoned Susan's number. She was not in London for it was her voice answering him. He explained what he was doing.

"Gareth! What's happened to him? Is he ill? However did he get up there?" Susan's voice was taut with anxiety.

"He's perfectly all right, . . . just tired!" Gareth answered as calmly as he could, for the sound of her voice had set his heart beating double pace and his hand, holding the receiver, was trembling. "I'll explain when we arrive. There's nothing whatever to worry about. Just . . . an adventure."

"How long will you be?" came Susan's voice, quieter now.

"An hour . . . or thereabouts. I'm on my way now."

"Thank you, Gareth!" she had said, her voice barely audible to him now, and then she was gone.

An adventure! he had told her, but he didn't know as yet. Ted still slept . . . thanks to Jane's champagne.

But five minutes later, the boy beside him stirred and presently he was sitting up, rubbing his eyes and beginning to ask questions.

"*Uncle Gareth!* I knew I'd find you. But how did we get in the car? Have I been asleep? What's been happening?"

"Suppose you tell me your part of the story from the beginning!" Gareth suggested, relieved to see that the boy seemed to be suffering no ill effects from his initiation into the drinking world. He was touched, too, by the knowledge Ted's words gave him that he had come to find *him*.

With child-like simplicity, Ted recounted the story of Susan's birthday, the present he wanted to give her, the clue he had from the diary. He seemed unaware of the taut expression on Gareth's face when that diary was mentioned, the painful, desperate look in his eyes and the tightening of his hands on the wheel.

This was so much worse than anything Gareth had anticipated. How could he ever explain this to Susan? What must she feel to learn that her son had been reading her most private and intimate thoughts and, taking them factually, had transmitted them to him, Gareth!

'Oh, Susan, my poor darling!' he thought. 'I, too, have longed to pour out my heart on paper. I, too, have longed to see you more than anything else in the world.'

But he knew and understood her character too well to hope she might accept without loss of pride this revelation of her deepest thoughts. Somehow or other he must find a way to stop Ted from telling her. And there was no task more unpleasant to him, more hateful, than deceiving and disappointing a child. Ted had not realized he was doing wrong . . . had acted only from his love of Susan, from his desire to make her happy.

"Uncle Gareth, you're not cross I came and asked you, are you?"

Ted's anxious voice broke in on Gareth's reflections. He realized that he had not heard the end of the child's story, but he could guess it near enough. Jane had turned his untimely arrival into a fresh novelty for her party.

"I'm not cross, Ted, but there's something I think I must explain to you. You see, Ted, I shan't be able to come down again tomorrow to see Mummy. It isn't that I don't want to, but it isn't quite the same for me as it is, let's say, for Uncle Jim."

"Why isn't it?" Ted asked. "Why can't you come?"

"Because Uncle Jim has nobody else to think about except you and Mummy. And I have Aunty Jane. There will be lots of things she will want me to do for her tomorrow and other days, too, when Mummy might like to see me. It isn't that I'm not fond of your mother because I am . . . you must know that . . . very deeply fond. But I'm married to Aunty Jane, Ted, and it's up to a man to look after his wife and make her happy before he looks after anyone else."

Ted was looking at Gareth now with a hard, resentful stare.

"Then you mean you like Aunty Jane more than Mummy?" he asked bluntly.

Gareth bit his lip. What answer *could* he give this child?

"Perhaps you're too young to understand, Ted," he said helplessly. "Maybe when you're older you will understand better. You see, Aunty Jane is my wife."

"I see!" Ted said, almost shouting. "And I do understand. You do like Aunty Jane better and you don't care if Mummy's happy or not. She cried and cried when you went to live in London and I did too, and you just didn't care. You went on purpose 'cos you knew we'd be unhappy. And now you're doing it again. You don't want Mummy to have a good birfday and you don't care about it being my surprise that's spoilt, too. Well, I hate you. I just hate you. And I like Uncle Jim ever so much better'n you and I don't never want to see you again. So there!"

And he burst into tears.

For one awful moment, Gareth, too, felt near to breaking point. It was true that he had hurt Susan, hurt Teddy, too, and yet none of it had been his fault, of his own volition. Now Teddy, whom he loved as he would have loved his own son, hated him, despised him even. And his accusations were hardest of all to bear, those and the sound of the childish, choking sobs of disappointment from the little boy beside him.

But he understood, too, that Ted could not know all the truth. The boy felt that he, Gareth, had withdrawn his affection from them, deserted two people who loved him. He could not sense what Gareth had tried so hard and seemingly successfully to hide from him – that he still loved Susan . . . still remained with them in thought and in his dreams.

As Ted's sobs quietened into a hard, determined silence, Gareth felt that after all, this was only one more thing he must bear with. And he could, at least, try to save Susan's pride. Tentatively, he said, "Are you going to tell your mother . . . about why you came to London?"

There was no answer from Ted.

"It might disappoint her, perhaps, if she knew. If you don't mention the 'surprise' then she'd never miss it when it doesn't happen, would she?" he went on.

Again there was no answer from Ted.

"It would be a shame to do that, wouldn't it? And she mightn't like you looking in her diary. They are supposed to be private, you know. Nobody should read a diary. I think, if I were you, I'd just say you came to town to visit us."

"Well, you aren't me, and I'm jolly glad!"

And Gareth had to be content with that, for Ted would make no promises and they drove the remaining miles in uncomfortable and miserable silence. And Susan stood waiting for them at the garden gate.

Fifteen

Although Susan had been half crazy with worry when she had returned home from her day in London, to learn from Mrs Mendall that Ted was missing and searches for him had proved fruitless, once she had heard Gareth's voice, so calm, so blessedly welcome, she had lost all fear. In its place came a swift rush of joy . . . joy because the day which looked like ending so desperately, had turned out to have this unexpected surprise.

As she prepared supper, she found herself unable to think of anything else but that Gareth was coming . . . would be here within the hour. She could not fathom how Ted came to be with him. She knew only that for all she had hoped with every ounce of strength never to see Gareth again after their last good-bye, now that her heart was put to the test, she could scarcely contain the happiness that swept over her in those waves of emotion. She had expected never to see him again . . . not for many, many months at least, by when she imagined she might have been able to build some armour around that betraying heart of hers against her love for him and the knowledge of his need of her.

'It can do no harm to see him once more . . . just this once,' Susan told herself helplessly. 'He believes I am no longer in love with him, and I will do my best to strengthen that belief. Only . . . dear God . . . let me look once more into that face, hear his voice again, feel the sweet agony of my longing for him. Give me this much and I promise I will ask no more of You . . . of him.'

Growing more excited, more nervous and yet outwardly more calm as she busied herself in the kitchen, following in her mind's eye his car covering the miles between them, Susan felt no guilt but only surprise that love had the power so to weaken her will and determination. Vows, promises, pledges . . . all could be swept away in one second of emotion. It was a terrifying yet wondrous thought. For she knew that love could make her strong, too . . . strong for the object of one's love if not for oneself. For Gareth she would break no promises, would for his sake maintain the illusion she hoped he now had, that she cared for him but no longer loved him. This knowledge gave her more comfort than anything else could do. At least she could hope reasonably for his return to happiness . . . to his old life.

She had, in spite of the excitement, remembered to ask one of the neighbours to tell Mrs Mendall and others who were searching for her son that Ted was safe. Later she would have to thank them and apologize for the trouble she had inadvertently caused them. She could not believe that this had been just a boyish prank of Teddy's. He had been put on his honour to behave as he knew she would wish him to, and he had been proud at the thought that she considered him old enough to trust. He had seemed happy enough, too, at the prospect of remaining at home alone all day. The only reasonable explanation seemed that he had decided to go to London to try to find her. Yet it was such a big step for so young a boy as Ted to take alone. He had only been to London a few times . . . once to the pantomime last Christmas, once the year before for shopping, and each time he had clung to her hand as if he were a little afraid, in spite of himself, of getting lost.

Susan stopped trying to think what had happened, for soon now Ted would be home and he would tell her. It was one of his most endearing and praiseworthy qualities that whatever he did wrong, when she asked him to speak out and tell the truth, he always did. He had never lied to her in the true sense of the word and it had been her policy to lessen whatever punishment she had in mind for him, because he was prepared to own up and take what was due to him.

After three quarters of an hour, Susan could no longer watch the hands of the clock moving so slowly round its face. Impatiently, she went out into the garden where the sun still shone from the west and, for a brief moment, she was no longer just a girl waiting anxiously for a first glimpse of her lover, but was all mother, wondering what Ted had worn and whether he was catching cold, now that the heat of the day had given way to the cool, evening air. It was long past his bedtime, too.

The sound of a car coming swiftly along the lane struck all other thought from her mind but that here, at last, was Gareth. The colour flooded into her cheeks and her hand went instinctively to her hair, brushing it back from her forehead in an unconscious gesture of self-adornment. She ran through the garden and up the path and as Gareth's car turned the corner, she was standing waiting for them at the gate.

Ted, who had sat so quietly for the last half-hour, seemed suddenly all nervous energy. He jumped out of the car almost before Gareth stopped the engine and ran round the bonnet to his mother, making no effort to pull away from her as her arms went round him, drawing him close to her. To Susan's surprise, he buried his head in her shoulder and stood thus in silence. Across his dark, ruffled head, her eyes went to Gareth, who stood now watching them, one hand on the car door, one feeling in his pocket for his pipe . . . a cigarette . . . anything that might help to ease tension.

There was an expression in Susan's deep, brown eyes that confirmed her son's story an expression that gave him an equal measure of happiness and pain. For he was certain in this one instant that Susan still loved him . . . that she had inferred that change of heart for his sake. This knowledge thrilled him, even while it hurt him, once more to think that it was he himself, the man who professed to loving her, who was making her unhappy, denying her the things to which she was entitled, the love and admiration she merited. Ted had revealed what secret thoughts passed through her mind when she was alone, and he had struggled this last hour to disbelieve them. Now, in her face, he read the truth and felt a very passion of tenderness for her sweep through him, leaving him weak and trembling as no physical passion could do. His eyes went to Teddy's back and silently he prayed that the boy would keep silent . . . not be the cause of hurting her pride . . . hurting her who so little deserved this pain.

But Ted continued to hide his face and, for the first time, Susan felt a renewal of her anxiety for him.

"He's . . . all right?" she mouthed the words over Teddy's head.

Gareth nodded.

"A bit tired, I expect, aren't you, Ted?" he said aloud, but there was no reply. Susan turned the boy slowly round to face her. His head hung low and she lifted it gently, so that his eyes looked into her own.

There was in them an expression of acute misery, such as one could see sometimes in the eyes of an animal . . . a desperate, suprised expression that held also an appeal. Susan bit her lip, conscious that something had happened . . . something which Ted could not speak of easily.

"Would you like to go straight to bed, darling?" she asked gently. "It's past your bedtime!"

The boy nodded his head but made no move to go.

"Run along, darling. If you hurry, Uncle Gareth will have time to pop up and say good night before he has to go," Susan encouraged him and was utterly unprepared for the venomous look that shot into Ted's face.

"I don't want him to. I hate him. I never want to see him any more," he uttered in a low, desperate tone, and with one last angry look at Gareth, he turned and ran quickly into the house.

"Gareth, whatever is the matter with him? What has happened?" Susan cried, all her maternal instincts to the fore now.

"Shall we talk about it . . . for a few minutes?" Gareth asked, hoping to find some explanation that would satisfy Susan about her son's odd behaviour.

"Indoors? Or out here on the lawn?" Susan suggested.

"The lawn, I think! It's been a ghastly day in town. It's

wonderful to smell the clean pure air of the country . . ." he broke off awkwardly, and followed Susan's slim upright form to the deck-chairs under the gnarled old apple tree.

"I know. I was up there shopping today. I . . . I don't like London."

There was a moment's silence as they seated themselves and then Gareth took the plunge.

"About Ted," he said nervously. "I don't think you should punish him too much, Susan. He's had rather a disappointment. You see, he took it into his head apparently, to pay Jane and . . . . and myself a visit. He came to tea, I think. But the journey took him longer, no doubt, than he realized and it was nearly six-thirty when he arrived. Of course, I popped him straight in the car to bring him back and . . . well, he took a poor view. I suppose I spoiled him a bit when . . . when we lived here and he'd hoped I'd let him stay awhile. But Jane was giving a cocktail party and it hardly seemed the best place for him. Besides, when I learned you didn't know about the jaunt, I realized how anxious you'd be."

"I was desperate!" Susan admitted. "Mrs Mendall came over at four to get his tea and there was no sign of him. She thought at first he was out in the fields and waited for half an hour before she really started to worry. When I got back at five she was frantic. She hadn't liked to leave the house in case he returned and she didn't know what to do. There seemed no clue as to where he might have got to except one remark he had made about writing a letter. We thought perhaps he'd gone up to the village to post a letter and Mrs Mendall went off to look for him. Others joined the search but he just wasn't to be found. I simply can't understand, Gareth, what made him go to London. He's never done such a thing before and I left him on his honour to behave. It seems so incredible that he should decide all in a minute to go to tea with you and Jane."

"Kids do do impulsive things at times!" Gareth said, he hoped convincingly. "Perhaps he'd even planned the trip for some time."

"Then why didn't he tell me he wanted to go?" Susan parried.

"I was going to town for the day, and he must have known I'd have taken him to Jane's with all the will in the world. Besides, last time Jane asked him up for the day he said he didn't want to go."

Gareth bit the stem of his pipe and looked away from Susan to the gentle slope of the lawn, so fresh and green and cool! It made him long desperately to be living again in the country. The hot, smoky atmosphere, the dreadful hurrying after mad rounds of gaiety and excitement, the endless, meaningless chatter of their friends . . . this was no life compared with the quiet peace of the countryside, the contentment to be found from living close to nature, amongst the things which grew, flowered, fruited, faded only to be renewed once more in the full flower of their beauty when the winter turned again to spring. There was no death in the country, for life was everywhere . . . not the life of bright lights and hot pavements and hustling, irritable crowds; of stuffy offices and breathless cafés, cinemas, dance halls . . . but real life. Here, women never lost their beauty nor spoiled it by artifice. They grew old gracefully with a pride to match their years . . . pride in their homes, their cottages, their children, their grandchildren. Age brought no disillusionments, only reverence from the young who learned from the old.

For the first time in months, Gareth remembered his own home. He had been one of three sons and two daughters living in an old rambling vicarage in Cornwall. His father, as his grandfather before him, had been vicar of the small parish. Gareth's elder brother had now taken over from his father and in time, no doubt, his son would do the same. There had never been much money. The vicarage was always in need of repair and during their childhood his mother and father had always found it hard to make ends meet. Five children incurred many expenses in food, education, clothes, and yet they had been happy . . . wonderfully and perfectly happy. They had run wild in the holidays, playing, learning from the old fishermen their skill in handling rod and line, boat and nets. Learning from the farmers how to till the land, grow wheat, shoe a horse, mine tin. They had learned how young things were born, mated, whelped or foaled, completing the circle of life. They grew up with life all around them, part of it as it was part of them. And they had been happy.

It had been entirely through unselfish motives that Gareth, when he grew up, had left this life behind him. His uncle had offered him a place in his firm if he cared to leave home and go to London. At first he had declined the offer, but by then he was old enough to see that his parents were growing old and needed his help . . . financial help. His father had never saved for his old age. Any money that he had to spare he gave away to those worse off than himself. Now, Gareth had decided, was his chance to give his father and mother security in their old age.

So he had joined the firm and because he had the will and a quick intelligence, as well as a way with men which made them respect and like him, he had climbed the ladder quickly. His uncle had talked of retiring when Gareth returned after the war and now he held only a nominal directorship, leaving Gareth in charge. And Gareth had become a moderately wealthy man. He had sufficient means to send home all the money that they needed . . . to send his younger brother to Dartmouth for his training for the navy, to keep Jane in all the luxuries she found so necessary for her happiness. He had sufficient, too, to realize the dreams that had lain dormant in his heart ever since he had left home . . . to buy a house in the country where he could live once more the life of his childhood when the day's work was done . . . to live it, perhaps with his own children.

These ambitions he had realized for those few brief months before their return to town. For that he could not blame Jane alone, since he had himself chosen to leave to avoid the close proximity to Susan. But he would have wished to move elsewhere in the country, instead of which he had found himself leading the artificial life of London society, and never more than at this moment, in the cool of a summer's evening, had he hated it so much, found it so empty and unbearable.

And but for Ted's unfortunate wish to bring his mother her heart's desire, he would not be here now. He must go soon, in any case, for he and Jane had been invited to a supper party which he could not ignore without a show of bad manners, since the numbers had been carefully pre-arranged.

Gareth did not dare turn and look at the girl sitting so quietly at his side. Every nerve in his body was taut with a longing to kneel at her feet, to lean his head in the cool freshness of her skirt and feel those soft fingers on his burning forehead. She could, he knew, bring him peace of mind and body as the country could give his senses peace. He longed for her quiet spirit and the life which she alone could give him. And, most bitter of all the resentment he felt against Fate, was the fact that he had no right even to touch her . . . that while taking nothing he could in turn give nothing . . . only pain.

And he had, through no will of his own, hurt Ted, too. The boy was angry with him, perplexed because he was too young to understand or be told the truth. His affection which he, Gareth, had so treasured must also be forgone, but this time, at least, for Susan's sake. From her last words to him and from Ted's behaviour when he and Jane had come to tea last week, Gareth had known that the child was hurt by what he imagined to be Gareth's desertion of him. He had trusted Gareth to do this one thing to make his mother happy on her birthday and failed to understand why it could not be done. Gareth dared not do it . . . for all their sakes as much as for the fact that his duty to Jane forbade it. It would be better for all of them for him to see no more of Susan . . . if only Fate would leave them all alone.

Susan, unable to wait longer for Gareth to speak, broke in on the thoughts which she imagined had taken him so far away from her and Ted.

"I can't understand, Gareth, how he got the money. He must have gone by bus if not by train. He only had sixpence that I know of."

"He paid his bus fare anyway," Gareth said. "Perhaps he had a little money saved, Susan. He did mention something about your birthday present."

"My . . . birthday!" Susan echoed. "You don't think he can have gone to London to find me something? But why London?"

"I can't answer for him, Susan. Perhaps he will tell you himself. But . . . don't . . . question him too closely. He's tired . . . and upset. I'm afraid I've failed him . . . again."

The pain so apparent in the tone of Gareth's voice as the last words were wrung from him, went straight to Susan's heart. Impulsively and without thought, she put her hand on his arm and automatically his fingers closed over hers. They were both trembling now and Susan's words of comfort, "It isn't your fault, Gareth . . . I'm sure of that!" were only whispered.

"I . . . I ought to go now, Susan. It's been . . . lovely to see you. Don't . . . worry . . . about Ted. I'm sure he didn't mean to do any wrong," Gareth said, his words coming unevenly as he fought to keep them mundane.

"You won't stay to supper?" Susan asked, but it was more a statement than a question, for she knew he would not stay; knew, also, that she could not trust herself to keep to her promise if he should do so. With an immense effort, she withdrew her hand and said lightly, "I ought to go in to Ted now. Thank you again for bringing him home. It was very good of you."

"No trouble!" Gareth said quietly as he got to his feet. "I'll be pushing off now. Good-bye, Susan, and the best of luck . . . for the future, I mean."

He turned abruptly on his heel and she stood watching him as he walked away from her. His words rang in her ears, words that proved she had not failed him after all. He might still love her but he could forget her now . . . or soon, for he believed she no longer cared for him except as a friend. She had not betrayed herself. By remaining here against every instinct which cried out to her to run after him, she could prove to him and to herself that this time it was all over . . . for always.

"Good-bye, my dearest!" she whispered, her eyes never leaving him as he climbed into his car, started the engine and moved slowly away.

Never once did he turn his head to look at her nor wave his hand, but she could understand and be glad that she could gaze her fill without his knowledge.

Only when the car had disappeared from sight and nothing remained but the hum of its engine through the quiet call of the birds as they went to roost, did Susan turn away, knowing that her heart once more had gone with Gareth, leaving only her poor, tortured body and her suffering soul behind.

'Each time he leaves me I die a little death!' Susan thought as she walked slowly towards the house. 'I am numb now as if I were dead, without feeling, without hope!'

And yet life did not seem to cease because a heart was breaking. And somewhere within her, part of her heart remained intact, the part that was held so surely in her son's small hands. Feeling could not die in her while the strongest of all human emotions, her maternal love, remained. Nor could the future be quite hopeless, quite empty, when Ted was there to share it with her.

Her footsteps quickened and her head lifted as she entered the house and ran up the stairs to her son's room.

Ted lay with his head buried in the pillow. He made no sound and Susan knew that he was not crying. Gently, she sat down on the bed beside him and instantly he swung round and his arms went round her waist as he clung to her.

"Shall we talk, darling, or just sit like this?" Susan asked, not wishing to force his confidences but longing to receive them for her own peace of mind. She had never before known Ted in this strangely adult mood that was yet so very young and defenceless.

"Like to tell me all about it?" she asked again as he did not at first answer her.

"You're not . . . cross with me, Mummy?" came his voice, muffled by the folds of her skirt.

"Ought I to be cross?" Susan parried.

He looked up then, with a sideways glance at her face.

"P'haps for being late home!" he said carefully. "And . . . maybe for not asking if I *could* go."

"I'd like to hear more about it first," Susan said, trying not to be weak with him, to promise forgiveness before she knew what he had had in mind.

"I didn't mean to be late home," Ted said anxiously. "It took longer than I thought to get to London."

"It does take quite a long while!" Susan agreed, concealing a smile from him. "What made you decide to go, Ted?"

He looked away from her then and a dark flush spread across his face. He no longer spoke freely but only muttered.

"Don't really know!"

Susan's tone sharpened a little. It was unlike Ted not to own up.

"You must have had a reason, Ted."

He did not answer her. Susan tried once more.

"Did you want to see Uncle Gareth?"

He nodded.

"What for, Teddy? Just for tea? For the fun of going?"

"Just 'cos!" Ted said evasively.

"That's no reason, Ted. You could have asked me and I would have taken you up for the day with me and left you at Aunty Jane's. Why didn't you ask me if you could go?"

"Didn't think of it till this afternoon!" Ted replied quickly. This much, at least, he could admit without giving anything away.

"Where did you find the money for your bus fare?" Susan asked.

"My pocket money and my money-box, and Uncle Jim gave me some money."

"You neither of you told me. You know you mustn't touch your money-box without asking me first."

"It was to get you a birthday present," Ted said, half defiantly.

Susan's face softened.

"And is that why you went to London?" she asked. "Did you want to buy me something up there?"

Ted remained silent once more. His small face looked white and strained and his fingers were playing with the wool blanket.

For a moment, Susan wondered if she should cease questioning him tonight and let him sleep, but somehow she did not feel he would settle down until he had spoken the truth. He would lie awake worrying. And in the morning he would wake with a cloud over his head to start a new day.

"Tell me the truth, Teddy!" she said gently. "I shan't be cross."

"But you'd be disappointed!" the words slipped out of Teddy's mouth in a rush. "Uncle Gareth said so. And you would, too."

"Disappointed? Uncle Gareth said so?" Susan echoed, shaking her head a little, unable to make sense. "Teddy, tell the whole truth . . . all of it. I'd rather be disappointed than have you keep anything back. You know I don't mind anything so long as you tell me the truth. That's more important than anything else."

She had said it to him a hundred times and Teddy was in no doubt about the fact that his mother meant it. But somewhere inside him, he had been impressed by Gareth's pleading that he should tell his mother nothing of the diary. It was not so much what he had said, but the way he had said it. He might hate Uncle Gareth, but he still respected his advice. He had never known him to be wrong even if his actions were hurtful and seemingly unjust.

The conflicting appeals from the two grown-ups raged inside him. He felt a little sick . . . very uncertain, and his head ached. He wanted to cry . . . to be punished . . . anything that would end this horrible day and leave him in peace with Mummy's arms around him as she kissed him good night and told him it was all over . . . that it would all be forgotten tomorrow.

His longing for peace of mind overcame his former determination to keep silent as Gareth had bade him. Relief at the thought of his coming confession brought the tears. Instantly Susan's arms went round him and she held him tightly for a moment while his words came at first incoherently and then more audibly. Slowly the story came out and comprehension brought the colour to Susan's cheeks, receding slowly, taking with it all the warmth from her body, leaving her deathly cold.

"... I didn't mean to read what I didn't ought to have ..." she heard Ted's tearful voice. "I didn't know you'd mind till Uncle Gareth said so and I just wanted to s'prise you ... honest I did. Uncle Jim said you'd like something I'd chosen more'n what he chose and I wanted it to be somefing you wanted very badly. I wanted it to be nicer'n what he's giving you and that's special 'cos he said so. It's in a little square box and he says its something to wear on your finger and I wanted you to like my present much more'n what his is. So when you said in that book you ..."

"That's enough, Teddy!" Susan broke in, unable to hear him repeat those terribly private thoughts she had never meant another soul to read. "No more ... *please!*"

Ted looked at her white face anxiously. He could not tell from the rigid expression on her face if she were cross or disappointed or neither. He felt apprehension replace the relief of confession.

Presently, Susan looked down at him and with an immense effort, she brought herself sufficiently back to normality to say, "I understand, Ted. I'm not cross and I'm not going to punish you. I know now you only did all this for my sake. So you can forget all about it, darling, and not worry any more ... only one thing, Teddy ... never, never read anyone else's diary. It belongs to the person who wrote it and it isn't meant to be shared ... like other things people have. Promise me?"

"I promise!" Ted said, and flinging his arms round her neck he drew her face down to his and kissed her. For a moment Susan clung to him, allowing herself the fleeting comfort of his embrace, then she released his arms and tucked him in for the night. Like an automaton she drew the curtains, opened the window and closed the door behind her. Her feet carried her to her bedroom and then only did she give way to the burning shame that her son had so unmeaningly brought to her.

She lay down on the bed and buried her face in the pillow. Never again could she look up from that darkness to face the world around her. Her pride lay broken into a thousand pieces at her feet. Gareth ... of all people ... knew the secret intimacy of her diary; knew perhaps the childish outpourings of her heart laid bare on paper but never meant for human eyes to read. He had tried to spare her . . . to prevent Ted telling her the truth. He had tried, for her sake, to stop her questioning her son. And in spite of that she had insisted on knowing 'the truth' . . . the truth which would make it impossible now for her to look Gareth in the eyes again. She had, so cleverly, she'd imagined, convinced him that she no longer cared . . . had denied the truth in her heart and been so proud of her success. And all the time Gareth had known. How easily he must have seen through her pathetic pretences!

'What can I do? What can I do?' Susan cried into her pillow.

And quite suddenly the answer seemed to be spoken into the room.

"Uncle Jim is giving you something special . . . in a square box. I think's it's a ring . . ." (Her son's voice.) A ring . . . an engagement ring. Jim was coming tomorrow hoping to combine a birthday with an engagement celebration. She knew it as surely as she knew that her pride and her illusions had been most soundly shattered. And with the certainty of Jim's determined proposal tomorrow, she could see a way to undo the unfortunate actions of today. She could accept Jim . . . agree to marry him. It would make Jim happy, please Teddy, release Gareth and at least, if it could not bring her happiness, it could restore a little of her pride.

Slowly the taut muscles of her body relaxed and a little warmth returned to her hands and feet. She raised her face from the pillow and looked once more at the world . . . the little world of her room. Tomorrow she could, after all, face the bigger world outside, for she had made up her mind quite definitely as to what she would do.

Sixteen

Jane stretched out on the *chaise longue* and settled herself more comfortably against the cushions which Marie had arranged behind her back. The room was warm with the airless hothouse atmosphere of over-much central heating but Jane was enjoying the heat for she was clad only in the flimsiest of *négligées* . . . a pale pink creation of tiny frills and tucks which became her little-girl prettiness very well.

A silver cigarette box lay on the little table beside her and from this she took a Turkish cigarette and placed it in the long amber holder . . . a new affectation she had recently acquired, copying someone in the smart set in which she now moved. She felt that the sophistication of smoking from a holder enhanced the demureness and innocence that was so much part of the Jane she presented to the world . . . particularly to the male world, and which, for all she might imagine otherwise, was still much of her true self. The pout that curved her scarlet lips, the discontented droop of her fair head, the irritable way she had been 'bossing' Marie this morning because she was in one of her 'sulks' . . . all these might have been true of the child Jane remained at heart . . . the spoilt over-cosseted little girl who was not, at the moment, getting things all her own way.

"Think it over, Jane, for this time I'm serious!"

Those words of Gareth's had been the culmination of a long scene and the beginning of this 'mood' from which she had not found it so easy to escape. For in her heart, she had been a little frightened of Gareth . . . certain that this time he meant what he said.

The scene had begun late one night. For some months . . . ever since they had come to the flat, in fact, she and Gareth had shared separate rooms. It had begun when she had thought Gareth had caught Ted's infantile paralysis and he had slept in his dressing-room. Since then, almost as if neither were aware of the change, Gareth had continued to sleep alone and gradually moved most of his belongings from Jane's room into his own.

Curiously enough, Jane found she enjoyed regaining her privacy. Now she could be as untidy as she liked and there was no Gareth around to fuss about her clothes lying all over the room because he could not find a stud or collar amongst the disorder. She had slept better, too, for she liked to curl up her legs and spread her arms sideways, taking all the big bed, and she had no fear now of waking Gareth when she turned.

And even more curiously, perhaps, she did not miss Gareth's physical presence . . . those moments of intimacy they had once shared . . . that last friendly chat before the lights went out, the times Gareth would sit watching her while she brushed her hair or come up behind her to drop a kiss on the back of her head. She simply never thought about them now, for with Gareth's absence, Jane had introduced Marie to her life and Marie now put her to bed, brushed her hair, even undressed her when she was very tired. She liked Marie . . . enjoyed the little French girl's obvious admiration of her looks, her figure, her popularity. With Marie as a willing listener, Jane would recount the day's adventures, successes, disappointments. Marie was, in fact, the recipient of all that went on in Jane's heart . . . and Marie soothed, comforted or encouraged according to what her mistress desired her to do.

In one thing only did Marie fail to understand Jane . . . that was her indifference to *"l'amour"*.

"Je ne vous comprends pas, Madame! Monsieur . . . he is so 'andsome . . . so *distingué* . . ." she shrugged her shoulders in a typically French gesture . . . "and you do not love him . . . *mais c'est incroyable!"*

Jane was amused.

"I'm very fond of him, Marie. But perhaps I *am* different from other women. Certainly *that* side of marriage doesn't particularly appeal to me. Frankly, Marie, I've come to the conclusion sex is very over-rated. I can manage very well without it, thank you."

"*C'est possible, Madame*, that you can manage without, but I not understand why you so choose. In France, perhaps one marries not so often for love as in England. But *Monsieur* . . . he is the true lover such as any girl in her dreams might long for."

"I agree he is attractive!" Jane admitted. "But there it is, Marie. I like being petted and kissed . . . yes! But otherwise I am indifferent. It's the way I'm made, I suppose!"

Marie looked at her young mistress helplessly. Could it be possible, she asked herself, that a woman so attractive, so full of the coquette, of everything that must appeal to the true man . . . could yet be unresponsive to that side of nature her appearance invoked? If it were true, it must indeed be another of nature's examples of contrariness.

So it was that Marie replaced Gareth for those nightly "chats" and Marie was a good listener and never, like Gareth, reproved her. Jane could, too, be so much more frank with Marie. In all, the arrangement suited her . . . until she had decided that afternoon, when Jim had visited her, to amuse herself by making Gareth fall in love with her again. Her vanity had been piqued to learn that Gareth, whom she had imagined to be once more her slave, still longed for Susan, of all people. She had, when they still lived in the country, had some suspicions, but later on, when they came to the flat, she had begun to notice how Gareth avoided any conversation in which Susan's name appeared . . . how he had invariably made excuses not to visit Susan when she had suggested it . . . how he had said he would not be home if Jane suggested a day to invite Susan and Teddy to town.

She had, even then, believed it impossible . . . had thought it was just Gareth's way of showing her, Jane, that he was annoyed with her. Then Jim had truly let the cat out of the bag. She had pretended, of course, that she had known all about it but it wasn't altogether true. *She had not been sure* . . . and it had shaken her a little to think that her power over Gareth had lessened to such an extent.

So she had decided to win Gareth back . . . for the fun of it as much as to satisfy her pride. It had not, however, turned out to be so easy. Gareth had pretended not to hear when she suggested he share her room that night. In consequence, Jane had planned a midnight invasion of Gareth's dressing-room. He had been asleep when she went in and only wakened when she climbed into bed beside him. She knew he was awake, but he had spoken no word and Jane herself had remained silent, feeling a little out of her depth and uncertain of herself.

It had been a strange, wild and almost frightening experience. Gareth had shown a side to himself that was hitherto unknown to her. He had shown none of the usual gentleness and consideration, the tenderness and control that had characterized his love-making in the past. Instead he had possessed her body with a hard, cruel determination . . . with a primitive indifference to anything but his own desires. And for the first time in her life, Jane had been really afraid of him and, at the same time, unusually responsive to this side of her marriage.

Long after Gareth lay sleeping once more at her side, Jane had lain awake, her mind as active as her body was relaxed. She could think of little else but the revelation that this night had brought of the man lying at her side her husband. Though a stranger now, he had yet never come so close to winning her as when he had ceased to care for her. Only now had her body awakened to those physical desires to which she had always believed herself indifferent.

She had felt both surprised and triumphant, for she did not yet understand Gareth nor the mood in which he made love to her that night. She thought that his wild and uncontrollable love-making had been his surrender to her . . . born of his old need of her and her love. She mistook for the passion she believed she had aroused in him, the hopeless, desperate, nearly savage quality of his possession of her. And when morning came, he was bitterly and dreadfully ashamed.

Jane was sleeping deeply, and with the utmost caution Gareth had slipped out of bed and, taking his clothes to the bathroom, dressed in there. By the time Jane was awake, Gareth was already at his office and trying to forget his home affairs in an orgy of hard work.

Jane had been both surprised and disappointed when she awoke to find Gareth had gone. She called to Marie to bring her a cup of coffee and had snuggled back under the bedclothes feeling that at any moment she might purr like a contented kitten. She was at peace with the world and particularly with Gareth. He was hers . . . all hers again and no doubt this evening when he came home, there would be flowers for her and a good deal of spoiling and the moment would be ripe to reopen the request to go abroad in the autumn. Gareth had said a hundred times he couldn't get away from the stupid old office but Jane felt sure she would be able to persuade him into it now. And a holiday abroad with Gareth in this new guise, would be exciting and interesting or at worst a change from the domestic rut into which, on reflection, Jane had decided they had descended.

Jane had been pleased by the expression on Marie's face when she brought the breakfast to Gareth's dressing-room. But for once Jane was not prepared to satisfy the girl's curiosity and waved her out of the room, so that she could day-dream a little longer on the success of her plans to win Gareth's love away from Susan and back to herself.

'I have only to lift my little finger!' she thought with a toss of her bright curls on the pillow, 'and he comes!'

So she had been quite unprepared for the shock in store for her when Gareth returned home from the office, later than usual, that evening. Jane had spent most of the day preparing for his homecoming. She had had her hair washed and set, a face-do, a manicure, and had gone out especially to buy the pink *négligée* she was wearing at this moment. She was, in fact, armed with every weapon that might win her the battle for the trip abroad she so much wanted.

She had greeted Gareth with a long look from beneath her lashes and waited for him to come over and kiss her. Instead, he had gone to the little cocktail bar in silence and poured himself and her a drink. Presently, while she watched him surreptitiously, he sat down with his face turned a little away from her and lighting his pipe, said in a low voice, "I hope you will forgive me, Jane . . . for last night. It was unforgivable . . . and . . . I'm very ashamed."

"Forgive you? Ashamed?" Jane repeated puzzled. "I . . . I don't understand!"

"Don't you, Jane?" Gareth's voice had replied, low, controlled, almost hard. "I hoped I wouldn't have to explain in detail."

"I can't see what you are trying to quarrel about, Gareth," Jane had tossed back at him, sensing from his tone that all was not well, as she had believed.

Gareth bit his lip.

"I'm not trying to quarrel, Jane. Far from it. But I do think it is time we came to some sort of understanding. We have been acting as if nothing had happened to our marriage. If we are going to make a success of it in spite of everything, then I feel we must be absolutely honest with each other."

"I see!" Jane said, but she did not yet understand what he was trying to say. Irritation mounted slowly in her to think that perhaps after all, Gareth was not quite so easily won back to slavish adoration.

"You know I believe that . . . that I'm in love with Susan?" Gareth's voice was so low she had to lean a little towards him to hear the words.

"Jim told me you had a crush on her!" Jane replied childishly. "I hardly think it's anything to be proud of, Gareth."

"I'm not proud of it, Jane, although I am not ashamed of my love . . . only for the betrayal of my heart. I made certain vows on the day we were married and I always look on those vows as sacred. Unfortunately my heart played me false. For that I am deeply ashamed, Jane, and I wish to do everything in my power to make up to you for that mental unfaithfulness."

"Guilty conscience, I suppose!" Jane said tartly. It did not in the least appeal to her to hear Gareth confessing his love for Susan. "And I should think Susan owes me an apology, too. Of all the dirty tricks, scheming to take another woman's husband away!"

"Be quiet, Jane! I will not listen to you saying such things!" Gareth's voice was like cold steel. It stung Jane into silence. "You know in your heart that Susan is incapable of such meanness. The idea never entered her mind . . . nor mine. The moment we discovered how we felt, we resolved never to meet again. You made that impossible, Jane. First by turning me out of the house when you thought I might carry infection into it; later by forcing me to go to tea with Susan when you must have known I didn't want to go. You wished to see how we would act together, didn't you?"

"Perhaps!" Jane said, thoroughly angry now. "I don't see why I should always be the loser."

"You lost nothing that you ever wanted, Jane. You never really wanted my love. You were indifferent to me except as a nominal husband, as a provider of the things you wanted whether they were things money could buy or sops to your vanity. You lost only the power you had over me when I ceased to love you."

"And last night . . . am I to believe that it meant nothing to you?" Jane asked triumphantly.

"Only a complete debasement of all that love means. I shall always regret last night, Jane."

"I see! So what is to be done about it? I presume you have some idea in mind?" Jane's voice was full of sarcasm.

Gareth turned to her then and his face softened as he looked at this girl who, although he no longer loved her, was still his wife and who, in thought anyway, he had wronged.

"Don't let us be bitter with one another, Jane. I fully realize that I am to blame for this state of affairs and I want to make amends as best I can. I want to know that if our marriage is to continue it is because *you want it to as much as I do* . . . that you are prepared to fight for it as hard as I am."

Gareth's face was very serious, his voice pitched low and vibrant.

Jane returned his gaze indignantly.

"I like that, Gareth! I call it the limit, honestly I do. *You* ask *me* what I intend to do about our marriage. Just *who* is the guilty party, I'd like to know?"

"I suppose in a way I am guilty . . . in thought if not in deed," Gareth admitted. "But if you will be honest with me, Jane, I'm sure you will admit that a little of the failure lies at your door, too. I'm not trying to excuse my own behaviour in any way, but can you say truthfully that you have done everything you could to make our marriage a perfect union?"

"In what way have I failed?" Jane asked, her voice still indignant and petulant, too, for she knew now to what Gareth referred. "I suppose everything is *my* fault because I won't have a baby. Well, lots of married women don't have children and, as far as I know, their husbands don't go on about it all the time."

"Perhaps those other husbands you refer to don't want children any more than their wives. But it isn't only that, Jane. I was so very much in love with you . . . so ardently desired to make you happy and know that you loved me as I loved you. Isn't it true to say that you have slowly grown more and more indifferent to me . . . to anything, in fact, that did not directly lead to some newer, more exciting entertainment? Has it made *you* happy . . . this wild chase after gaiety . . . the parties . . . drinks . . . the stupid chatter of the set we now move amongst? Are you content in your heart with our life? I cannot begin to say that I am."

"I've had a lot of fun up here," Jane broke in. "And anyway, it was just as much your idea to come back to town as it was mine. I can't help it if you don't like my friends . . . you certainly don't make any of your own!"

It was an unfair thrust, for Gareth had, in the past, frequently requested that Jane should entertain some of his men friends and their wives . . . mostly people he met through his work and who were slightly older and more seriously minded than Jane's set. After one or two such dinners, Jane had complained so ceaselessly that they were 'boring', "dull", 'stuffy' that he had given up asking these friends home or accepting invitations from them. It had been the same with his family. After one visit to the vicarage in Cornwall, he had known that Jane would never fit in with the quiet simplicity of his home. His brother, now vicar of the parish since his father's death, his two unmarried sisters who kept house had done their best to understand and like Jane, but although they had admired her prettiness and petted and spoilt her, within five days the novelty of their village life had palled and Jane had been asking petulantly if there wasn't at least a cinema to which they could go.

Gareth had not suggested they should spend another holiday there and Jane had never mentioned it. Gareth had slipped away for a night from time to time to see his family, usually when Jane had some heavy social engagement that she did not think required his presence.

"I think we are getting a little away from the main point," Gareth said at last. "Our friends are not nearly so important as ourselves. They are only important because we are not satisfied with each other's company. We used to do things on our own once, Jane . . . occasional theatres, dinners, dances . . . or spend evenings at home together by ourselves. Lately we seem to have to have the company of others. I think that indicates failure to appreciate each other."

Jane swung her feet to the ground and walked crossly to the bar to pour herself another drink.

"What are you suggesting we do about it, Gareth?" she flung at him over her shoulder.

Gareth shrugged his shoulders helplessly.

"I don't know, Jane. That's the problem I hoped we might solve together."

"Perhaps you'd like a divorce so you can marry your girl-friend!" Jane retorted with a desire to hurt him.

"No, I don't want a divorce unless you do, Jane. You are my wife and, as I said before, I meant the vows I gave in church the day I married you. But I cannot go back to the old life . . . somehow, I don't think it was the right way for either of us. I gave in too much . . . spoiled you, perhaps . . . so that you ceased to respect me. I was your lap-dog, Jane . . . slave to your whims and fancies. That was no more a marriage than this present state of affairs. We should be equals, Jane . . . with the same rights, the same ideas, working towards the same goal."

"And just what goal are we working for?" Jane asked.

Gareth stood up slowly and took a step towards Jane so that he could look straight into her wide, angry blue eyes. His voice was urgent as he said, "We haven't got a goal, Jane, and we must have one. It's what we both need. A child would bring us together in a way that nothing else could. It would give us a common interest, something to work and live for. Won't you consider it, Jane? You can have no idea how grateful I should be to you . . . And I would do everything in my power to make things as pleasant as they could be for you. You'd have the best of everything, nurses, doctors, anything that would ease the restrictions motherhood might put on you. And after the child was born, you could choose any holiday you want . . . go to America, the South of France . . . anywhere in the world for a month to recuperate."

For the first time, Jane was prepared to consider seriously what Gareth was saying. She sat down in one of the armchairs and looked at him through her lashes.

"I do want to go abroad, Gareth!" she said, appealing to him in a voice now soft and full of sweetness. "I was going to mention it again this evening only you started this silly quarrel. I want to be friends again, too. Honestly I do. I don't really mind about Susan. I knew you'd never do anything about it and I suppose in a way it was my fault. But I'll be different, Garry darling. Really, I do love you, you know!"

Gareth looked into the blue eyes, opened wide with a childish candour. Hope sprang into his heart and in an instant he was beside her chair, his hands holding her arms and his whole mind filled with a longing to put things right between them . . . to make up to her in every way possible for the love he could not give her, but hoped desperately she would reawaken in him.

"Then you will agree?" he asked.

Jane wriggled uncomfortably in his grasp and turned her face away from him.

"To what, Gareth? That we're not going to quarrel any more?"

"To have a child, Jane!" Gareth said bluntly.

Jane's lips curved into a pout. Gareth was staring at her now, his face taut with disappointment. For that one instant he had believed she had acquiesced, mistaken her vow that she loved him to mean that she cared sufficiently for him to grant his dearest wish . . . a wish that must surely bring them together again. *But she had not meant it.* She was searching now for a way to tell him and he could read the evasive words she was about to speak in that hard, young face.

Slowly, he rose to his feet.

Jane watched him covertly. She was anxious not to lose this chance of pressing home her point about the holiday abroad. If she could only find some way to get round her side of the bargain . . . a way of saying she would have a baby but not yet . . . so that Gareth would be convinced she meant it even if she did not.

"I . . . don't want to promise, Gareth, but perhaps in a little while . . . ?" she began, staring at the back of his head and wishing she could see his face, read the reaction to her words in his eyes. But he refused to turn.

"I would like a promise," Gareth said quietly. "You see, Jane, I cannot in my heart feel that you love me as you say you do while you can deny me what lies nearest to my heart. Not that I have any right to expect your love, but at least as man and wife we should each desire the other's happiness if we are to make our marriage succeed. I desire your happiness with all my heart, Jane, and if it is a holiday abroad you want, then have it. But until I have your promise that you will keep your side of the bargain, I would not come with you."

Jane's dawning gratification turned at his last words into a new frown.

"But Gareth, I can't go *alone*! I should be lost travelling around by myself."

"You can take Marie . . . or a woman friend," Gareth said quietly.

"Well, I know, but I don't want that. I should be bored to death without . . ."

". . . A man about the place to pet and spoil you?" Gareth finished for her.

Jane tossed her head.

"Well, there's no need to be nasty, Gareth. Of course I want an escort. You're my husband . . . it's up to you to look after me."

"You're my wife, Jane, and it's up to you to bear our children. Until you do, our marriage can never mean more to me than a mistake we have both made . . . a mistake which was more of my making than of yours, for I persuaded you to marry me. I believed I could win your love. I have succeeded not at all. But I have tried, Jane, as far as I am capable, of being a good husband to you. I think the future lies in your hands now . . . *our* future, perhaps I should say. Either we both fight for it . . . together, or neither of us do. I cannot go on fighting for it alone. In the event of your deciding against children then I feel I must lead my own life . . . at least part of the while. We will present a face to the outside world of married bliss . . . if you choose. But we shall be strangers to each other in the house. You can have your friends . . . I mine. But I hope this won't happen. I hope, Jane, that we can grow close to one another again. The barrier between us can so easily be pulled down by this one gesture on your side. It is all I ask of you. Grant me this and I will lay the rest of the world and my heart once more at your feet!"

"But Gareth, that isn't fair!" Jane cried as he turned towards the door. "You're asking me to give up much more than you're going to. I shall have to grow fat and ugly and never see anybody for months and months, and then suffer that dreadful pain. It isn't fair. I don't like babies and even if we had a nurse you'd expect me to look after it on her day off. I should be tied to the house, grow dull and old and matronly. And you'd be the first to stop loving me when I looked old and fat and ugly."

"You would not seem ugly to me, Jane . . . only beautiful!" Gareth said quietly. "And I should love the mother of my children as I could never love anyone else. Think it over, Jane. I do not ask you to decide this minute. If you are frightened of childbirth, go to your doctor and talk to him about it . . . let him convince you there is no danger, and very little pain these days. And when you've made up your mind, Jane . . . let me know."

"Where are you going, Gareth?" Jane called after his departing figure. She didn't want to be left alone with this ultimatum. She wanted time to talk Gareth round . . . to win him back to her own way of thinking . . . to persuade him to go with her on her holiday and forget about stupid babies. This was a Gareth she could not understand, could not submit to her will. She was the wronged party . . . and yet Gareth had made it seem as if she were to blame. It wasn't fair . . . and it wasn't in the least the kind of evening she had envisaged.

"It's nearly dinner time and Marie has cooked something special!" she added.

For a second Gareth paused and turned to look at her from the door.

"Forgive me, Jane, but I'm going out for a while . . . for a walk I think. I don't want any supper."

"But Gareth, we haven't finished talking," Jane pleaded.

For a moment . . . just for one fleeting instant, a smile crossed Gareth's face.

"Oh, Jane!" he said. "Is there anything more we can say which would make things different?"

And when she remained mute, he turned away from her and went quickly out of the door.

'Think it over!' Gareth had said. Well, she had been thinking ... for an hour at least ... and Gareth was still not back. She had thought and thought, but all the time, at the back of her mind, she had known what her answer would be. She wouldn't have a baby, not for Gareth or anyone else. And if it came to the worst, then they'd just have to live as he had said they would ... as strangers. It wouldn't really matter very much. Gareth would still be host at her parties, her escort when they went out. He would still provide for her and she *could* find some girl friend to go on that holiday. After all, did she mind so much if Gareth was indifferent to her? Apart from last night, she had never really *needed* the love he used to shower on her. She wouldn't be the loser of anything that *really* mattered, since she would still have her social life, her friends, her position as Gareth's wife. "In name only" ... wasn't that the right description for what their marriage would be? And why not? Gareth would make no demands on her and she had very few to make of him that were not purely financial!

'Well, he's asked for it. Let's see how he likes it,' Jane thought. 'He'll suffer a lot more than I shall!'

No, she had nothing serious to lose since Gareth would not consider divorcing her unless she asked him to do so, or, of course, if she were unfaithful to him. But that event was unlikely, since men didn't appeal to her senses in that particular way. Their admiration she enjoyed, their companionship, their tributes and harmless little flirtations. And those she could still enjoy.

Now she was tired of thinking ... and bored with sitting alone.

'I'll ring up the club,' she thought, 'and see if Bim is back from his trip to America!'

But before she could do so, the telephone rang and, as if by telepathy, it was Bim's voice she heard, excited, eager, almost incoherent in his effort to impart some 'terribly important news'.

"Are you alone, honey? Shall I come to the flat? Or will you come here? No . . . can't tell you over the wire. I just gotta see you in person . . . don't waste any time then, honey. I'll send a car for you right away. Oh, baby . . . are you or are you gonna get one great grandmother of a surprise!"

Seventeen

Because her vanity superseded even her curiosity to hear Bim's 'news', Jane kept the hired car he had sent to fetch her waiting a full twenty minutes while she changed from the *négligée* into a smart, silk cocktail dress. It was cornflower blue in colour and became her better, perhaps, than anything else in her now extensive wardrobe. The colour seemed to reflect in her large eyes and the softness of the material draped so skilfully round her slender figure gave her the appearance of a young Venus.

With her fair curls swept up on top of her head, a stole of white fur round her shoulders and long white gloves reaching to her elbows, Jane knew that she would evoke that pleasant whistle of approval from Bim; or an admiring glance from any man who looked her way. The chauffeur of the car gave her just such a glance as he helped her into the back seat.

Driving round to Bim's club, Jane felt a little thrill of excitement at the unexpectedness of this summer's evening. Only a few moments ago, so it seemed, she was feeling thoroughly down in the dumps . . . angry with Gareth, bored, frustrated with life in general. And now she was on her way to meet Bim . . . one of the few men Jane knew who had remained her friend. The platonic basis of their friendship had been founded when she had married Bim's best friend and although Jane knew he both liked and admired her and thought her the most attractive English girl he knew, he had never tried to make love to her, never complicated their dates by falling in love with her. There was an element of fraternal affection in his treatment of her, combined with the admiration she so much enjoyed.

And apart from her own pleasure in seeing Bim again, there was this surprise to look forward to. Bim had sounded very excited and try as she might, she could not imagine what the surprise might be.

Bim was waiting for her in the foyer, and having told the chauffeur to wait, he hurried Jane into the lounge and instead of taking her to the bar, found a corner settee as far away from anyone else as he could.

"I just gotta talk to you somewhere quiet," he explained. "Now what'll you have to drink, gorgeous? Something to buck you up. You'll need it!"

The tension in Bim was like an uncoiled spring, and yet there was a serious expression to his face that Jane could not remember noticing before. She could hardly contain her curiosity while the waiter served the drinks Bim had ordered.

At last they were alone and Bim, lighting cigarettes for them both, inhaled deeply and took a long look at Jane.

"Gee, you're a swell-looking girl, Jane," he told her. "I'm certain sure you grow lovelier every day. Seems you're hardly the same kid I used to know in the old days . . . remember?"

"Of course I remember, Bim," Jane said, dimpling at the compliment. "But let's not talk about me. I want to hear your news."

"It concerns you, honey. And it concerns the good old days, too. I hardly know quite how I'm gonna break this piece of news. You see, so much depends on . . . on the old days . . . on how much they meant to you."

Jane looked at her companion with a sideways tilt to her head.

"You know what they meant to me, Bim. I don't understand what you're getting at."

Bim shrugged his shoulders helplessly.

"I guess I'm not making myself clear. What I really mean, Jane, is . . . well, what would you give to be back in those days?"

Jane's eyes widened.

"With Ham, you mean? I don't know, Bim. It seems so long ago, and yet I really loved Ham. I've never loved anyone else the same way. I was terribly happy and at times terribly unhappy . . . worried. I . . . I just don't know what I'd do if I could go back. But what's the use of talking about it?"

"I just wanted to try and get some idea . . . of how you felt about things. Your husband, for instance. I know it's none of my business, but Jane . . . do you love him? Really love the guy, I mean?"

Jane drew a deep sigh.

"It's funny you should ask me that, although I still don't see what you're getting at," she said. "But since you've asked, the truth of the matter is we've had a bust up. In fact, just before you telephoned it all came to a head. Gareth wants me to start a family and I don't want to. It may sound selfish and all that but I just don't like babies. Besides, I'm much too young to settle down and be matronly. It's not in my nature to be one of those domesticated women like the girl Gareth seems to have fallen for. It's an awful mess, Bim, and I sometimes wonder if I ever should have married Gareth. It isn't that I'm in love with anyone else but just that we're bored with each other. We aren't suited. Gareth thinks it's my fault and I think it's his."

It was a relief to be able to confide in Bim and he was listening attentively to every word she said. She felt that his sympathy might soothe her ruffled feelings, and at the same time ease the tiny pang of conscience which she only half-admitted to herself, for to her behaviour to Gareth. Deep down within her she knew that all he had said to her had been true. She had never really wanted all the love he had showered on her. She had enjoyed the spoiling and the life he had given her . . . had enjoyed the position she had as his wife; but of Gareth himself, the man, she had demanded very little because she had never stopped to consider how she would feel if he didn't love her . . . nor how much she valued his love.

Certainly she had never been prepared to make any sacrifices for him nor go to the trouble that at one time she had exerted for her young American husband. Ham had only to lift a little finger and she would rush off to obtain whatever it might be he wanted. He had only to raise one eyebrow, with that funny little smile at the corner of his mouth, to send her scurrying into his arms. At times, too, he had treated her badly . . . been late for dates, disappointed her over some promised treat, forgotten her birthday . . . once even forgotten he was meeting her at a railway station and gone off with a party of his own friends. But he had only to ask her forgiveness with that quick, ready smile and she had forgiven him and forgotten her grievance as quickly as she had been ready to laugh with him and join in some fresh, mad idea that he had thought up to amuse her.

And she had been jealous of Hamilton, too. Jealous of every look he gave another pretty girl, for he had had a 'roving eye' like so many American G.I.s, and although he had loved her, was her husband, he could, so he once teased her, enjoy other feminine charms from a distance. But it had not paid to be sulky and petulant with Ham. He liked to see her always laughing, always cheerful and something that was in him had kept her nearly always so. He knew her faults but he had been amused by them . . . calling her 'Vanity-puss' and 'his spoilt baby' and 'my girl with the come-hither eyes'. But for every fault she had, Ham had had his share and so often they were the same. They had understood one another and been amused to think how alike they were. 'We're almost too alike,' Ham had said just before they were married. "We're bound to fight a lot, honey, but oh, boy! what fun we'll have when we kiss and make up!'

Yes, life with Ham had been fun . . . never a dull moment, and even if he was 'the boss' he had loved her as much as she had loved him, and quarrel though they did, as Ham had predicted, it had been wonderful fun making up just as it had been exciting to fight with him. Their whole short married life had been exciting from start to finish and it had dashed her down to earth with horrible sharpness when Ham had finally been drafted overseas and she had been alone once more. She had lived in her memories then, only keeping cheerful because she knew they could be together again one day soon, and when this certainty had been replaced by hope and at last by hopelessness, Jane had felt that the future must remain permanently empty for her.

It was then that Gareth had reappeared in her life and he had been a great consolation to her . . . filling the void with flowers, phone calls, parties, attention, admiration. Not the varieties that had been Ham's, but a more serious, persistent courting that had, in its way, been exciting just because Gareth was so obviously serious.

She had known that she was playing with fire but somehow she had never got burnt. She had grown fond of Gareth, used to him, in a way dependent on him and eventually married him. But she never had in the past and never would feel the same towards him as she had once felt towards her wild, dare-devil Hamilton.

"Perhaps Gareth is too old for me!" she said aloud to Bim. "I really don't know what's wrong, Bim, but there it is. Neither of us is happy!"

Bim took a swift drink and studied Jane over the rim of his glass.

"You wish yourself unmarried to him now?" he asked.

"Divorce him?" Jane said, and shook her head. "There doesn't seem much point to it, Bim. I'm not in love with anyone else and what would I do with my life without anyone to look after me? I'm fond of Gareth in a way and I must admit he does take care of me."

"You're a funny girl, Jane," Bim remarked, more to himself than to her. "You look such a soft-hearted kid and yet in a way you're hard. Don't think I'm criticizing you. I'm just trying to get at the truth. I like the sound of your husband. He seems a nice enough guy and yet you don't really give a damn for him underneath, do you? I don't think you ever did."

"But I *am* fond of him, Bim, except when he gets in one of his moods," Jane cried petulantly.

"But you don't love him . . . not the way you loved Ham. I remember how you used to act around *that* guy. Nothing was too good for him, too much trouble to do for him. You were crazy about him, Jane. Those days you really were soft-hearted! You took plenty of punishment from him and still came back smiling and ready for more. You could only have done that if you'd loved him."

"He was such fun!" Jane cried. "No matter what happened we could always laugh together. And I was never bored. Perhaps when he was killed something of me went with him. Maybe that's why I'm hard now. I don't know."

For a moment or two Bim was silent. Then he said abruptly, "We often used to wonder just what did happen to Ham, didn't we, Jane? We always wondered just *how* it happened. Neither of us ever wondered if it really *had* happened."

Jane gave him a startled glance.

"But, Bim, there wasn't any doubt. He was officially presumed killed. You told me yourself that they wouldn't presume someone dead if there was the slightest chance they might be alive."

"That's right, unless some guy had been taken prisoner and we'd not been notified. Or lost his memory or gone underground."

"And we went on hoping till the war in Europe was over. By then, whoever came into that category would have turned up. You said so, Bim. You . . . you haven't heard any news . . . you couldn't have . . . ?" she broke off, staring at Bim as if she could not take her eyes off him for an instant.

"I *have* heard something, Jane. It's so darned difficult to tell you. It's so fantastic . . . yet it's true all right . . ."

"You mean . . . *he's alive*?" Jane broke in, her face chalk white and her hands trembling so violently that she had to put down the cigarette holder.

Bim nodded his head.

"But where? How? Bim, for heaven's sake tell me. Don't try to break it gently. Tell me what's happened? Is he ill? What's he doing?"

"Steady up, honey. I'll tell you all I can. Firstly, he's not ill. Not hurt in any way. I want to tell you what happened before anything else. I'm afraid you won't like it, Jane, so try and keep calm, honey. Just take a grip on yourself and bear with me."

"I'll keep calm!" Jane whispered. "Only tell me quickly, Bim. This suspense is dreadful. Please tell me!"

"It was like this," Bim said, looking down at the table and speaking slowly and clearly. "You'll recall when Ham went missing after that reconnaissance? Some guy stepped on a mine and four of the six were blown sky-high. Two got back and reported what had happened. Next day they found the bodies . . . three of them . . . or sufficient to identify them. But they didn't find Hamilton . . . nor his identity disc nor any other identification. They hoped he might have got away and didn't report him missing till the week after. But he didn't turn up. Eventually they reckoned he must have been nearest to the mine and presumed him killed. It was the obvious answer and nobody thought to doubt it. You weren't given the full details as they weren't very pretty, but I found all that out. I guessed you'd be happier just believing he'd been killed in action."

He lit another cigarette and went on without a pause, "He wasn't killed in action, Jane. He went out on that reconnaissance and slipped away from the others in the dark a few minutes before that guy hit the mine."

"Slipped away?" Jane asked. "You mean . . . ?"

"Deserted!" Bim said briefly. "Perhaps when you remember Ham's nature, it doesn't seem quite so bad as that word sounds. You know how restless he was. He got fed up with army life . . . hanging around camps and taking orders. Ham never much cared for discipline, did he? He was a roving kind of guy and even the occasional 'sorties' weren't sufficient excitement for him in the end. He wanted action . . . action all the time. He'd expected hand-to-hand fighting instead of which he hardly ever saw the enemy. He volunteered for anything that held a spice of danger . . . got a reputation for being the bravest man in the unit. And he was brave. It wasn't cowardice that made Ham desert. And he didn't run until after that reconnaissance. He went closer in to the enemy that night than any of the others and passed the information on to the officer in charge. Then on the way back he suddenly realized that there was a way of escape for him, escape from the boredom and discipline and frustrations of the life he had grown to hate. You know Ham, Jane. The idea came and two minutes later he transmitted it into fact. He just slipped away and hid until the others were well out of sight."

"But why? Where did he want to go? What did he go *for*?" Jane asked.

"He didn't know then. Didn't care. It was enough for him to know he was a free agent again. He made his plans as he went along. Got civilian clothes from some farmer, eventually teamed up with the resistance movement and fought against the Germans with them."

"But why didn't he stay with the American army if he wanted to go on fighting the Germans?" Jane asked. "I don't understand."

"It was more dangerous with the guerillas, more the kind of fighting Ham had wanted. Danger and more danger and the hand-to-mouth kind of life in caves in the hills that appealed to him. He liked the men he lived and fought with, learned the lingo, and although he was wounded slightly once, he always seemed to come out of the most dangerous situations unscathed. Gradually, the men kind of looked up to him as a sort of cat with nine lives. One day the leader got killed and Ham was voted in his place. From then on he planned the raids, gave the orders, was the chief. He had power, freedom and at the same time he was killing more Huns than practically any other man in the Allied armies. The army awarded him the Purple Heart for gallantry . . . posthumously. You hold the decoration, Jane, and believe me, Hamilton deserved it. He was quite fearless. He was almost a legendary figure out there and tales of his dare-devil fighting are still told . . . only he assumed another name and no one thought it might be Hamilton the guerillas spoke of, when they talked of their Yankee leader."

"He never wrote!" Jane said. "He could have let me know!"

"And risked having the army after him? They shoot deserters, Jane, in war-time. Or else imprison them. But he should have told us . . . you anyway."

"He didn't trust me!" Jane said. "Or else he didn't care."

"He cared, Jane. But you were a long way away, and he was living in a different world. I don't think he ever expected to come out of it alive. He gave no thought to the future . . . just lived from day to day. Then suddenly it was all over and he had to think. He was a hero all right but that was all. And he hadn't a dollar to his name. If he'd stayed in the army he'd have had a big bank roll. But no one paid the guerillas . . . they just looted when they wanted anything. And suddenly looting became taboo. By then Ham had got into Germany. He'd taken care to keep out of the way of the Allied armies. He had been living underground and he stayed there. He knew well enough that there was money to be made and he wanted money then. He wanted to get to America and start in business over there."

"You mean he went into the black market?"

Bim nodded his head.

"Just that! He'd tag on the end of the queues of G.I.s outside the P.X. stores and collect his ration along with them. No one asked for his identity cards. He was an American all right and he had a fine selection of G.I. uniforms. He'd do the round of the P.X. stores, army, air force, paratrooper, and take the stuff back to his hideout. The Huns would pay anything for a cigarette and Ham had plenty. He reckoned the army owed him some pay and he didn't give a damn about fleecing the Huns. They'd killed too many of his friends."

"And he's still there?" Jane asked, her hands gripping the edges of the table.

"No! Things got pretty hot. The military police got wind of him and he decided to beat it back to America. He got a passport of sorts and booked a passage back. You could still buy most things in the black market in those days, though it cost plenty, but Ham had plenty. By then he had dollars, too. But things weren't so easy in America. He might have given himself up to the army authorities but he was scared they would gaol him or something. Cost of living had gone up and his money went pretty fast. He'd put some capital into a small garage business which went bust and next thing he hadn't a nickel. He got a job but couldn't stick taking orders after so many years of giving them. He quit and got in with some bad guys. Next thing they framed him for a small robbery he hadn't done and the police were after him. Then he really got scared. Someone had turned in a description of him and he was afraid the police would discover who he really was. He got a job on the next boat out of New York as a steward and came to England. He's here now, Jane. He found out I was over here and tracked me down . . . reckoned I might know where to find you and that one or other of us might help him. He's in my rooms, honey, and it's up to you now. I didn't know if you wanted to see him or not, so I said I'd try to find you but wasn't sure I could. You can choose what to do, Jane. Remain as dead to him as he once was to you or else go to him. Which is it to be?"

"Here! In London! I can't believe it!" Jane whispered. "I never imagined anything like this. It's all so utterly incredible, Bim. He's alive. And here, in this country . . . in London . . . it just doesn't seem to make sense!"

"There's something else that'll be hard to reconcile yourself to, too," Bim said. "You've committed bigamy, Jane. You're not married to that husband of yours . . . whether you want to be or not. You're still married to Ham!"

"Not married!" Jane gasped, suddenly realizing this new fact and yet still unable to credit her own ears. "But Gareth . . . I mean . . . Bim, I just can't think straight. What am I going to do?"

"Try and keep calm, honey!" Bim said, smiling for the first time since he had started his story. "I know it's a shock. Believe me, I needed three neat whiskies when I set eyes on that guy. I needed another three when he told me what he'd been doing. I'm his friend, Jane, and I'll help him all I can, but that doesn't stop me admitting he's done wrong. He hasn't played fair by you or by his country, and he's broken American law. It's hard to judge him because he's such a singular guy, one doesn't seem to make the same rules for him. He sure must have got a touch of gipsy in him, I guess. He should have lived in the days of highwaymen or something. I don't know! But turning up the way he has done, although in a way typical of him, has certainly upset your life for you. And there's your future. I've no right to advise you, Jane, as I don't know what Ham's going to do with his life. But this much I do know for sure . . . if you don't want to share that life with him, I certainly wouldn't blame you. You owe him nothing at all. As for the legal side of the business, I guess you could get a divorce from him easily enough. The trouble would start, of course, once the authorities found out he was still alive."

"What . . . would happen to him?" Jane asked.

Bim shrugged his shoulders.

"Hard to say! The war's been over a long while. There's been an amnesty for deserters but Ham didn't know about it in time to get himself straightened out. Now the law is after him. They'd get him for that if not for desertion. You couldn't very well ask for a divorce from a man presumed dead unless you could prove he was alive. And as soon as you do that, out comes the whole incredible truth about him."

"I think I could do with another drink . . . a strong one!" Jane said. "I just don't seem to be able to grasp all this. I'm not dreaming, am I, Bim?"

"Guess not, honey, unless this whole life's a dream. Ham's no ghost, anyway. He's sitting in my rooms as large as life. But see here, Jane, as far as I'm concerned, if you want it that way, Ham can remain as dead to the world as they think him. If you just want to forget this all happened and go back to your Gareth, I shan't open my mouth and I'll see Ham doesn't. He owes it to you not to make trouble for you. I'll see him out of his present difficulties somehow or other. But he has no right to mess your life about now, after all this time."

"I would be committing bigamy knowingly then," Jane said slowly.

Bim shrugged his shoulders helplessly.

"It's one awful mess, Jane, I agree. Take your time and think it over. If you like, go home and talk it over with this husband you aren't married to. Ham can wait. He kept you waiting long enough."

"Tell Gareth?" Jane echoed. "No! I don't want to do that yet, Bim. I want to think it out myself. I don't know what I want to do about anything yet, but I do know I must see Ham. I have to see him, Bim. No matter what wrong he's done, it just doesn't seem to make any difference to my wanting to see him. Perhaps when I've done so I shall know what I feel about everything. Maybe it'll sort itself out. But I'm afraid, Bim. I'm terribly afraid."

Bim put out a hand swiftly and took Jane's cold fingers in his.

"There's no need to be frightened, honey. Nothing can happen to harm you. I'll be there alongside you. Besides . . ." he gave a grin . . . "Ham's no dangerous character for all he sounds like a bold bad villain. He really was framed in that robbery. The worst he's ever done was to pinch some stuff off a lorry, and when you remember that at one time it was his patriotic duty to do just that from the Germans, you can partially forgive him for doing so. He was always an unsettled kind of guy and the war completed the job. I guess there's plenty of fellows like him all over the world, Europe in particular, who are finding civilian life hard. They were heroes during the war and now they are law-breakers for doing just what they did then . . . killing, looting, smuggling, stealing. And Ham just hadn't the stability in his character to stand up to it all."

"My mind is whirling!" Jane said confusedly. "None of this seems real. I'm sure I shall wake up in a moment. It's like a kind of nightmare mixed up with dreaming. It's so wonderful that he's here . . . alive . . . and yet the things he has done . . . *and the way he's treated me*. It wasn't fair of him, Bim. If he'd loved me truly he'd have written to me . . . or if he couldn't do that, he could at least have sent for me when the war was over."

"To live underground in Germany? Conditions were appalling, Jane. You, least of anyone I know, were unfitted for the life he led out there."

"Then when he went to America!" Jane persisted. "But he'd forgotten all about me. And I was his wife!"

"Sure, honey, but it was several years since he'd seen you, remember? And what about yourself? You hadn't forgotten him, maybe, but you'd got over his 'loss' sufficiently to marry again."

"I thought he was dead!" Jane said. "That was different."

"And for all Ham knew, you, too, might have been dead. The bombing was pretty bad in this country and Ham had heard about it. But I'm not trying to put his case to you, Jane. I honestly don't want to influence you in any way at all. I'll leave Ham to speak for himself if you really mean to see him. It's between you and him now and all I have to do is to tell you again that I'll stand by you, Jane, whatever you decide to do. I have a feeling your Gareth will stand by you, too."

"Gareth!" Jane echoed, realizing that she had almost forgotten his existence. "Oh, Bim, what a ghastly muddle! If I'd been sure I loved Gareth I would know what to do. But I'm not sure. And I'm not sure about Ham either. Perhaps after I've seen him . . ." her voice trailed away uncertainly.

"Well, if it's to be tonight, I reckon we'd better get a move on," Bim said. "I think it would be a good idea, too, if we had something to eat first. You'll need to keep your strength up for the coming ordeal!"

For the first time, a smile flitted across Jane's face and a little colour came back into her cheeks.

"You will stay with me, Bim? Don't leave me alone with him. I'm so afraid . . ."

"Of falling in love with him all over again?" Bim asked with sudden intuition. "I see your point, Jane. It can't be much fun knowing that the guy you love isn't all you'd imagined he was. Ham has a lot to atone for . . . to you and to others. And you can't tell what the future will be, either. On one side you have a guy you don't really love who can offer security and a decent home and all the rest of it. And on the other . . . who knows?"

"What will he do, Bim?" Jane asked. "Will he give himself up? Would he have to go to prison? Or will he stay in hiding? What would I do with him? Besides, I don't even know that he wants me back. He probably doesn't give a row of pins for me now."

Bim smiled again and gave Jane's hand a quick squeeze.

"That's one thing I guess you needn't worry about," he said. "Just take a look in the glass, honey, and tell me if any man could resist the reflection? You were a pretty enough kid when he married you . . . and Ham wasn't the marrying kind, remember? . . . Now you're twice as pretty and you've got something else . . . poise, sophistication, worldliness . . . call it what you want. You're not the same perky little girl just out of school. *You* could manage *him* now . . . hold your own. He'll be nuts about you, Jane, leaving past sentiment out of it. But I guess that won't help you any. It's yourself you have to consider . . . and the guy you aren't married to after all."

"I know, I know!" Jane said. "But somehow Gareth doesn't seem to come into it, Bim. Maybe I'm selfish but I can't think of anything else but me just now . . . and Ham. And the fact that I feel all weak inside me."

"Nerves, excitement and hunger!" Bim diagnosed, pulling her very firmly to her feet. "We're going to eat, Jane, and then we'll take that car round to my rooms. So for the next quarter of an hour, don't think of anything else but food. You'll feel better when you've eaten. All set?"

"All set!" Jane said, collecting her handbag and gloves, and with her hand tucked firmly under his arm, she allowed herself to be led from the room, walking automatically and unable to stop that sinking sensation as if she were, after all, merely living in a dream.

Eighteen

After his talk with Jane, Jim found himself undergoing a variety of different emotions. For the first time in his life he actively disliked his young sister, and he could willingly have put her over his knee and spanked her, had he imagined it would do any good. But their interview had been pretty conclusive, Jim decided. He knew Jane too well to be under any deep delusions about her. She was, and always had been, a selfish and self-centred girl and now he knew that she was utterly egotistical as well. The whole world must revolve around her or else she was dissatisfied with life. No one could be more charming than Jane when she was the centre of the picture, but the charm gave place to a sullen, petulant determination to get her way at all costs, if she were not actually doing so.

But an hour or two after leaving her flat, Jim found himself a little less heated and a good deal calmer. He realized that his own impulsive actions had possibly only strengthened Jane in her determination to keep Gareth at all costs. But he had never for one moment when he had decided to go and plead Susan's and Gareth's cause with his sister, imagined that Jane already knew of their love for one another, far less accepted it and decided to ignore the whole thing.

It had shocked Jim to find Jane so callous . . . so utterly indifferent to anyone else's emotions but her own. He had been prepared to champion her always; to protect her and in this instance to comfort her and do his best to help her through what he realized must be a difficult period of her life. He had even foreseen her in tears, telling him that she loved Gareth too much to lose him . . . begging him, her brother, to help her win back Gareth's affections. But this had in no wise come to pass. Jane knew that Gareth loved Susan . . . knew, moreover, that Gareth had been doing his utmost for some time to put that love in the past and try to make amends to his wife. But Jim now knew that Jane no longer loved Gareth, if she ever had. He had wondered at her indifference, her hardness on occasions when he had noticed her treatment of her husband, but he had put it all down to temporary tiffs and Jane's selfishness and the spoiling she had always received. He had felt fairly confident that they would adjust themselves once Gareth stopped spoiling Jane and took a firmer hand with her.

Now it seemed unlikely that this could ever happen. Gareth would be suffering from a guilt complex and do everything in his power to make up to Jane for the loss of his affections, and Jane, in her turn, would be taking advantage of it whenever she possibly could. It seemed an unlikely prospect for future happiness for them. And Jim's sympathies were entirely with Gareth. He had seen Gareth's efforts to make Jane care for him, to settle down to a real marriage with possibly a child or two . . . had seen Jane in her light-hearted, uncaring fashion brush Gareth's love aside and welcome it only when she wished to gain something from it. Gareth had not seemed to worry too much at first and Jim believed that in his heart, the older man had always hoped Jane would "grow up" a little and settle down. He had seemed sensible and patient enough to wait for this event, when suddenly love had overtaken him in a way he could never have foreseen. Once that had happened, for a man of honour (as Jim well knew his brother-in-law to be) Jim could foresee nothing but the present impasse which had arisen. Jane did not intend to release Gareth nor would Gareth ask for his freedom. And Susan would have no part in sending any marriage on the rocks.

'If only they were both just a little less honourable and decent,' he thought with a wry smile, and with his heart hardening, 'and Jane more considerate of others!'

Nevertheless, Jim could not find it in his heart to condemn his sister's actions completely. No matter how she might choose to go about it, her efforts to keep her husband were only what every woman *should* do . . . try to find a common footing for the future, to keep the marriage intact. This he could understand and applaud, had Jane's motives in doing so really been for everyone's good and not just for her own. She had resolved to keep Gareth tied to her but not because she disapproved of divorce, not because she loved him, not because she intended to do all she could to win back his love. No, only because Gareth was useful to her, maintained her in a high standard of living such as she could not afford as a single woman, because it suited her to have him as an escort or host when she needed him, because she did not intend to let some other woman be as happy as she had failed to be with the man she had married.

'And what of the future?' Jim asked himself as he dined alone in his rooms. 'What of Susan, for whose sake I've been at loggerheads with my indescribable sister?'

Could he, he wondered, now consider himself justified in pressing his own suit with Susan? Would it be reasonable to suppose that there was no longer any hope for her and Gareth, and that consequently, he himself could at least make up to her a little for the blows life had dealt her? Would it be fair for him to try to get her to marry him . . . to win her affection if not her love?

For a long time Jim sat alone, thinking out the answer to this problem. At the back of his mind, he felt that Susan might in the end be persuaded by the very persistence of his own arguments, his love for her, to marry him. He felt that it was in his power to persuade her against her own judgment and for, this reason, he knew that the responsibility of doing so would be enormous. Her whole future as well as his own . . . not to speak of Teddy's, would lie at his door. If things went wrong only he would be to blame and although he himself did not consider divorce harmful between a man and woman who did not get along, his views differed where there were children. It could not do Ted any good to grow attached to him as his new father only to lose him again later.

But for all Jim argued with himself, deep in his heart he knew that he *must* ask Susan once more to marry him, must take that chance. He had tried his utmost by seeing Jane to make things right for Susan without thinking of himself, knowing that if Jane agreed to divorce Gareth, he himself would lose the one woman he had ever wanted to marry. But he had loved Susan sufficiently to put his own feelings aside for her sake. Somehow, now that he had failed to achieve anything but failure, he could not rid himself of the thought that this was what Fate intended . . . that now he had done what he could, it left him free to try to get Susan to marry him if she would.

Until the early hours of the morning, Jim sat by the open window of the tiny sitting-room overlooking the rooftops of London. It was a hot, airless night and even when darkness fell there was a restlessness in the warm night air that was not conducive to sleep even had his mind been able to relax. He had studied closely a snapshot of Susan and Teddy taken one weekend at her cottage. She was wearing one of those cool, crisp, cotton frocks that made her look younger and at the same time more poised, more graceful than ever. The short dark hair fell boyishly over her forehead and yet in no way detracted from her femininity. Susan was one hundred per cent a woman . . . the kind of girl whom one might see pictured in those exotic glossy-paged American magazines. Sometimes they would be short, slight, blonde girls with laughing eyes and mischievous gamine expressions and sometimes . . . those Susan reminded him of . . . tall, slender, mysterious . . . with eyes that seemed to contain the world's secrets, and a wistful mouth that bespoke both sadness and a sympathetic understanding of life. Perhaps he only imagined that "haunting" quality . . . having seen Susan only when she had been endeavouring to hide her love for Gareth and her unhappiness from the world. Certainly he had only glimpsed occasionally those brief moments of gaiety when her dark eyes widened into a smile and her face became radiant and glowing. At these times she had seemed to him more beautiful, more dangerously attractive than ever. He wanted to be the man to bring back the smile to her eyes for always, to hear her soft, low laugh, and see her face filled with happiness.

'I can do it!' Jim told himself. '*I must do it!* It does not matter that she loves Gareth. In time she will forget him and my love will be sufficient for us both. Somehow I shall win her love . . . make her happy!'

Then the die was cast, for he knew now that he must at least try to do these things he so ardently desired . . . that he could no longer prevent himself from proposing to her again and again if need be . . . until she had really destroyed all his hopes by her unending refusals.

So it was that a determined, serious-faced Jim set off in his car the following day to put into action the first plan of his campaign.

Today was Susan's birthday, an event he had been looking forward to until he had learned the truth and decided to try to bring Susan and Gareth together. He had, over a month ago, bought an elaborate diamond and emerald engagement ring . . . one which he hoped Susan would accept as a birthday present if she refused to accept it for its real purpose. Before he had been to his sister, he had locked the ring away, believing he would not after all have the pleasure of presenting it to Susan. Now it lay in his breast pocket and with the new, bright, sunny day, his hopes were high and his heart was beating swiftly. Gone was last night's indecision. In its place was a determination to fight for the woman he loved with everything in his power, just as he would do everything possible to make her and her son happy, if she ever agreed to marry him.

His arrival at the cottage was greeted with a rather wan smile from young Ted, who looked pale and tired and in no way his usual energetic, buoyant self. Susan was not in the garden and in spite of his impatience to see her, Jim forced himself to stop for a moment or two for a word with Ted.

"Is Mummy having a nice birthday so far?" he asked, putting a hand on the boy's shoulder.

"I'd rather not talk about it!" was Ted's mumbled reply.

Jim's eyebrows shot up.

"Wasn't the present a success?" he asked, and as there was no reply, he tried again with a jocular, "You never told me what you finally bought for her, Ted."

But the boy tugged his arm away from Jim's restraining hand and to his surprise, darted off down to the far end of the garden into a clump of bushes and out of sight.

It seemed unfair to follow him, since the boy so obviously wished not to talk to Jim, so he left him alone and went slowly into the house. There was no sign of Susan in the sitting-room and it was only as he crossed the hall that Jim knew where to find her. His heart sank together with his hopes, as he paused uncertainly, listening to the low sobbing that came from the kitchen. Susan . . . crying . . . it seemed so utterly despairing, so hopeless that it struck a cold shiver down his spine. He remained hesitantly in the hall, not wishing to intrude and yet longing to go to her . . . to try to comfort her . . . to hear what it was that had further distressed her.

Impulsively, he took a step or two forward and the next minute he was striding into the kitchen and Susan's dark head was on his shoulder as she clung to him, grateful for the strong pair of arms that went around her, for the comforting flow of words he poured into her ear.

"Don't, darling, please don't!" he was saying. "You'll make yourself ill. Nothing can be as bad as all that. It'll all come right. I'm going to take care of you from now on. Nothing shall hurt you again. Only please . . . darling, please don't cry."

Gradually the tension within her eased and the tears fell more slowly. Jim released his hold of her and tried to raise her face, but she kept it bowed with a typically feminine gesture.

"I must look frightful, Jim!" she whispered in a small, choked little voice.

"Then pop upstairs and repair the damage if you want to, my sweet!" Jim said with a grin. "While you're gone I'll put the kettle on for a cup of tea. I'm told that is the remedy for any woman's ailments!"

"You're a dear, Jim!" Susan said, and hurried away to her room to freshen up her face.

She felt terribly ashamed that Jim should have found her in such a state, but somehow the sleeplessness of last night, together with the burning shame of Ted's so very much misplaced good intentions and his unhappy little face over the breakfast table when he wished her a happy birthday . . . had all been too much for her. She had wanted to appear happy, cheerful, unaffected by what he had done, but her smiles were as forced as her words and Ted knew her too well to be deceived. Her own unhappiness she could bear . . . give way to in the darkness and privacy of her bedroom, but to think that she was responsible for Ted's white face, for the dark circles beneath his eyes, for the questioning, anxious way he looked at her . . . had sapped her control, and when he had disappeared into the garden, she had sat down at the kitchen table and cried as if her heart could no longer hold the pain it had to suffer. Jim's arrival, if untimely, had nevertheless forced her to take a hold of herself and now she could feel a little better for the relief of those tears . . . filled with fresh determination to make this birthday of hers a happy one for Ted's sake. Birthdays were so important to him . . . even other people's. And with Jim's help, bless him! . . . the day could yet be turned into a success instead of continuing the failure it had begun.

'Dear Jim!' Susan thought, as she walked slowly downstairs to rejoin him. 'He's so very good to me and I *am* fond of him. In a way I almost love him . . . even if it isn't the same kind of love I feel for . . .' she broke off her train of thought quickly. Gareth's name must never be mentioned again . . . not even to herself. Once she had been able to think of him without pain, without any loss of pride, for there had been no shame in loving him when the secret was her own. It seemed that for always in future the hot colour would flood her cheeks when she thought of Ted's behaviour yesterday. Half the tragedy had been that he had, after all, only desired her happiness . . . wanted her to have what *she* most wanted. She had tried to deceive Gareth into thinking she no longer cared . . . had imagined she had succeeded only to have Ted reveal the secret out-pourings of her heart. She would never know how much Ted had read of her diary . . . how much he had understood or repeated. She could not bear to ask him nor face any further loss of pride. It was bad enough that Gareth knew the truth and so much worse if Jane, too, had heard the reason for Ted's unexpected visit. She had not asked Gareth if Ted spoke to Jane alone, for she had not known until after Gareth had gone what had happened up there. Now she would never know, for she would not talk to Ted about it further. Best that he should forget the whole incident . . . forget it as she must do and as she hoped Gareth and Jane would do.

Jim had made the tea when Susan returned and she drank it gratefully, a little of her natural colour returning to her face as she did so. She sat down in one of the basket chairs beside Jim's and lit the cigarette he gave her.

"Please forgive me, Jim! I'm very ashamed of myself!" she said.

Quickly, Jim's hand covered her own and he held it for a moment as he said, "There's nothing to forgive, Susan. Do you want to talk about it? Perhaps if you told me it might help?"

Susan shook her head.

"Just . . . general depression!" she said. "It's best forgotten. It was silly of me to give way like that . . . and Teddy'll be upset if he sees I've been crying. He thinks birthdays are a special kind of magic when everyone is simply bound to have a good time."

"He didn't seem any too happy just now," Jim admitted. "I asked him what he'd given you for a birthday present and he shot off like a rabbit without saying a word."

Susan bit her lip.

"We'd both rather you didn't mention that. He . . . chose something . . . rather unfortunate. It upset him . . . and me."

"That's a shame!" Jim said, forbearing to ask for further details. "Do you think it would make him feel better if he could get something else? Something you do want?"

"That's a sweet suggestion, Jim, but I don't really want anything. Still, it might help matters."

"We'll go together, just he and I, and choose something in the village," Jim said. "But before we do that, I've something for you myself, Susan. I doubt this is the right moment to give it to you but . . . well, I don't suppose any time is the right one in one way. Anyway, here it is, Susan, with all my love and my best wishes for this year and the years to come."

And he took the small parcel from his pocket and handed it to Susan.

She did not open it at once but held it in her long, slender fingers, staring at it as if she were trying to guess its contents. But she knew what it must be . . . as Jim knew she must know. Neither of them spoke until at last Jim said, "Won't you open it, Susan? It would make me so happy if you'll wear it. I know what you are thinking . . . that it would be unfair . . . I've thought of all your arguments in advance. But don't consider my side of it, Susan. I can take care of myself. I know how you feel and if I still wish to do this, surely it is my responsibility and not yours to worry about my side of it! It is your feelings that matter, Susan . . . whether you are fond enough of me to bear with me, to give me a chance. I know I'm no superman! I can't even offer you very much except my love . . . and a promise to do everything in my power to make you and Ted happy. I'm only asking for a chance to do this, Susan. Won't you give it to me?"

"Jim! I don't know what to say. Last night I decided that I would agree to marry you if you still wanted me to do so. But my motives were selfish." Susan's hands clenched round the small box as she remembered her feelings. "That was unfair of me and this morning I know that that reason doesn't count. Don't ask me to explain what it was, for I can't speak about it."

"The reason wouldn't matter, Susan, my dear sweet child!" Jim said with a smile. "It would be enough for me that you said 'yes'!"

For a moment a smile fleeted Susan's face, only to recede and leave her serious and thoughtful once more.

"Can it ever be right to marry someone you don't . . . that you aren't in love with?" she asked, her voice so quiet Jim had to strain forward to catch her words.

"How can I answer that question for you?" he countered. "I've had no experience of marriages, Susan! Except those of my friends. Sometimes it seems to me that the happiest marriages are those which are marriages of convenience arranged by parents."

"But then neither partner loves the other!" Susan said.

"Maybe love doesn't always make for happiness though," Jim argued. "Perhaps a marriage based on affection stands a better chance. I'm hoping so because that is all I ask of you, Susan. I think you are . . . fond of me?"

"I am, Jim!" Susan said fervently. "Too fond of you to help you to do something either of us might regret. You are guided right now by your heart and I am trying to be guided by my head."

"But it is what *your* heart says that matters!" Jim cried. "Surely that is the only thing that matters, Susan."

"My heart does not belong to me!" Susan whispered. "Gareth took it into his keeping without intending to do so. Now I would give anything in the world if he would only leave my heart alone. He does not try to imprison it and yet it is as surely with him as if he asked for it in words. It has no right to be there, but against both our wills it remains there. I have no heart to feel with, Jim, no heart to offer you."

"I know that, Susan. I know you love him. Somehow I can't hate him for that as that I suppose I should. I've always liked Gareth and the trouble is I can see all too clearly why you do love him. But that is now, Susan, today; what of the future? Time, surely, will help? And I want to help, too . . . in any way I can. Couldn't you ever forget?"

"I don't know, Jim. That's the whole trouble. I've tried, God knows! And yet I do not seem able to do so."

"Because you are too much alone. You live too much in your thoughts. And this place has far too many memories. Let me take you away, Susan. I'll fill your life with new things . . . new thoughts . . . help you to start again."

"I wish I could be sure that it would be right of me to let you do those things, Jim. I want to forget, I've been bitterly unhappy, lonely, miserable. I would like to be able to laugh again, to enjoy life as I used to do, to be carefree and at peace with myself and the world. You are opening a door, perhaps, to all these things and I am so very much tempted to forget what it is you are really offering me . . . marriage. One should not marry to escape something unpleasant. One should marry because one wishes the happiness of the other more than anything else . . . because happiness for oneself is impossible apart from them, as would be theirs apart from you."

"And if you refuse me, Susan, what then?" Jim asked quietly. "Will it be more 'right'? Will you be happy continuing as you are? Will I be happy without you? Will even Ted be happier than if you married me? And if the answer to these questions is no, then logically it must be right to do as I suggest."

Again that quick smile brightened Susan's face as she said, "Somehow I do not think you are a very logical person, Jim! But that is hardly important. I am fond of you . . . deeply fond. I think perhaps we might find a certain happiness together. But what worries me always is that where there is no alternative for me (for as you say I cannot find happiness in my present life), for you the chances are much greater. You are very young, Jim . . . and handsome . . . no, don't joke about it . . . you must be attractive to many women, and you are so very, very nice. In time you would get over me, find some other girl . . . someone who could love you as you deserve to be loved."

"But those girls . . . women . . . they wouldn't be you, Susan. It is *you* I want to marry. If you care to put it this way, in spite of all the disadvantages you speak of. To see you happy would mean more to me than the love of fifty other women!"

"Oh, Jim, don't flatter me too much or you'll make me cry again!" Susan cried. "I wish you didn't love me quite so much . . . that we could just be the best of friends. I don't want to be responsible for hurting you!"

"Then open my present to you and wear it, Susan, because if you don't you'll hurt me dreadfully!" Jim said triumphantly. And as she still hesitated, he took both her hands, holding them tightly in his own. "This needn't bind you in any way, Susan. It is only an engagement ring and you can name the duration of that engagement . . . a year, if you wish, longer. If at any time you feel it wouldn't make you happy . . . or wouldn't be right to go through with it, then you have only to say so . . . I wouldn't try to hold you to an engagement. I just ask that you should look on it as a period of trial . . . of seeing in all sorts of little ways if you think it will work out. Surely that can do no harm, my dear, cautious, serious Susan! At least if in the end you decide not to marry me, I shall have had the satisfaction of knowing I was engaged to the most wonderful girl in the world, and that you cared sufficiently for me to give it a trial."

Jim's ardent, persuasive words brought down the last of Susan's defences. She was still not convinced that she was doing the right thing . . . still not certain that it was fair to Jim . . . that she herself really wanted this. And yet, seen in the light of a trial, the engagement did not after all appear so binding, so serious a matter. It would be between Jim and herself . . . no public notices or celebrations attached to it. It could, if it didn't work out, be as quietly broken as it had started.

"All right, Jim!" she said softly. "And . . . I'll try . . . to make it work . . . to make a fresh start!"

Her eyes were very bright and she was never closer to loving him than when he pressed his lips to her hands, and though he must have longed to do so at this moment of her surrender, he forbore to kiss her lips with an instinctive understanding that Gareth's kisses were yet not far enough in the past for her to want them from some other man.

When Jim raised his eyes to hers he saw a tenderness in them which gave him a swift surge of joy.

"Open it, Susan. Then I can take that small son of yours down to the village to choose you another present and make him happy, too!" he begged.

But as Susan's fingers felt for the string round the little parcel and Jim stood expectantly beside her, the shrill ring of the telephone intruded upon them. It rang again . . . and a third time, each time seeming louder, more insistent.

"I'd better answer it," Susan said. "I can't understand who can be ringing. I won't be a moment, Jim."

As she walked swiftly out of the room, Jim rose slowly to his feet and without being fully aware of it, his hand went out as if even now he would restrain her from leaving him. For in his heart there was another bell ringing . . . a warning that had no reason and yet which would not be denied. The ring was not yet on Susan's finger, and this could be Fate having decided it had no right to be there. Only a moment ago they had been so close, mentally as well as physically. Now it seemed as if every moment widened the gap between them.

Jim stood rooted to the same spot, unmoving, holding in his hands the parcel which Susan had thrust back at him as she hurried away to answer the phone.

Nineteen

In spite of the sustaining meal Bim had forced her to eat, Jane still felt empty . . . hollow in the pit of her stomach. She had not, since her wedding day . . . the day she had married Ham, felt so nervous and completely unsure of herself.

Now, as she stood beside Bim in the lift that was carrying her upwards towards the man who had once (no, was still) her husband, she felt the palms of her hands damp within the long white gloves and knew that she was trembling.

"Steady!" Bim said quietly, his hand on her arm. By the nerves jumping beneath it, by Jane's pallor and unusual gravity, he had guessed more than a little of the strain she was undergoing. It could, after all, be no easy decision for her. Everything he had himself recounted to her of the years since she had last seen her husband could only point to the fact that Ham was hopelessly unstable . . . that the laws of man took second place to the laws he made for himself which were, in fact, the outcome of his nature. Hamilton had always been restless . . . a rolling stone who, but for the strength of purpose and intelligence, would undoubtedly have 'gathered no moss'. But the strength of character that vied with the weak, unstable side of his nature, had provided him with the impetus to excel at anything he undertook. He must do things well or he did not care to do them at all . . . and once begun, he would see a job through until he felt he had mastered it. Ham must be the master . . . the one to rule his own life, for he could not be ruled by others.

And what, Bim asked himself, had the results of this contrary nature brought to the man? Not ultimate success. Brave as had been his exploits with the guerillas, these were long over and, by most ordinary people, long since forgotten. The world could so easily forget the sacrifice men made in wartime . . . the courage and daring and initiative they had shown. Already it was once more a commercial world. The successes were the men who stuck at their jobs, made money, attained important positions in official or business circles. And far from doing this, Hamilton had defied the law, was a "wanted" man . . . wanted by both the army and the American civil courts, whose laws he had thrust aside. Maybe even now the police knew of his escape to England and had started the finger of English law pointing in Ham's direction.

Undoubtedly, Bim decided, most men would condemn Hamilton. He had thrown away the advantages given him at birth, the exceptional intelligence, the ability to do well at practically anything he undertook, his immense good health and physique. Perhaps he would have succeeded better had he had to fight a little harder for the things he had wanted in his youth. Maybe success had come too easily to Hamilton and he had ceased to respect the ordinary man in the street and the laws made for his benefit.

Bim shrugged his shoulders in a gesture of indecision. It was so easy to condemn, but when one knew a man as well as he had known Hamilton, one could so easily make excuses. For one thing, he had an unusual charm which enabled him to make many friends among men and which made him irresistible to most women. This charm was partly due to the fact that whatever the results, his motives were well meant. He wanted others to be happy as much as he desired to be happy himself, and he would go to as much trouble for a friend as he would to achieve his own immediate idea of happiness.

It was this charm, this desire to please that had won Jane so inevitably to Ham's side. Bim had watched the romance blossom and in his turn been surprised that two such happy-go-lucky people should take one another so seriously. But they had fallen in love, each for the first time in their lives loving another more than they cared for themselves. The spoilt, pretty child that

Jane had been, developed into a woman with only one object in life . . . to keep her young husband happy and content and herself as near to him as she could. It had been part of Ham's temperament to have a 'roving eye' but in his heart he loved Jane, and Bim had known she need have no cause for jealousy of other women even if she had not known it herself.

The surprising thing, Bim considered, was that Hamilton had put all thought of Jane aside when he decided to desert from the American Army. And later, his actions had proved that he had no intention of sending for her nor returning to her. Of course, neither of these actions would have been easy under the circumstances and no doubt Ham had found his life full enough without women on the path he had chosen for himself. But he had conveniently thrust aside any responsibilities he ever had for his young English wife and for this reason, Bim felt that Jane's decision was indeed a hard one.

He did not doubt that Jane still loved her husband . . . that she was afraid of the repercussions of a meeting after all these years. She quite clearly did not love the man she had later married believing Ham to be dead; and even before she knew of Ham's existence once more, she had been discontented with her present life. There was nothing to keep her with Gareth . . . away from Ham other than the knowledge that with him she could have a guarantee of a secure and settled future. Hamilton had no definite future . . . unless one considered the idea that he should give himself up to the authorities, serve whatever punishment was due to him and start again. And it seemed improbable that a girl of Jane's nature, having led a life of comparative luxury these last years, would have the strength of character to stick by him, wait for him, help him to begin again.

Alternatively, Ham could remain "in hiding" . . . go across to Europe where he would be unlikely to be traced among so many millions of displaced persons. He could start afresh there and try to make something of the life so wasted until now. And this again must mean insecurity for Jane.

These thoughts flashed through Bim's mind in the few minutes before he stood with Jane outside the door of his rooms where Hamilton was waiting for them. Many similar reflections had crossed Jane's mind but with less clarity, for she found herself reverting always to the present . . . to the moment when she would actually see Hamilton again. Even now she could hardly believe it was all true . . . that he was there, behind the door, her rightful husband.

Then Bim's hand was on the door knob and as it swung open, a man turned quickly from the open window, looking over Bim's shoulder to where Jane stood, unmoving, behind him.

For a long moment they stood thus in silence, the three of them, only Bim's head turning from one face to another as they gazed deep into one another's eyes. He heard Jane's whisper as she spoke Ham's name, noticed that all the colour had returned to her cheeks which were now flushed a feverish pink. Then Hamilton stepped past him and as Bim turned away, took the trembling girl into his arms. Silently, Bim went out through the open door and closed it softly behind him.

"Oh, Jane, Jane, my little honey!" Ham cried, pressing her closer to him only to release her almost immediately to stare down into her face. "It is you . . . really you!" he murmured, and his finger traced the delicate contour of her face, as if by touching her, feeling her, he could remember her the better. "You've changed . . . you're more beautiful than ever . . . oh, Jane . . . I'd surely forgotten how lovely you are!"

She could not speak yet . . . only in her turn study the suntanned face of the man who was a stranger to her and yet so very familiar, his burning dark eyes, flashing with that vitality and excitement that found its echo in her own heart. But those eyes had deep lines around them now as there were around that mischievous little-boy mouth. Ham, too, had changed, grown older, become more a man and less the boy she had married. Even the short, square nose, bridged with freckles, was now set deeper, so it seemed, into his face. He was thinner, and with a pang in her heart, Jane felt rather than saw that so much of his former buoyancy had gone.

Her heart began to stifle her with its hurried beating. Every nerve in her body seemed acutely aware of the touch of his hands, his arms as they held her. There seemed to Jane to be a current of electricity between them, flaring, startling, exciting . . . drawing them closer and closer until his face blurred before her eyes in that instant before his mouth came down on hers in a hard, compelling, desperate kiss.

'I love him!' Jane thought. 'I've always loved him. I had forgotten what this meant to me . . . what power he has over me. Oh, Ham, Ham, how could I have forgotten. I love you, love you.'

Against her lips he murmured the same words.

"Only you, Jane . . . never anyone else. I thought I had forgotten. I thought I didn't need women in my life but I need you, want you, my darling . . . Oh, honey, I love you . . . so much . . . so much!"

He led her across to the deep armchair and took her on his lap, marvelling anew at the smallness of her, the light fairy quality that had entranced him when first he met her. His hands moved over her body, remembering, delighting, awaking her to a response that she herself had hardly believed herself capable of feeling.

She clung to him, her heart still too full for her to speak, her eyes, her lips telling him all that he longed to know. He had come to England in the main to escape, but at the back of his mind he had hoped, not only for help from Bim, but for a sentimental reunion with Jane. He had not entirely forgotten her, nor the power she had once had to attract him as no other woman had ever done. Often in the war he had thought of and longed for her physically, only to forget her again in some new more immediate activity until solitude brought her once again to his mind.

That she must by now have remarried he had never stopped to consider until he decided impulsively to come back to her country . . . to places where she might be found. Then questions had flooded through him . . . unanswered until Bim had given him the story of her life. He had felt a wild, acute jealousy of the man she had married whose wife she still at that moment believed herself to be. He did not know how much he still loved her then, and now . . . seeing her again, holding her like this . . . it was as if the years between had never existed. She belonged to him as she could never have belonged to any other man. She was his wife, *his* . . . and although he could see the force of Bim's reasoning that she owed him nothing after the way he had treated her, nevertheless he knew that he could not step out of her life now without a fight. She might cling to him at this moment of reunion, surrender herself to his impassioned embraces, offer her lips to receive his kisses, but he wanted more now than this physical surrender. He wanted complete possession of her heart once more . . . to bind her to him as he had done the day he married her . . . he who had once believed himself incapable of marrying!

Abruptly, he released her and with hands that were strong, determined and yet curiously gentle, he turned her face upwards so that he could look deep into those cornflower blue eyes.

"Jane, I must know . . . I must hear you say it . . . you don't love . . . you can't love . . . ?"

"Gareth?" Jane finished for him. Her eyes dropped and her fingers went childishly to the buttons on his shirt, moved to the collar that opened at the neck, revealing the brown throat. She felt her heart twist anew at the pulse throbbing there . . . throbbing in time to her own breathless heart. *This* man was her husband . . . the man she loved. Gareth now seemed the ghost . . . the unreality. For her, as for Ham, the years between this moment and their last parting were non-existent. And yet still she could not speak of this. She could understand Ham's jealousy of Gareth, for she herself had felt her heart lift when he had told her there had been no other woman in his life. Yet he deserved to suffer a little . . . suffer as she had done when she had believed him lost to her for ever.

"He's been . . . a wonderful husband to me!" she murmured, looking at Hamilton through her lashes and seeing the shot go home.

"He was never your husband, Jane. Don't torture me, honey. I know I deserve it, but tell me you hadn't quite forgotten me . . . that you still care a little bit?"

"I was heart-broken when I thought you had died!" Jane said slowly. "I thought my life was over . . . finished. Gareth picked up the pieces and put them together for me. You destroyed my happiness, Ham. He renewed it."

"Then you do love him? You are happy with him?" Ham asked, between lips that had set in a hard line of disappointment. "This means nothing more to you than . . . than just that physical bond between us?"

"We were always attracted to one another in that way, weren't we?" Jane countered adroitly, happy and yet miserable in the knowledge that he was indeed suffering now. "It is something that we feel whenever we look at one another . . . and yet so easily forgotten out of sight."

"That isn't true, Jane. I've remembered a thousand times. But that can't be all . . . it can't be. I love you, Jane. I've treated you abominably . . . I've been a heel and I've nothing to offer you now, nothing at all. I can't ask you to come away with me . . . start life again. I haven't the right, but I must know if you still care . . . still love me just a little. Tell me only that and I'll disappear again and leave you alone. Is that what you want me to do, Jane . . . to go away and leave you to resume the life you have made for yourself without me?"

Jane was silent, knowing that this moment was not after all one for evasions, for toying with Ham's feelings, for "getting her own back" on him for his treatment of her. He had, when she considered it, been a bad husband . . . turned out to be anything but reliable . . . a quality which was foremost in Gareth's character. As Ham himself had said, he had nothing to offer her, no right even to ask her to leave Gareth and all *he* gave her; to go to Ham now would mean an end to the life she had so carefully built around herself . . . her friends, parties, extravagant mode of living, her fashionable clothes, her social position. Ham was not only penniless, he was a kind of criminal. To go with him would be madness and yet was it not, after all, just this very uncertainty that attracted her? Wasn't it this side of Ham's nature that had so attracted her to him . . . his sudden unpremeditated plans to do this or that . . . go here or there . . . throw up into the air the tickets for the ballet and in the next instant buy new ones for an ice show? It was this never quite knowing what the next day would bring, that had made her life as Ham's wife so exciting, so utterly free of the boredom these last years had so often threatened. Had she not, after all, built this new, secure, frivolous society life about herself just to counteract that boredom . . . that security?

'But he might leave me again!' a voice whispered caution in her ear. 'I could not be sure that he would not tire of me . . . disappear again and leave me to make my own life once more without him.'

But at the back of her mind, her vanity would not permit this thought. She was older now, more experienced. This time she would know how to keep Hamilton firmly at her side. There would be no war to force the initial parting. Where he went, she too, could go. She could make his life so happy, revolving around her, that he would find he could not do without her.

'It's madness even to consider it!' spoke that voice again. 'Everyone would say I was crazy! Even Bim would think so!'

Nevertheless, the world could not know how her heart could throw those cautions to the winds. "Go with him!" it said. "You love him . . . you need him as he needs you. You were meant for one another . . . you were always happy with him. Give him another chance. You could not face the old life with Gareth whom you don't love . . . not now you know *he* is alive."

Impulsively she flung her arms round his neck, pressing her cheek against his, her voice low and vibrant as she cried, "I do love you, Ham. I always have. I always will. Nothing else matters but us. Nothing else. Don't leave me . . . ever again. If you go, I'll come with you. I don't mind anything else so long as I can be with you."

For a long instant he held her triumphantly, victoriously, his heart aflame at her words. She was his . . . all his . . . as much now as on the day he had married her. She loved him . . . would go with him in spite of everything. It was a moment of supreme glory for him . . . of exultation. Then as she lay pressed against his heart, his own feelings betrayed him. Jane . . . his Jane . . . was still such a child. Beneath that new sophistication she had not, after all, altered so much. She was still the happy-go-lucky kid fearlessly throwing her lot in with his . . . guided by her emotions and not by reason. A new and unaccustomed feeling of responsibility assailed him. He felt bitterly ashamed and remorseful for the way he had treated her. No matter how often circumstances had led him further and further from her, he should have returned to her; or at least let her know he was still alive. He knew she had suffered . . . been lost, lonely, unhappy as Bim had told him. And now he was contemplating taking her away from that life she had built up for herself without him . . . taking her away from some other guy who no doubt took good care of her, treated her better than he, Ham, had ever done. He was taking her to a life about which he knew nothing whatever. He had no plans, no money, nothing but a will to make something of his life after all. It would mean work . . . hard work, self-denial . . . many hardships, and it was this life he had without thinking, persuaded Jane to accept.

"I can't do it, Jane!" he said aloud, all the life gone from his voice, which was almost expressionless, so dead did it sound. "It wouldn't be fair to you. I had no right to come back into your life . . . to upset it in this way. I should have remained 'dead' to you. I can't take you with me . . ."

She was sitting upright now, staring at him with a face white with anxiety and apprehension.

"Then you weren't serious? You don't still love me after all?"

"Love you!" Ham cried. "That's just it. I've only this moment realized I love you far too much, honey, to let you throw everything away for me. Don't you see, Jane, I've nothing to offer you, *nothing*. Even my name I can't use . . . I must be ashamed of. Deserter . . . criminal . . . those are the tags on the end of that name I once gave you so proudly. I'm no good, Jane . . . no use to myself, let alone to you."

"But if you love me, I don't care about anything else!" Jane said wildly. "I don't mind about names . . . or anything like that. It's you I want, Ham. It's you I love no matter what you've done!"

He caught her to him then, straining her close against him with a desperate strength, for he felt in his heart that having found her so newly it must in the end only be to lose her once again.

"Fool, fool that I was!" he murmured brokenly. "If only I had foreseen . . . thought that one day . . . Oh, Jane, Jane, what are we going to do?"

She felt instinctively that he was weakening . . . that he, who had always been the stronger of the two, was at this moment the weaker. This reawakened love for him, so much deeper now that she was older, gave her strength to fight for it, for herself, for the man she loved.

"We'll find a way somehow, Ham. If we love each other truly nothing else matters . . . nothing! Bim will think of something. We'll go away . . . start again . . . anything you like . . . only I couldn't bear it if you left me now."

The cry came from her heart . . . the heart that had remained so deaf to Gareth's call. Her thoughts were now all for Ham, regardless of herself, she, who had always been so self-centred, so selfish! Love . . . true love, lent her qualities that were not basically part of her nature. For Ham she could brave all things . . . be all things.

Her eyes blazing, her face alight with determination, she released herself from Ham's grasp and ran swiftly to the door. She flung it open and nearly fell over Bim, who was sitting patiently in the hallway smoking a cigarette. The sight of him squatting on the floor gave her a momentary desire to laugh hysterically, but she controlled herself.

"Guess I thought it better not to intrude!" he said, grinning up at her.

"Oh, Bim, you fool!" Jane said, holding out a hand to assist him to his feet. "These are your rooms . . . and you sit in the hall!"

"Then it's okay to come in now?" he asked.

"I've come here to fetch you, Bim!" Jane said eagerly. "You've got to help us. We must think of something. You see . . . I love him, Bim. I was afraid . . . but that doesn't matter now. We love each other. You've got to think of an idea for us . . . tell us what to do."

Bim walked into the room and with a friendly grin at Ham, said, "You sure don't deserve this, my lad! But seeing that the damage is done, then I'll do my best to help you both. But first I want a drink!"

A few minutes later they were seated beside one another, Jane and Ham holding hands tightly, and Bim was speaking to them with an unusually serious expression on his face.

"It's this way, Ham!" he was saying. "To my way of thinking, and I'm going to be frank, you've made a pretty awful mess of things all round. First, you shouldn't have deserted, doggone it! Then, having done so, you should have given yourself up. Failing that, you owed it to your wife to let her know, somehow, you were alive. Failing that, you should have returned to her when the war in Europe was over. Failing even that, you should never have gone to Germany but come back to the States and given yourself up then. In fact, you've gone from the frying pan into the fire all along the line. And lastly, you had no right to come back at *this* stage, for Jane."

"But that wasn't my motive for coming over here . . . not the reason I came . . ." Ham began, but Bim interrupted him.

"Nevertheless, over here, you had to give way to sentiment and without thought for the future once more, you insist I produce Jane for you. Well, that's that! I guess I know when to throw in my hand. Cupid shines in both your faces! But what I'm trying to get at is this, Ham. You've done a lot of harm to a lot of people, yourself, too, and Jane not least. It's within your power to make amends . . . to start again . . . if you've got courage . . . and I think you have it in you. Give yourself up, Ham. Take what's coming to you like a man and start over again. If Jane really cares about you, she'll see you through . . . wait for you, help all she can. If she doesn't . . . then that's your misfortune. But you'll go on being a failure . . . perhaps go downhill altogether unless you get back on the right road pronto! That's my advice and nothing either of you can say will alter it!"

There was silence while Ham stared down at his hands, lost in thought and oblivious to Jane's and Bim's gaze on him. Presently he looked up at Bim and said, "Then I must take the rap for the job I didn't do? I really was framed in that robbery, Bim. Honest to goodness I hadn't a thing to do with it! I know I've plenty else to atone for but I feel pretty bitter about a gaol sentence for something I didn't do!"

"If you didn't do it, Ham, a good barrister will prove it. I'll put up the necessary for your defence . . . do everything I can to help you."

"I . . . I can help, too!" Jane said soberly. "I shall have a little money. Gareth would . . ."

"He won't do a darned thing!" Ham said violently. "That's asking a bit much of him, Jane. I couldn't accept a nickel from him."

"You won't need to," Bim said reassuringly. "I've plenty. Now how about it, Ham? What's your answer?"

"There's no . . . alternative?" Jane asked quietly. "I mean . . . if we went to Europe as you said . . . ?"

The look on Bim's face caused her to break off into silence.

"It's no basis for building a new life. Running away never helped anyone, Jane. Besides, he hasn't done so much harm. We can even hope to get him off completely when the record of his service in Italy is known. When it's all over, you can go back to the States and he can get a job. Whatever you do, you can succeed, Ham. You know you can. And I'll be right behind you both."

"I'd . . . be . . . waiting . . . too," Jane said slowly, "if you did have to . . ."

"Let's hope it won't come to that!" Bim broke in. "Now, come on, Ham. Make up your mind. Or rather, don't think . . . do what your heart tells you. I'll bet my bottom dollar that's in the right place!"

"It's in Jane's hands!" Hamilton said. "Let her decide!"

"Me?" Jane looked from one to the other aghast. "But I can't decide for you, Ham. It's your responsibility. I think . . . maybe Bim's right . . . but you must decide finally."

"She's quite right!" Bim said. "It's your responsibility, Ham, and time you started facing up to that and all the others."

Ham took a deep breath and looked for a moment at Jane, who reached out and held his hand in her own. A brief smile went across his face as he said, "Okay, then. I'll give myself up. Sounds like a movie drama, doesn't it?"

Bim clapped him on the back and looked immensely satisfied. "You're doing the right thing. I'm sure of it, Ham."

"But not until tomorrow will I denounce myself!" Ham said. "I want this evening . . . what's left of it . . . with Jane . . . with my wife!"

"Oh, Ham!" Jane whispered. "You make it sound as if you're going to the gallows!"

He laughed outright then, and the colour came back to her face and a smile with it.

"Say, what about that illegitimate husband of yours? Does he know where you are?" he asked her.

"Gareth!" Jane cried. "I'd forgotten all about him! Bim, what time is it?"

"Ten-thirty p.m.!" Bim said laughing. "There's the telephone, honey. Shall we leave you to it?"

"No . . . yes . . . no, I can't face him alone. What shall I say? It'll be a shock to him . . . no, don't laugh. This isn't a laughing matter," she said, as the two men laughed at her confusion.

"Just ring up and tell him whatever comes into your head, honey!" Bim advised. "He's not liable to go jump in a lake or anything frightful?"

"Oh, no! We're . . . we haven't been very good friends lately.

As a matter of fact, he's in love with another girl. Perhaps I could just tell him I'm going to free him so he can marry her!"

"Sure thing!" Ham said, still laughing. "And he won't even have to pay for a divorce. Gosh, honey, how does it feel to be a bigamist?"

"Oh, Ham, don't tease!" Jane said, lifting the receiver. "It was all your fault . . . you know it was!"

"Then I can be glad of one thing . . . that my return will make four people the happier!" Ham announced. Then they both fell silent as Jane dialled the number of her flat and spoke Gareth's name.

Twenty

Susan lay on the rug beneath the shady old pear tree, her hands behind her head, her eyes staring upwards through the green leaves to the cobalt blue of the sky beyond. Only the barest breath of a breeze stirred the hot haze of summer sunshine that flooded the garden. It was a perfect English summer's day . . . warm, drowsy, somnolent, with nothing but the call of the birds to break the stillness.

And in Susan's heart this same warmth and peace was reflected.

Only one day had passed, yet this transition from acute and desperate unhappiness, from uncertainty, to perfect and utter contentment was as complete as it must be permanent. Never again would she know that loneliness of spirit, that unrest of her body, that agonizing longing of her heart. Today Gareth was coming . . . he would be here in time for tea and soon . . . so soon he need never leave again!

Starry-eyed, her heart beating with ever-increasing excitement as she lay here in glorious anticipation of Gareth's arrival, Susan had no idea how utterly beautiful she looked. Only yesterday she had no colour in her cheeks; even her hair had been dull, lifeless, her soft mouth drooping in fatigue, uncertainty making her nerves taut and near to breaking point. Now the colour in her cheeks was rose-pink, her mouth curving with the happiness that seemed to spill over from her dark, brilliant eyes.

Even now, with Gareth's arrival no more than an hour distant, Susan could scarcely believe that she was not dreaming. Could it have been only yesterday . . . her birthday . . . that she held Jim's engagement ring in her hands, uncertain if she could agree to wear it, to betroth herself to him whilst he assured her that an engagement need not be binding? Only yesterday that the telephone had rung and Gareth's voice, deep and husky with excitement, had said without a word of warning, "Susan, I've rung up to ask you to marry me!" No warning, no explanation . . . just those words which she had never dared hope to hear. When emotion permitted her to reply, her words were as simple, as unquestioning as his. "Gareth, you know I will!" Then had come the questions . . . the explanations . . . the wonderful news that not only was Gareth free to marry her but that Jane herself had made this possible; Jane and the American husband she had believed dead. For Susan could never have found true happiness with the man she loved had there been any doubt in her own mind that she was depriving Jane, her friend, of something she valued, wanted . . . even if she had in this new light of circumstances, no legal right of possession.

But Jane was in love with her Hamilton, Gareth had explained. The man had been in trouble and, in spite of this fact and the insecurity of the future, Jane intended to stick by him. Gareth himself was giving them every help he could. He had insisted that it was for him to finance the legalities attending the dissolution of his marriage, or whatever the peculiar circumstances required. He had also insisted that Jane accept a large sum of money from him, which would enable her to have something to fall back on if things did not go too well for her in the new life she had chosen. Gone were all traces of bitterness towards her. They were more friendly now, Gareth told Susan, than they had been for many months. Each could appreciate the other's desire for freedom; understand the call of love. Jane had wished Susan and Gareth every happiness and that one day they might all four meet again.

It had been hard to take in the details from that long telephone call. Gareth had talked like an excited schoolboy which, indeed, he felt. He was intoxicated with the good fortune that had given him the right to do as his heart dictated and this knowledge alone made him feel ten years younger.

"When can I see you, Susan?" he had begged her. "I cannot

wait long to tell you in person how much I love you. Darling, answer me! Tell me again that you do love me . . . that your heart belongs to me as surely as my heart is yours!"

How long they talked, Susan could not afterwards remember. In a daze she had returned to the kitchen, trying unselfishly to find a way of imparting her incredibly wonderful news to Jim without hurting him, disappointing him too greatly.

But one look at her face must have given Jim an indication of the news she had received. She had not been able, even had she wished, to wipe the radiance from her face, dull the glow of her eyes.

"What's happened, Susan? Don't be afraid to tell me! Whatever it is, if it has the power so to transform you, I shall be glad. To see you happy is compensation . . . for I can only assume that my idea . . . is off!"

So she had told him simply and directly that Jane's American husband had returned, was alive after all; that Gareth was therefore not married and had asked her, Susan, to marry him as soon as she could.

Jim had been wonderful, Susan thought, remembering. He had hidden his own disappointment, congratulated her, planned with her what should be done with Teddy when she went on her honeymoon.

"He shall spend those days . . . weeks, with me!" Jim had said. "We'll be two bachelors in town together! We'll go to Lord's and the Zoo and the Royal Tournament . . . and it will be next best to having you, Susan dear! Instead of being a father I shall be a favourite uncle and no doubt the rôle will suit me far better!"

He had joked, laughed, covered up his own feelings until the last moment before he left. Then, as he stood in the hall about to go, he had put his arms round Susan and held her tight against him for one brief instant.

"I shall never forget you!" he had said softly. "You'll be my ideal, Susan . . . my most treasured memory!"

"But I shall be more than that, Jim. I hope I shall be your friend. You speak as if we shan't meet again!"

"I would rather not . . . for a little while at least," Jim said in a low voice. "Maybe in time I'll get over you but until then . . . well . . . there it is, Susan. I can't help loving you any more than you could force yourself to love me. You're a wonderful girl!"

And he had kissed her lightly on the cheek.

There was nothing Susan could find to say in reply that she felt would make him happier. But she reached up and returned his kiss and almost before she knew it, he had spoken an abrupt "good-bye" and was gone.

So Jim remained the only cloud in the brilliant blue sky of her thoughts. It hurt her to think that he was miserable, wretched as she had been. Yet deep down in her heart, she could not altogether believe that Jim's love for her had gone as deep as her own feelings for Gareth. Somehow, she felt convinced that before long Jim would find another girl – someone perhaps a little younger, more amusing, who would laugh him out of his sentimental mood and bring him the happiness he deserved.

A shout from the garden gate broke into Susan's reverie and she watched her small son scamper across the lawn towards her, his satchel and school cap clutched in one grubby hand.

He looked hot and breathless as he flung himself down beside her and said, "Thank goodness school's over for today! Gosh, I wish I didn't have to go to school like you don't, Mummy!"

Smoothing the damp, dark hair off his hot little forehead, Susan thought, "I must tell Teddy what is happening. He'll be hurt if I decide our future without consulting him! How happy he will be. He has always loved Gareth . . . admired him so much!"

She was totally unprepared for the scowl that spread over his sun-burned face when she announced that Gareth would shortly be here with them . . . in time for tea.

"What's he coming for?" was Ted's only comment.

"To see us!" Susan said. "And to ask us something very important. You see, Ted, he wants to marry me and be your new father."

The scowl deepened and Ted scuffled his shoes in the grass but said nothing.

"Aren't you glad, Ted? I thought we would both say yes!" Susan spoke again.

"I don't like Uncle Gareth. I thought you were going to make Uncle Jim my father."

"Don't like Uncle Gareth?" Susan repeated, ignoring his last remark. "But why, Teddy? You used to be so fond of him."

"'Cos he's nasty. He doesn't care whether we're happy or not," came her son's answer in a flow of angry words. "He makes you cry and he broke his promise. He said he was always going to live here and then just because Aunty Jane wanted to go away he went too. It wasn't fair!"

Light dawned slowly, and Susan was silent as she realized how much a small boy could sense of the atmosphere grown-ups created around him, no matter how one might imagine him to be ignorant of the facts. Instinct told him a good deal and because Teddy had always championed his mother, been unhappy if he knew she was, he had resented the causes he believed were responsible. Duty, loyalty, marriage . . . these were things he could not fully comprehend, but a broken promise he understood . . . a refusal by Gareth to visit them, to put her, Susan, before his wife, Jane. Perhaps she ought to have told him more, tried to explain what was going on, but she had never imagined Ted knew of her unhappiness until the episode of the diary and this she could not have discussed . . . even with him.

Was it too late now to remedy all this? Or would Ted always feel this resentment against the man he believed had made his mother and himself so miserable? Soon Gareth would be his father and, whatever happened, she must try to put their relationship on the right footing, else her son might do irreparable damage to all their chances of happiness, more especially his own. She could not bear that he should dislike the man she loved so much; misunderstand the fineness of his character, the sacrifices he had made for her sake as much as for Jane's. She had hoped that between them, she and Gareth, instead of making Ted a little jealous of this new interest in his mother's life, might make him feel doubly loved, doubly wanted.

"Darling, I want you to listen to me for a moment," she said gently, talking to the back of his head which he had turned away from her. "You're quite a big boy now and old enough, I think, to understand what I am going to try to explain to you. Maybe I should have told you before, but I didn't think we should see Uncle Gareth very much . . . and I thought it best for us both to forget all about him. You see, darling, he was married to Aunty Jane. Now when two people get married, they promise in church to the minister and to God to love each other always. They also promise to take care of each other always, no matter what happens. The minister then tells everybody that God has said that no man or woman must ever part them. Do you understand all that?"

Ted was interested now and his face was turned once more towards her. He nodded his head.

"Well, when Uncle Gareth and Aunty Jane were married, they made all those promises. Perhaps one day you will make the same promises when you get married. They were very happy at first but after a little while they got a little cross with one another . . . just the way you get cross with me sometimes and I with you when we aren't doing just what the other one wants. But because of the promises, they made up the quarrels and became friends again. They came to live down here and you and I both became very fond of Uncle Gareth, didn't we?"

Again Ted nodded his head and Susan felt encouraged to continue.

"And Uncle Gareth grew very fond of us. Now being fond of people and loving them is very nearly the same thing, and after a little while, Uncle Gareth started to love us and we started to love him. Now you know how nice it is to be with people you love, so you will understand why we wanted to be with Uncle Gareth as often as we could and he with us. There was nothing wrong in this for you because Uncle Gareth could love you just as if you were his own little boy and you could love him like your own daddy. But it was wrong for me to love him and for him to love me."

"You mean because he had promised God to love Aunty

Jane?" Ted asked, and when Susan nodded her head, he added, "But why couldn't he love you both?"

"Because the more you love one person, the less love you have left over for anyone else!" Susan said adroitly. "So that meant that every time he loved me a little bit more, he loved poor Aunty Jane a little bit less. So we talked it over and we decided that it would be the right thing to do not to see each other ever again and try to forget all about each other."

"Is that why Uncle Gareth went away?"

"Yes! He didn't want to go. You see, it meant he had to leave you, too, and that made him very unhappy. So we were all unhappy. And Uncle Gareth had to break his word to you because his promise to God was more important."

"Then how can he come and see you today without making God angry?" asked Susan's son, with a frown creasing his forehead.

"Well, my poppet, that's another part of the story. You see, a long long time ago, before you were born, Aunty Jane was married to someone else, just like I was married to your real daddy. And just as your daddy was killed in an aeroplane, so everyone thought Aunty Jane's husband had been killed fighting in the war, too. Now God didn't mean men and women to live all by themselves, so once a husband or a wife died and went to live in heaven with Him, He said it would be all right for the one who was left behind to marry someone else. So Aunty Jane married Uncle Gareth."

"Why didn't you marry anyone, too?" Ted interrupted.

Susan smiled and took Teddy's hand in her own.

"Because I was so busy looking after you when you were a baby that I never had time to think about it until you were growing up and going to school. Then I became lonely and then I met Uncle Gareth."

"Well, I still don't see how Uncle Gareth and Aunty Jane can break their promise now!" Ted said, when he had digested Susan's statement.

"Because, Ted, Aunty Jane's first husband . . . the one everyone thought was dead, was still alive after all. But he was in America . . . ever such a long way away and nobody knew he was alive. Then quite suddenly, the day before yesterday, he came to England to find Aunty Jane. Now God doesn't allow people to have two husbands or two wives, so He said that the very first promises are the ones that must be kept. So you see, Aunty Jane will go away to live in America, I expect, and Uncle Gareth won't have a wife any more and he wants you and me to love him and look after him."

"You mean we'll go to church and promise to love him like God says?" Ted asked.

Susan nodded and waited for Ted to speak. She could see from the expressive dark eyes, from the crease on his forehead, that he was thinking over with great seriousness all she had said. She had provided him with an answer to many things which had troubled him and as he understood them, slowly the resentment and hurt that had gathered in his heart since Gareth's departure, gave way to a new rush of affection for the man who was once his idol . . . whom he knew that he still loved better than anyone else but his mummy . . . better even than Uncle Jim, whom he liked 'a lot'. As he recalled that Susan had said Gareth would become his new daddy, a great wave of happiness swept over him, for one moment making him want to cry. For now he would have someone to boast about as the other boys at school boasted. He would be able to tell them about his father's 'smashing sports car', that he was 'bags taller' even than Jack's father, who so far held the record; that *his* father was teaching him to swim, play cricket, taking him to a football match. Yes, he would really have something to swank about . . . someone to be proud of . . . someone, too, who would really understand. Mothers were all right but sometimes they just didn't see what a boy meant . . . how a boy thought about things like tree climbing and putting worms on hooks for fishing. Mothers were squeamish and even his mother, who was a pretty good one anyway, fussed over him as Uncle Gareth would never do. He could really talk to Uncle Gareth . . . and this time he would be there for ever and ever because they would all be promising God that they would. It was an exhilarating and stunning thought.

"Do you think we should say 'yes' when Uncle Gareth comes to ask us?" Susan broke in on his thoughts, bringing him back to the present.

Ted turned his glowing face to hers.

"I guess it's all right with me!" he said gruffly, for his feelings went too deep for words. Abruptly, he jumped to his feet and without looking at Susan, he rushed across the lawn and started to turn somersaults with breath-taking speed.

Words of caution rose to Susan's lips but she forced them back and watched him silently, a smile on her face. She knew her son so well . . . could understand that this daring exhibition was but an outlet for the great joy within him; a joy which echoed again and again in her own heart.

"It's all right, Gareth!" she whispered aloud. "He loves you in his way as much as I love you in mine!"

She lay back once more, this time her eyes closed, her heart again in perfect peace. She did not see her son tiptoe back across the lawn, passing within a yard of her as he made his way back to the gate and out on to the road. His mother might be able to wait patiently for Uncle Gareth to come, but he just *had* to go and meet him.

So it was that Gareth stopped the car about half a mile from the house and picked up the small, hot little boy who flung himself into the seat beside him.

"I came to meet you," was his shy remark, with a glance at Gareth from beneath his lashes.

"Jolly nice of you, old chap!" was Gareth's comment, for he sensed by the boy's face that all was well once more between them but that the boy had not the words to express all that was in his heart, in his eyes. In turn, Gareth gave no verbal indication of his own emotions. His love for Susan was all-important, all devouring and yet in his heart there was a place reserved for her son . . . for the small boy who epitomized the son he had longed for and never had. Ted was part of Susan, her flesh and blood, and he had loved him and gained his first understanding of Susan through him. Soon he would be the boy's father and with every fibre of his being, he intended to be as good a parent to him as he could ever be to his own children. Perhaps before long, this desire, so long repressed, would be realized, but for all they were part of him, too, he would allow no difference between them and Ted.

"Mum's waiting in the garden for you!" Ted said as Gareth restarted the car. "She's on the lawn . . . and I think she was asleep but I don't acshully *know*."

"Then perhaps I'll give her a surprise and wake her with a kiss as the Prince woke the Sleeping Princess, remember?" Gareth replied with a smile.

He stopped the car out of earshot of the garden and hand in hand with the delighted Ted, went silently past the gate. He could see the bright colours of Susan's frock in the shadow beneath the tree . . . see the white curve of her arms behind the dark, curly head. His heart started to beat with suffocating swiftness.

"Go on!" Ted urged with a grin.

"Not with you watching, you young rascal!" Gareth said. "How would you like to have someone watching you kissing a girl?"

Ted, quite understanding Gareth's masculine embarrassment, turned away with a grin and disappeared into the house in search of something to eat, for he had a distinct feeling that this was a very special day and a very special occasion . . . hardly one, for instance, when anyone would notice if a few jam tarts were missing.

He strode into the kitchen and with his face wreathed in smiles began tucking into some tea.

In the garden, Gareth moved silently across the grass until he was standing beside Susan, silently looking down into her face. Her eyes were still closed and the dark lashes lay softly on her cheeks. With a jolt of his heart Gareth was reminded of that other time, many months ago, when he had sat at Susan's bedside the day she was ill and he had surprised her sleeping . . . the moment when he had first realized his great love for her. So long ago and they had suffered so much since then . . . never hoping for an instant that the day might come when they would be free to express that love to one another without guilt . . . without a sense of wrong-doing.

For a long moment he gazed down at her and then, gently, he sat down on the grass beside her and leaning over her, kissed her softly on the lips.

Instantly her eyes opened and as recognition dawned in them, a light came into them and slowly her mouth curved into a smile of welcome. Her arms moved from behind her head and with unconscious simplicity, went round his neck, drawing his face down to hers once more.

"Oh, Gareth, my darling Gareth!" she whispered. "It is really you at last?"

She held his face between her cool white hands, staring long into those blue-grey eyes, tracing once again the remembered lines, touching for a brief instant his strong determined jaw, his lips. Then only did his arms go round her, pulling her fiercely towards him, holding her ever closer to him until her cheek lay pressed against his own, her heart beating tumultuously against his.

"Susan, Susan!" he said in that deep, low voice which seemed to thrill through every nerve of her body. "I, too, can hardly believe I am not dreaming. I love you, Susan . . . my dearest, *dearest* one. I can say it now . . . I have the right at last. I love you . . . love you . . . *love you*."

"And I love you, Gareth . . . for always. Never leave me again!"

For answer his mouth came down to hers, not gently this time but with all the pent-up desire and emotion that had lain so restlessly in his heart. He kissed her mouth, her eyes, the soft throbbing pulse in her throat and gloried in the swift response that thrilled through her at his touch.

"It's been so long!" she whispered against his lips.

"But soon we shall be married!" Gareth cried exultantly. "You will be my wife, Susan . . . *my wife!*"

"For always!" Susan repeated and clung to him once more as

if in her heart she was still afraid that something might again take him from her.

It was Gareth who unwound her arms from about his neck and said breathlessly, "My darling, this is hardly the way for us to behave in front of that small son of yours on a summer's afternoon!"

She smiled at him shakily and curled her fingers round his own.

"Oh, Gareth, if you only knew how much I loved you!" she said.

"And I, you!" Gareth replied. "I tried to forget you, Susan . . . tried the impossible. You are part of me . . . and without you I was completely and utterly lost. I wanted to do what was right . . . to make amends to Jane . . . start again . . . but it was all so hopeless! I could not put you out of my thoughts and I could not even make myself want to."

"It was the same for me!" Susan cried. "I tried to convince myself . . . as well as you! . . . that I could forget . . . build a future without you. But . . ." she looked at him shyly with the colour coming again to her cheeks ". . . you know from Teddy what I really felt. I was so ashamed when I learned what had happened. I wished I could die, Gareth. Now I am glad you knew . . . glad that you can never believe I ceased to love you."

"I never did believe it, my darling!" Gareth said tenderly. "You told me so and yet my heart told me otherwise."

They were silent for a moment, holding hands, content just to be near one another.

Then Susan said dreamily, "I'm so very happy, Gareth!"

"So shall we both be for the rest of our lives!" Gareth prophesied. "Ours is a love that cannot be denied, Susan. Heaven knows we both tried to live without one another . . . but it was only an existence. What I should have done if . . . if things had not worked out the way they have . . ."

"But it has all come right for us, *darling* Gareth," Susan broke in. "And for Jane, too. I hope she will be happy, Gareth. I wish it with my whole heart."

"And I do, too!" Gareth agreed. "I'm pretty sure she will be, Susan. When I saw her yesterday, I hardly knew her. I think she is really and truly in love with this American. He sounds a bit of a bounder in many ways, but in spite of everything, she's quite crazy about him. There's no doubting the fact. It was a new Jane I saw. She wasn't thinking of herself . . . of what would happen to her . . . only of him. And I believe she genuinely wished us every happiness, too. She . . . she did not even want to accept the financial help I offered her . . . said she didn't deserve it after the way she had treated me. But I over-persuaded her for I'm certain she will need it. She took it as a parting present."

"I'm glad!" Susan said. "And if she needs help in the future, Gareth, we'll do whatever we can, won't we?"

Gareth nodded.

"It's a funny world!" he said. "Love can make so much difference to people . . . raise them to higher standards . . . to greater sacrifices. It enables them to be better people, more tolerant, more understanding. I saw a new Jane yesterday and I don't think I was ever so fond of her as at our good-bye. I admired her courage and respected her for throwing over security, which she always wanted, for a man who could offer her nothing."

Susan sighed.

"I shall never understand how she could leave *you*, Gareth."

"Because she didn't love me, my darling, as you do. You look at me through rose-coloured spectacles. And more important still, because she loved her husband. I think perhaps she had always loved him and that was why our marriage was doomed to failure."

"I'll write to her!" Susan said. "We must keep in touch."

"I rather think she will go to America," Gareth said. "But write by all means, darling. Now let's talk about us! When shall we be married?"

"Soon! As soon as possible!" Susan said from her heart.

Their eyes met in a long, deep look and passion rose once more between them like an electric flame. Gareth would have taken Susan into his arms but for a timely interruption from Ted as he shouted from the kitchen window, "Hey, Mum! . . ." and with a mischievous grin on his jammy face . . . "Hi, Dad! Aren't you *ever* coming in to tea?"

Susan looked at Gareth and a slow, deep smile spread across his face. Laughter welled up inside him and with a spontaneous gesture, he jumped to his feet, pulling Susan up beside him.

"The little devil!" he said, his voice full of affection.

And with their faces wreathed in smiles, they walked hand in hand across the lawn, towards their son.